1942

1947

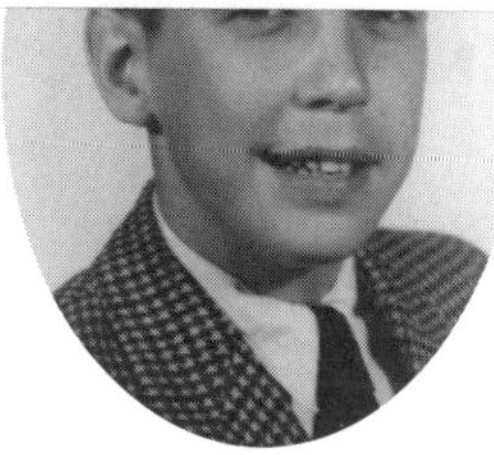

1956

1942: Above: Dr. Gruner (Baba) and Nicholas.

1947: An oil portrait painted by his grandmother, Mary Mullally, when he was 5-1/2.

1956: Second year at D'Arcy McGee High School in Montreal, Quebec.

1945

1945: Jessie Gruner holding Nicholas. Behind from left to right are his brothers Michael, Peter, Christopher, Anthony.

1955

1955: The Gruner family in their garden on Caledonia Road in Montreal. Front left to right are Nicholas, Pinocchio their dog, Cecilia, Jessie, Jennifer, and Malcolm. Back row: Anthony, Christopher, Peter, Michael.

1964

1962

1962: Nick Gruner, center, chief deck steward on S.S. Richelieu.

1964: Nicholas Gruner graduating from McGill University in Montreal, Quebec with Bachelor of Commerce Degree.

1919: Drawing of the chapel at Hartley as envisioned in Oscar's dream. See account of his dream in the Appendix.

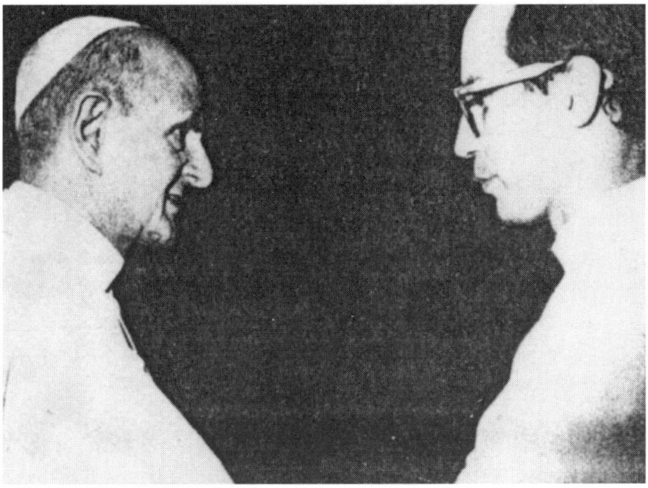

1971: Nicholas Gruner as a seminarian, in conversation with Pope Paul VI.

1972: Seminarian days at San Vittorino. Left to right: Andrew Winchuck, Brother Gino, stigmatist (with the wounds of Christ), Ron Tangen and Nicholas as he completed his final year of his Bachelor Degree in Theology. Brother Gino dubbed him "Doctor".

1968: Nicholas Gruner (left with a beard) kneels for Padre Pio's blessing. Padre Pio, at 81, is pushed in a wheel chair towards his room as he greets the pilgrims. While he worked nearby, Nicholas resided for seven months in San Giovanni Rotundo to be near Padre Pio and to receive the help of his powerful prayers and counsel.

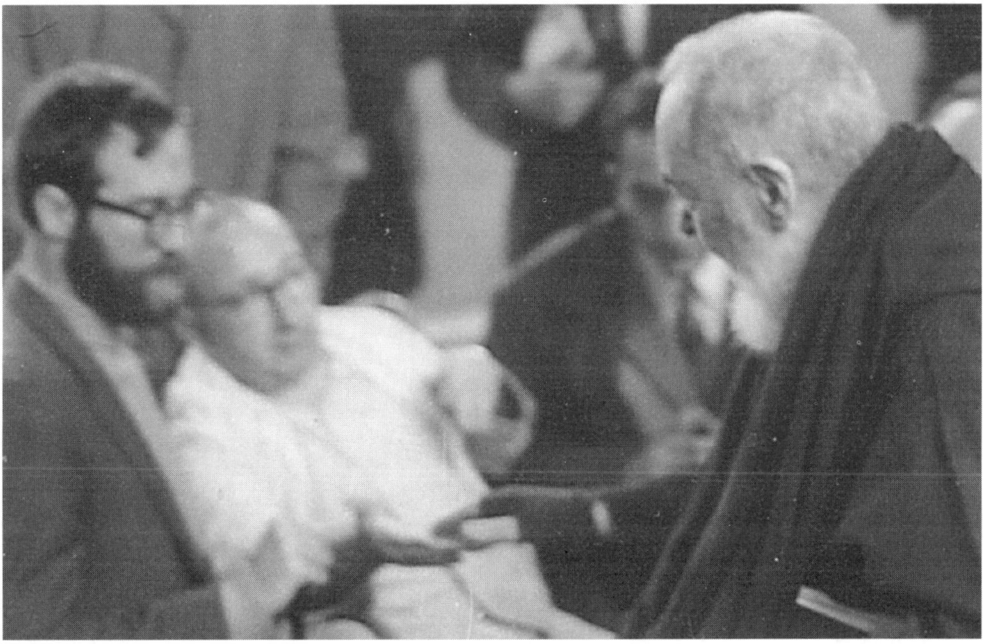

Above: August 22, 1976 - Ordination of Father Nicholas Gruner by Bishop Pasquale Venezia, Bishop of Avellino, at Frigento, Italy in the Diocese of Avellino, in the Conventual Franciscan Sanctuary of Our Lady of Good Counsel. Father Gruner, center, kneeling. Left to right: Vicar General of the Diocese, a newly ordained young priest, Father Stefano Manelli, Bishop Venezia, the Pastor of Frigento, Father Gabrielle Pelletier and Father Alphonsus (William) Sutton.

1980: Father Gruner holding the Rosary blessed by His Holiness, Pope John Paul II, personally given to him inside the Vatican by the Pope's secretary, Father John Magee in February 1980. This picture appeared in the *Catholic Register*, the Canadian national Catholic paper.

1975: Above, Nicholas Gruner, S.T.L., teaching Religion in Erlanger, Kentucky in his year of pastoral training. He taught in the Diocesan Seminary of St. Pius X as well as at Holy Cross High School and St. Henry's High School.

Even lack of electricity did not stop Father from meeting the deadline to get *The Fatima Crusader* to press under impossible odds.

Father Gruner and Father Nault (front) and Father Michael Jarecki (behind the altar boys) lead the procession at the official opening of the Fatima Center.

1994 Official Opening of the Fatima Center near the Peace Bridge between Buffalo N.Y. and Canada.

On August 22, 1994, Father Nault, Father Gruner and Father Victor Soroka in front of the plaques listing the thousands of supporters who made this dream possible.

Bishop Paul Vasylyk, Ukrainian Bishop imprisoned by the Communists several times for defending the Catholic Faith and Josyp Terelya a prisoner of conscience for 23 years, pictured here on the TV set of Fatima: "The Moment Has Come." It was Josyp who had an appointment for Father Gruner and himself, in January 1990, to meet the Pope, and after paying the expense to get there, the meeting was cancelled mysteriously by someone the day before the meeting.

Father Gruner with Father Victor Mroz on the 50th anniversary of his ordination to the priesthood. Father Mroz was one of St. Maximilian Kolbe's original friars and felt the crusade to consecrate Russia was more important than even the work of St. Maximilian. Father was with Father Mroz, praying the Rosary when he died. St. Maximilian had prophesied the time of his death.

Bishop Aloysius Balina, Bishop of the Diocese of Geita, Tanzania, one of the bishops who have come to visit the Fatima Center in Fort Erie.

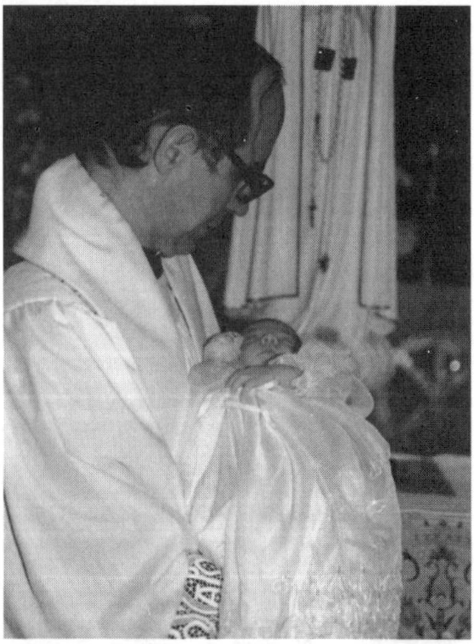

1990: Father Nicholas Gruner is holding Nicole before the Pilgrim Virgin Statue after baptizing her. She is named after Father Nicholas and his patron Saint.

1985: Father Gruner giving a keynote speech at the All India Laity Congress with lay Catholics attending from all over India. Father was invited on three different occasions to speak at this Congress and share the podium with various bishops and other dignitaries including Bishop Ignatius D'Cunha, Bishop of Aurangabad and Bishop Thomas Dabre, Auxiliary Bishop of Bombay.

Center: The Pilgrim Virgin statue blessed by Pope Paul VI acts as a magnet drawing large crowds. Everyone wanted to venerate Her and honor Her.

Bottom: Father Gruner surrounded by several assistants as he invests more than 100,000 persons in the Brown Scapular during one of his five mission visits to India.

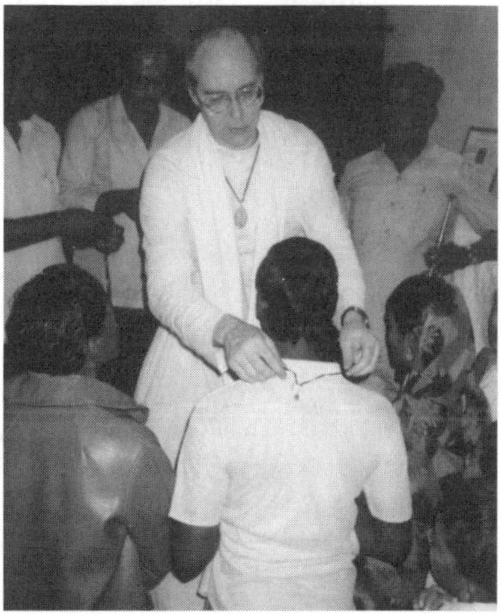

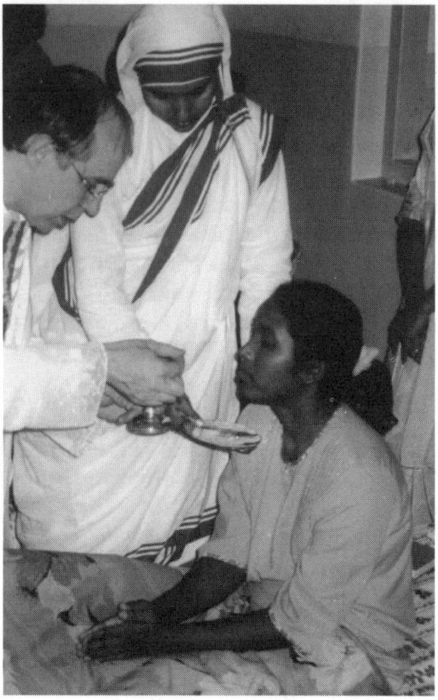

Above: November 1991. The Sisters of Mother Theresa welcome the Pilgrim Virgin statue into various convents and houses of charity where their great love and devotion is most edifying. Mother Theresa, herself, promised to pray for Father Gruner.

Right: Father Maschio, Father Gruner and Father Nault. Father Maschio, a legend in his own time, spent more than 40 years in Bombay and other parts of India establishing great works of charity and piety. Father Maschio predicted that many bishops around the world would be helped by Father Gruner's efforts to explain and promote devotion to Our Blessed Mother.

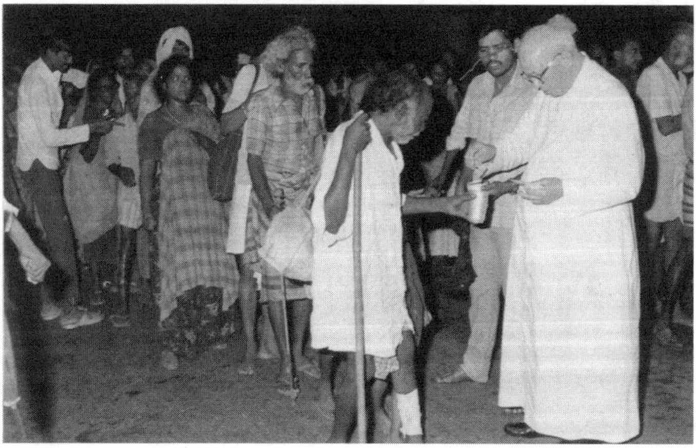

Father Maschio at work feeding the poor in India.

Above: Archbishop Limon, S.V.D., in his cathedral at Dagupan, Philippines, after the Mass and public procession in 1989. On October 7, 1992, he joined Archbishop Toppo of India and Archbishop Jose Cordoso Sobrinho, O.C., of the Archdiocese of Olinda e Recife, Brazil, when the Bishop of Fatima gave his blessing to Father Gruner's Conference at Fatima, October 8-12, 1992.

Father Gruner with some of the Brazilian children that he and his apostolate help feed each month.

Father Gruner in November, 1995, blessing some of the orphans at the Immaculate Heart Orphanage founded by Archbishop Arulappa and Father Gruner. At back of the picture is the Sister in charge and standing to the right, Anthony Sebastian, General Manager.

More of the orphans in their school uniforms

Reproduction of the March 26, 1984 issue of *L'Osservatore Romano*. See enlargement of Pope John Paul II's words. This has been reproduced and published three times in *The Fatima Crusader* over the years because the opponents of the consecration of Russia have conveniently, since 1984 to the present, continued to omit to report what the Pope actually said when he clearly indicated he had not done the consecration. Below, we reproduce the undisputed evidence published again in February 1989, in *The Fatima Crusader*.

L'OSSERVATORE ROMANO

GIORNALE QUOTIDIANO POLITICO RELIGIOSO

Liberaci dalla fame, dalla guerra

Tre eventi

Madre della Chiesa! Illumina il Popolo di Dio sulle vie della fede, della speranza e della carità! Illumina specialmente i popoli di cui tu aspetti la nostra consacrazione e il nostro affidamento. Aiutaci a vivere nella verità della consacrazione di Cristo per l'intera famiglia umana del mondo contemporaneo.

CONTINUAZIONE DALLA PRIMA PAGINA

On December 8th, 1983, Pope John Paul II wrote to all the bishops of the world, asking them to join in with him on March 25, 1984, in consecrating the world to the Immaculate Heart of Mary. He included with his letter his prepared text of consecration. On March 25, 1984, the Pope, making the consecration before Our Lady of Fatima, **departed from his prepared text to add the words highlighted here.** As you can see they were reported in *L'Osservatore Romano*. The words he added at this point indicate clearly that the Pope knew then that the consecration of the world done that day did not fulfill the requests of Our Lady of Fatima. After performing the consecration of the world proper, a few paragraphs above, **the Pope added the highlighted words which translate: "Enlighten especially the peoples of which You Yourself are awaiting our consecration and confiding."** This clearly shows he knows Our Lady is awaiting the Pope and bishops to consecrate certain people to Her.

"Maintain Humanity under 500,000,000 in Perpetual Balance with Nature"

Father Gruner (below) has personally delivered to the Vatican, tens of thousands of petitions asking the Holy Father for the Consecration of Russia.

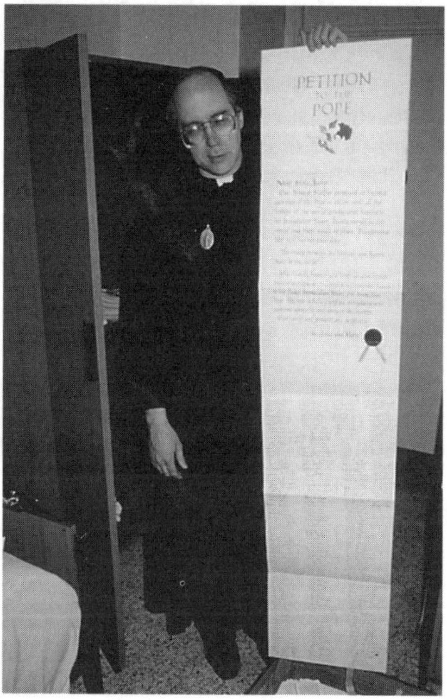

Above (left): New World Order obelisk erected in Elberton, Georgia in 1980 stands 19'3" high and weighs 237,746 lbs. The stone inscription in 8 langaugеs (photographically reproduced above) outlines their satanic call to wipe out 9/10ths of humanity, reducing it from the present 5.5 billion people down to 500 million, calling for the extermination of 5,000,000,000 people. You can be sure that unless you apostasize, you and all believers in Jesus Christ are targeted for slaughter in the near future by these God-hating militant atheists. This obelisk is spoken of in the Chapter entitled *Why The Open Letter?*

❶ **The International Fatima Rosary Crusade Symposium held in Vatican City in the Aula Magna (Great Hall) of the Pontifical Institute of the Augustinianum, inside Vatican City, November 24, 1985.**

Eminent Fatima scholars addressed the prestigious audience. From left, Professor Christiani, Frère Michel, Hamish Fraser, Father Caillon, Father Gruner.

❷ **Part of the audience attending the conference. A number of priests, religious and laypersons attended. It was advertised on Vatican radio. The Symposium was held on the opening day of the 1985 Extraordinary Synod.**

❸ **November 24, 1985, in the foreground, Latin Rite Patriarch of Jerusalem, His Beatitude Giacomo Giusseppe (James Joseph) Beltritti, patron of this symposium, listens without earphones as he understood all languages of the various speakers. His Beatitude spoke out on the Synod floor on the need for the consecration of Russia. He encouraged Father Gruner to continue publishing this important request and he promised to work behind the scenes towards realizing this goal of achieving Our Lady's Triumph through the consecration of Russia in the exact manner She requested.**

❹ **Below: Fatima, Sunday, October 11, 1992; in the hall of Paul VI Pastoral Center after Fr. Fox's lecture. Brother François at the microphone denounces in the presence of Fr. Kondor (right) and Fr. Fox (seated left), the apocryphal character of the five letters from Sister Lucy dealing with the act of March 25, 1984 which was published by them. Br. François stated "These letters are false...I am prepared to justify my accusations..." The following day, the Abbé Laurentin was to express surprise on learning that neither Fr. Fox nor Fr. Kondor had any answer to make to Br. François. The session was simply swiftly closed.**

Above: Bishop Pestana addressing the First Bishops Conference. At every bishops conference at least one bishop addressed the whole assembly of bishops.

Above: ❶ Archbishops Toppo and Sobrinho; and some of the over 60 bishops ❷ who attended the First Bishops Conference in Fatima.

His Grace Telesphore Toppo, Archbishop of Ranchi, India and His Grace Jose Cardoso-Sobrinho Archbishop of Olindo and Recife, Brazil obtained the blessing of the Bishop of Fatima for Father Gruner's Conference in Fatima, October, 1992—although permission was not needed. This points out that the published statements in *L'Osservatore Romano* by Cardinal Sanchez and Archbishop Sepe are false. For more information see Petition to the Holy Father by Coralie Graham, Mairead Clarke, Mary Sedore, in the Appendix section.

Right: Father Gruner (center) walking in procession in Fatima on the 13th of October in happier days.

Father Gruner enrolling a number of the various translators who were responsible to see that all the speeches were translated into Italian, French, Spanish, Portuguese, at the Second Bishops Conference in Mexico City (Guadalupe). At break time, after the talk on the Scapular, they all asked to be enrolled.

Archbishop Milingo in an impromptu speech at the Mexico Bishops Conference, denounces the underhanded and illegal maneuvers of the anti-Fatima forces in the Vatican which caused the letter he is holding to be sent to all the bishops around the world to prevent many of them from coming. For the text of his speech, see Appendix. To know why this letter is illegal, also read the Canonical denouncement of these tactics in the Libellus, (formal Canonical Petition to the Pope) full text of which is in the Appendix.

Center photo: In the foreground with white beard, Cardinal Padiyara, walking in procession from the concelebrated Mass on October 9, 1992. Father Gruner is following immediately behind to assist the frail Cardinal who was his guest at the Fatima Peace Conference. None of the shrine authorities objected, yet only a day later, on October 10th, while again assisting the Cardinal, Father Gruner was attacked.

Below: Photo of Father's injuries, shortly after being assaulted by two young men. One disappeared right after this attack; the other stayed around to admit to Father Pacheco's interrogation that he did this attack under orders from Msgr. Guerra, Rector of the Shrine at Fatima at that time.

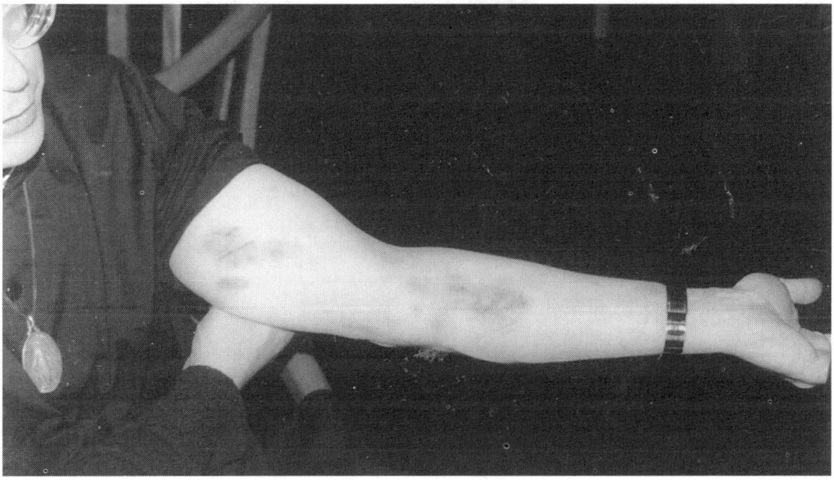

On November 20, 1996, Our Lady's worker, Joseph Cain, asks the Holy Father to please consecrate Russia. He also handed him a petition (Libellus) signed by a number of lay Fatima apostles. It was prepared according to Canon Law requirements, and which details and documents the illegal and unjust acts of several Vatican bureaucrats including Cardinal Sanchez and Archbishop Sepe, and solemnly requests the Holy Father to intervene to stop these abuses of authority by those powerful persons.

At the close of Fatima 2000, the third Bishops Conference in Rome, Italy, Bishop Lopez led the Congress in prayer. We pray His Holiness will receive sufficient support and consecrate Russia before it is too late.

Father Gruner listens while His Grace, Archbishop Milingo speaks to the bishops and delegates about exorcisms and the existence of satanic worship that is taking place right inside the Vatican.

Below the Italian press coverage of Fatima 2000 focused on Archbishop Milingo's speech. The largest Rome daily, *Il Messaggero* gave him front page headlines. Various other newspapers also featured this revelation. The Archbishop called a press conference a few days later and reconfirmed his accusations that satanists are indeed active today in the Vatican.

«Seguaci di Satana in Vaticano»

Il vescovo Milingo attacca la Curia, dall'America confermano l'accusa

Cronache dall'Italia

Mercoledì 27 novembre 1996

L'EX ARCIVESCOVO ESORCISTA DI LUSAKA CONFERMA TUTTE LE «ACCUSE»

Milingo: Satana è anche in Vaticano

'Già nel '75 Paolo VI disse che il Maligno era entrato in quelle stanze. Non risulta ne sia uscito'

LA NUOVA SORTITA DELL'ARCIVESCOVO A UN CONVEGNO SU FATIMA

Milingo: 'Satanisti in Vaticano'

L'esorcista Milingo: «Rivelate il terzo mistero di Fatima»

«C'è il diavolo in San Pietro»

Il Maligno non risparmierebbe neppure sacerdoti e vescovi

L'ombra di Satana nel Vaticano

Above: A painting depicting the apparition of the Child Jesus and the Immaculate Heart of Mary, Who, with Her hand resting on Sister Lucy's shoulder, promises salvation to those Catholics who practice the Five First Saturday devotions.

At Fatima in the Capelinha, Father Gruner touching the original statue of Our Lady of Fatima in one of the rare moments when the glass casing was removed.

Right: Sister Lucy, in her Dorothean habit standing beside Bishop da Silva in 1946 where she was asked why we must wait until 1960 for the Third Secret to be revealed. She replied: "Because it will be clearer then."

An official newspaper photo of part of the 70,000 witnesses to the Miracle of the Sun on October 13, 1917.

Father Gruner leading a pilgrimage at the Loca Do Cabeco, where St. Michael the Archangel appeared two times.

Above: On October 11th, 1990, Carolina, the blood sister of Sister Lucy, shortly before she died, told Father Gruner that she had visited Sister Lucy in the Carmel of Coimbra for more than 40 years and never had she been able to speak alone with her sister in the same room. They were always separated by a grill and many other sisters of the convent were in attendance at all visits. Unlike the hand-holding session in the same room by someone claiming to be Sister Lucy in October 1992.

Jacinta, Lucy, Francisco, photographed before August 13th by Father Joachim Antonio do Carmo, in the garden of the Marto family a few days before they were kidnapped and put in jail by the masonic mayor of Orem for their crime of reporting what Our Lady of Fatima said.

Father Gruner with John Marto the brother of Jacinta and Francisco in the house the seven Marto children all grew up in.

Above: Part of the crowd March 13, 1922 protesting the attack at Fatima by the Masons. See arrow where the chapel was bombed.

FATIMA PRIEST

Priest, Prophecy and Peril . . .

The Vatican Key to Peace or Terror

by FRANCIS ALBAN

Good Counsel Publications
Pound Ridge, N.Y.

Distributed by:
ANGELUS PRESS
2918 Tracy Ave
Kansas City, MO 64109 USA
1-800-966-7337 • 1-816-753-3150

Good Counsel Publications
P.O. Box 203
Pound Ridge N.Y. 10576

Printed in U.S.A.

This book is respectfully dedicated to
Our Lady of Fatima
and to all cardinals, patriarchs, bishops, priests,
religious and lay persons
who have dedicated themselves
in humility and love to Her service.

"Suppose, dear friend, that Communism (Russia and Russia's errors, in Fatima terms) was only the most visible of the instruments of subversion to be used against the Church and the traditions of Divine Revelation ... I am worried by the Blessed Virgin's messages to Lucy of Fatima. This persistence of Mary about the dangers which menace the Church is a divine warning against the suicide of altering the Faith, in Her liturgy ... A day will come when the civilized world will deny its God, when the Church will doubt as Peter doubted. She will be tempted to believe that man has become God ... In our churches, Christians will search in vain for the red lamp where God awaits them, like Mary Magdalene weeping before the empty tomb, they will ask, 'Where have they taken Him?'"

. . . Pope Pius XII

"Through some crack the smoke of satan has entered into the Church of God."

. . . Pope Paul VI

"We must admit realistically and with feelings of deep pain, that: Christians today: in large measure feel lost, confused, perplexed and even disappointed; ideas opposed to the truth which has been revealed and always taught are being scattered abroad in abundance; heresies, in the full and proper sense of the word, have been spread in the area of dogma and morals, creating doubts, confusions and rebellion; the liturgy has been tampered with; immersed in an intellectual and moral relativism and therefore in permissiveness, Christians are tempted by atheism, agnosticism, vaguely moral enlightenment and by a sociological Christianity devoid of defined dogmas or an objective morality."

. . . Pope John Paul II

Table Of Contents

BOOK II ~ IN HIS OWN WORDS

BOOK III ~ TESTIMONIES

Author's Foreword

A life founded upon truth is unshakeable. Only a loss of the truth can make us tremble. The Patriarchs and Prophets trembled at the thought of losing God, of not fearing Him enough, of not serving Him enough. They trembled also at seeing His truth denied. Their spiritual children, the saints of the Church, in defense of His truth, strode singing into blood-drenched arenas, bowed gracefully to the headsman's axe, skipped up the steps to the guillotine, chanted His praises before firing squads. The catalogue of names, numbering in the thousands of thousands who willingly surrendered their life in defense of the truth is a cornerstone of our Catholic heritage. Smiling at death has been the last earthly act of our spiritual ancestors.

Each and every one of them, however, before they could smile at death, had an obstacle to hurdle. They had to harness the force that overcomes the mind and heart of man when truth is denied, a force human nature has in abundance, a force with which the Patriarchs and Prophets and Saints, as Sacred Scripture and Church history thoroughly testify, have been richly supplied by the Creator. They had to harness their anger.

There is great anger upon the earth today, most of it bearing the hallmark of chaos and unrelenting grief that are the gifts of Lucifer to his earthly cohorts. There is also being raised, however, a sizeable murmur, born of *holy* anger, that echoes of blood-drenched arenas, the whisper of the swinging axe, the sigh of the plummeting blade. For a lie has been told, a great lie that slanders God. A lie that cuts like a knife. It identifies the friends of God by the wounds they bear after it passes them by. The cutting edge of this fatal whisper is made of three simple words: "*Fatima is finished*".

The purpose of a lie is to hide the truth. The result of a lie is the wounding of those who are seeking the truth, the assaulting of those who are defending the truth, or the discrediting of those who are passing on the truth.

Our entire lives are built upon truths heard at our mother's knee, truths intoned gently at our bedside in childhood, truths absorbed from family tradition. Upon these foundations rest our past, our present, and our future.

There are those in the Church and State today who, for unique and specific reasons, conspire to spread the Lie by obliterating the credibility of those who defend Heaven's truth. In their wake, a plague of wounded hearts cries out to Heaven. Our Sacred heritage itself is suspect. Were we lied to at our mother's knee? At the bedside of our childhood? Is the Church not Our Mother? Did She lie to us? Most stagger under the weight of their suspicions. Some crumble. Some begin to disbelieve Heaven itself. Those who neither stumble nor fall under the blow of the Lie, but stay upright, are salting the earth anew with the secret of the Saints — the knowledge that Heaven does not lie.

When it comes to the Message of Fatima, the stakes are so high, Lucifer himself seems now to be taking a personal hand in attacking Fatima's defenders. In the forefront of the battle, constantly brandishing the banner of Fatima before the ranks of the enemies of Heaven, the International Fatima Rosary Crusade refuses to retreat, withdraw or surrender. Those who have tried to level the Apostolate in the past know that it will remain a formidable foe of the Lie for as long as Father Nicholas Gruner, its founder and director, remains its driving force. Their task then, is to obliterate Father Nicholas Gruner.

To accomplish this requires silencing a man whose insistence on the necessity of the Pope and bishops of the world to obey the requests of Our Lady of Fatima has made him, arguably, the most controversial priest in the Church today. Who is he? What is he? Why is his destruction important to the enemies of Fatima? Why are they spending so much time, money and energy to eliminate him from the scene? We must look at his personal history to discover the answer.

... Francis Alban

BOOK I

THE PRIEST AND THE PROPHECY

PART ONE

IN PERSON

Chapter 1

The Stars At Noon

In Old Montreal there is a spot beloved of all generations of Catholics in the Province of Quebec where the stars can be seen at morning and afternoon as well as at night. On the deep blue ceiling of the great church of Notre Dame, in silver and gold, handpainted stars by the thousands look down on the faithful below.

Many a child has gone home from Notre Dame with aching neck wrought from standing on kneeler and pew, turning, turning, and gazing up at that magnificent rendition of Heaven brought indoors. That the glory of the Church it represented could possibly fade in the span of a few short years would have been considered an outrageous idea in the 1940's in Quebec. The province known as the Province of St. Anne appeared as securely set in the Faith as were the stars in their blue—painted firmament.

It has been said that never in history had the Social Kingship of Christ been reflected so totally and completely on earth as it was in the kitchens of Quebec Province in the first half of the 20th Century. Here the Faith came from its supernatural height and permeated every aspect of life. To those who suggest the Church was a smothering, oppressive force in the lives of the people of Quebec it might be noted that the unique culture of the Province of St. Anne exists today precisely because of the Catholic Faith; the Church having provided the prime bulwark against assimilation by Protestant Britain.

(In fairness to Britain it can also be said that the conquest of Quebec by Britain in 1759 undoubtedly saved the province from doing a brisk trade in guillotine blades when revolution turned Mother France into an abattoir a mere thirty years later.)

Whatever may be said about the history of Quebec, it is indisputable that Montreal, in 1942, was very much the center of a vibrant *La Belle Province*. To be in Montreal was to be instantly part of the most cosmopolitan city of the hemisphere outside of Rio.

The Town of Mount Royal within the greater city of Montreal was indeed an ocean removed from the sounds of the cannonade in Europe, but the soul of Quebec resonated thoroughly with the dangers to France from the first moment of Hitlerian madness. The Fuehrer's broadcasts could shake radios in Northern Quebec and inner city Montreal just as readily as it did the radios of France. The fantasy of the Maginot Line came crashing to earth along the St. Lawrence as well as along the Champs Elysées. And who can doubt that the dreadful rhythm of stormtroopers marching past L'Arc de Triomphe chilled hearts in the shadow of St. Joseph's Oratory.

Even so, to be born in Montreal in the middle of the Second World War was to have one's eyes open to the most critical era of human history and yet view it from a special vantage point of security and safety. Few Canadian mothers in those dark years were unaware of their blessed distance from ringside as the curtain rose on what has appeared as Act Two of the Apocalypse.

Jessie Gruner had already borne four children to God and her husband Malcolm by May of 1942. Michael, the first, was born on the feast of St. Athanasius, that great Saint who, in defense of the Church and the Faith, justly opposed even the Pope. Peter was next, then Christopher, who was born on the eve of St. Nicholas' feast day, and then Anthony. This newest one would be called Nicholas.

Nicholas Gruner was christened in the parish of St. Malachy's, according to the tradition and law of the greatest teaching institution in the world, the two-thousand-year-old Roman Catholic Church.

He was named after St. Nicholas of Tolentino, a Catholic priest and miracle worker, on whose feast day his parents Jessie Mullally and Malcolm Gruner had married, September 10, 1930.

Is it mere coincidence that Nicholas Gruner and another Nicholas, Van der Flue, share both a name and some very similar life patterns? Nicholas Gruner, the fifth son, became a priest, as did the fifth son of St. Nicholas Van der Flue. Both, also, would oppose abuse of authority and irresponsible judgements.

In Nicholas Van der Flue's day he gave Switzerland the solution to an "unsolvable" problem. The Swiss Constitution is his masterpiece and it still stands today. Nicholas Gruner was destined to publish to the world the solution to an "unsolvable" problem, the only means of obtaining world peace.

Malcolm Gruner was one of the original five Catholic men who petitioned the Archbishop of Montreal to found the parish of the Annunciation of Our Lady where the family would live for forty years. Malcolm then served as a warden of this parish for about 30 years. Two of the children would be baptized there, three receive first Holy Communion, another three would marry there, and in time the parents would there celebrate their fiftieth wedding anniversary.[1] Malcolm was also instrumental in founding the local parish school of St. Joseph and at least four of the children went there. It had classes for both English and French Catholic school children for as long as Nicholas went to school there. More continuity. More tradition.

In 1942, Catholic continuity, tradition and law were the birthright of any future priest, all gifts he would need in abundance when, in future years, under the pressure of so-called "reformers", the Church would jettison these and other precious treasures of its sacred heritage.

Indeed, continuity and tradition marked the Gruner homefront. A statue of the Sacred Heart, displayed in the most prominent place in the house, the head of the stairs, dispensed blessings and urged caution. Year after year children navigated those stairs passing by the Sacred Heart who, as in Catholic homes everywhere, with one hand cautions don't run, and with the other says I'm here if you fall. Running on just such a staircase as this, St. Therese of Lisieux suffered the intersection of youthful emotions that would change her life forever and lead inevitably to sainthood.

In front of the image of Our Mother of Perpetual Help, in Jessie and Malcolm's bedroom, the children were taught the Memorare, that portal of rescue in times of despair.

"*Never was it known that any who implored Thy help or sought Thy intercession were left unaided...*"

Fighting the odds and testing frontiers seemed part of the family background. Grandfather Dr. Emmet J. Mullally was a prominent physician in Montreal and one of the first English-speaking commissioners on the Catholic School Board. Dr. Mullally was instrumental in founding D'Arcy McGee High, the first English-language Catholic highschool in Montreal. Being an avid historian of the Irish legacy in Canada, Mullally had it named D'Arcy McGee after the dynamic Irish parliamentarian who was assassinated on Sparks Street in Ottawa in 1868. Later, a grade school in Montreal was named after Mullally himself, in acknowledgement of his contribution to education in the city.

"We had a happy, stable home," Father Nicholas Gruner remembers today, "a mother who stayed home, a father home every night and on weekends. My parents never disagreed in front of us. We took vacations as a family to Prince Edward Island and sometimes in St. Joseph de Mont Rolland, 45 miles north of Montreal, where a house was lent us." It was there Nicholas learned how to swim in a hurry shortly after his brother Peter threw him in the water and he almost drowned.

Not a word of swearing was ever heard in the house, neither blasphemous talk nor gutter language. "The worst my father ever said was 'bloody'."

His brother Tony recalls that before Nick was born, Peter had learned some swear words when he was two, from a maid and that when he used them in front of his mother, she figured out where it came from and immediately dismissed the woman. Father relates, "My mother took her duty as a Catholic mother very seriously and saw to it that blasphemy was never even whispered in her home.

"Although we might have been considered among the upper-middle class," Father Gruner notes, "we didn't have any excess. I remember father saying if he had wealth, he would share it generously. But he was not wealthy and we knew it. We were conscious of not having excess and of working for what we had. We had to earn our own way. My sister Jenny, the youngest, recalls that when she was 10, even though our parents could have afforded to buy her a bicycle, they insisted she earn her own. When Tony accompanied my father out of town to a big construction site, he ordered only a hamburger for his meal and told my father, 'I know you don't have much money so I didn't want to be a burden.'

"We paid our own way through school, lived at home for university, but worked in the summer to pay for it.

"We were all very different, all individual, all quite aware of our independence and our own point of view." Father recounted that the person who used to babysit him was a certain Madame St. Laurent, who told him that he did not speak until he was four. But when he spoke he knew exactly what he meant. He expressed himself very explicitly and objected if he was significantly misquoted. It is characteristic of how Father Gruner speaks today.

All of the Gruner children have post-graduate degrees, except for Michael, the eldest. And, indeed, both parents put a high value on education.

Father Gruner remembers: "My father came from a long line of inventors and engineers. He had an engineering degree himself and turned down a scholarship because others more needy than himself needed it.

"His middle name and my own is Nightingale. Alice Nightingale, my father's mother, insisted that we were related to Florence Nightingale, the famous nurse.

"My mother had a great sense of justice. She was supportive if we were in the right but not if we were in the wrong. For example, despite pressure from the angry car owner, my mother would not let Tony pay for a windshield broken during a baseball game because he was not actually playing in the game but merely watching. She had been a school teacher before she married and continued to take an active role in our education. In my first year at McGill University she made me redo a paper on economic history even though I thought it was quite adequate. She said it wasn't good enough and made me work harder on it.

"Her family was well known in Montreal. Grandmother Mullally's family came to Canada in 1842, during the potato famine in Ireland, landing in Montreal.

"Grandfather Mullally could remember when Louis Riel was executed by the Government of Canada (for leading the Metis rebellion of 1885 in western Canada) and how his father explained that the hanging of Riel was bad for Canadian unity.

"Grandfather Mullally's mother knew her own mind and was very strong-willed. She was a MacDonald and despite very strong family opposition, she was the first Scot in PEI to marry an Irishman.

"Doctor Oscar Cameron Gruner, who was known to his grandchildren as 'Baba', was also a medical doctor who specialized as a pathologist and a researcher in cancer. Early in his life, his mother, Eleanor, a very strong-willed, artistic woman, determined that her son would become a famous surgeon." Her role model was that of Sir Barkley Moinahan. Sir Barkley was a competent surgeon to Queen Victoria. He wrote a text of surgery. In that text there was a section on the spleen, which at that time was still a considerable medical mystery. It was Oscar who wrote the chapter on the spleen though he was not given credit for it.

In 1910, Oscar, who was an assistant professor of pathology, and Alice came to Montreal with their two children, Malcolm and Douglas. He co-authored articles on pathology of various tumors with a Dr. Emmet James Mullally which were published in reputable journals such as the *American Journal of Pathology*. Mullally was a McGill graduate, and in one of the first groups of doctors to do what they now call a surgical residency. In 1913 the signs of war were obvious and Oscar felt he should be back in England. He returned and joined the British Army Medical Corps and worked as a pathologist.

Dr. Gruner pioneered a scientific test on the early detection of cancer by a simple but accurate count of white cells in the blood. He showed it to Nicholas when he was a child and taught Peter, then a teenager, how to use it. Peter is now a doctor himself.

Indeed, Oscar had a very original mind in medicine and cancer research. His work in 1915 was decades ahead of his time. Indeed, it wasn't until 50 years later that the scientific community caught up with his research. They finally recognized his work and he received an award in 1965.

He, himself, opposed some of the medical establishment and was critical of contemporary theories of medicine treating the human body as if it were simply a machine. He also thought that too many medical practitioners were in the back pocket of the drug companies. He was a quiet man and would never get into a fight, but, as a researcher, held on to the truth.

In 1949, he proved that cancer can be cured. A German man called Mr. Fookes, who worked for Malcolm, had cancer and Dr. Gruner cured him with medicine discovered by another researcher in Canada.

Malcolm Gruner, born on August 22, 1905, attended Leeds Grammar School where he did quite well academically. Although encouraged by his father to study medicine, he was never really interested. Oscar was a renaissance person and intrigued by many aspects of the then new world. Malcolm was especially interested with the new finds in the various Egyptian excavations and was a well-read Egyptianology buff. One of the digs revealed the mummy of an Egyptian princess. The archaeologists sent her ringed hand to Malcolm for evaluation.

In 1926, Malcolm, a graduate engineer, emigrated to work in Montreal at Vickers. He re-introduced himself to his father's old friend and colleague, Dr. Mullally. In so doing he re-met Jessie Rosalie. Malcolm returned to England but much correspondence ensued between he and Jessie. Jessie visited England with her father and brother James in 1928. Here, Jessie and Malcolm became engaged. They would be married in Canada.

Malcolm had exhibited, early in life, a readiness not to shrink from what he perceived as a 'call'. In Rome in the 1920's, the young Malcolm, not yet Catholic, was so moved by the life of St. Cecilia, the noble Roman virgin who professed her faith courageously and gave her life for Christ, that he was converted in the very place Cecilia was martyred.[2]

His conversion is recalled by Father Gruner: "My uncle Douglas had already turned Catholic but my father was adamant in refusing to do so. Then Malcolm was invited to Rome by his parents during the Holy Year, 1925. He said he would go, not to see Christian Rome but as an avid student, interested in archaeology, to see the ruins of pagan Rome. He made his way to the Church of St. Cecilia in Trastevere because of its archaeological interest and his great love of music, St. Cecilia being the Church's patron of music. When he was in the cellar of the ruins, he heard the story of how St. Cecilia died. (She was sealed in a steam room, but she remained alive. The executioners then attempted several times to behead her but the neck wound was not immediately fatal — she lived two more days while she dictated her spiritual will, giving her house to the Roman Catholic Church so that it could be converted into a place of worship. St. Cecilia was also a great apologist for the Church.)

"When I asked my father what converted him he said he was so moved by the story of St. Cecilia, who was rich and beautiful and had everything the world could offer, but out of love for Jesus Christ gave it all up and became a virgin martyr. In 1946, true to his promise made some 21 years before, the first daughter in the Gruner family would carry her name, so that, as in all Catholic families, the spiritual legacy of the early martyrs would inspire and strengthen and direct the offspring. But whether St. Cecilia's sacrifice would actually affect Malcolm's family in future years was being determined in the late autumn of 1943 by a hand writing in a far country.

§

God must surely be the greatest storyteller of all. He certainly knows how to keep a reader's attention. No one ever put the Old Testament down out of boredom, rather it is out of the exhilaration of trying to absorb the twists and turns, plots and counterplots, throughout the whole history of God's revelation of Himself to the chosen people that causes the reader to seek rest for the eye and the soul now and then. But throughout it all He holds the reader's attention as He held the attention of the Hebrews by one perfect tactic — a promise. He promised them a Redeemer. And He held their attention for centuries until He fulfilled that promise. It was only then that the jaded, to whom He had entrusted the promise, looked the other way. And God's treasure went elsewhere.

Every teacher knows the surest way to capture a naughty child's attention is to promise something is going to happen to him soon. To the cynical, over-indulged, spoiled and arrogant people of the Twentieth Century, God presented a device that would rivet their attention year in, year out, decade after decade. He gave them a Secret. Not "to" the world at large, but "for" the Catholic faithful in the world at large. Through His Mother at Fatima, He entrusted that Secret to three illiterate peasant children, Jacinta Marto, aged seven, her brother Francisco, nine, and their cousin Lucy dos Santos, barely ten.

A vocation from God can enter the heart of a child long before adolescence. God is not restrained by lack of faith in children. He knows what their future holds. God knows His own, knows that shepherds in Bethlehem would not hesitate to enter a cave, knows too that the child seers of Fatima, Jacinta and Francisco, would spend the rest of their short lives burning with love for Him. And He knows too that Lucy, the last remaining Fatima seer, would be obedient to Him and His Mother all her long life on earth.

In the spring of 1917, all of Portugal was electrified to hear that three nondescript children had apparently seen the Virgin Mary, in a pasture north of Fatima, on the 13th of May. She promised to meet them there on the same day every month until October.[3] There would be six meetings in all. Only the three children were at the first, 70,000 men, women and youths from all walks of life and every corner of Portugal were at the last. What was played out in between was some of the richest drama in the entire 2000 year history of Catholicism.

The Blessed Virgin told the children that God was much offended by the sins of mankind and asked if they would willingly make sacrifices to console Him and for the conversion of sinners. They were promised they would go to Heaven. (Jacinta and Francisco would die within three years, Lucy, the oldest would live for the rest of the century.) For six months the three withstood scorn, police threats, mental torture at the hands of the authorities, anger from their own families, and the suffocating adulation of enraptured spectators. Because of their faithfulness to grace, and with Our Lady's help, they survived it all. They were also helped by the two most famous ingredients of the entire phenomenon — they had been promised a great miracle in October and had been told a Secret in three parts.[4]

Over the decades, as Heaven allowed it, the first two parts of the Secret were made known by Lucy dos Santos, upon orders from her bishop, after she entered religious life.[5] The first part of the Secret contained a vision of the damned burning in Hell for all eternity, the fate awaiting many people in the world if man does not cease offending God.[6] The second part said that if mankind did not stop in its offences against God and His law, a worse war (World War II) would break out in the reign of Pius XI and that the world would continue to be punished by means of war, hunger, persecution of the Church and persecution of the Holy Father. The Virgin stated She would return to ask for the consecration of 'Russia' to Her Immaculate Heart, by the Pope and the bishops of the Church, to prevent Russia from spreading "... her errors throughout the world".[7] The third part of the Secret, which has yet to be revealed, was written down by Sister Lucy on twenty-four lines on one sheet of paper.[8] It has been in the Pope's possession since 1957[9] and has fascinated and challenged Catholics for the balance of this century.

As for the miracle promised for October, who was going to pay any attention to a wild prediction made back in July by three peasant children? They couldn't read, couldn't write, had no social graces whatsoever and seemed downright backward when you got a good look at them.

It was too ridiculous! They even announced the day it would happen, October 13th, and the time, noon,[10] the same hour the Virgin had supposedly been appearing to them since May. Who could fall for such nonsense?

Seventy thousand people did. At noon hour, October 13th, 1917, the approximate resident population of Jerusalem on the day Christ wrote with His finger in the dust, were standing ankle deep in mud, in the pasture north of Fatima, in a downpour that had lasted all night.[11]

"Look at the sun", Lucy cried at the prompting of She who had just revealed Herself to be Our Lady of the Rosary.

The rain stopped, the clouds disappeared, the sun appeared silvery, as easy to look at as the moon. It began to send out waves of color not seen since creation, to recreate the complexion of those upturned faces and of earth itself. Then to the stupefaction of the thousands transfixed below, it began to spin. Suddenly, it tore free from the heavens and threw itself earthward in a zigzagging plunge, a great ball of blazing heat, threatening to scorch the terrified spectators back into the dust from which they had come.

At the height of the terror, it stopped, just overhead, hung there for a moment, the great pendulum of time had ended its swing. Then time began again, the sun drew up, away from the thousands, and made its way back into the sky. In moments it was what it had been since it was created and once again, no one could look upon it.[12]

The seventy thousand were dry — clothes, hair, shoes, umbrellas and earth, all dry,[13] dry as the dust on the Temple floor that Christ had written in before He sent away the woman with the words, "Neither do I condemn you." Homeward bound the multitudes went that October day in 1917, hearts soaring, filled to the brim with an unparalleled reminder of God's forgiveness. Indeed, what man must do to earn that forgiveness is what Fatima is all about.

When the first two children died, the sole custodian of the Secret was Lucy dos Santos. There, within the soul of this peasant girl, the Secret has been allowed to remain out of the reach of evil men until the time was ready for it to be revealed.

By 1941, that life had already obediently shouldered the burden of her Fatima mandate for 24 years. That summer she was commanded to write what we now know as her Third Memoir.[14]

In that memoir she revealed for the first time that the Great Secret of Fatima was divided into three parts. On this occasion she also revealed the contents of the first two parts of the Secret.[15]

Lucy dos Santos, having relived the entire six months of 1917 through the writing of her Third Memoir and revealing the first two parts of the Secret by June, 1943, became ill with bronchial ailments which led to a serious case of pleurisy.[16] In September, alarmed by the prospect of the seer taking the third part of the Secret back into eternity with her, her bishop, Bishop da Silva of Leiria, expressed the desire that she write it down.[17]

She explained to the bishop that on such an important matter she preferred to await an order to do so.

Finally, in mid-October 1943, Bishop da Silva gave in writing to Sister Lucy the order she requested from him.[18]

Still she could not comply.

She felt for almost three months, "a mysterious and terrible agony. She related that each time she sat at her work table and took her pen in order to write down the Secret, she felt prevented from doing so."

She wrote her director that, "Although she had tried several times, she was unable to write what had been commanded her, and that this phenomenon was not due to natural causes."[19]

1943 ended. The day after New Year's Day, 1944, Our Lady appeared to Lucy in the infirmary of Tuy. There she confirmed: "... that it was indeed the will of God and gave her the light and strength to accomplish what had been asked for."[20]

In the Chapel at Tuy, the same place where she had received on June 13, 1929, the vision of the Most Holy Trinity, Lucy wrote down the Great Secret of Fatima told to her one July day in 1917, a day when witnesses noticed the sun grow so dim that the stars could be seen at noon, a Secret so vital even the stars had come out to listen.[21]

Note: For the reader who wants further background on Fatima before proceeding with this book about the Fatima Priest, please refer to Appendix I.

Chapter 2

The Beauty Of Thy House

Growing up in Montreal, it would be hard for a Catholic child not to be inspired by the career of Brother Andre, the humble religious who spent his life honoring St. Joseph. So many healing miracles were worked in St. Joseph's name through the prayers and hands—on ministrations of Brother Andre that even in his lifetime he was known as the "Wonder Worker of Montreal." Brother Andre's passion for his great patron, St. Joseph, knew no bounds. Overcoming demonic hostilities inside and outside the Church, the uneducated religious solicited the aid and financial assistance of the great and not-so-great in his grand plan. His determination and holiness caused to rise on the slopes of Mount Royal, the great edifice that would be known round the world as St. Joseph's Oratory.

Like so many others throughout the first half of the century, Nick Gruner went to the Oratory on the slope of Mount Royal many times and prayed to the famous servant of the great Saint Joseph. Also, like so many other boys in Quebec in the first half of the century, he was a Latin Mass altar boy by the time he finished second grade.

There, amid the high drama of the Immemorial Mass, once again like many before him, he underwent a special transformation.

There was a moment, in the Mass of the Ages, when many an altar boy made the transition from being just a child listening to the "blessed mutter of the Mass" as it issued from the lips of the priest, to becoming, at heart, a priest himself. The transition took place in the heart, on that landscape of innocence and trust, where, like a deer searching for a running brook, he had yearned for God, without knowing it, all his young life.

The moment was marked by the sound of running water. As he poured water over the fingers of the priest, he heard the priest whisper,

'*Lavabo ...*' . At the sound of that word, decade after decade, since the Mass of the Ages was formulated, century after century, that word '*Lavabo ...* ', washed the world forever from the altar boy's heart and ushered him into the priesthood.

That moment of grace would remain a mystery all of his life, perhaps only in later adulthood could one pinpoint with accuracy the moment when the altar boy became a prisoner of Christ. Still, there must have been a moment of recognition shuddering through his soul the first time he heard the translation of the words into his own tongue.

"I will wash my hands among the innocent;
And will compass Thy altar, O Lord,
That I may hear the voice of Thy praise;
And tell of all Thy wondrous works.
I have loved, O Lord, the beauty of Thy house;
And the place where Thy glory dwelleth.
Take not away my soul, O God, with the wicked:
Nor my life with men of blood
In whose hands are iniquities:
Their right hand is filled with bribes.
But as for me, I have walked in my innocence:
Redeem me, and have mercy on me.
My foot hath stood in the direct way:
In assemblies I will bless Thee, O Lord." (Ps. 25)

Of all the moments of nurturing that demonstrated the sheer genius of Holy Mother Church none surpass that moment when the Bride of Christ, so breathtaking in Her grandeur, nemesis of principalities and powers, terror of tyrants and ideologues, turns all Her attention to the littlest of Her children, the pure and trusting boy on the altar, and gives him an embrace that makes of his past, present and future, a love story unequalled in the annals of romance, the pure and utter thralldom that can exist only between a young man and God.

Powerful enough to wed time to eternity, nevertheless the love that enters a boy's heart at '*Lavabo ...*' remains within, without a pulse, until, as surely as the head is hinged to the shoulders, the boy, following an impulse he could not fathom, nor scarcely even acknowledge, leans his head back and looks up at the body of the Son of Man hanging above the tabernacle. His eye follows the line of those tortured limbs, all four of them drawing the eye toward their point of intersection, that Sacred Heart hidden within the constricted chest, and the altar boy's heart begins to throb, beating out the rhythm of the realization that floods his soul, the rhythm of the answer to the question that has haunted him since first he saw that Body on the Cross on the wall above his crib —

'Why'? For a moment the boy is lost in the silence of the Cross, but then the ticking seconds are pounding, pounding, pounding within his own chest. And he knows the answer.

Somehow, he makes his way through the remainder of his duties, changes into his own clothes, rushes out into the cold winter air of morning and flies headlong homeward through the snow crying, "For me. For me. For me." And he is in love. And called to be a priest forever.

A mandate from God can come any time and when least expected. The Virgin in Nazareth was not expecting Gabriel. The shepherds in the fields of Bethlehem were not expecting a choir of angels, yet they were mandated to go seek a child wrapped in something special and laying in a manger. The shepherds on the slopes of Bethlehem, drowsy, cold, probably hungry and cranky wanted nothing more than to doze off and be left alone. The most introspective of them might have sat gazing eastward over Jordan toward the Mount where he had been told since childhood that Moses was buried. Stories told in childhood glow with a sacred warmth that is never more welcome than in the cold heart of middle age. But, instead of being left to their rest, the shepherds were called upon to witness nothing less than the arrival of God on earth in the most unexpected of wrappings, the flesh of a baby child.

Far away from those famous shepherds in time and geography, three other shepherds — aged seven, nine and ten, had nothing more on their mind one spring day in northern Portugal, in 1917, than to rush their way through noontime prayers, when suddenly they were mandated to contemplate nothing less than the future of mankind.

So it is that greatness can enter the heart of a child and shape its future even as a boy runs home after early morning Mass, bursting to tell his mother what has just happened to him. He rushes into the kitchen, finds her at the stove, as he does every morning after Mass, but, instead of blurting out the news, he stands there speechless.

Only then does he realize the thing so recently planted in his chest is a secret, between him and God. He cannot even tell his mother. How does he know this? Well, how did the Wise Men know they could not return to Jerusalem and gossip? Heaven flooded them with the wisdom of doing otherwise.

The mother glances back from the stove to the doorway and sees the altar boy returned. Sees the snow melting from his cap onto his brow, coursing in miniature brooks down either side of the face. In a second of time so tiny only angels could measure it, she has recorded the change in him. She looks at the light in his eyes, the words shaped on his lips but arrested there by some mysterious grace with which she has always been sharing this child. "Don't drip snow on the floor," she might say.

Then, perhaps, "Breakfast is on the table."

Simple banal words, spoken since time immemorial at this time of a winter morning, between mother and son. But this time by a mother to a priest.

Faith comes through the mother, said De Maistre. It always has. It always will. Who can doubt that the Three Wise Men had three wise mothers?

Padre Pio received the faith from his. Cardinal Mindzenty from his. Father Fuentes from his. They grew into three of the most persecuted priests of the Twentieth Century. One can easily suspect that it was in those silences between a mother and her son, a boy with his secret, a mother with hers, that Pio, Fuentes and Mindzenty gained the strength to stand alone against the most horrific forces this century could throw at them, and emerge with their defense of the Cross intact after years of vilification, betrayal and persecution. Is there a boy at your kitchen door? Look closely before you answer. Could he be a Fourth Wise Man, perhaps an inheritor of the mantle left on the river bank by Pio or Mindzenty? The Catholic child standing at the schoolhouse door on his first day of school in 1948 was a new creature on earth, one living under the threat of the nuclear annihilation of whole nations, unaware that his Church, too, was an endangered species.

§

A child entering grade school in Catholic Quebec went prepared with five or six years of home catechism. When Nick Gruner was five, his mother said she wanted all her children to grow up to be not just nominal Catholics, but good Catholics. She taught them about the Immaculate Conception at home, before school. It is the wise mother who reserves this precious teaching for herself in those early childhood years. The child accepts the Immaculate Conception with the greatest of ease. What, after all, to a pure child could be more natural than for God to create perfect purity to be the Mother of His Son? To learn of this treasure from a mother is to be awarded a trophy of the faith that cannot be lost to any adversary, on any battlefield.

Like Catholic children the world over, Nick learned the story of Fatima at home, long before he ever saw a school door. Just across the street from the Gruner home lived Mr. Leonard Hynes, future President of C.I.L., his wife, Jessie, and their four children, each aged within a year of four of the Gruner children, including Nick. One day, in their house, during a recitation of the Rosary, he heard them inserting at the end of each decade the "O my Jesus ..." prayer formula dictated to Lucy by Our Lady of Fatima. He objected to it since he hadn't heard it said before. It was then that they told him about the Message of Fatima. He took the details home and inquired about them of his mother.

It was in the 5th grade of St. Joseph's School in Montreal that the teacher told the Fatima story to the class. After hearing it, he had gone home and announced that he was pledging to say the Rosary every day for the rest of his life. He was reminded by his mother that such a pledge was a solemn promise to the Mother of God and should be entered into with great caution and even greater resolve. The presence of the Mother of God in one's life was not to be taken lightly.

Father Nicholas Gruner would later recall the legacy of Marian devotion left by his family: "On my father's side of the family, devotion to Our Lady was quite deep. My father had been an Anglican and heard the arguments against devotion to Our Lady. Still, when I was in my twenties, he defined for me his attitude towards Mary — namely, that just as a king delights in honoring his queen, Jesus, who is King, delights in honoring Our Lady, who is His Queen.

"Grandfather Mullally had founded a hospital in Montreal and named it St. Mary's, after Our Lady. He had been born in Prince Edward Island and his uncle had been a sea captain. Once, the captain had to get rid of a drunken sailor who was causing trouble. As he was about to leave the ship, the sailor cursed the captain and the crew and the ship. Afterwards, off the coast of Newfoundland, a storm destroyed the ship. Nevertheless, not one of the men were lost, for, when the ship went down, my grandfather's uncle had them all praying the Rosary.

"My grandmother, Mary Mullally was an artist who painted pictures of Our Lady, including Our Lady of Fatima, which I now have in my house. When an art exhibit in Montreal once displayed a broken lily, symbolizing the artist's denial of the virginity of Our Lady, my grandmother severely upbraided the curator, taking him to task for including it in the display."

In the late Forties, when Nick was in early grade school, the essentials of the Fatima story and the beauty of the characters were known to nearly every Catholic. What was not known, and could not have been at that time by the father and mother catechizing their children in far away Canada, was the drama that had been still unfolding within the Church regarding both Our Lady's Message and, in particular, the Third Secret.

What Pius XII knew about the Great Secret can only be a matter of conjecture. However, in 1950, he performed a unique and vital act of leadership. On November 1, Pius XII declared as infallible teaching of the Church that Mary had been assumed body and soul into Heaven upon Her death.[1] The Dogma of the Assumption would give a world living under the shadow of extermination a reminder that life did not end here, that no matter what evil man might bring into the world, the company of a loving God for all eternity was our true destiny.

Chapter 3

Wound In The City

Nick Gruner was in high school from the fall of Hungary to the fall of the Church Militant. From 1955 to 1959 he attended D'Arcy McGee High School, the same school his grandfather, Dr. Mullally, had founded 25 years earlier.

Few young men of that era could savor such continuity in family tradition. For Nicholas Gruner it would last a lifetime. Indeed it would have to, for tradition as it was known by home, school and family, was about to be swept away by a wind created outside of nature.

Nick had always been considered serious in nature even as a teenager. Not that he was totally immune to stimuli, but fads never seemed to touch him. Rock and roll, for instance, was popular, but it seldom consumed his interest. Fonder of Chopin and other classical favorites that Malcolm Gruner played at home in the evening, he became even more appreciative as he grew older.

"He was a bit of an entrepreneur in school," his brother Tony recalls, "organizing ski trips, selling magazine subscriptions to raise money for school projects. He wasn't into a lot of sports but he did play hockey in the Parish hockey league after he left high school." He had two sisters younger than himself. The last and seventh born, nine years Nick's junior, was named Jennifer. A classic moment of sibling co-existence is contained in her childhood memory of him.

"He was very good to me. He even taught me to ride a bike. I used to make him sandwiches, three cheese sandwiches every day. He'd pay me 10 cents. It was my first job. He was my first employer. But he'd complain to classmates when he got tired of them. By the time my older sister joined him in school she was jokingly blamed for making those sandwiches."

As a family, they followed the practice of visiting seven churches in one day the week before Easter on Passion Sunday. It was one of the first great Catholic family traditions swept away by the changing times.

At university, Nick was voted in as president of the Newman Club, winning by one vote. He put a lot of effort into it, showing his characteristic willingness to lead the way even when unpopular, against opposition.

Though there was little time for it in his always busy schedule, he enjoyed playing hockey and football.

Always, he exhibited a lifelong character trait.

"He had a strong sense of right and wrong," Jennifer recalled. "When Jehovah's Witnesses came to the door there was a strong family tradition of talking to them, not just for courtesy sake, but at length, to teach them. He seriously defended their attacks against Our Lady's virginity to which they were unable to argue. He would talk to them and they would go home to check out what he said, hopefully to think things through. But he did not talk about the religious life in the sense of his being interested in it."

Looking back and reflecting on those early days forty years later, Father Gruner explains some of this secondary family and school formation: "I learned to 'make it on my own' very early on." As the fifth child and the fifth son, he was in the middle of the family. "Of course, my sister's friends were not my friends. My older brother Tony was, and still is, a charming man. He made friends easily and was invited everywhere but, as older brothers are wont to express, he did not want his younger brother tagging along. Plus, we had different characters. As a result, I made my own way.

"That continued after leaving grade school. All my companions went to Loyola, which was run by the Jesuits. But my father insisted that, unlike my older brothers, I would not be taught by the Jesuits. Reputedly, they did not excel at teaching math and, as there was a possibility that I might go on to engineering as he had, he felt I would fare better at D'Arcy McGee, the school my grandfather Mullally had founded. It was then run by the Christian Brothers.

"D'Arcy McGee was in the heart of downtown Montreal, quite a different setting from where we lived. We weren't a rich family but we lived in what might be called a good neighborhood in what had originally been my grandfather's home. Though we wanted for nothing, and the house was well kept, we still did not have the extras that the neighbors had. Going to school in downtown Montreal at the age of 13, having no friends there, forced me to adapt to people of different cultures and diverse backgrounds."

It might be said that like many who are considered more mature than their years, there were certain stages of growing up he never went through. The trajectory of his future career had already begun, one that would constantly pit him against superior numbers.

He came by the dynamic honestly, as Tony Gruner relates — his parents tended to be politically Conservative in a province that was, at that time, historically Liberal, the Gruners taking advantage of the option of voting against the party in power. Even as he entered school, he was developing a resistance to being outnumbered, no doubt in part a result of being raised in a non-French family surrounded by the French-speaking population of Montreal.

§

Montreal itself had been founded by a special act of providence, although most Montrealers would not know that today. It began as a missionary outpost, the result of a dream interpreted as coming from God, the seeds of Montreal being sown by a small population of French pioneers who accurately believed their endeavors, sacrifices and sufferings were in the service of the Gospel and the Catholic Church.

As a Montrealer, it was not lost on Nicholas Gruner that his native city could have had a very different history had Louis XIV consecrated France to the Sacred Heart in 1689, as requested by Our Lord to St. Margaret Mary Alacoque.[1] If the powerful Sun King had obeyed, Protestant Europe might have been converted back to the Catholic Faith through France, and French North America might never have fallen to the English. As Nick Gruner learned later, these possibilities would dramatically parallel those promised by Our Lady of Fatima in return for the consecration of Russia. In retrospect, the parallels were even more poignant to him, when recalled, that his student days were lived during the collapse of the Church in Quebec. Would it have happened anyway? Would the Church in his native Quebec have withstood its almost total disappearance, along with the old Quebec, under longtime Premier Maurice Duplessis?

For all his faults, Duplessis understood the importance of keeping the province Catholic. He had even passed a law which kept the Jehovah's Witnesses out of Quebec. And, indeed, less savory aspects of Duplessis' reign made a profound impression on the young Nick Gruner.

A saintly Archbishop, the Most Rev. Joseph Charboneau, had confirmed him, the same bishop who soon got into trouble with the Vatican because he crossed a line drawn in the sand by Premier Duplessis. The famous strike of Quebec's asbestos workers struck the province like a cataclysm. It devastated incomes, starved families.

"Bishop Charboneau took the side of the union workers," Father Gruner today recalls. "I remember him as man with great courage and moral fortitude."

Experiencing a unique brand of hellfire, Charboneau raised money to feed the starving workers.

"He saved lives," Father Gruner points out. "Literally, Charboneau was a pastor feeding his sheep. Whether the strike was right or wrong did not matter, he would not see families destroyed by hunger."

Duplessis was outraged that a mere Archbishop should be siding with the union workers against the government. He apparently enlisted the aid of some well-placed Vatican bureaucrats.

Charboneau was removed, sent packing, a broken man, to Victoria, as a confessor of nuns. He was the Archbishop of Montreal yet he was summarily dismissed and replaced. His departure left wounds in the city for a long time.

Charboneau's feeding of the poor was his downfall. There can be little doubt that the incident still reminds one to be cautious regarding careerist Vatican bureaucrats. The reality at the bottom of the crisis should never be forgotten.

Charboneau's replacement was Paul Emile Leger, later to be made Cardinal. Leger's transformation throughout his career mirrors with sad irony the disintegration of the Church in Quebec. In the beginning, Leger's presence and determination were edifying. In the early Fifties he had caused a sensation at 10 o'clock one night by approaching a roadside pornography stand downtown, taking magazines off the racks and throwing them into a bonfire.

By the time he died, thirty-some years later, women in long priestess gowns stood along the steps of Notre Dame Cathedral holding aloft coffers of burning incense in their hands as his coffin was carried down the steps, at the avant garde Offertory, with baskets of bread on their head, all images of the post-conciliar Church Leger personally shaped in Quebec.

There were, admittedly, abuses of power executed by various Churchmen in Quebec over the centuries but overall this unique bastion of the faith in North America had been preserved. Then on October 8, 1958, Pius XII died. Pius had predicted Communism would strangle the Americas 'at the neck'. The noose was tightening before Pius was laid to rest. Few had seen it coiling into place. The election of John XXIII was felt in every city, hamlet and classroom in the world. Then came 1960. In Quebec, Duplessis and his two political successors died in the same year. It set the province spinning. On February 8, 1960, the curtain rose on the most catastrophic decade in the history of the Church. That day, the Vatican anonymously announced that the Third Secret of Fatima, the details of which Catholics worldwide had eagerly awaited, would not be publicly revealed that year.[2] The Sixties had started with a lie. Nick Gruner was still studying at McGill University in the critical year, 1963, when Pope John XXIII died, John Kennedy was assassinated, and Pope Paul VI reconvened the Second Session of the Council. Life seemed more serious suddenly.

Nick Gruner considered himself blessed to have gotten through the Catholic school system in Quebec before governmental attacks on education changed it forever. Ten years later, he would teach within that system, see how schools had been reorganized into large impersonal classes, both unwieldy and unwholesome. The public education system was not organized any better, and worse, it wasn't Catholic. By 1970 both systems would be destroyed, with few remnants of Catholicism surviving.

The priesthood had always been there. But even at 21, on retreat in Montreal, he had been cautioned, 'Finish your degree first and then consider the priesthood'. He was then two or three years into his degree, with no thought of abandoning his studies. Basic to his plans was to enter the seminary with a degree in business. He took his Bachelor of Commerce Degree at McGill University in Montreal, finishing in 1964. Then it was time off to see a bit of the world.

Chapter 4

Gethsemane

After graduating from McGill, Nicholas Gruner decided to head to Europe and visit places of importance to his father's English roots.

These were personal pilgrim years for Nicholas Gruner, filled with travels in honor of Mary's Motherhood of Men. He began his journey as a deck hand on a freighter to Europe, in 1964, cleaning and painting, until the officers' cook got sick and he took over the job.

Because Baba had a great devotion to Our Lady, he wanted his grandson to visit Aylesford, Kent, in England. He recalls why Oscar Cameron Gruner had such great devotion to Our Lady. "My uncle Douglas died in Australia when he was only 18 years old, trying to stop a team of horses that were running wild through the town. Douglas took after them on his motorcycle and the horses trampled him to death in January, 1926."

Many times it has occurred to Father Gruner that his father's sudden conversion was not only due to St. Cecilia, but also to Douglas, his brother, whom he believed offered his life to God to obtain this grace for Malcolm.

"This spirit of self-sacrifice is also reflected in my father who, after his conversion, made the heroic offering of allowing God to take all the merits and prayers for his soul in Purgatory to be offered to other souls before him.

"Shortly after Douglas' violent death, my grandfather Gruner had a dream about Douglas, who was the younger of his two sons. He described how, in his dream, he saw the way saints greet the newest one among them. First, the saints receive him, then afterward, Our Lady welcomes him to their number. He recognized Our Lady in his dream because She resembled the image of Our Lady as She is depicted in the chapel of Hartley, a small chapel in Kent, England. My grandfather described his special dream as follows:"

"The picture began by the appearance of a small glow of light... and the picture was of the altar rail and the altar of the Oratory here at Hartley... Very rapidly it became evident that there was a solitary young figure kneeling in the middle of the rail. It was Douglas. His head was bowed low over the rail...

"...The form of Our Lord became evident; robed in brilliant golden light; the raiment and He were one... the upper part of our boy's body being quite lost to view in the blinding light of Our Lord's presence.

"Then I perceived His Face, sharply visible in semi-profile, among the brightness which extended beyond and all round, almost like thick rays; and as He stooped over the boy, and seemed to embrace him, his shoulders, He seemed to be soothing him and comforting him, and embracing him, as a father might...

"...One felt absolutely secure; it was not an atmosphere; it was peace itself; it was living peace...

"...That odor of Peace was all between the place I saw, and right across the gulf down to me, and I was filled with it during the whole time His Form was visible...

"...Suddenly, at his left side, appeared the form of a most beautiful Lady; Her face was in semi-profile; there was a wonderful expression on it; infinite motherhood; the face was not young; the light She gave round Her was extremely intense, much more than that of the angels; and yet it was less intense than that of Our Lord, different really, it was not that peculiar sense of Almighty—security.

"She stooped down to our boy and seemed gently to lift him up, his head lying in Her left elbow; I could not see his features; he was like a babe; and yet I was sure it was still he — still Douglas; he seemed to be sleeping, and yet aware of being in Her arms. His form was indistinct. As She held him thus, the circle of angelic forms rose a little with Her, and there seemed a movement of them all — away from the rail, and towards the Gospel side of the altar, and it was as when a person is carried from among a crowd and the crowd slowly makes as if to follow. At the same time She stood erect, nearly; and was in full profile; and for a moment I saw that Her profile was now exactly the profile of Our Lady of Hartley; but it was not a fancy; She was living; one could tell it was not a statue. The light of the whole scene centered in Her as She moved from the altar rail.

"The details became indistinct for a short time now; but when it was all clear again, I saw that Our Lady had handed the soul of our boy into the care of a great multitude — a very great multitude of bright forms, forms like the angelic ones at the altar, but paler; where their features were visible, one could see they seemed sad — but a happy sadness.

"They seemed to move greatly as She came; they moved eagerly forward to their new companion; it was a very active movement; and yet they did not seem to move away from their place. It was the movement of a sudden intense interest and eagerness to minister to the newcomer. But when the newcomer was among them he became like unto them; not like a baby—form; and he was quite lost to view to me; so dense was the crowd of beings who came round him..."

(The full text of Oscar Gruner's dream, which he entitled "The Message of January 28, 1926", can be found in Appendix II).

Father Gruner remembers: "When Baba heard of my trip to England, he insisted I go to Aylesford, which is also in Kent, where Our Lady of Mount Carmel appeared to St. Simon Stock and presented him with the Brown Scapular in 1251.[1]

Saint Simon Stock's cell was flooded with light when Our Lady appeared to him. She held the Scapular in Her hand, even as She wore it full size on Herself, and She made this, the Scapular, a sign of Her special love and protection for them.

She said to Saint Simon, "This shall be to thee and to all Carmelites a privilege that whosoever dies clothed in this (Scapular) shall not suffer eternal fire. It shall be a sign of salvation, a protection in danger and a pledge of peace."

"My grandfather had always been gentle with me but was unusually adamant in insisting I go to Aylesford. So I went there, staying from December, 1964 to March, 1965. I was enrolled in the Scapular during that time and have not taken it off since. That was the beginning of my pilgrimage to Marian shrines." And since putting on the Scapular, Nicholas almost immediately started to pray the Rosary daily. He has only missed a few days over the last thirty years.

He lived as a volunteer at the shrine for three months, until March '65. From there he crossed over to France, heading for Rue du Bac, Lourdes and also to Garabandal.

§

Can any priest look back over his shoulder at the grace that has shaped his life and pinpoint with exact precision the moment he first recognized the call to the priesthood? What is the call? What exactly is it calling the young man toward?

A priest is set aside from other humankind by one single fact, he is born with a vacant chamber in his heart that he can fill only after giving it a name.

Breathes there a man who claimeth not
One lonely spot
His own Gethsemane,
Whither with his inmost pain
He fain
Would weary plod,
Find the surcease that is known
In wind a—moan
And sobbing sea,
Cry his sorrow hid of men,
And then —
Touch hands with God.

(*Gethsemane* by Edmund Leamy)

The young man who touches hands with God never forgets the touch, and spends the entire treasure of his life force trying to earn that touch again.

Once, in Paris, shortly after visiting the shrine of the Miraculous Medal on Rue du Bac, praying before the incorrupt remains of the silent Saint, Catherine Labouré, and contemplating the famous chair in which Our Lady sat and held Catherine's head in Her lap, Nick Gruner made his confession to a French priest, not in the chapel itself, but in a makeshift confessional corner.

The priest asked about his vocation and explained, "When God created each individual human being, He, at the same time, gave that soul a vocation. Now if we are faithful to God's call, we will, in fact, be much more happy in this life because we shall fulfill in our lives what God intended us to be." The priest emphasized, "God created us in a way in which we will be more fulfilled, more ourselves, if we accept the call from God. It is a great obligation, a high vocation, but there is sacrifice."

The priest put a uniquely French perspective on it, 'la gloire' — sacrifice. Added to it was the promise that if one does what God wants, one will become more of what God wants one to be, and ultimately more happy.

Father Gruner would remember this promise throughout his life. By 1965, he was in Portugal, where he tried to hitchhike to Fatima but was unable to catch a ride. Eventually, he made his way north to Pontevedra and Tuy, from there to Santiago. He went to Garabandal in March, where he stayed for several days. He came back to Garabandal on June

18, 1965, when St. Michael reportedly gave the last message which told us to have greater charity and more love for the Most Blessed Sacrament and which also warned that many Cardinals, bishops and priests were on the way to hell and dragging many more souls with them.

His journey there really began to take more definitive shape in July, upon returning to Aylesford for Cardinal Carmel Heenan's official re-opening of the Shrine which had been lost to the Church since 1549 under the Protestant revolt in England. While walking behind a young pilgrim couple, he overheard the woman say to her husband, "I'm not sure about this Garabandal business. Is it really Our Lady appearing here? The miracle hasn't happened yet." Nick introduced himself and said, "You don't have those problems with Fatima. Fatima is approved. The miracle has taken place. The popes have approved it. Fatima is valid, Fatima is good." Nick also said, "If we listen to Fatima then we need to pray the Rosary, wear the Scapular, these are the message of Fatima. So at least you can resolve to obey Our Lady of Fatima. If you do all She said at Fatima, you need not worry about any, as yet, unapproved apparitions."

Yet even as he said those words, he was conscious of the difference between Garabandal and Fatima. Fatima was so uncomplicated because it was approved by the Church and thus so easy to promote.

At Garabandal, a pilgrim put into his hand a booklet on the Rosary by an American. It contained the statement of Our Lady regarding Russia, "If My requests are not granted Russia will spread her errors throughout the world raising up wars and persecutions against the Church. The good will be martyred, the Holy Father will have much to suffer, various nations will be annihilated."[2]

Interestingly, it was the only thing about Fatima in the booklet, amid meditations on the mysteries of the Rosary. He became preoccupied with what Our Lady's Fatima requests actually contained.

He finally returned to Montreal in August of '65. His brother Tony notes that although even in high school, Nick was similar in nature to what he is now, serious, with his humorous moments, after he came home from Europe there was a difference in him.

"In Europe, he had made the decision to become a priest."

He entered the seminary that September and was sent by the diocese of Montreal to Resurrection College in Kitchener to do his year in philosophy. He took as many courses as time would allow, passing them all with flying colors. In September, 1966, he went to the Grand Seminaire, the major seminary in Montreal, for his first year in theology. Most of the classes there were conducted in French. While there, he expressed himself emphatically about the outright atheism on the campus at the University of Montreal, to which the "Grand" was affiliated, and argued forcefully against a group of students, with modernist leanings, who were promoting the idea that Catholic divorce would be permitted in the future.

They claimed that Cardinal Garrone, the new Prefect in the Vatican in charge of all Catholic Seminaries, was on their side. Undaunted by prestigious names, Nick Gruner said, "I don't care if 10 Cardinals hold that position, it is still heresy. Divorce for Catholics can never be approved by the Church." The rector, in May, 1967, told Nicholas he did not agree with his intellectual position though he acknowledged they were argued intelligently and forcefully, but were not shared by him, and told him to try his vocation elsewhere.

By 1968 he was once more in Italy. He was, in fact, riding a train to San Giovanni Rotundo when he first heard of *Humanae Vitae.* He vigorously defended it against the naysayer. It was probably the first papal encyclical since the *Syllabus of Errors* that raised tempers in trains, buses and coffee shops worldwide.

He was to live in San Giovanni during the last six months of Padre Pio's life and was present for the funeral of the man called 'a living crucifix' who had suffered so cruelly from the ill will of Vatican bureaucrats, the indifference of Pope John XXIII and the financial exploiters of his name. Few men in this century suffered more for the love of his priesthood, few men were subjected to more suspicion and vilification, than the pious Franciscan of San Giovanni Rotundo.

His lesson to all seminarians might well be that any priest contemplating a new apostolate receives no peace on this earth. Vilification, libel and slander will rain down upon him with relentless force. Only knowing that Christ suffered worse slander allows men like Padre Pio to find strength to continue.

The list of priests, some of whom would later be canonized, who have so suffered is endless. St. John Vianney, St. Louis de Montfort, St. John Bosco, Damien the Leper. Is there a good priest alive today who has not been subjected to the malice of the relentlessly pious of today's Church and most especially from that ingredient of Church life few priests escape — the Catholic matron who considers all she needs to be canonized in her own lifetime is the friendship of a unique man of God, preferably one much in demand and the center of world attention?

Padre Pio showed all too clearly what fate lies in store for the priest who becomes a lightning rod for pious assassins ever active on the phone lines of the current day Church. Nick Gruner lived in San Giovanni from April till September 1968, when Padre Pio died.

On October 13, 1968, he saw Fatima for the first time. The most startling characteristic of the shrine in the Cova da Iria is its masculinity. This is no mere gathering place for sentimental housewives. Here, uniformed Portuguese soldiers, having returned home from the horrors of Angola, did the army crawl on their stomachs from the edge of the esplanade to the azinhiera tree to thank the Madonna for bringing them home safely. Here young men walk along the highway in packs with all the panache and swagger of gangs in any big city in the world, but here they carry Rosaries. Here men, young and old, join the women petitioners for the long sojourn on their knees, along the Penitential Way, from the edge of the Cova to the capelhina. Men walking the street with a Rosary in hand is as common as men fingering worry beads in Greece and the Middle East. Men come here to lay down their lives for God. Some never leave, content to pass the remainder of their days, living saintly hidden lives, serving the Virgin in the shadowed laneways spreading out from the shrine. Nicholas Gruner would come back many times. But for now there were more pilgrimages, to Lourdes, to La Salette, and finally to the Holy House of Loretto, in Italy.

§

During the years when Vatican II had been in session, Nick, like most of the world, did not follow it daily. He was aware of it, but was preoccupied with his seminary studies at that time. Indeed the sacrifice spoken of by the priest confessor at the Rue du Bac had not been long in coming, for by the Sixties the attack on the seminaries was already in full swing. The domino effect, the Council inadvertently set in motion for Catholic education and theology itself, was already threatening to unbalance the spiritual and intellectual foundations of the priesthood. It was during these years that the ideologies that had haunted the Church since Pius IX ceased being mere specters and seized control of seminaries, colleges, high schools, and even began to filter down to the Catholic grade school level. Americanism, Leo XIII had labelled it. Modernism, Pius X had called it. Democratic socialism and secular humanism were its classroom euphemisms.

In the resulting confusion spreading everywhere in the dogmatic, hierarchial, sacramental Church, a seminarian had little but his own spiritual instincts (*sensus fidelium*) to help him discern what was true from what was not. Our Lady had promised those who prayed the Rosary daily, would not fall into heresy. Father Gruner reflected in later years, "How fortunate I had rediscovered the Rosary as an adult, before entering into the seminaries in those days of confusion."

For him the determination to always fight for what was true had been founded long ago. His entire educational trajectory reveals an independent mind prepared to stand alone regardless of the cost.

Political and organizational abilities which would be so crucial to his own future apostolate had been already in evidence as early as 1956, when he became president of the ATC (Annunciation Teenagers Club).

Throughout those years, his sister Jennifer recalled, Nick remained thoroughly involved in the normal activities of day to day life. In 1956, he became president of Annunciation Teenagers Club. The older teens were letting it close down but Nick took it over and made it flourish for many more years, despite jeering opposition from the older teenagers.

> "The older teens basically despised the efforts of the founder, a Mr. Coleman, a Vice-President of Kraft Food in Montreal, and talked about closing the club down. I wrote that we would like to keep it open. As a result of that letter, I was elected president and we were allowed to try one more time. In spite of the jeers of the older teens, we were able to revive the club, making it active within the parish once more." This initiative of his also helped others, he recalls, "I recruited Eric McLean, who was one year lower in school, to work on our executive committee. He became the next president of ATC and later went on to join the Jesuits. Today he is the Provincial for the English-speaking Jesuits in Canada."

At McGill University, he became president of the Newman Club, winning the election by one vote — that of the returning officer, who had the deciding vote since the vote had been tied. He found himself in a leadership role responsible to and for people who had, to some extent, opposed him. The experience foreshadowed future battles.

In October 1970, he was offered a position with a small Mexican religious community housed in Rome. He took them up on the offer, staying a year. While there, he completed his second year of theology, taking his courses at the Pontifical University of St. Thomas Aquinas.

That brief stay with the Mexican Community would ultimately involve Nick in the drama of initiating a new and unique seminary. At the Mexican Community, the founder, Father Morelos, urged the novices to work on Sunday in the orchards. Gruner chose not to engage in physical labor on Sundays and so, after exams, in June, he departed, at the insistence of Father Morelos. Thereafter he was left to find his own way, relying on some money he still had left in his bank account from teaching.

As Father Gruner recalls:

> "In the summer of 1971, I used to go to Mass near St. Paul's Outside the Walls, and pray there every day with some Franciscan

friars who were just beginning to form their own community. I had just left St. Paul's Basilica to go back to my room when I noticed the car from the Mexican community that I had left one month before.

"I met a Father Carlos and two other visitors to Father Morelos' community, Ron Tangen and Les Stelter, who had come looking for me at my previous address, having been directed to me by a friend in London, England. They were looking for a seminary.

"I told them about Brother Gino, a religious well known in Rome as a stigmatist and miracle worker and, as many said, the successor to Padre Pio. Some days later they came by and wanted me to bring them to Brother Gino, which I did. I translated for them and told Brother Gino they were looking for a seminary, and Brother Gino suggested that all three of us join his Order, the Oblates of the Blessed Virgin Mary (O.M.V.), and study there, at San Vittorino, where Brother Gino lived. Ron was overjoyed with the suggestion. Brother Gino told me to be their 'guardian angel'. I refused to translate this at first, since it wasn't addressed to them, but at the guys' insistence I finally translated what Brother Gino had said. Brother Gino told us there was going to be a general chapter of the order in mid August and to not apply now, but come back after the general chapter had been held.

"Brother Gino had the gift of foretelling the future sometimes and was a prudent counsellor. They took his advice. As Brother Gino appointed me to be their guardian angel, they invited me to go with them to Garabandal, Fatima and Lourdes. They had a third companion, Mike Larshack. They were all over six feet tall and somehow all fit into a Fiat Seicento, much smaller than a Volkswagen. I took the fourth seat.

"On the pilgrimage trip that followed, we travelled over 1,000 miles and we stopped at a number of places including San Damiano, where it was reported Our Lady was appearing. There we met Andy Winchek and picked him up to bring him to Rome. In Garabandal we met Jim Shelton from Ohio, who was 39, 10 years older than I and we brought him back to Rome as well. In Rome, we met a third American, Jim McArdell, from New Jersey. They all agreed to join the Oblates.

"Although Brother Gino suggested we stay at San Vittorino, and we were welcomed when we went there every so often, we continued to be stationed in Rome at the OMV parish of St. Helen's.

"Shortly after joining the Oblates, five of us English-speaking seminarians went on another trip to Eastern Europe with Father Michael, the priest in charge of the seminarians, along with three other

Italian speaking seminarians. We visited the OMV house in the same city where the Council of Trent was held. We also visited Austria where the Oblates had a parish and a house in Vienna. From Austria we went to Hungary."

It was during their stay in Hungary, September 1971, that Father Gruner gained a first-hand view of what Communism was really like.

"Early in September, 1971, eight of us seminarians and a priest drove to Hungary. Visas to enter the country were only issued for 36 hours and the fee was the largest I had ever seen for such a brief visa. As we approached the Austrian-Hungarian border, I took a closer look at the landscape. In both directions the fields were ploughed up and mined and steel watchtowers were planted every half mile or so. The whole country was like a giant prison camp with miles of barbed wire fencing. The sentinel scrutiny towers seemed high enough to watch for anyone trying to make a run across the minefields, making escape virtually impossible.

"There was a heavy steel barrier at the Hungarian border that you would not dare to try to run through with your vehicle. As if that wasn't bad enough, once inside that barrier you found you were trapped between that and yet a second steel barrier. We noticed something very unusual when the immigration compound was changing guard. There were not just two military border patrol men being replaced by two others. There were three guards, all with machine guns drawn, replaced by three other men, also with guns drawn. The third, Father Michael told us, was to shoot the first two guards if they should ever try to escape. Was he serious? I don't know. But none of us were about to start testing them.

"After some time, we were finally released and allowed into the country. We had 36 hours to drive to Budapest, look around and get out before we were officially breaking the law and liable to some fine or imprisonment. We drove to the capital and noted how empty the streets were, hardly any cars. But there were long line—ups of people at the grocery stores waiting their turn to buy bread.

"That evening, around 9:00 p.m. we went to a restaurant. Again, hardly anyone was there except for an older woman who started to speak to us. She raised her voice and spoke excitedly in Hungarian for a minute or so. Quickly she was surrounded by two or three men in trench coats and without ceremony hurried out of the restaurant. No one moved or did anything — and, we did not see her again. We decided, right then and there, not to experiment in free speech in a public place.

"The following morning five of us went to the American Embassy to see if we could visit Cardinal Mindzenty. It was watched by two Hungarian plainclothes police who paced in front of the embassy all the time. I had never had any trouble entering an American Embassy anywhere else around the world, but here I was not allowed in as I was not an American citizen. I was told it was because of the ever watchful Communist police who were looking for some pretext to accuse the Americans because of the high profile exile, Cardinal Mindzenty, who had been living inside the embassy for the last 15 years.

"The Hungarian Communist police outside were there as spies to ensure that Cardinal Mindzenty did not escape and to see who was going in to visit him. He represented a real and continuous threat to the morally bankrupt regime that had imposed itself on the Hungarian people for the past 25 years.

"That one man represented such a threat shows what moral authority the Church had and would have if it would follow the courageous example of that great witness to the Catholic Faith.

"I learned afterwards that not even the four American seminarians who were let inside the Embassy were able to meet Cardinal Mindzenty. Obviously, access to him was near impossible. Cardinal Mindzenty had come freely to the Embassy in 1956 when he was released from the clutches of his Communist torturers and prison guards during the brief Hungarian uprising. He stayed there as a symbol of resistance, resistance against the religious and civil oppression his countrymen had been and still were undergoing.

"The Cardinal was, no doubt, treated humanely inside the Embassy, but it was clearly a crucifixion for him. May he pray for us today, now that he is in Heaven. I believe his case will be introduced shortly for sainthood. We need many more Catholics of all levels from laypeople to Cardinals like him.

"One of the Americans with us spoke German, which is the international language of Eastern Europe and thus we were able to communicate and find the address of an old acquaintance of his living in Budapest. The man and his wife had not dared have their children baptized because they would have lost their good paying jobs. They both were like middle managers in a State run concern, part of a small fortunate group who would own their own home after paying the mortgage on it over 35 years.

"This home was a very small apartment on the 8th floor of a very large and run down apartment complex. The toilet top was made of wood with tin to prevent the water leaking out of it. The concrete beams and columns in the stairwells were crumbling to dust. We estimated the building would not be standing in 35 years, but this was the 'workers paradise'.

"Obviously they were getting neither the kingdom of God nor much else on earth. It is indeed sad that people do not realize how true Our Lord's statement is: 'Seek first the kingdom of God and all things will be added unto you'. One could say, by way of implication, 'Seek first the paradise of man on earth and you will get hell here and hereafter'. To us this point was clearly made in Hungary.

"On Saturday morning after we went to the U.S. Embassy we looked at more of the sites in the city. The historic Church of St. Stephen had been turned into a museum by the Communists. We saw it for the historical record of what it had been in the past and also to see what Communism did to famous churches. Creeping secularism in the West also has the effect of turning our famous cathedrals into mere tourist traps and quasi-museums, but in Hungary the effect was achieved by a deliberate state policy.

"Saturday afternoon, our Hungarian host took us to the monument built in honor of the Russian soldiers who 'liberated' the city. It is a massive monument placed in the prime location of Budapest overlooking the Danube River which runs through the city. It is an historic spot, not just because of the 'liberation' monument, but because it is symbolic of the glorious days of Hungarian history before Marx, Lenin and Stalin were even heard of. Here at this monument stand not only several giant statues of Russian soldiers laboring to take over Budapest, but also several live flesh and blood Russians with real guns standing guard.

"Les Stelter decided to have his picture taken in front of the Russian monument. There he stood, 6'2" with his arms upraised holding in his hands a giant sized wooden rosary for all to see. Several pictures were taken when our Hungarian host called me over to him and quietly but firmly said, 'Tell your friend to take down his rosary. You see that Russian solider over there?' 'Yes' I said. 'Well he might think your friend is mocking the Russians and he will have me imprisoned.' Les took his rosary down in this city supposedly 'freed' by the Russians, yet not free enough to display a rosary in public.

"We left that afternoon in a hurry because our 36-hour visa was running out. Thanks to our two guides, we had seen more than most in that short period of time. We made it back to the border with only half an hour to spare. After our luggage was thoroughly inspected and rummaged through, we were allowed to leave."

When they returned they saw first-hand that the writing was on the wall for conservative and orthodox seminarians. Father continues:

"We went to St. Helen's parish where Father Michael was in charge of seminarians in Rome, 25 km from San Vittorino, in the Casalina district of Rome, close to the heart of the city. They were renovating the seminarian's chapel. The altar was not going to be left against the wall but put in the center. Father Ron, who had spent four years looking for a good seminary and had been invited by Brother Gino himself to join the Oblates, was not about to take this chapel renovation lying down. He objected quite strenuously and went to Brother Gino and told him his objections. Brother Gino told us to ask to be transferred out to San Vittorino and take seminary training there and take a car in, every day, to the Angelicum.

"The Superior General, Father Ottello Ponzanelli, who was about to leave for a three-month tour of the Oblate houses in South America said he did not want the seminarians to go to San Vittorino. He left the decision to us English-speaking seminarians but strongly counselled against it. I said I would stay with the majority, since I was the translator.

"Then Ron and Les and a third seminarian decided to go to San Vittorino, I then said I would go as translator. The other two Americans also then agreed to go. This was the beginning of a seminary that would rock the Vatican.

"By September, 1972, we had 50 new seminarians and would have had 100 had the Oblate middle-managers allowed us to accept the Nigerian applicants. I was authorized by the Superior General to speak on behalf of the Oblates, in the summer of 1972, on vocation-gathering trips in the U.S. and Canada. I acted as the official translator and travel companion of Father Capello. He was opposed to what we stood for, was very 'modern' but I suppose that was the Superior General's way of maintaining control and placating the strong opposition he was getting from some of the 'modern' Oblates.

"My role in the founding was getting professors who were orthodox and conservative, the distinction between conservatism and traditionalism hadn't been made yet. We found Father Buckley, Father de Voss and Father Vansteenkiste to teach philosophy.

"Basil, Ron and I drew up and printed a brochure about the seminary, with the Superior General's approval. Ron wrote a letter explaining his experiences. He started as follows, 'I am writing before the Blessed Sacrament exposed' and went on to describe his experience looking for a seminary for four years, and how they were all bad ones, and how his dream was fulfilled by going to San Vittorino. Over several months, it got published in eleven small journals. We circulated our brochure, especially in Ron Tangen's mailings, to prospective seminarians who had written him as a result of his letter being published. The brochure explained that the seminary was based on the rule of the saintly Father Lanteri, a humble Italian priest from the Piedmont district of Northern Italy, who lived through the troubled period during and after the French Revolution, and died in 1830.

"One of the purposes of Father Lanteri's congregation was to fight current errors. Alas, the modern Oblates' attitude was, 'We don't fight current errors anymore.' Father Lanteri spoke of St. Thomas as the first choice of teacher of dogmatic theology and formation, and St. Alphonsus for moral theology, to fight the current errors, both being Doctors of the Church.

"During the fall of 1971, while living at San Vittorino, I heard from my friend, Nimal Mendez, about his brother Basil's plight. Basil had been a professor of philosophy in Ceylon, who decided to become a priest, and entered a diocesan seminary in Ceylon.

"Basil's agony was not unlike my own persecutions at the hands of seminary administrators. I told Brother Gino about Basil, and in keeping with Father Lanteri's spirit, Brother Gino agreed for us to pay for Father Basil's plane ticket to bring him over. Father Basil had fought against heresy in the Ceylon seminary and told the Cardinal there, quoting St. John Eudes: 'When heresy is taught in the seminary, there will be blood flowing in the streets.' And indeed, sad to say, there has been blood flowing in Ceylon almost ever since Father Basil left the country. In fact, even recently, they had a strike in nearby Madras, India, in sympathy for bloodshed going on in Ceylon."

In their brochure, the young seminarians promised a rich prayer life to others interested in the priesthood: 15 decades of the Rosary every day, and one hour before the Blessed Sacrament, Mass and Communion; and a spiritual apostolate afterwards, giving the sacraments, preaching the gospel, saving souls, as well as being taught St. Alphonsus and St. Thomas.

"The brochure struck a nerve." Father Gruner recalls, "We got hundreds of letters. The seminary was written up around the world, thanks to the prayers and sacrifices of Brother Gino and, of course, the fact that we were offering a genuine Catholic training to serious young men who knew that finding a true Catholic seminary was becoming very difficult.

"We operated our outreach on a shoestring with only a few dollars donated here and there which, after six months, started to be more sizeable. By October, 1972, one year after we had started to recruit seminarians, we had collected and spent $25,000 to promote Oblate vocations. This was only one quarter of what the Archdiocese of New York had, just for their vocation outreach."

Nick, Ron and Brother Gino had demonstrated by October, 1972, that there was no lack of vocations in North America.

At the same time, in 1972, the North American College in Rome, sponsored by the National Bishops Conference of the USA, was openly talking about closing down because they couldn't get enough seminarians to fill it. The whole hierarchy of the USA couldn't find enough seminarians to keep the North American College going, even though at the College each seminarian had a private room, bathroom and office, which by any seminarian's standards are palatial. The Archdiocese of New York alone had a $100,000 budget per year to find seminarians but was not successful in finding many, if any, while that year with only $25,000 the Apostolic zeal of these Oblates brought in fifty new seminarians.

Then the fight began. As has happened so very often in this century, a success story attracting the attention of the Vatican upper echelon spelled trouble. Specifically, it brought into the picture Cardinal Garrone, at that time the head of the Congregation for Education. Father Gruner continues the story:

"When I returned to San Vittorino on the feast of St. Francis, September 17, Vini Young, a personable young seminarian, said how relieved he was that I was back. Four seminarians suspected of being Communists, and who were not part of the movement we had generated, had turned the Superior against the vast majority of seminarians. They insisted we remove all outward signs of piety, such as medals worn on the outside, crosses on our briefcases, and what have you.

"Our Lady helped us in this crisis through Brother Gino. God gave Brother Gino a vision of the Communist seminarians phoning a Communist priest in the Vatican at 2:00 a.m. Brother Gino went downstairs and surprised these communist infiltrators as they were on the phone in the kitchen where they thought no one would find them at that late hour.

"After this, Brother Gino took me aside and said, 'If you don't stand up to them now, you will lose the seminary you want to form. Stand united'. That's how Communists work, a small number can overwhelm a larger number too intimidated to stand up.

"I explained his words to the others and we did stand united." The four Communist seminarians saw the ranks closing in on them, saw that they could not carry the day in modernizing the seminary and finally gave up. They were ultimately shown the door."

Brother Gino said later, "Because of the presence of one person (Gruner) and the absence of another, (who had supported the four), we were able to get rid of four Communist seminarians."

Brother Gino was asked by the seminarians, after the Communists left, why this was allowed to happen. He replied that it was because God wanted them to be trained and aware that these things were going on. "The training was not lost on us and not lost on me today."

The lesson was: be too successful and they'll try to shut you down. Either by infiltrating your operation or ...

"We wanted to have philosophy as well as theology at the seminary taught by orthodox professors. Not all professors at the Angelicum were orthodox. There were among them professors who taught heresy, even though the Angelicum was reportedly 'the best' of the other Roman theological universities. Our aim was to get a degree from the Angelicum with our own professors. The Dean of Philosophy agreed to it, as did the Dean of Theology, the rector of the university, and the Superior General of the Oblates. A confirming vote by the Senate of the Angelicum was merely a formality in such a situation.

"Thus in the spring of 1972, we took their word for it and did what they told me. Then a few days later, the closed door meeting of the Senate was held and shot down our proposal. I had not been invited to be present. The Dean of Philosophy apparently stood up and said the Congregation for Education under Cardinal Garrone would not accept it. With that remark from the Dean of Philosophy, no one else said or did anything in our favor and then the Senate voted us down.

"When I found out the next day, I asked the Dean of Theology, Father Salguero, what happened. I reminded him that he personally had told me not to worry about our proposal for Angelicum professors teaching at our seminary and that he had reassured me that the Senate, the supreme governing body of the Angelicum, would easily accept our proposal.

"I believe it was Father Salguero who then told me that it was the Dean of Philosophy who had intervened, as I described above, to shoot it down.

"I then went to the Rector Magnificus, Father Gieraths, and I asked him why I had not been told of the problem before the meeting. Perhaps I could have done something to prevent the negative vote.

"The Rector Magnificus, Father Gieraths, told me I should have talked to the student president beforehand, who could have represented our proposal, had he wanted to. No one ever told me that before our proposal was torpedoed, and I did not even think the student president had much to say in anything, up to that time. Well, I decided the Rector cannot have it both ways, when it came to the election of the student president a few years later.

"The upshot was we could not give degrees for those studying theology in the internal school. They had to go to the Angelicum and be exposed to heretical and less-than-orthodox teaching but we kept our hopes that in September we could have an internal school for theology and philosophy.

"We knew from the Legion of Christ that their Superior General had gone into the dean of philosphy office one day and said, "Get rid of that professor or I will take my students out tomorrow." Only then did the dean get rid of him. This proved we knew what we were talking about in choosing our own professors.

"We didn't need their degree to be ordained. The Oblates had the right to train their own and they didn't have to graduate with university degrees to be ordained. But come September, we ended up studying theology at the Angelicum but managed to save our philosophy school by having philosophy under Father Buckley and Father deVoss, but even that wasn't acceptable to the powers that be. Over the next three months they managed to have Father Buckley removed and then over the next few months succeeded in totally closing down what remained of our internal philosophy school. But they did not rely only upon internal agents in the seminary to close it down, the Vatican's Cardinal Garrone got involved.

"Cardinal Garrone was reliably reported, at a meeting in the Vatican, to have become angry upon hearing in early fall 1972, that there were 50 seminarians at the school, and of all the things we were trying to do. 'That place must be closed' he said, pounding the table with his fist. At first, the young seminarians could hardly believe this report, but in time it was proven to be true.

"Before 1972 was over, the Superior General of the order came to visit me in the Novitiate near Turin, after his visit to South America." Father Gruner recalled, "I was in far Northern Italy because by October, I was identified as the leader in getting the seminary started and holding it together, plus, I did have a track record for getting rid of the four bad seminarians that Father Cappello had sided with. Thus the local Superior insisted I do my Novitiate up North.

"I did not know much of the details of what was going on in San Vittorino after I started my Novitiate on November 21, 1972. I got my largest dose of news in December from the Superior General, Father Ponzanelli.

"The Superior General said the pressure on him was tremendous. Even though he was somewhat modernist, he was sympathetic to getting vocations. Father Buckley was bounced. An investigating team from the Vatican came to look at what was going on in the seminary. There was nothing to investigate. (The investigation was merely window dressing for what they intended to do).

"By the spring of 1973, our internal school was closed. All the seminarians had to go to the Angelicum with good and bad professors.

"In September 1973, I was still in the novitiate of the Oblates of the Blessed Virgin Mary. The Superior General had just come back from some lecture where a professor denied that Christ rose physically from the dead. He agreed with this heretical teaching and repeated it to me and as well to all the Fathers and novices, including Basil. I simply said, 'That is heresy.' The Superior General repeated his point and I repeated 'Heresy'. He still kept it up and after the third time I remained silent as this was not a child's game. A few months later, I was out on my ear, a conclusion that is not surprising. In reference to my saying it is heresy, their reasoning was 'Since you have no confidence in your superiors, it is not reasonable you stay on with this order'.

"In the mid 1980's, Father Basil, now editor of *Christ To The World,* a small journal sent to 1500 people, published an article by an English priest demonstrating that Garrone's tenure in charge of Catholic education around the world was a disaster. Garrone was furious and expressed his fury in a letter to Father Basil. Shortly after, Garrone was replaced."

Long time friend Jean Fioretti of New York recalls meeting Gruner in those early days when he was not yet 'Father', merely 'Nick'.

"My husband Bob and I knew another seminarian who was studying at the Oblate seminary in San Vittorino who invited us out for a visit. That was in November of 1972. There was a gathering at which Brother Gino received people from many different countries. Nick, as it turns out, was Brother Gino's interpreter and right hand. We became friends and remained in touch with him throughout his studies and his ordination.

"It's a custom in Italy for seminarians to go home for the summer and so, sometimes, he visited with our family here in New York. Many of the young men stayed at our home in the summer. The other seminarians all used to say Nick was too rigid. But nobody could argue with him and prove him wrong. They had all gone into the seminary with a very strong faith. But it was the Seventies. Things were changing."

§

By 1975 Nick was in St. Thomas Aquinas University in Rome, where once again he found himself in the role of challenging election irregularities — a candidate with the lesser count of votes had been declared the winner. The vote was 66 to 63 on the first two ballots with only two candidates running. Still the Dean and Rector called for a third ballot.

"It meant challenging the Dean of Canon Law and the Rector, Father Gieraths; addressing the 'fixing' of an election; studying the existing constitution and discovering the law was on our side; petitioning against the validity of the election, then, appealing over the heads of the Dean and Rector to the Master General of the Dominicans who still upheld the Rector."

Undaunted, that encounter saw Nicholas Gruner taking the kind of direct and positive action that has long since become his trademark.

"We sent the documentation to *Si Si No No* when Father Putti was still editor and publisher there. Whether or not this had anything to do with the future of the Angelicum, the fact is the Rector, Father Gieraths, was never re-appointed."

Gruner received his Bachelor's Degree in Sacred Theology and the Licentiate Degree in Sacred Theology from the Pontifical University of St. Thomas Aquinas, in Rome. Achieving ten out of ten on all courses and papers save one,where he obtained a nine out of ten, he successfully completed all required courses for his doctorate in Sacred Theology. His doctoral thesis alone remained.

The subject of his Licentiate thesis was Mary's Motherhood of Men in the Supernatural Order of Sanctifying Grace. A good part of the thesis dwelt on this teaching of the Church prior to and during Vatican II and the post-conciliar teachings of Pope Paul VI. In part it read:

"'For the glory of God' and at 'the most solemn and most opportune moment', Pope Paul VI proclaimed Mary Most Holy to be 'Mother of the Church'. The Holy Father did this to satisfy his own desire, and the requests of many Council Fathers, to make an explicit declaration of the maternal function which the Blessed Virgin Mary exercises towards the Christian people.

"Paul VI gives the dogmatic foundations of this title: 1) It is a title widely used by the faithful and the Church; 2) Her Spiritual Maternity is based on Mary's Divine Maternity. Because She is the Mother of Christ, She is also the Mother of the Mystical Body of Christ.

"It seems to me", Nick Gruner wrote, "that this affirmation by Pope Paul VI that Mary's Divine Maternity is the foundation of Mary's Spiritual Maternity should stop all further discussion which tries to say that Mary is only the most excellent member of the Church and no more, since only She is the Mother of the Whole Christ."

As an elected student representative at St. Thomas Aquinas for the doctorate year in Theology, this meant being invited to faculty meetings and he found himself with a vote in the election of the dean.

> "When the current dean, Father Salguero, stated with, shall we say, 'official humility', that he should not run again, I took him at face value and began to seek other members of the faculty's help in getting a better dean. Even so, I was soon prompted to bear in mind that they still had some say in whether I graduated or not.
>
> "In faculty meetings, we student representatives had not only a consultative but a decisive vote. In other words, our vote would count toward whether or not a decision would be made. Father Salguero, Dean of Theology, wanted to appoint Father Barnabus O'Hearn, C.P., as a visiting Professor of Scripture, in the Angelicum. I enquired around about him and was given an article by a priest, a recent Doctoral graduate, which was published in the *Wanderer,* against O'Hearn, by Msgr. Bandas, who had impeccable theological credentials. His degrees included a degree higher than Doctor of Theology. He pointed out that O'Hearn was suspect of heretical writing. When the item came up on the agenda at the next meeting, the Dean of Theology asked if there were any objections to appointing Father O'Hearn. I then proceeded to distribute copies of the article. After reading his copy, Salguero became very angry and yelling at me, said, "Gruner, don't ever bring anything like that in here again." I was centered out and felt like crawling under a table. The dean regained his composure and insisted on a secret ballot. When the vote box had only been three-quarters circulated, some of the voters opened the ballot box and saw the votes up to that point, thus making the vote invalid. The dean however declared it valid and that the vote went against us. We lost the battle but we won the war because O'Hearn, some weeks later, claimed health problems and did not come."

A former dean of the faculty, Father Lemeer, who had participated in the meeting, told Gruner afterward that he agreed with him that the article he had circulated was fair comment and his circulation of it did not deserve the criticism it got. Nicholas Gruner reflected on that: "I wondered to myself why, then, did he not stand up at the meeting in defense of the article and my position."

The reality is — the way business is conducted at faculty meetings demonstrates clearly why professors who are orthodox, and know better, do not stand up when they should. They are simply afraid that they themselves will be thrown out, as was Father Giuliani, an orthodox professor of Christology, who was dismissed by the modernists who were in control.

Personalities on staff at the Angelicum merely confirmed the unhealthy dynamics at work in Catholic education in that era: "A visiting Spanish Professor of Theology went out of his way every class to take many shots at St. Paul, saying St. Paul discriminated against women, basing it on his admonition that women should obey their husbands." After hearing this many times, Nicholas Gruner felt it his duty to speak out, even though he was endangering himself. He countered with, "Do you have to obey your superior? Do I have to obey a legitimate order from a bishop? Is that discrimination against us?" The debate, conducted in Italian, in class, ended after 20 minutes, with the Professor left with nothing to say. Except for one or two passing remarks, he never spoke about it again in Nicholas Gruner's hearing. Neither did he return the following year.

Father Gruner reflecting on this incident, says: "The victory was all Our Lady's — I was so mad at his scandalous comments that I prayed one Hail Mary after another — asking for the right words, and they came to me even as I was speaking, just an instant before I needed them."

In mid 1975 his spiritual director was the famous Father Gabriel, a Servite Father who had a following of thousands of faithful in Rome. He advised Nicholas not to join any religious order unless they obtained his ordination first. When the Conventual Franciscans of Frigento offered to take him in, he told them the conditions laid down by Father Gabriel. Gabriel had the reputation of being a holy, gifted man, so they conformed to his advice and found a bishop for him on November 21, 1975, the Feast of Our Lady's Presentation in the Temple, in the diocese of Avellino. In the same manner, they had already ordained one Father Paulo, a seminarian from Padua, whom Gruner had met on pilgrimages around Rome.

The Bishop of Avellino, Pasquale Venezia, a short, little man, five-foot-five, had a heart attack shortly before Nick Gruner arrived for his incardination. The whole diocese had turned out en masse to pray for his recovery. When the young seminarian was incardinated into the diocese on April 15th, Holy Thursday, 1976,[3] the Bishop jokingly said,

"I blame all the priests. It's your fault. If you've got me for longer now, it's your fault because you prayed for me."

On the Feast of Our Lady's Queenship, on the Octave of the Assumption, August 22, 1976, his father's birthday, and also the day designated by Pius XII in 1946 as the Feast of The Immaculate Heart, at the Sanctuary of Our Lady of Good Counsel in Frigento, Italy, Nicholas Gruner received Holy Orders, conferred upon him by Bishop Pasquale Venezia.[4] Among those present at the ceremony were Malcolm and Jessie Gruner, as well as Fathers Manelli, Pelletiere and Sutton.

§

Immediately after, Malcolm Gruner, whose early years in Italy, and his conversion at the tomb of St. Cecilia, had forever linked his family to that country, celebrated his 71st birthday by receiving Communion from his own son's hand at his first Mass. It is the moment the parents of a priest await for their entire life. Much of the salting of the ensuing apostolate had already been determined by the people and the events of that day.When Malcolm had converted, under the influence of St. Cecilia, the faith came to him with its abundance of treasures in a sudden flash of knowing, so that soon after, he was able to say to those who charged that devotion to Mary competed with devotion to Jesus, that it was Jesus Himself who delighted in honoring His Mother.

As it so often does with a new priest and his parents after ordination, the ensuing months were devoted to family. All priests know that time will never come again. In this case, they went on pilgrimage to the shrines of St. Anthony of Padua, St. Francis of Assisi, St. Michael of Mount Gargano, St. Leopold in Padua, St. Gemma Galgani's burial place, St. Peter's in Rome and St. Nicholas of Tolentino, to commemorate the Saint on whose feast day, September 10th, in 1930, his parents had married and in whose name he had been christened.

After ordination to the priesthood, but before entering the Novitiate, Father Gruner lived and worked in the house of Our Lady of Good Counsel, Casa Mariana, the Marian House of the Franciscan Friars, under the direction of the local superior, Father Stefano Manelli.

The work included some travel, with permission from the bishop. He entered the Novitiate on October 4, 1976, and received his name, Father Nicholas Maria. He remained at the Novitiate of the Franciscan Friars until February 1977. At that time, he began inquiries, with the permission of the provincial, to see if he could continue his Novitiate in North America, in one of the provinces of the Conventual Franciscans.

With permission of his superiors, he travelled to the USA and Canada.

By May, after talking to and visiting with Provincials of two of the four Franciscan provinces, he was directed to Marytown in Kenosha, Wisconsin. The provincial there could not promise that he would incardinate him. He would only consider it after he completed his Novitiate in Italy. But there were language difficulties, for, in Avellino, the bishop would not let him preach unless he had written out everything. And to hear confessions in Italy, the bishop wanted him to first learn the difficult local dialect. That would have taken years.

§

The possibility of forming an English house in Italy, at that time, seemed pretty well hopeless. There was nothing left for Father Gruner to do but write to the Bishop in Avellino, asking permission to seek a bishop in North America.

He travelled across North America introducing himself and seeking incardination, seeking a bishop who did not order his priests to give Communion in the hand: Washington, D.C., New Mexico, Texas, Florida, North Carolina, New York, Kentucky, Wisconsin, all to no avail. Then in August of 1977, acquaintances in Ottawa asked him to come help save a Fatima Apostolate centered in that city. He arrived on the Feast of Saint Clare, August 12th, 1977.

By 1977, little remained of the pontificate of Paul VI. In the sixteen years since John XXIII's 'inspiration' the Church had become barely recognizable. Virtually nothing remained of the moral authority it had wielded in the past. A sneering triumphalism was assumed by the enemies of the Bride of Christ. Any attention paid to spokesmen for Roman Catholicism by the Left Wing establishment of the Ecumenical Church was an exercise in sheer condescension.

In the waning months of Paul VI's life, traumatized Catholics hoped and prayed for a successor who would strengthen the primacy of the Chair of Peter and promote the rights of Christ over those He redeemed with His Blood on Calvary. The knowledge that Paul VI was nearing the end spurred many who had suffered myriad varieties of martyrdom in defense of the faith during his pontificate. Restoration movements sprang up around the world. In anticipation of the inevitable conclave, grief-stricken Catholics, began offering nothing less than the balance of their entire lives for the salvation of their sacred heritage.

On June 5, 1978, Bishop Pasquale Venezia officially granted Father Gruner written permission to live and work outside the diocese of

Avellino.[5] With that blessing, Father began his full time commitment to Our Lady of Fatima's Apostolate.

On August 6, 1978, Paul VI died. Grief was the legacy left the Church. Grief for the passing of treasured aspects of the faith that were consigned to oblivion. Grief that the truths of the faith had been lost by poorly educated clergy in theology chairs.

Those fatal years coincided with the most dangerous time in history for the unborn children of the planet. A New World Order was on the horizon. Population controls were on the agenda of world health organizations. The new missionary to the Third World was the contraceptive salesman. A slaughter of the innocents of the world was about to be launched supposedly to harness mankind's growth down to a manageable number. In the Western hemisphere, mass infanticide would be launched in the most unlikely country on earth.

Chapter 5

Whose Hands Are Full Of Bribes

The results of a mid 1960's survey run by the *New York Times* claimed that the three most boring words in the English language were 'weather, budget and Canada' but not necessarily in that order.

Even the people of Canada were amused, demonstrating that at least the non-violent, non-revolutionary, non-strife ridden country north of the 49th parallel still had a sense of humor.

By 1968, Canada would have another distinction. It would be the first country in North America to legitimize the murder of children in their mother's womb. A high price to pay to be interesting.

If ever a country needed a soul-stirring, it was in those years leading up to the fatal act of entrenching judicial slaughter of innocent babies in the Canadian Constitution.

In June, 1978, Father Gruner became the Vice-President and Executive Director of the National Committee for the National Pilgrim Virgin of Canada[1] and shortly thereafter published the first issue of *The Fatima Crusader*. Immediately after, in this position, he launched the first of his nation-wide Rosary tours.

During those early pilgrimage days of 1978, crisscrossing Canada with the statue of the Pilgrim Virgin, the true heart and soul of Marian devotion revealed itself to be very much alive in Canada. In the warm reception afforded the statue of Our Lady of Fatima, it was clear that the romance of Catholicism still remained in people's hearts, that same yearning that once prompted artisans to raise the great stones of Chartres above the plains of France.

Those escorting the Pilgrim Virgin on the mid-Canada portion of the tour must surely have thought, from the evidence, that it was not too late for the world to return to God. There was the procession through the streets of half English, half French Hawkesbury, on the Quebec-Ontario border, recalling to mind the great Corpus Christi and Christ the King processions of now distant memory. Then, in Ottawa, a triduum at St. Mary's, with Father Whelan, the all-night First Friday, First Saturday vigil at St. Martin de Porres, with Father Heffernen.[2] At St. James Church, in Oakville, Father Lima's parishioners lined up for one and one-half hours to venerate the statue. At Cobourg, the parishioners asked to accompany the statue's travels, in their own vehicles, to the next town of Port Hope.[3]

The recollection of the Pilgrim Statue visit to the parish of St. Stephen the Martyr, in Dowling, Ontario, by the pastor, Father Marcel Nault, provides a close-up of Father Gruner's early priesthood days.[4]

"It was 1979. He called me and said, 'My name is Father Gruner and I have with me the Pilgrim Statue of Our Lady of Fatima. I go from church to church wherever I am travelling. Would you like me to come to your church?'

"I asked why he wanted to. He answered, 'Because people know you as a Marian priest'.

"I could not help but smile when I saw him getting out of his van wearing a black cassock. I was not in the habit of seeing a priest in a cassock.

"I helped him bring the statue of Our Lady inside, all his scapulars, everything. He had not yet celebrated his daily Mass and asked permission to say it there.

"I invited him to say either the Mass on Saturday night or Sunday morning for the Parish. He said, 'If you don't mind I prefer to say it by myself.'

"I then said, 'If you're not saying Mass, will you help me distribute Holy Communion?' He said, 'I'd rather not, if you don't mind.' You see, he would not give Communion in the hand.

"I thought, what kind of a priest is this? I found out the answer as I watched him say the Tridentine Mass, with his own chalice and his own traditional vestments, listening to him when he was praying the Rosary on his knees, teaching the message of Fatima, giving out the Brown Scapular to my parishioners, praying with his hands extended over the head of those being invested in it. All his prayers were in Latin.

"I took note that he was very serious about everything he was doing, especially in teaching the message of Our Lady. He was outside of the new way of saying Mass. I was inspired not to condemn him just because of it.

"He asked permission to visit the two schools in the parish, one French and one English, to distribute hundreds of Brown Scapulars.

"A year later, in 1980, he asked again to come back to my parish. This time, after his visit was finished, I shook hands with him and said, 'Father Gruner, I have the feeling Our Lady of Fatima wants me to work for Her.'

"Later, he invited me to preach in Montreal at a conference at the Sheraton Hotel. I talked on the Catholic dogma of hell and he printed it in his *Fatima Crusader* magazine.

"When he asked, 'Why don't you come and work with me?' I decided to wait for a sign from the Lord. Then he invited me to go to Fatima and there I had the privilege of addressing Cardinals and bishops on the dogma of hell. I decided to work with him."

Father Nault was instrumental in establishing one of the most noticeable characteristics of Father Gruner's appearance. As Father Gruner recalls, "Father Nault assigned me the penance of wearing the miraculous medal outside of my cassock. I still wear the one he gave me to this day. Our Lady promised that those who wear the medal would get great graces. I began wearing the medal around the time I started to write on the issue of the Consecration of Russia. Is it because of these special graces, for wearing the miraculous medal publicly around my neck, that I have been able to concentrate on the consecration? Is that why I was selected to do this job? If so, I wish more priests would wear it, then more work on the consecration would get done."

On the tour of Western Canada, the statue arrived in the diocese of Mackenzie—Fort Smith in the Northwest Territories, geographically the largest diocese in Canada, by way of a special courtesy, free air passage given on all jet flights for Our Lady's travels in the north.

At Black Lake, people flew in from over 1000 miles away. Hundreds received the Sacraments during the visit. The parish priest, Father Mowka, O.M.I., kept saying it was like Christmas or Easter. Father Mowka heard confessions all day for three days. "I only saw him briefly during meals. He was always hearing confessions. I could not help because I didn't speak the Indian languages. When it came time for us to fly out to our next scheduled visit, the entire town came to see the seaplane off and to wave a final farewell."[5]

At Fort Norman, they gathered at the landing strip to greet its arrival, then walked back to the church in procession. Once inside, they individually chose to approach the Pilgrim Virgin statue on their knees, to pay homage and petition for favors. Official government meetings scheduled for the district had to be cancelled because of the great numbers who chose instead to go to the church to see the statue.[6]

In Prince Albert, at the Cathedral, Bishop Morin crowned the Pilgrim Virgin and formally consecrated his Diocese to the Immaculate Heart.

Forty parishes were visited by the Pilgrim Virgin when Edmonton hosted the tour in November.[7]

She travelled 20,000 miles. Thirty-eight thousand Scapulars were given away. Twenty-two thousand Rosaries. One hundred and seventy thousand leaflets, forty thousand pamphlets, ten thousand *Fatima Crusaders*, thousands of Peace Plan booklets.[8]

During stop-overs of the Pilgrim Virgin, the Blessed Sacrament would be exposed all day to the accompaniment of those ingredients of Catholic life that are, alas, now but a thing of memory — school processions, five-hour vigils, all-night vigils. At Holy Trinity, in Vancouver, the Stations of the Cross were said at 2:30 a.m. These are the things by which Catholic culture was once nourished.

With such style were the signs of a vibrant traditional Catholicism made evident that in 1978, Bishop Remi De Roo of Victoria would give his "...wholehearted support for the further promulgation of the devotion to Our Lady through the practice of the Fatima Rosary."[9] My, how times would change! In a mere ten years, a marathon 'people's synod', lasting just slightly shorter than the Jurassic Period, would conclude that Remi De Roo and his Diocese of Victoria were on the cutting edge of a New Church, that Thing set up to replace the Church of Rome.

"I am not a lackey for the Pope," De Roo would repeatedly claim while blithely and heretically announcing that, "Transubstantiation was a thing of the past." His diocese, the synod said, would no longer be needing input from Rome. Would no longer, in fact, have any need of the Pope. But that was still one pope away.

The Pilgrim Statue was in downtown Vancouver when news flashed around the world that the newly-elected Pope, John Paul I, after reigning only thirty-three days, was dead.

§

Meanwhile, back in Ottawa, the Trudeau government, who in legalizing homosexuality had declared that, 'the government had no place in the bedrooms of the nation,' had proposed omitting a clause in the long-awaited new Canadian Constitution. That omission in effect said not only did the government have a place in the wombs of the nation, but that once it got there, it could do whatever it darn well pleased to the unborn voter slumbering peacefully under its mother's heart.

His 1968 Omnibus Bill had, as far as Trudeau was concerned, justified abortion. Before '68 it had been recognized in law for the crime that it was in fact. Trudeau decriminalized it and by 1981 was attempting to enshrine the murder of unborn babies in the Canadian

Constitution by leaving out the necessary clause protecting the unborn.

Canadians who recognized the omission for what it truly meant were traumatized and propelled into action. One of the most daring and, it turned out, most troublesome of all the obstacles thrown in the path of the government brought attention to Father Nicholas Gruner from people in rather high places.

1981. Parliament was preparing to vote on the Constitution. With little time and a meager few hands to help, Father Gruner set about to make the Catholic Members of Parliament an offer they would not soon forget. In a twenty-five page letter informing Catholic Members of Parliament of the real meaning behind the constitutional terms, Father Gruner quoted Pius XI's *Casti Connubii* condemnation of abortion and made the point that it was a parliamentarian's moral obligation to defend the unborn. Failure to do so would make them guilty of the abortion death of Canadian babies through the sin of omission. With the help of an unnamed Member of Parliament, Gruner managed to place on the desk of every Catholic MP the reminder that if they voted for the proposed constitution, that was without protection for the unborn, they were going to be guilty of mortal sin and would end up in Hell, eventually, unless they truly repented.

To succeed in positioning an outside paper on the desk of each MP was almost unheard of and the reaction from the Speaker of the House was swift. In his bruised and battered mini-office in downtown Ottawa, Father Gruner received a phone call from no less a personage than Jean Sauve, then Madame Speaker of the House, who demanded to know how he gained access.

Jean Sauve was Catholic. Prime Minister Pierre Trudeau was Catholic. Cabinet Minister John Turner, later to be Prime Minister, was Catholic. Jean Chretien, another future Prime Minister, was also Catholic. All of them, together, were about to carve in stone a constitution that did not protect the unborn, in direct opposition to the requirements of their Faith. All of them proceeded to make it *de facto* legal to suffocate, burn and scissor a baby in half inside its mother's womb. The image of a cassock-wearing priest gaining access to the inner sanctum of Parliament to challenge the consciences of Catholic MPs was intolerable to them.

After all, had not Archbishop Emmett Carter of Toronto, a spokesman for the Canadian Conference of Catholic Bishops, himself pulled back from challenging them by telling his brother bishops in Canada that they had no business interfering with government? Yet Father Nicholas Gruner had published, to the embarrassment of His Eminence, the fact that twenty-four Western bishops had condemned the lack of protection for the unborn.

It is now part of Canadian history that Cardinal Carter, shortly after, was granted the highest honor in the land, the Order of Canada, by Trudeau, Sauve, Turner, Chretien et al. It can be truly said that the government of Canada never forgets a favor. Nor, for that matter, would they ever forget the cassock-wearing troublemaker who had almost upstaged them in their triumphant moment, and to whom possibly might go the blame for causing their critical vote to be delayed a few hours. Not to worry, it was passed into law anyway. And Canada was, at last, interesting.

The errors of Russia, where legalized abortion had been enshrined for six decades, had seduced the quietest, most peaceful country on earth and lulled it into becoming the blood-spattered midwife of a soon-to-be eugenics industry. Hitler would have blushed.

What the Parliamentarians of Ottawa had encountered in that month so crucial to the abortion holocaust in the West was the new reality of the Catholic Church. The defense of Roman Catholicism was now up to the man in the street, and to the priest with a sense of purpose.

Chapter 6

Power Play Of A Locket Cult

Perhaps the years of touring had been too successful, had drawn too much attention, not from, say, a hostile media, but rather from hostiles within the Church, specifically, in Ottawa, where the Trudeau, Sauve, Turner, Chretien abortion endgame was in play. The high altitude from which the first invectives were launched at Father Gruner conjures up images of hotlines and unlisted numbers and secretaries dialing.

The first attack had actually come in October of 1978, when Father Gruner was on the road with the Pilgrim Virgin. In Edmonton he received a letter from Archbishop Angelo Palmas, the Papal Pro-Nuncio in Ottawa. The letter was in French, even though Msgr. Palmas knew Father Nicholas Gruner spoke English as his first language. In it, Msgr. Palmas accused him of being a 'vagus', that is, a priest who is not incardinated anywhere.[1]

In fact, Msgr. Palmas didn't address him as Father Nicholas Gruner in the letter at all, but as Father 'Colas' Gruner. Father Gruner phoned Ottawa, objecting strenuously to the accusation, telling Msgr. Palmas he most definitely had permission from his bishop, Pasquale Venezia, in writing. He asked if Msgr. Palmas wanted him to come back to Ottawa immediately, to set the record straight.

Msgr. Palmas told him, "No, no Father, stay where you are. As soon as you complete your statue visits we'll talk about it."

Meanwhile, Father Gruner sent Msgr. Palmas a copy of the letter from Bishop Venezia which granted him official permission to be away from the diocese of Avellino. The document was a mere five months old, still perfectly valid, and eliminated *any* possibility that he was a 'vagus'.

The trail of this first notable complaint lodged against Father Gruner by the Pro-Nuncio, led, incredibly, to a strange fringe group claiming allegiance to the anti-Pope, Clemente Dominguez Gomez, a Spanish so-called 'seer' living near Seville.

Of all the factions, movements, groups, that had come into existence to fill the void in Church leadership, few were more bizarre than this Spanish cult that had founded a foothold in Ottawa in the 1970's. Its symbol was a locket worn around the neck. A very special locket.

Clemente supposedly had a vision of the Blessed Virgin, soon after which he enthroned himself as 'Pope' Gregory XVII. And so was added to the arsenal of the anti-Catholic press yet one more bizarro who discredited yet anew any authentic mystic soul. This same group was dabbling in what Father Gruner perceived as satanic sacrilege against the Holy Eucharist. Who were these people?

Among other titles, they called themselves the Brothers of Saint Joseph, and also the White Army. The 'Army' was founded by one Maria Concepcion, whom the Portuguese bishops once charged with sacrileges against the Blessed Sacrament. There was also a Madame Bouff, who based herself in Marseilles, and who would go to visit Maria Concepcion every so often in Portugal. At the center of their cult were supposedly consecrated hosts which Maria Concepcion said she got from the Archangel Michael, who, during an apparition, was supposed to have dropped them on the ground. Concepcion picked them up, so the story goes, and in time began sharing them with Madame Bouff from Marseilles.

Madame Bouff visited Canada in 1975 and again in 1976, recruiting people into the White Army. The "Army" had a hierarchy, a commander general for Canada, who was higher than the rest of the Canadian members, the next rank underneath were the 'apostles'. The 'apostle' was to wear a locket which could be bought in any ten cent store. Madame Bouff bestowed upon each 'apostle' a Host, allegedly consecrated. Inside the locket she would affix the host with glue and, once bestowed, the Body and Blood of Christ was, supposedly, thereby transmitted through the daily workaday world. The "soldiers" the next lower rank, were to gather around an "apostle" and to adore the contents of the locket.

Father Gruner's first-hand knowledge of the cult came about when one of the 'apostles', reasonably enough suspecting there was something not quite proper about the required item of apparel, asked Father Gruner if he would relieve him of his locket. He did so, opening it up himself. Inside was a piece of Host about thumbnail size.

Father Gruner recalls vividly that, during his possession of the locket, he sensed pains in his chest that he had not experienced before or since. He considered the locket to be 'of the devil'. Besides the pains Father Gruner experienced, he had already come to this conclusion for 9 different theological reasons only after reflecting on the locket story and Maria Concepcion's tale. He told two other priests, each of whom had more than 30 years' experience, of his findings and they concurred that the locket was diabolical. One of the most compelling reasons that told him the locket was of the devil was the fact that the White Army types order their followers to never tell any priest outside the White Army about the lockets. St. Ignatius says such a command of secrecy about the spiritual life is one of the strong signs that a mystical experience is of the devil.

"Just as the Church has sacramentals," Father Gruner comments, "the devil too has 'his' sacramentals. The locket clearly represented a sacrilege against the Blessed Sacrament."

The locket, Father Gruner perceived, was literally a devilish sacramental. Was it a consecrated Host that had been desecrated? He could not be sure. Was it something that gave the devil power over the people? Most definitely yes.

An unsettling string of horrific physical accidents befell locket wearers. Marriages were rent asunder. Families broke apart, polarized into hate camps, children were lost, seemingly forever, to their parents.

Father Gruner's first precaution was to bury the locket in salt that had been blessed with the blessing in the Roman Ritual which is used particularly to control the power of the devil. Then he asked another priest to relieve him of it and dispose of it according to the rites required by the Church in cases such as this. The priest who received it from him was so afraid of the evil aspect of the locket he drove the forty miles back to his home on a four-lane highway at twenty miles an hour. Once home, he took the Host out of the locket and put it in a jar of water to let it dissolve. There was no way of ascertaining that the Host had, in fact, been consecrated. The safest thing to do was to assume that it had been and treat it as such. As well, the priest in question put a second host, unconsecrated, of comparable size, in a second glass of water. After five days, the second one was dissolved. The first one lasted another 15 days.

When Father Gruner denounced the locket cult publicly, in Catholic papers in the U.S. and Canada, he instantly became the cult's number one enemy. He was soon vindicated when the cult was publicly denounced by Archbishop Plourde of Ottawa in the front pages of the *Ottawa Citizen*. The *Montreal Gazette* followed up with a lengthy series of articles about this bizarre aberration.

One of the locket wearers declared her intention of destroying Father Nicholas Gruner, boasted, in fact, that she would have him run out of the country and immediately proceeded to shop for a journalist who would print her personal rendition of Father Gruner's concocted failings. Nothing suited her purpose more than to have at her disposal the ultimate tool for discrediting Father Gruner at every turn, the vague and scary-sounding term 'vagus'.

§

The tour of Western Canada had drawn considerable attention to the young priest. The actions of his enemies would ensure that everything he would do in the future would attract even more attention. Ironically he was generating a public profile that belied the personal conditions under which he labored. A uniquely qualified witness to the spiritual climate of Ottawa in those days, Father Victor Soroka, rector of the Basilian Seminary in the late 1970's, recalls the conditions under which Gruner toiled.

"He worked in one room rented from an elderly lady. In the front section of the room he slept on a bed without springs. There were hardly any facilities. He had to ask neighboring pastors for a place to say his Mass. At that time he was publishing *The Fatima Crusader* with the help of one pious lady by the name of Debbie. But when it came to sending out the issues, he rented a hall basement and asked for volunteers to help with the envelopes.

"He was our guest quite often at the seminary. It was not possible for him to stay there as we had twenty-six seminarians then and all the rooms were occupied, except when we had a vacancy. (The seminary has since been destroyed by fire.)

"His finances were so slow in coming he could never pay in full for one edition, he was always running behind, and had a lot of trouble with the post office. They didn't want to give him the right rate, said he wasn't entitled, which wasn't true.

"Father Gruner went to different bishops but he didn't find any co-operation. Why? Because of jealousy. You see, he hardly had enough for food and yet he was promoting Our Lady through *The Fatima Crusader* and the Pilgrim Virgin Statue. He was willing to live in a rectory and help out but no one would have him. Why? Because they didn't want to acknowledge Marian devotions or have the Rosary in public. Churches neglected the Stations of the Cross and they were all giving Communion in the hand. His biggest crime was saying the old Mass. He was probably the only priest in Ottawa who did so at the time.

"He never made a cent, and he drove one of the poorest cars on the road. Everybody said, 'let's let him have it.' And they let him have it. But he won after all these years. Just look at what he's accomplished in contrast to them."

For those who wanted to destroy him, Father Gruner himself had provided the necessary ammunition. The focus of his apostolate was Mary. The agenda of his apostolate was simple and direct — take Mary's message straight to the people. After 18 years of the smoke and mirrors of some modernist bureaucrats who were smothering the Church, Rosaries and Scapulars were practically revolutionary. The response of the people to the Western Canada tour suggested that such a 'revolution' was, though unwelcome by the powers-that-be, apparently not unthinkable. The thing to do then was to stop it.

Why? Because of Mary, that's why. There was no place for Mary in the plans of those who were deforming the Church to fulfill their own agendas. Mary had to go. To understand clearly why Mary had to go, one has only to turn to one of the most fascinating Scotsmen of the 20th Century, Hamish Fraser.

Hamish had been a devout Communist until 1947, responsible for the work of the party in the west of Scotland, especially responsible for seeing to it that the soul of the labor movement remained forever opposed to the government of the day and the Church of all time. In 1943 his conversion began.

By 1947 he was a Roman Catholic. By 1950 he was attending Fatima Conferences.

In the January 25, 1953, issue of *L'Homme Nouveau*, Abbé Richard, later to become President of the Blue Army in France, recounts a moving incident in which hereafter Hamish would be dubbed "The Dove Man".

"Is it impossible that the cosmic rays of charity should bring about the resurgence of authentic humanity in a world made monstrous by brutality and hate? On the contrary, such a rebirth may be confidently counted on as the result of prayer, penance, holiness, and the consecration of ourselves to God through Our Lady. For these things are real, and, in consequence, have the power to set in motion, with a new vigor and a new orientation, all the potentialities of modern man.

"That is the lesson taught us once more at the Parc des Expositions by our friend Hamish Fraser, the Man of the Dove. ... A friend of ours, a priest of the diocese of Cherbourg, had in his possession two doves, the offspring of the doves which in such an extraordinary fashion accompanied the statue of Our Lady of Fatima during its progress in Portugal and Spain. This priest unleashed the couple, which had never known freedom, in the Great Hall of the Parc des Expositions at the very moment when, to the music of hymns, Our Lady's statue made its entrance. The doves, frightened out of their wits, flew two or three times about the hall, and then hid in the rafters.

"But one of them first circled around as if looking for someone, and, out of the thousands of people who filled the hall, selected Hamish Fraser and calmly perched on his head, in the midst of his bushy hair, and there it remained, apparently quite undismayed by the flashes made by the photographers who were vying with each other in their efforts to get a shot of the scene. Then, after about three minutes, it went along to rejoin its companion.

"Some moments later, Hamish Fraser was beginning his speech and declaring: 'I do not say that I believe that prayer can convert Communists; *I know* that prayer can convert Communists.' The dove seemed to have vouched for the declaration of this man in advance. A miracle? Not, certainly, a miracle for unbelievers. But, to adopt an expression of St. Paul, it may well be a sign for the faithful: *in signum fidelibus*."

Hamish watched the highjacking of the Church take place at the Second Vatican Council, saw the confusion being sown by confused theologians, witnessed the humanists outwit the bishops, observed the misguided modernists planning their strategy. Saw it all. He wondered why others could not recognize what was occurring. The tactics of confusion and well-planned 'spontaneity', the endless appeals to the dignity of man, for compassion, for liberty, equality, the endless insertion of brotherhood slogans into speeches, the relentless demands for more involvement of the people — all this was a strategy he knew and recognized. It had been his job to make this very strategy work within the labor movement in Scotland.

At the bottom line of all the changes these strategies wrought in the Church, he pointed out, there was one single prime directive, the necessary effort required to move Mary out the Church door, for according to the Communists, if Mary goes, the Catholic Church, sooner or later, will go.

Why did Mary have to go? Hamish explains:

"It was necessary to assault the Mother of God for the simple reason that there was no other way possible whereby the Son could be effectively exiled from Society and Man. Get rid of Mary and you would have dismantled forever any notion of institutionalizing within the Church the Social Kingship of Christ." Which would mean annihilation of Communism.

"Mary had to go because there was no other way of uprooting the Incarnate God from the consciousness of the people.

"Mary had to go because it was in Her womb that God had become flesh and blood.

"Mary had to go in order that God could be transformed into a meaningless abstraction. An impersonal being remote and entirely divorced from the affairs of the work-a-day-world.

"Mary had to go because it was from Her womb that God issued forth into human society.

"Mary had to go because She had mothered and suckled the author of the old moral order of society, which the revolutionaries were seeking to destroy.

"Mary had to go because She was the mother of Christendom, the mother of unity of Christians.

"Mary had to go because no less than the Mass itself, Her Immaculate Conception was literally an insuperable barrier to the rise of the lay state.

"Mary had to go because Her blessed name was the last remaining obstacle to the development of that 'laissez faire' society wherein relations between man and man were no longer based on brotherhood but on the cold and utterly forbidding cash nexus.

"Mary had to go because the reformers recognized Her for what She was and is," what the popes have always called, "... the Mediatrix between God and human society".[2]

And once She was gone, anyone who dared try to bring Her back would have to be annihilated, i.e. Father Gruner and The National Pilgrim Virgin Apostolate. The last thing the new Church needed was another Blue Army.

§

For decades, the original Blue Army, the militant-sounding association of Catholics devoted to Fatima, had been impressing upon popes and princes the worldwide interest of Catholics in the cause of Our Lady of Fatima. Its organization was firmly entrenched in Fatima with an impressive onion-domed headquarters just east of the edge of the Cova da Iria. It was situated in that direction from the azinhiera tree where the light first flashed in the sky to announce the impending arrival of the heavenly Visitor to the Cova. It had been difficult enough for the enemies of Mary to infiltrate the Blue Army. They didn't want another Fatima Apostolate and feared Father Gruner might prove to be just that.

They were wrong to expect him to form another Blue Army. In the beginning, however, relations with that historical organization had begun cordially enough, and with the best of intentions. However, the movement begun by Father Nicholas Gruner would ultimately neither represent, operate the same, nor imitate the Blue Army. In time, his own Apostolate would come to oppose the Blue Army's U.S. leadership's disinformation about the request of Our Lady.

With time, the Blue Army and *Soul Magazine*, its official publication, had lost its edge, its leadership had aged, mellowed, and seemed to lose its independence from the Ostpolitik (the political overture to the East) of the Vatican. They became willing participants in a nearsighted vision of the future:

A few months before the Second Vatican Council began, Vatican diplomats negotiated an unprecedented restriction on its deliberations: Metropolitan Nikodim of the Orthodox Church, a puppet of Moscow, would accept the Vatican's invitation to send Orthodox observers to the Council, if the Council would refrain from any condemnation of Communism. A written agreement to this effect was signed between Nikodim and the Vatican's representative, Cardinal Tisserant. The Orthodox observers, KGB operatives in the garb of priests, waited in Moscow for Pope John's opening speech, which promised a new era of "dialogue" with the world and an end to condemnations. The next day the observers arrived at the Council.

The "Vatican-Moscow Agreement" established Ostpolitik, "East politic", as the touchstone of Vatican diplomacy, influencing the Holy See's relations with the entire world. In exchange for silence in the face of evil, the Council would be favored with the presence of KGB operatives representing a puppet church controlled by the Kremlin. Where once there had been steadfast papal condemnation of Communism, there would now be dialogue and negotiation with the forces of world atheism.

The properly filed written canonical request of over 450 Council Fathers that communism be placed on the agenda of the Council was somehow "lost" in the conciliar bureaucratic apparatus. During the Council Cardinal Tisserant would rise to silence any discussion of Communism by a council Father, saying that it was forbidden. A human plan of diplomacy had collided with the divine imperatives of Fatima. Some 16 years later Father Nicholas Gruner and the Apostolate would enter the zone of collision. Not so the Blue Army.

In matters of the Vatican-Moscow Agreement, the Blue Army seemed to be almost too agreeable, too eager to toe the party line. Its new sense of compromise, its currying of favor with the Secretariat of State earned it the epithet — The "Bl'Army", and the chunk of the Berlin wall enshrined in glass on the edge of the Fatima shrine's esplanade — the "Bl'Army Stone".

Father Gruner and *Soul* and the leadership of the Blue Army had gotten along very well in the beginning. An occasion for collaboration in the early 80's demonstrates the case clearly: For years the International Council of the Blue Army had observed the fragmentation of its leadership in several countries, Canada among them. John Haffert in *Soul* magazine wrote: "At first we attributed Canadian fragmentation to French-English differences. But as we look back over thirty years of experience, many other factors emerge ..."

In January 1980, Mr. Setz-Degan, the International Secretary, invited Father Gruner to the Blue Army meeting in Rome to help the International Council resolve problems in Canada. Father Leoni, chairman of the Blue Army in Montreal, was not able to be there, but Father Nick Gruner was. Asked his opinion of Father Leoni, by the vice president of the Blue Army, Monsignor Galamba, Father Gruner remembers answering, "He's a nice guy."

In retrospect, it now seems what really lay behind the effort to unify the various Blue Army groups in Canada was the desire to bring *every* Fatima apostolate under the influence, if not control, of the Blue Army, which in turn would be controlled from the top through the Vatican's Secretary of State.

Father Gruner's instinct was to aid in the effort to create a unified Fatima Apostolate in Canada. As was reported by John Haffert in *Soul* magazine, "Father Gruner ... gave an overall report of his meeting with various Canadian leaders." (Gleaned from his touring the Pilgrim Virgin across Canada ...)[3]

The Council Officers decided that Father Peter Leoni, President of the French Section in Montreal, "... be given full authority to bring the various factions in Canada together and to prepare a single National Executive Committee ..." with the help of Father Gruner, "whose proven devotion, availability for the work full time, and his ability to speak English, French and Italian made him the ideal choice."

The Canadian leaders from Montreal, Toronto and Ottawa agreed to meet on January 17, 1981, at St. Mary's Cathedral rectory, Kingston, midpoint between the cities under the chairmanship of Father Leoni. One of the Canadian leaders, Mr. Wally Stafford, refused to go, holding to the position that he was already the Blue Army president of Canada.

A National Executive of the Blue Army in Canada was formed with full power to form a national center, to publish its own magazine, to call for recognition from all Blue Army Centres in English-speaking Canada and to establish Toronto as the National Blue Army Centre in Canada for the time being, with Father Nicholas Gruner being chosen President of the National Executive Committee in English-speaking Canada.

In July of 1981, the Blue Army met in its Fatima headquarters for the election of officers for its international organization. Although the meeting had been planned for some time, it was conducted in the traumatic climate immediately following the attempted murder of the pope.

At the time, Father Gruner, with one secretary, was occupied full time with the Apostolate, working out of a small, cramped office in the ground floor of a monastery in Ottawa. In advance of this gathering, Father Leoni, (President of the Blue Army in Montreal), after a visit to the Pro-Nuncio, Msgr. Palmas, in Ottawa, paid a call on Father Gruner and insisted in a friendly manner that he accompany Leoni to Fatima, offering him one of the two votes allotted to Canadian delegates that year.

Father Gruner was unprepared for a trip to Fatima at that exact moment, to the point of not even having a current passport. Leoni, however, insisted, offering to pay Gruner's way, including the hotel expenses. Father Gruner did not at first see the importance of it but a priest friend, Father Victor Soroka, advised him to go.

Neither of them could possibly have dreamed that the long arm of the locket cult was already stretching ahead of them, all the way to Fatima. Unknown to Father Gruner, Father Leoni was carrying a letter in his pocket indirectly connected through its writers to the locket cult, a poison pen manifesto of former disgruntled volunteers.

It would be a summer of confusion and crisis. It seemed that the progress Father Gruner was making in serving the cause of Fatima was eliciting nameless and faceless opposition. Just before leaving for the Fatima meeting, he was informed by a priest serving in the diocese of Avellino, where he himself was incardinated, that word was out that he, Father Gruner, was about to be suspended.

Once again, as seemed to be becoming habitual, the enemies of Fatima were guaranteeing that his attention would be divided at crucial moments in the history of the Apostolate.

Father Leoni and Father Gruner flew together from Montreal, landing first in the Azores, then proceeding on to the mainland and to Fatima. Seated together, they talked for about ten hours throughout the trip. What was not spoken about, however, was that a meeting had recently been conducted from which Father Gruner had been excluded, at the insistence of John Haffert, and decisions made in the Kingston, January meeting had been overturned.

Monday, in Fatima, Father Leoni rose to announce not only in his own name, but also in the name of Father Gruner, certain supposed changes from the January meeting in Kingston. Listening to Father

Leoni, Father Gruner now realized that the trip to Fatima was intended to get him to acquiesce to these unauthorized changes.

Father Leoni also had another card to play. In the event that Father Nicholas Gruner should be nominated as a candidate for *any* position during the elections, Father Leoni had come prepared. The *coup-de-grace* to any such plans was in his pocket. Taking Father Gruner aside at one juncture, Father Leoni informed him that he was carrying a letter, received in Canada, that contained accusations by some disgruntled persons in Ottawa. Father Gruner and Father Soroka had already replied in person to these libels sent to Father Leoni several months earlier. Father Leoni had indicated his satisfaction then but now he was going to use this letter as a concocted blackmail weapon to make Father Gruner conform to Father Leoni's orders. A rear-guard action, and relentless phone calls to the Pro-Nuncio by Father Gruner's White Army opponents in Ottawa, had brought the ugliness of Ottawa politics to Fatima. 'The Letter', Leoni stated, 'would be revealed if necessary.' Later on the letter writers were to become plaintiffs against Father Gruner but all three of them dropped their claims.

'The letter' ploy is one well known to anyone who has tried to establish an apostolate in the service of the Church. Pious opportunists, poison pen letters, the telephone, are the nemesis of many a volunteer organization. This 'letter' had been circulated with the thoroughness at which poison pen letter writers are wont to excel, one copy of it having gone to the Nuncio in Ottawa.

Father Gruner was compelled to resume a familiar role, that of measuring and weighing the procedures of the elections as in the seminary days in Rome several years earlier. In attendance were some illustrious veterans of the Cold War. One of the more notable, Bishop Constantine Luna, had been a prisoner of the Red Chinese in 1951. Father Peter Leoni himself had been in a Communist prison in Russia in 1955. Yet, in spite of their histories both were, from their vantage points within the Blue Army, supporting the Vatican-Moscow Agreement forged from the 1962 meeting of Nikodim and Tisserant.

When it came to the issue of elections, three names were nominated for the post of president — Luigi Scalafora, (the future president of the Republic of Italy), Father John Power, from Ireland, and Bishop Luna. In what seemed a clearly overt attempt to control and direct the voting, some twenty plus delegates who had been guaranteed a vote were disenfranchised when Mr. Setz-Degan and John Haffert announced the vote would be limited to one vote per country instead of the two. Setz-Degan, as international secretary, had formally promised, in writing, there would be two votes per country, in the official notice of the meeting, dated January 1981, six months prior to the meeting.[4]

To this obvious infraction Father Gruner voiced a legal objection on constitutional grounds, speaking in English, French and Italian.

"The unilateral decision to disenfranchise half the delegates was totally illegal, even if it was backed by the majority of those who kept their votes. I would not have wasted my time, had I known that Haffert and his cronies would change the rules of procedure and of elections as it suited them and without any regard to law, justice or charity.

"One delegate from Brazil, who was a lawyer, talking to those beside him said plainly, 'This is a circus'. I urged him to speak up to all the delegates but he refused. He later on was elected as one of the members of the international board of directors.

"During this manipulation of the Blue Army and its highest governing body, which claimed itself as the Vatican-approved Fatima apostolate, the fact emerged that despite its founding in 1947, it did not by 1981 have a constitution that had been ratified by the Vatican.

"So not feeling bound by its own rules and with no one overseeing its proceedings, it continued to change the rules as it suited the insiders, who were clearly afraid of the democratic rule which they so proudly proclaimed.

"The election of officers and directors came. Instead of having one vote all at once, each office was nominated and voted on one at a time. It was not long before a new fraud was attempted by Setz-Degan.

"The constitution absolutely called for a clear majority of votes in the first ballot. With the 50 originally promised votes, the majority would have been 26. Even with Setz-Degan's elimination of half the votes down to 25, a majority would have been 13. With all this maneuvering, Bishop Luna still only got 12 votes, Father John Power of Ireland and Mr. Luigi Scalafora between them got 13 votes. Yet in total disregard for their own constitution, Setz-Degan tried to claim that Bishop Luna had thereby been elected."

It was at this juncture Father Gruner felt bound to speak once more. This time he did not expect them to understand or follow fundamental rules of procedure or laws since they had shown dismal lack of understanding and respect for it in his first intervention.

He said again in English, French and Italian, "I don't care what you do, but in case you are interested, you are breaking your own rules that you claim you are guided by, your own constitution calls for an absolute majority in the first ballot."

"Then, Setz-Degan said, 'We are all friends here, let's not go through another ballot, let's not bother with formalities. Let's just declare Bishop Luna as elected.'

"Obviously Setz-Degan and his close personal friend, John Haffert, wanted Luna to be the new international president.

"This was even more obvious because they had insisted on nominating him despite the fact that it was publicly announced that Cardinal Rossi, the Cardinal in the Vatican in charge of the Council on the Laity, had formally told the Blue Army leaders, 'We do not want any bishop to become International President.' They formally went against this order while they claimed to be so obedient to the Holy See. They further acknowledged this Congregation as having jurisdiction over them since they, as a body, were seeking a special recognition which they had not, as yet, received.

"Despite all this, they went ahead and nominated Bishop Luna. John Haffert, in public, said in French several days later to the Bishop of Fatima that there were no other qualified candidates. This was clearly not true since Luigi Scalafora, then a member of Parliament in Italy, and who later became the President of Italy, had allowed his name to stand for nomination."

In response to Setz-Degan's appeal to break the rules again, the famous Spanish priest and Fatima archivist, Father Alonso, rose and spoke out plainly and with controlled but obvious anger. He told all present they could not change the rules in mid stream. After Father Alonso spoke, they held a second ballot and gave 15 votes to Bishop Luna.

Later, Father Gruner, himself, was nominated for one of the next ranking positions. It was then that Father Leoni pulled out the letter in question and told him that, if he ran, he, Father Leoni, would make public 'the false letter' causing sufficient confusion to lose the vote.

So Bishop Luna was finally elected with a majority after several ballots. That he would toe the party line, play down the worldwide petition campaigns to the Pope for the consecration of Russia, do nothing to upset the directives coming from the Secretary of State, was proven later in an all-day meeting between Father Gruner and John Haffert in the spring of 1985. Haffert was an open admirer of Cardinal Tisserant, prime architect of the Vatican-Moscow Agreement. Father Gruner offered to publish a positive news story on Cardinal Tisserant in *The Fatima Crusader* magazine in exchange for Haffert restoring in *Soul* magazine, the campaign of petitions for the Consecration of Russia. Haffert replied, "I can't. Luna won't let me."

Had the Blue Army by that time been subverted by the Secretariat of

State to the point where it had lost its independence? There was no way to prove it. Father Gruner, however, resigned in protest from the organization.

In 1986, the President of the Cleveland, Ohio division of the Blue Army also resigned over the illegal maneuvers used to keep the National Council of the Blue Army from discussing and resolving to promote the Consecration of Russia. He said "It is quite apparent that the Blue Army is controlled by a few entrenched people and is not governed according to its constitution." The facts surrounding this continued to raise suspicions in this regard.

The attempt to silence Father Gruner with the letter-in-the-pocket trick, no doubt, at other times in Church history, had sent other priests running for cover, never to be heard from again. The attempt was a study in the arrogance of old power, power corrupted from being too long in office, revealed in the tired tactics of men who were unaccustomed to being challenged. They presumed one opponent of the Vatican-Moscow Agreement had thus been dispensed with. They presumed too much.

§

Rome, August, 1981. Within days of the Blue Army meeting Father Gruner was in the Eternal City, following up a letter of appeal sent through Father John Magee, at that time personal private secretary to the Pope. It was intended for John Paul II. It was read to him in the hospital in early summer, 1981.

Before Father Gruner's letter reached the Pope, His Holiness was already learning more about Fatima. Pope John Paul II had sent for and read the Secret of Fatima immediately after an assassin's shot rang out in the Piazza of St. Peter's on May 13, 1981.[5] The exacting requirements of the terms of the Consecration of Russia that would, apparently, ward off the consequences of the Third Secret were also detailed to him at that time.[6]

As Abbé Caillon, head of the Blue Army in France, explains: "The question of the consecration of Russia to be made by the Pope in union with the bishops is governed by two texts written by Lucy a long time ago. The first important text: 'The Good God promises to make an end of the persecution in Russia if the Holy Father deigns to make, and orders to be made, by all the bishops of the Catholic world, a solemn and public act of reparation and consecration of Russia to the Most Sacred Hearts of Jesus and Mary and if, in return for the end of this persecution, His Holiness promises to approve and to recommend the practice of reparatory devotion (the Five First Saturdays)."

"Lucy gave this text to her confessor, the Portuguese Jesuit Father Gonçalves, on May 29, 1930. As Father Gonçalves posed still further questions, Lucy gave him another text a fortnight later, on June 12, 1930, along exactly the same lines. As for the Bishop of Leiria, Msgr. da Silva, he decided to write to Pius XI in March 1937 reproducing exactly what she had said. This text is therefore beyond all doubt." Father Caillon continues:

"Let us recall that between 1929 and 1939, Stalin was at the apogee of his cruelty. All the Russians whom one met in Paris or elsewhere, at that time, spoke with one and the same voice, in effect saying: 'Lenin was responsible for 20 million corpses in seven years; Stalin has been responsible for 46 million in 29 years; i.e. a total of 66 million corpses. Lenin is therefore worse than Stalin.'

"Pius XI was therefore informed in 1937 of the duty of effecting the collegial Consecration of Russia. He did not do so. And we have had corpses in tens of millions.

"In May 1936, in the course of an intimate communication, Lucy asked Our Lord why He would not convert Russia without these two so difficult conditions: that Russia should be the sole object of the consecration; and that this consecration should be made by all the bishops of the world, on the same day, each bishop doing so in his own cathedral in a solemn public ceremony.

"Our Savior replied: 'Because I wish all of My Church to recognize this consecration as a triumph of the Immaculate Heart of Mary, in order, thereafter, to extend and place alongside devotion to My Divine Heart, devotion to this Immaculate Heart.'

"Lucy replied: 'But, my God, the Holy Father will not believe me if You do not move him by special inspiration.'

"Christ replied: 'The Holy Father! Pray much for the Holy Father. He will do it, but it will be late! However, the Immaculate Heart of Mary will save Russia. It has been entrusted to Her'."[7]

It has been broadly reported that Pope John Paul II wept when he read these lines shortly after the attempt on his life.

The Pope, at the time Father Gruner presented the letter to Msgr. Magee, had returned to the Gemelli hospital for further rest after initially being discharged. As Msgr. Magee testified later, he read the contents of Father Gruner's 15-page letter to the Pope. The letter outlined the threat of "suspension" that Father Gruner had been subjected to, and the fact that there was no crime committed and only anonymous accusers. The pressure was being applied against him by nameless bishops of various ranks who were against Our Lady of Fatima. Father Gruner's letter had concluded with a promise to correct any errors if there were any with a reminder that he could not stop spreading the truth just because he was subjected to pressure politics.[8] The letter was sent by the Pope to the Secretary of State who sent it to the Congregation of the Clergy.

Father Gruner then proceeded to the Congregation to find out, in person, why he was being harassed. At that time, Msgr. Usai was the official in charge of the file. He told Father Gruner that it was not the Congregation that wanted to intervene, that, in fact, the Congregation was really not interested in the matter, but that the Pro-Nuncio to Canada had spoken face-to-face with its head, Cardinal Oddi, about him. Msgr. Palmas apparently had told Cardinal Oddi that no Canadian bishop would have Father Gruner. (Prior and subsequent facts demonstrated that Msgr. Palmas' claim was false.) Msgr. Palmas had strongly urged therefore that Father Gruner should be made to return to Italy.[9]

Father Gruner immediately sought out his bishop, Pasquale Venezia, who had incardinated him in Avellino. Bishop Venezia also made clear that it was the Pro-Nuncio, Msgr. Palmas, (and by extension the Secretary of State) who was interfering with his efforts to find a benevolent bishop.[10]

When Bishop Venezia was asked by Father Gruner to make a contract between Father Gruner, Bishop Venezia and a benevolent bishop, for a period of five years, Bishop Venezia said he could not do that. "The Nuncio," (meaning Msgr. Palmas) "will not let me do that."

Father Gruner returned to Rome to speak to the third in command at the Congregation for the Clergy, Under-Secretary Msgr. Gugliermo Zannoni. Msgr. Zannoni told him, "The Pro-Nuncio cannot forbid your bishop from making a contract with you and another bishop — it is none of his business. It is strictly a matter for you and the two bishops concerned."[11]

Nevertheless, the pressure brought by Msgr. Palmas on Bishop Pasquale Venezia held. It would result, from 1981 to 1989, in Father Gruner not being allowed to find, without hindrance, a benevolent bishop to incardinate him.[12] Still, during most of this time, he obtained faculties from local bishops to preach and hear confessions.[13]

Chapter 7

Before Communism Changed Its Name

To Father Nicholas Gruner, the moral authority of the Catholic Church worldwide was tragically neutralized through the disastrous Vatican-Moscow Agreement of 1962. The Agreement, arrived at in Metz in 1962 between Cardinal Eugene Tisserant, representing the Vatican at the explicit direction of Pope John XXIII, and Metropolitan Nikodim of the Russian Orthodox Church, paved the way for Russian Orthodox representatives to sit as observers at the Second Vatican Council on the condition demanded by the Russian Orthodox, that no condemnation of Communism would take place at the Council,[1] such a condemnation being equated by the KGB puppet Nikodim as a condemnation of the Russian people themselves.

Father Gruner elaborates on the dismal failure of this Agreement to protect the Church in the East, or around the world, wherever Communism held power: "No part of the Catholic Church existing in the territory of Communist control exists in freedom at all comparable to anywhere in the West. Persecution has not disappeared. Catholic priests are forcibly detained by Communist agents on a regular basis simply because they are Catholic priests; loyal Catholic lay people because they practice their Catholic faith are discriminated against, unable to work at the jobs and at the pay that they are due; the Church has little freedom in appointing bishops. All this in those countries which have negotiated with the Vatican.

"Communists in these countries have temporarily lessened some of their fury against the Church which they displayed at the time of Stalin. This apparent lessening of persecution in some countries had been granted in return for some extremely significant concessions given by the Vatican

"But in those Communist-dominated countries which have not been willing to negotiate with the Vatican, the persecution of Catholics continues as ruthless and relentless as anything that existed under Stalin. In Albania, China, North Korea and Vietnam the Catholic Church suffers open, bold and vicious persecution."

To this Father Gruner applied one specific indisputable explanation: the Consecration of Russia still remained undone.

In recent years, so much has been said about the 'Consecration' of Russia, from so many points of view, so often, with such passion and with such futility, people scarcely listen when it is mentioned. The controversy over its format and substance had divided the Church and ignited internecine warfare. The degree of bordom exhibited whenever it is mentioned represents a major triumph for the anti-consecration forces. But, in fact, in the early 1980's many people had never heard of the consecration. It was in great part through Father Gruner's efforts that it was brought to the world's attention.[2]

In spite of the familiarity of its terminology, the copious rhetoric for and against, it is necessary to include the details of the consecration 'requirements' here and now. The need to do so highlights a much-overlooked fact in the career of Father Gruner, namely, that his enemies like to paint the picture that he is isolated, alone in his opinions, and therefore to be ignored. But Father Gruner is anything but alone. His beliefs regarding the Fatima Message and the consecration are thoroughly confirmed and strengthened by the most respected and familiar names in the entire Fatima arena. For example, to secure the exactitude Our Lady deserves, one need only turn to the testimony, insight and research of two of Her greatly respected servants, Abbé Caillon of the Blue Army in France and Father Joaquin Maria Alonso, for many years the official Fatima archivist.

One year to the day after the attempt on his life, His Holiness Pope John Paul II, at the shrine in Fatima, consecrated the world to the Immaculate Heart of Mary. Sister Lucy herself was there to witness it. *Soul* magazine, the Blue Army of USA's official journal, reported that at last the consecration of Russia was completed according to the requirements. Surely the Pope wouldn't come to Fatima and not follow the criteria set down by the Virgin. But Abbé Caillon shows why the act of May 13, 1982, did not, in fact, meet the demands of Heaven.

He begins by recalling the events leading up to the Pope's shrine visit May 13, 1982.

"Item No. 1: In March 1982, Pope John Paul II wanted to know precisely what he should do on the occasion of his pilgrimage to Fatima."[3]

And so a special envoy for the Pope, the Lisbon Nuncio, Archbishop

Santo Portalupe, was sent to Coimbra.

"This historic interview which took place during the afternoon of Sunday, March 21, 1982, lasted for two hours. On the one side of the grille there was Lucy; on the other side there was the Lisbon Nuncio, the Bishop of Leiria, Cosme do Amaral and Dr. Francis Lacerda."[4] When it was proposed by Bishop Amaral that the consecration the Pope had already done was indeed what Our Lady had asked for, Sister Lucy while not saying a word, did wave her finger back and forth, making it very clear that no, it had not been done properly.

Sister Lucy then made crystal clear what was required: to the question what exactly should the Pope do, Lucy explained that "the Pope must select a date on which to order the bishops of the whole world to arrange for a public solemn Act of Reparation and of consecration of Russia to the Most Sacred Hearts of Jesus and Mary, each in his own cathedral and at the same time as the act of consecration effected by the Pope.[5]

In spite of the high-level involvement of men hand-picked by the Pope to hear these words from the seer "... in the text which was sent to the Holy Father by diplomatic bag, it was not spelled out that each bishop must, each in his own cathedral, and on the same day as the Pope, arrange for a solemn public ceremony of the consecration of Russia."[6]

Why was the exact message not passed on to the Holy Father? On March 21st of 1982, when the Pope's envoy, Archbishop Santo Portalupe went with Bishop Amaral and Dr. Francis Lacerda to see Sister Lucy, John Paul II knew that Our Lady of Fatima had saved his life. He was asking through Portalupe, 'What does Our Lady want of me?'

Father Gruner, in reporting the causes of the misinformation, said: "After the visit, Archbishop Santo Portalupe sent his message back to the Vatican. However, Bishop Amaral intervened to see to it that the full message was not sent in the papal diplomatic bag, and that the requirement ordering the bishops to join him was not included." In fact, Abbé Caillon, in November 1985, in Rome, told Father Gruner point blank that Bishop Amaral had told Portalupe not to put into the message to the Pope any mention of the bishops joining the Pope in his act of consecration.

"This same kind of interference in 1952 caused Pope Pius XII to be badly informed. In 1952, Pope Pius mentioned Russia specifically, the only time that a pope has ever done so.

"What he lacked was the bishops. In 1982, Sister Lucy specified there must be the bishops, it must be the same day, the same hour, either all in Rome or Tuy or anywhere else they want, one location all together or they can be in their own dioceses, in their own cathedrals, and do it at the same hour of the day."

Abbé Caillon takes up the story again following the May 13 consecration by John Paul II at the Fatima shrine: "In the days after May 13, 1982, a Brazilian advocate, the Blue Army Representative for Brazil, presented himself at noon one day at the Carmel at Fatima (where the 75-year-old Lucy who had travelled there for the papal event still rested, before returning to the Carmel at Coimbra) seeking to be received by Lucy in order that they might know precisely what to make of the act of consecration ... effected on that day.

"Poor Lucy, having no authorization to speak concerning the essentials of the matter, could do no more than make some trite observations that would sound encouraging, appeasing and hopeful. But the Brazilian advocate believed that from these observations it was possible for him to infer that a statement based on what she said could be broadcast worldwide. In effect, his text was reproduced almost everywhere, misleading opinion everywhere."[7]

As a result, diverse sources began to report that the May 13, 1982, consecration fulfilled Our Lady's request for the Collegial Consecration of Russia to Her Immaculate Heart, this, in spite of the fact that the Pope himself was saying otherwise: In the Bull of January 6, 1983, announcing the Holy Year, the Pope seemed to be taking his cue from what Lucy said to the Lisbon Nuncio on Sunday, March 21, 1982. Clearly the Pope was planning for the future:

"A special ceremony of prayer and penitence could be celebrated by the bishops of the entire world in their respective cathedrals on the same day, or on a date which would follow immediately, in order that after the solemn inauguration of the Jubilee, the entire episcopate of the five continents with the clergy and the faithful could manifest their spiritual union with the successor of Peter."[8]

But he still made no move to order the bishops to do it. The Holy Father only said 'could be'.

Father Gruner recalls that year, 1982, as the one in which the consecration emerged in its full importance to him: "When I heard for the first time in 1980, in Toronto that the consecration of Russia would bring peace to the world, I thought, that's too simple. It doesn't fit. What about all these other works that need doing. So I more or less dismissed it."

In the summer of 1982, John Haffert in the Blue Army *Soul* magazine added immeasurably to the confusion of the general public by publishing a supposed interview with Sister Lucy by an 'unidentified' anonymous interviewer saying that the consecration was done.

"About a month later I read Hamish Fraser's comments on the *Soul* magazine statement saying that John Haffert had done great work in promoting Our Lady of Fatima up until then but all the good Haffert had done previously was outweighed by the evil of publishing as true this false statement. Hamish stated Haffert had it all wrong. But how could he get it all wrong?"

Father Gruner had known Hamish since 1969 and John Haffert since meeting him in Rome in 1971-72. He published both their stories in the same issue of *The Fatima Crusader.*[9] The John Haffert piece was the only time the *Crusader* ever carried an article declaring the Consecration was done. From that point on, the issue of the Consecration would remain center stage of Father Gruner's apostolate.

From a much respected voice in Rome came a complete refutation of the Blue Army's claims. Father Joseph de Sainte-Marie was a Professor of Sacred Theology at the Theresianum. It was he who had drafted the speech delivered by John Paul II at Fatima during his 1982 visit. Father Sainte-Marie addressed the misleading statements in a letter to Hamish Fraser January 16, 1983.

"I profoundly deplore all these more or less authorized declarations made in the wake of the Pope's visit to Fatima on May 13 last. Until now, they have given rise only to confusion of minds, a division of hearts and the dissipation of forces ...

"It is therefore necessary to confine oneself exclusively to statements by the Blessed Virgin ... They are known, and concerning what we are at present discussing, the consecration of Russia to Her Immaculate Heart, the two principle ones are the following:

July 13, 1917: 'To prevent it (war, hunger, persecution of the Church and persecution of the Holy Father), I shall come to ask for the consecration of Russia to My Immaculate Heart, and the Communion of Reparation on the First Saturdays ... In the end, My Immaculate Heart will triumph. The Holy Father will consecrate Russia to Me; it will be converted and a certain period of peace will be granted to the world.'

June 13, 1929: 'The moment has come for God to ask the Holy Father to make, in union with all the bishops of the world, the consecration of Russia to My Immaculate Heart, promising to save it by this means'.

"On May 19, 1982, on his return from Fatima, in the course of a general audience, the Pope declared: 'I tried to do everything possible in the concrete circumstances to emphasize the collegial unity of the Bishop of Rome with all his brothers in episcopal ministry and service in the world.'[10]

"Reading this," Father Caillon continues, "we observed that, curiously, the Pope had made no allusion to the necessity of proceeding to the consecration of Russia according to what had been prescribed by the Blessed Virgin Mary, both in 1917 and 1929, and transmitted by Lucy. But we could not imagine that on May 13, 1982, the Pope did not already know what we ourselves know clearly and what is also known by millions of rank and file Catholics who are somewhat familiar with the history of Fatima. We can still less imagine that, after having made investigations, the Pope was as badly informed as all that ... We know, moreover, that the Pope was to meet Lucy on May 12. He was prevented from doing so by a delay in the implementation of his program. Lucy could speak to the Pope only just before the ceremony of May 13. The interview lasted 30 minutes. No one knows what was said, but by then the Pope's talks had already been printed. It would have been difficult to change anything."

Abbé Caillon takes up the story again in the spring of the following year.

"A second historic interview also took place. Sister Lucy was sought out by Archbishop Portalupe again. (This time Bishop Amaral was excluded, very likely, because he had caused the 1982 message to be incomplete in its version sent to the Pope. He was replaced by a priest instead, Father Messias Coelho.)

"The Lisbon Nuncio, accompanied by two Portuguese experts, returned to see Lucy the afternoon of Saturday, March 19, 1983. This interview at which Lucy, the Nuncio, Dr. Lacerda and Father Messias Coelho were present lasted for two and a half hours, from 4 p.m. until 6:30 p.m.

"Lucy had prepared a text which was read officially and on which she commented. The Consecration of Russia (it made clear) had not been effected because Russia was not clearly the object of the consecration and because each bishop had not arranged a public, solemn ceremony of Russia's consecration in his own cathedral.

"The text prepared by Lucy concluded with these words: 'The consecration of Russia has not been made as Our Lady has demanded. I could not say so because I did not have the permission of the Holy See'."[11]

Father Gruner points out that much of this confusion continues to exist today because Sister Lucy is not allowed to speak in public. "When allowed to speak, she has consistently said the same thing - in 1929, 1931, 1935, 1940, 1943, 1946, 1952 and again in 1983 - *always* the same thing. The message is very clear, very specific."

Father Alonso completes the picture, demonstrating again that the conditions for the consecration are exact and well known. Father Alonso presented the following texts which are certainly composed by Sister Lucy herself, at different dates:

June 13, 1929 - "The moment has come in which God asks that the Holy Father make the consecration of Russia, in union with all the bishops of the world."

May 29, 1930 - "If the Holy Father deigns to make and command that the bishops of the Catholic world do it likewise."

April, 1937 - "... if Your Holiness deigns to make and commands that all the bishops of the Catholic world do it likewise ..."[12]

§

There it is. No one can doubt or deny the conditions. Even the reader with the most rudimentary knowledge of Fatima can judge for himself whether the consecrations that took place in 1982 and 1984 meet all of these requirements.

"Make it known to My Ministers," Our Lord said to Lucy, "given they follow the example of the King of France in delaying the execution of My command, like him, they will follow him into misfortune. It is never too late to have recourse to Jesus and Mary".[13]

In spite of all the specifics available, all the confirmations required, and the living eyewitness testimony of Lucy herself, whom Heaven has seen fit to leave on this earth for the purpose of contradicting error and thwarting interference, the bishops of the world have not met Heaven's demands.

Again and again, Father Gruner has published and broadcast on radio and TV that warning to the 'ministers' of the Church that the scaffold of the King of France looms on the horizon unless they fulfill the demands of Heaven.

"The word 'bishop' is Greek for watchman," Father Gruner reminds us. "The prophet Ezechiel, in the Old Testament, was told of the duties of the watchman. God said to Ezechiel: I've appointed you watchman. Now, if I put you as watchman on the watchtower and you see the enemy coming and you do not sound the alarm, you do not warn your fellow citizens that they are in danger, then I will hold you, watchman, personally responsible for the deaths of any one of your fellow citizens.[14]

"What's that got to do with the Vatican-Moscow Agreement? It has everything to do with it. Each and every bishop has a duty to cry out when he sees the enemy of the city of God, the Church of God, being attacked. He is in a watchtower. He can see them coming and if he doesn't warn his fellow citizens, then the deaths, spiritual or even physical, of his fellow citizens, are held to his account.

"What our watchmen did in 1962 was make a compact, an agreement, to not cry out when they see the enemy coming. Communism is an intrinsic evil." That is a definition of Pius XI speaking as a representative of Christ. "He who hears you, hears Me",[15] Christ said. "Communism is intrinsically evil and no one who would save Christian civilization can co-operate with it in any way whatsoever."[16] So spoke Pius XI.

He also said at the same time, "During Our Pontificate We too have frequently and with urgent insistence denounced the current trend to atheism which is alarmingly on the increase. In 1924 when Our relief-mission returned from the Soviet Union We condemned communism in a special Allocution which We addressed to the whole world . . . to this hour the Papacy has continued faithfully to protect the sanctuary of the Christian religion, and that it has called public attention to the perils of communism more frequently and more effectively than any other public authority on earth."[17]

In 1937, he said it was his duty to raise the cry again. If it was the duty of Pius XI to raise the cry again, how can we countenance an agreement from 1962 to 1997 in which Communism has not been denounced?

During the Second Vatican Council, four hundred and fifty bishops went through the legal procedures to put the topic of Communism on the Council agenda[18] yet, the petition was illegally sabotaged so that it would not be brought to the floor.[19]

From the very beginning, in 1962, it was understood by the parties to the agreement that for the agreement to have its effect, it could not be revealed nor could any denouncement be tolerated from any corner of the Church, particularly from bishops, but also from priests.

There, in the simplest terms, is the reason behind the targeting of Father Gruner from the highest levels of the Vatican bureaucracy. Even in the early days of his apostolate for Fatima, unbeknownst to himself, he was breaking the Vatican-Moscow Agreement by denouncing Communism. Couple that with the fact that Father Gruner has focused on delivering this message repeatedly to the bishops and the pot begins to boil over.

Father Gruner has written to the bishops of the world thirty-five times and, out of all that correspondence, less than twenty-five bishops have actually said they disagreed with him about joining the Pope in consecrating Russia. This is less than one percent of the world's bishops. For all intents and purposes, aside from these few negative replies, there appears to be no opposition outside the Vatican.

Does this mean they would join in the consecration if the Pope demanded it? Father Gruner believes they would. The vast majority who respond are positive. Of the 1700 bishops who have written to Father Gruner, 1500 positively support, in general, the Fatima initiative of Father Gruner. It seems whatever opposition there is, is in the Vatican bureaucracy itself. The obvious preoccupation of a small group of bureaucrats with Father Gruner's apostolate suggests that he must be making some serious headway in gathering support for the true consecration. To effect the Consecration of Russia as it was requested clearly requires the dismantling of the Vatican-Moscow Agreement. A deliberate breaking of it.

How could John Paul II do this when in 1981, being pressured by Cardinal Casaroli, he accepted and renewed the Vatican-Moscow Agreement?[20]

"We can't make a promise to do evil," Father Gruner points out. "Such a promise, vow, or oath is not binding. I can't take a vow to disobey God's law, to not denounce evil. It is my sworn duty. By becoming bishop, by becoming pope, one has taken on the job of watchman.

"Why pay the man in the watchtower who won't sound the alarm? It would be a betrayal of the sacred office of the papacy, of the sacred office of the bishop, to engage in or agree to or to carry out the terms of the Vatican-Moscow Agreement. There is no moral obligation to live by it. In fact, there's a moral obligation to break it. Every Catholic priest should denounce it publicly, not just by saying how terrible it is, but by pointing out that Communism, as evil, is still here. We can't take a vow to do nothing in the face of evil."

Chapter 8

The Scaffold Rises

It is an oft-repeated fact of history that one single individual working out of one single room can change the course of history. St. Philip Neri, St. Therese of Lisieux, Marie Curie, Louis Pasteur, Alexander Graham Bell, Edison, Marx, Lenin.

Father Gruner had made his entrance onto the international stage and the Message of Fatima was being spread around the globe as a result. The conditions under which all this was being generated deserve special note.

From the very beginning, volunteers invited to undertake key roles were overwhelmed by the Apostolate's need for the basic necessities. This was not merely an operation with its ribs showing, this was one round of bare bones for everyone.

Jane McAuley, who met Father Gruner on his tour with the Pilgrim Statue in Niagara Falls in May of 1983, answered his call for help and soon found herself arriving at the Ottawa bus terminal later that year, at 5:30 on a July morning, with nothing but his phone number on a scrap of paper to indicate what the future might hold.

He was living and working out of four small rooms on Rochester Street, two up, two down. She remembers the windows were covered with a faded purple material someone had given him.

"I'm not in Purgatory yet," was her first remark.

Working conditions seemed to contradict her words. He had a small workroom for himself with a desk or two, the kitchen housed three filing cabinets, a refrigerator, teacher's table, an oil stove and sink with a chipped mirror cabinet. Her new boss ate one meal a day.

"Got any rules?" she asked, to which he replied, "Three Rosaries a day and daily Mass."

Forces natural and supernatural gnawed at the nerves of the workers on a daily, hourly basis. The Old Boy with the red tail was always on the hunt to get the volunteers in-fighting, fill the rooms with tension, jettison patience, crave escape from co-workers. And the devil was not above staging a little high drama.

> "After doing a mailing one day, Pearl Garneau, her daughter Cathy Sene, and I went out for food," Jane relates. "I was driving, missed my turn, and took another. Suddenly there was a person in the middle of the road ahead of me. They yelled, 'Stop, you're going to hit him!' But I knew I wasn't to stop. I said, 'No, I'm not. I'm going to go right through him'."

And so she did, but not before glimpsing an image that has stayed with her to this day.

> "A ball of fire came out of the mouth of this man and straight at the van, then he was gone. Just like that. I drove through where he had been standing, without even slowing down. In the morning the windshield wipers were twisted."

Down and dirty melodrama, however, didn't need the devil as executive producer. It came quite readily from one of those piety-dripping antagonists who lurk on the fringe of new Apostolates, bent on destroying them if the game is not played their way. This particular individual, infamous for the thoroughness with which that person habitually shredded the reputation of priests who failed to recognize that person's own oft-self-confessed sanctity, adopted the strategy of following Jane around town.

> "Trying to psyche me out," Jane recalls, "when we went, for example, to the post office. They would sit in the parking lot watching our every move."

The tactic is a familiar one, a staple maneuver of the pious assassin who feels compelled to let people know they are being watched and considered 'suspect' in an attempt to un-nerve them. But it didn't work.

> "We learned how to outwait that person and it finally stopped".

By mid 1984, though no one knew it at the time, the later relocation of the Apostolate from Ottawa to Fort Erie, Ontario, (across Lake Erie from Buffalo) was being initiated by people and circumstances in small, seemingly insignificant ways.

Coralie Graham, editor of *The Fatima Crusader*, describes the preliminaries leading up to the move.

> "Our little group (in Fort Erie) worked at bringing the Rosary and devotion to Our Lady back to our church and privately prayed for a Tridentine Mass. We organized a Wednesday night novena to Our Mother of Perpetual Help at St. Michael's Church along with Father Patrick Norton. We were not the most welcome addition to the church schedule and had to carry the five foot statues of St. Joseph and Mary

back and forth from home every week. We wanted some traditional material for the people attending. Through St. Michael's Cathedral in Toronto we encountered Father Gruner's booklet called *Our Lady's Urgent Appeal.* The phone number listed on it was Shirley and Don Pennel's, who told us about Father Gruner and gave us his number in Ottawa.

"After phoning him we received *The Fatima Crusader* and booklets we ordered to give out along with cartons of books on St. Alphonsus. Father could never resist the opportunity to promote St. Alphonsus' holy work. That was the beginning of the book service in Fort Erie.

"I was attending daily Mass at the Redemptoristine Convent on the Niagara Parkway every morning, by special permission of the bishop, before going to work. Father Norton, who was chaplain and was preparing to go to Ireland for a trip, announced one morning that a visiting priest would be bringing a statue of Our Lady of Fatima to the convent and would be saying Mass in his absence.

"The visiting priest was Father Gruner. My first introduction to Father Gruner was a Godsend as he proceeded to offer the Tridentine Mass. I was giving my thanksgiving before Communion, for this wondrous answer to my prayers, when I felt a tremendous enveloping warmth filled with peace and glowing happiness. It literally permeated the room. It was so intense, I looked up from my prayers as if I were expecting to see what I so intensely felt. But I could not determine the cause. Minutes later, as I fell in behind the Communion line, it hit me like a thunderbolt. All except one or two of the Contemplative nuns that normally received Communion in the hand, standing, were kneeling and receiving the Host on their tongue. It is as crystal clear in my mind today as it was at that moment that Our Lord gave a sign of how pleased He was at this appropriate act of adoration and respect. The statue of Our Lady of Fatima, as always with Father Gruner, was prominently placed at the foot of the cross on the altar and Her sweet smile seemed to also radiate with warmth and pleasure at this small act of adoration.

"With such an introduction to Father Gruner, my future working for Fatima, it seems, had already been decided.

"Father Gruner continued his pilgrimage through the Niagara Region to the various churches and our little Rosary Group attended the first one. Then the second, then the third, until we were attending all of them. The combination of Father Gruner's Mass and the appeal of the Pilgrim Virgin Statue was a magnet drawing us in spite of times when we had not planned to go at all, for God had answered our prayers, we had Mary back and the Tridentine Mass.

"In May of 1984, he took me up on my offer to do volunteer work for the Apostolate and called from Ottawa to ask if I would handle Canadian book orders. I converted my spare bedroom into an office. Two others, Bernie Dumelie and Frank Timms offered to list orders on their computer. By autumn we had a smooth enough volunteer operation going to prompt Father Gruner to consider establishing the Apostolate in Fort Erie."

They went to Ottawa to see what his set-up there was like. It was as Jane McAuley had described it — bleak.

"In one small apartment he had a card table, metal shelving along the wall piled with paperwork, and a door off its hinges, propped up on cartons of *The Fatima Crusader*, as his desk. In his fridge was a bowl of rice and a can of tuna which he did not hesitate to offer to share with us."

Father Gruner went through a period of doubt about moving to Fort Erie and for a time considered crossing into the States to work out of Constable, New York, instead. Jane McAuley encouraged him to choose Fort Erie, adding that her relatives there also would act as volunteers.

In March of 1985, they moved the office to Fort Erie and Father Gruner followed a month later.

"I moved to Fort Erie with the Bishop's own personal permission," Father Gruner explains. "He knew I was coming not just for a visit, but to buy property for the Apostolate. Before coming to the St. Catharines Diocese, I wrote the Bishop of St. Catharines, Bishop Thomas Fulton. I said I was thinking of moving the office down here and did he have any problem with that? Basically, he wrote back asking who wanted us. I replied in person by going to visit him in the chancery office. I was relieved to find out when I met him, near Christmas 1984, his reply to my proposed moving of my office. 'It's a free country' he said clearly, indicating he had no objection to my proposed move. In fact, he then lamented I had not moved earlier so that he could have sold me some property the diocese had just disposed of. Later, he recalled to me his freely given permission when I went to visit him at his Chancery office in August of 1988.

"Coralie Graham, representing her Rosary group, also contacted Bishop Fulton and offered to furnish him with ample signatures of petition to allow the Apostolate and Father Gruner to settle here, to which His Excellency replied, 'That would not be necessary'.

"Regarding the permission, in August of 1988, Mary Sedore, a staff worker since 1986 and a personal friend of Bishop Fulton, together with Coralie Graham and myself, visited the Bishop of St. Catharines to discuss matters of mutual concern. During this discussion the bishop's permission of 1985 came up and Bishop Fulton, after reflecting on it a bit, did recall giving his permission to us to move the Fatima Apostolate to Fort Erie, within his diocese.

"After June of '85, as I was living down in Fort Erie by that time, the faculties in Ottawa expired. Bishop Fulton extended them to me, by phone, every month thereafter until November 1987. I finally got them in writing in November of '87, but only for six months, till June of '88. In January 1988, he then wrote me a second letter saying that there was a typing mistake by the secretary ... so he extended them to only three months and then he extended them again. In effect they went to June 1, 1988."

Coralie Graham recalls the early days after the move:

"A month after Father moved to Fort Erie I was volunteering evenings and weekends to ship books and do office work. Ultimately, I quit my job to work full time for the Apostolate. I have never regretted it nor even once looked back. Actually, I learned very fast that when you work for Our Lady your life becomes an express train."

There were major disappointments along the way. The Apostolate wanted to put in an offer to buy an abandoned school in Crystal Beach, not far from Fort Erie. At first they were stopped by the Town which was about to claim special privileges and purchase it for themselves so they could give it to a group in Fort Erie. Their plan was contested as contrary to law and abuse of municipal privileges. The town then withdrew.

The Apostolate was told the asking price for the school but a private consultant counselled to bid higher as the building and property were worth much more. The counsel was followed and a bid was made for several thousand dollars higher than the suggested figure.

The next day, the Apostolate found that the purchase was awarded to another group who bid a mere forty-five dollars above their own despite the thousands of dollars difference between their bid and the suggested price. This was suspicious, particularly as the Apostolate was denied the right to be present for the opening of the bids.

Father and the staff learned to measure how effective an issue of *The Fatima Crusader* was going to be by the amount of trouble encountered getting it out. Every *Crusader* worked on was beset by crises. They felt very close to the Curé of Ars. The very day they would decide to start on a *Crusader* pandemonium would ensue — staff off sick, water pipes burst, furnace breaking down, vehicles breaking down, the entire ceiling leaking from a torrential rainfall — once it was so bad they hired two students to empty trash cans full of water throughout the night. The electricity has been outed by storms — Father Gruner has worked on the *Crusader* by the light of vigil candles propped up on soft drink cans. When machines wouldn't work, the staff would tape a Miraculous Medal or St. Benedict Medal to them, have Father bless them, and they would start up again.

When Father was around, the devil worked overtime harassing him, then when he's away on business, the devil switched his focus to those left behind.

The editor of the *Crusader* recounts:

> "Before we grew to our present size, sometimes I worked until 2, 3, 4 in the morning, alone in the building. At times, others have worked with me but they went away saying, 'I don't know how you can work at night.' They kept hearing footsteps on the roof.
>
> "When Father is away and phones to ask, 'How are things going?', I learned that as soon as I said, 'Fine,' pandemonium would break loose again. If he called one hour after departing, it would start then. If he didn't call for three weeks after leaving, it wouldn't start until then. I began not answering, 'Fine,' to the question. But just recently, I slipped, said, 'Fine,' and 60 seconds later there was a line-up outside my office of people with grave problems to overcome."

Yet, Heaven always helps the Apostolate survive the gravest crisis, it seems, so long as they persevered and never gave up. Their faith did not let them down. When they owed $750,000 and had not a cent to pay for services or make a mailout, St. Joseph brought in the funds to bail them out.

A Director of the Apostolate tells us of a side of Father Gruner often not seen except by those working closely with him.

> "Father takes very seriously his position as 'steward' of the donations that come in. Though he does not have a spare minute to answer everyone's personal concerns, for years he helped open the mail himself. He would be quite overwhelmed at the hardships and sacrifices of our people and would be fierce at not allowing any volunteers or staff to squander a penny.
>
> "Father practiced what he preached. Since I met him, and 13 years later, to this day, Father has only drawn a paltry sum of $500 a month to live on, and this for laboring 18 hour days, hardly ever taking any leisure time off for himself. It has become a common practice for our *Crusader* staff, including Father, to work two days and nights straight through with no sleep to make our deadline. On at least one occasion

we even persevered to the third straight day. That was the time Denise, our Production Manager was so tired that when she stopped at a stop sign on the way home, she forgot where she was.

"No task was too menial for Father. He always joined the staff to lick stamps, stuff envelopes, drive trucks, whatever it took, to get the job done — to get another step closer to the goal to consecrate Russia.

"In the first year in Fort Erie, we rented an old factory that had been abandoned for ten years. The roof had leaked and on the floor were huge puddles of water. We moved in and Bernie Dumelie and Frank Timms, always there with their sleeves rolled up, did a tremendous cleaning job to make it as fit as possible. And Bernie's sister, Virginia Halbach, and 'mother', Martha Halbach, were our prayer powerhouse, offering Rosary after Rosary to pray us through our trials.

"Money was scarce and Father would not spend a dime more than necessary, so he made a room for himself in the warehouse. His first year there, he had no bathtub, no hot water, no furnace, no kitchen stove or sink. We put a small electric heater in his room. He had only the staff washroom to bathe in. His stove was an old oil heater in the office. His table was an old bed board propped up on cartons of *Crusaders*.

"Never did he complain. We all worried, but he just kept shuffling on, like St. Louis de Montfort.

"Now and again those who act like a pack of wild dogs tearing and pulling at a morsel of food would publish remarks, 'What does Father Gruner do with that money?' and I'd smile, thinking if they only came and saw. The donations Father Gruner receives go to promoting the full Fatima Message. Anyone who comes to visit can see it does not go to luxuries.

"When Rome bureaucrats tried to get Father Gruner out of the Apostolate and prevent him from preaching on Fatima by threats, innuendos, and branding him a 'vagus', we were an endangered species. But we are still here."

§

It is also a fact of history that the intensity of opposition directed at people who work for Our Lady is in direct proportion to the effectiveness of their efforts. The efforts to confuse and control Father Gruner's Apostolate was a mirror image of the confusion that was attempting to distort Our Lady's Message worldwide.

The Blue Army has long held an emotional hammerlock on the hearts of believing Catholics who remember when it started in 1947 and was the only voice propagating the Message. It still remains a formidable foe of the critics because of the historical sentiment that it earned from supporters over the decades.

In the early '80s, however, it appeared the Blue Army was losing its characteristic independence and fortitude. Most evident in their change of attitude was the manner in which, to the exacting demands of Heaven for the consecration, they suddenly applied a sort of political relativism.

In extracts from an interview with Sister Lucy, published September 1985 in *Sol de Fatima* (the magazine of the Spanish section of the Blue Army) the Fatima Secret was considered in the light of events unfolding within the Church in 1985. (The article was a vital one. The 1982 *Soul Magazine*[1] bogus interview had been exposed and ridiculed by Abbé Caillon and Father Paul Leonard,[2] among others.[3])

Extract From The Interview:

Published September 1985 in *Sol de Fatima*, Spain.

Question: At what moment of the Fatima mystery do we find ourselves?

Sister Lucy: I think we are living in the time when Russia is spreading its errors throughout the world.

Question: By that, are we to understand that Russia will take possession of the whole world?

Sister Lucy: Yes.

Question: John Paul II had invited all the bishops to join in the consecration of Russia, which he was going to make at Fatima on 13 May, 1982 and which he was to renew at the end of the Holy Year in Rome on 25 March, 1984, before the original statue of Our Lady of Fatima. Has he not therefore done what was requested at Tuy?

Sister Lucy: There was no participation of all the bishops, and there was no mention of Russia.

Question: So the consecration was not done as requested by Our Lady?

Sister Lucy: No. Many bishops attached no importance to this act.

So stood Fortress Blue Army before it underwent some fundamental changes in direction in 1985-86. The changes took place against the backdrop of very definite and very specific concerns of the Holy Father. Hamish Fraser explained:

> "Concerning one thing at least there is no possible room for doubt — the Holy Father's awareness of the need for the Collegial Consecration of Russia ... For already within two years he has three times consecrated the world ... and on the third occasion (March 25, 1984) he invited the bishops to join with him ... in making the Act of Consecration.

"Moreover, on each occasion he indicated that he realized ... the consecration demanded by Our Lady had yet to be made.

"Let no one therefore pretend that the Collegial Consecration of Russia ... is not very much on the mind of the Holy Father."[4]

Why then has it not been properly done?

"Given on the one hand the Holy Father's anxiety concerning the ... consecration ... and on the other hand the scandalous hostility elicited by the (his) request for episcopal participation in the consecration of ... March 25, 1984, it can be inferred, with moral certainty, that one thing in particular has so far prevented the Holy Father from ordering the Bishops of the Universal Church to join with him in ... consecrating Russia; *his fear that to do so might well provoke formal schism.*" (italics added)

Why are the bishops resisting Our Lady of Fatima? Once again Hamish Fraser provides a stunning explanation.

"There are several reasons why so many bishops quite literally see red whenever the Message of Fatima is mentioned:

"1) Fatima condemns the new catechetics! In many Episcopally approved catechetical texts, Hell is scarcely even mentioned, and certainly not as something to be taken very seriously, in spite of the fact that the Virgin in the Cova ... felt it necessary to give the three young seers a terrifying vision of Hell:

"2) Fatima Condemns Sex Education! Ignoring both *Humanae Vitae* and *Familiaris Consortio* which stress the necessity for modesty and chastity as well as the grave sinfulness of contraception, many bishops have imposed most questionable forms of 'Sex Education', some of which border on pornography, on the Catholic Schools for which they are responsible. Our Lady ... went out of Her way to emphasize the need for strict fidelity to the Church's moral teaching, and in particular the need for both modesty and chastity, telling Jacinta, youngest of the three seers: 'The sins which lead most souls to Hell are sins of the flesh.'[5]

As Jacinta herself subsequently reported: "The Mother of God wants more virgin souls bound by the vow of chastity. Woe to women wanting in modesty."[6]

Hamish continues, "The Pope's fear is grounded in his realization that material episcopal schism is already widespread in various parts of the world ... at a time when great numbers of the bishops are obsessed with the notion of collegiality, nothing rouses many of them to greater fury than to be reminded that the Queen of Heaven has demanded that, together with the Holy Father, they collegially consecrate Russia to Her Immaculate Heart.

"In other words, the first and foremost reason why Fatima is intolerable to so many bishops, and why they also intensely resent Papal authority, is that whereas prior to Vatican II the Popes had consistently condemned Communism as 'intrinsically evil', since Vatican II most episcopal conferences now appear to act on the assumption that it is not Communism but anti-Communism in any shape or form that is 'intrinsically evil'.

"Why has this change of Episcopal attitude dated from Vatican II? It is primarily because of the Vatican-Moscow Agreement which assured the Kremlin that if Russian Orthodox observers were sent to Vatican II, Communism would not be discussed at the Council. Nor was it. It is because of this criminal omission that after the Council, it became possible to pretend that Communism had become licit and to do so in the name of the Council. This criminal omission is why it became possible to advocate an alliance of Catholics and Communists and even to espouse a 'Theology of Liberation' that is simply revolutionary Marxism in a 'Christian' disguise.

"In short," says Hamish "if so many bishops detest the Message of Our Lady of Fatima it is because its reference to Russia's errors condemns the policies of virtually all Episcopally approved 'Justice and Peace Commissions' and also of Catholic 'Development Agencies' such as CAFOD (England), SCIAF (Scotland), Trocaire (Ireland) and CCFD (France). For these organizations today provide 'the revolution' with a basis for the kind of 'popular front' which it was at such pains to engender against the determined opposition of the pre-conciliar Church; a 'Popular Front' which everywhere promotes subversion by mobilizing Christians, particularly Catholics, in support of the Revolutionary Cause, but particularly in such areas as the Philippines, South Africa and Central America which Moscow is determined to destabilize in order to foster its imperialist ambition.

"To be perfectly blunt, if so far the Holy Father has not found it possible to fulfill the demands of the Queen of Heaven, it is because he realizes that, as a consequence of policies pursued by post-conciliar Nuncios and Apostolic Delegates, he has now to contend with a host of modernist bishops who are Catholic in name only.

"For that reason there is only one means whereby the Holy Father could now fulfill the demand of Our Lady of Fatima. He would be required to order all bishops to join him in collegially consecrating Russia to Mary's Immaculate Heart on pain of demitting office forthwith, in the event of their refusing to do so ...

"Indeed, it is doubtful if any Pope in history has ever been confronted with circumstances so prejudicial to the exercise of Papal authority as now exists in the wake of Vatican II. Certainly, no one who fully understands the present situation would be so foolish as to upbraid, or in any way belittle, the Holy Father, because so far he has not found it possible to do what is manifestly necessary in order to restore Catholic order.

"And this despite the fact that such action is manifestly necessary. It is imperative, because the longer material schism is tolerated, the more intractable will the bishops become, for each day they are becoming ever more greedily accustomed to having their cake and eating it; that is to having all the advantages of material schism with none of the disadvantages of formal schism.

"Moreover, the longer material schism persists, the greater the likelihood of those bishops being able to take their flocks with them in the event of formal schism."[7]

Hamish stated this in November 1985 at the first Fatima conference sponsored by Father Gruner held in Vatican City. Much has happened in the Church and the world in the past eleven years to change the bishops' attitude toward the Consecration of Russia. Not the least of which is the ongoing campaign by Father Gruner and his associates to teach the bishops about Our Lady of Fatima's command to them to consecrate Russia.

Hamish died in October 1986. No doubt today some bishops are still influenced against the Consecration for the motives Hamish outlines above. Nevertheless had he still been alive today, he might be inclined to conclude, as Father Gruner has from his extensive correspondence and personal visits with bishops, together with their participation in the Bishops' Conferences, that once properly informed about Fatima, most of the bishops would, in fact, join the Holy Father in consecrating Russia, if asked by him to do so. This point of view was publicly upheld by Archbishop Milingo in his talk at the Fatima Peace Conference for Bishops held in Mexico in November 1994. (See Appendix IV.)

In 1985-1986, in spite of all the evidence to the contrary, "semi-official" sources and the Blue Army began to publish and insist that the consecration had at last been completed as of March 25, 1984, in Rome.

Why then, with the evidence available, does the Blue Army continue to spread confusion? It would seem that the Blue Army had been infiltrated and compromised. According to Father Paul Leonard: "The leadership of the World Apostolate of Fatima (alias Blue Army) has stubbornly and impenitently falsified Our Lady's message, in their unholy campaign to bring the Fatima message in line with the Vatican-Moscow Agreement."[8]

The March/April 1986 Issue of *Soul Magazine*, on page 22, states, "The Collegial Consecration (was) ... made with the bishops of the world by Pope John Paul II in St. Peter's Square on March 25, 1984 ... There the Pope in union with all bishops of the world made the consecration to Mary's Immaculate Heart. *As requested in the apparitions of June 13, 1929.*

Then on page 9 of the same Issue — *Soul Magazine* states: "The Holy Father proceeded to consecrate the world to the Immaculate Heart of Mary ... in compliance with the request of Our Lady when She said 'I will ask for the consecration of the *world* to My Immaculate Heart ...'"[9]

At this point in the publication of such an obvious misrepresentation of the known facts, Father Leonard, encouraged by Father Gruner, hastened to the defense of Our Lady, stating dramatically and emphatically that Our Lady never asked for the consecration of the *world* but ... clearly specified Russia. Father Leonard saw the reasoning behind it in stark terms:

"Our Lady's real Fatima Message has been suppressed because it is at variance with Cardinal Casaroli's ... pro-Communist Vatican-Moscow Ostpolitik."[10]

The point that Father Leonard makes also is that this misinformation is deliberate so as to inject enough confusion into the consecration issue[11] as to dissipate the laity so that there be no groundswell of support for the Pope. This reminds us of what Father Joseph de Sainte-Marie said about the consecration confusion caused by the Blue Army and *Soul Magazine*, in 1982/83. *"Until now, they have given rise to confusion of mind, division of hearts and the dissipation of forces.*[12]

> This is "cunningly conceived to achieve a hidden but nevertheless very definite purpose to put an end to the public campaign for the Collegial Consecration of Russia to the Immaculate Heart of Mary,"[13] said Father Leonard, of the Blue Army leadership.

It seemed even the most highly respected of American bishops when under the Blue Army mantle, felt obliged to direct the faithful away from Our Lady's dramatic demand to the hierarchy for the consecration and to instead place the onus on the faithful who are already obeying Our Lady. U.S. Blue Army President, Bishop Jerome J. Hastrich, in *Soul Magazine* March/April, 1984, page 5 stated: "We might pray explicitly for Russia if we wish to do so, *but in our public message* avoid upsetting the delicate balance of international affairs which the Holy See is trying so hard to control and direct. We must desist from working for the fulfillment of Our Lady's request so as not to offend the Communists for even Russians who are not Christians may understandably resent any thought that they are in need of conversion."

In a statement that would make them few friends in the Vatican, Fathers Gruner and Leonard responded with the following summary, "The Blue Army has been turned into an instrument of Cardinal Casaroli's Vatican-Moscow Ostpolitik which would prohibit the Pope and bishops from fulfilling Our Lady of Fatima's request for the sake of the shortsighted politics of appeasement, compromise and surrender to Communism."

Father Gruner, throughout, continued to press home his main point: God demands the solemn public act of Consecration of Russia by the Pope and all the bishops of the world. God insists upon this solemn act in our time.[14]

The Vatican-Moscow Agreement in fact had raised a drawbridge between the Blue Army and Father Gruner's Apostolate.

"We cannot agree with Mr. John Haffert that the Vatican has outsmarted Moscow in this agreement and that, because of this agreement, the Church is better off.[15]

"Communism is conducting more than just a war of ideas. It is a total war on all fronts against God ...[16]

"The fight by the militant atheists of the East and West converges upon the Catholic Church. Both concentrate their efforts towards drawing the faithful away from the practice of their faith, away from the Word of God, from prayer and the Sacraments, the means of Grace necessary to save our souls."[17]

Father Leonard added, "Cardinal Casaroli, who as Secretary of State is at the head of the entire Vatican diplomatic corps, still adheres to the Vatican-Moscow Agreement. He recently demonstrated this when he made it clear that he had no responsibility for the anti-Communist content of the Instruction on Liberation Theology issued on September 3, 1984, by Cardinal Ratzinger and he denied that he was even consulted about the Instruction." [18]

Blue Army President for the U.S., Bishop Hastrich stated in that March/April, 1984 Issue of *Soul Magazine* (which came out before the 1984 consecration) that instead of praying for the conversion of Russia, "We are rather to pray that members of the Blue Army would so pray and fast that they themselves might be thoroughly converted ... to pray for the 'conversion' of Russia may seem like waving a red flag in front of a bull ... and so it might be more prudent to pray for peace in the world."

So intense was the craving to have the campaign for the Consecration over and done with, the wishful thinkers were willing to overlook anything the Soviets did. Or said. In late November 1986 Soviet leader Mikhail Gorbachev, in a speech in Tashkent, called for a 'firm and uncompromising struggle against religious phenomena'. So much for change in the Soviet Union. So much for the conversion of Russia. So much for the 1984 consecration.

Gorbachev declared, "We must be strict above all with Communists and senior officials, particularly those who say they defend our morality and ideals but in fact help promote backward views and themselves take part in religious ceremonies."[19]

The timing of the speech and the location reflected Moscow's concern for the Islamic fundamentalist revival, Tashkent being the center of a predominantly Islamic population. Knowing the media's fondness for Gorbachev, it was no surprise that they failed to publicize this gaff in the General Secretary's otherwise smooth public utterances. Yet imagine the headlines if he had made his pronouncement in, say, Rome itself.

There can be little doubt that even those bishops still entranced by the disorientations resulting from the Vatican-Moscow Agreement would have found reasons to applaud Gorbachev's speech.

In response, Father Gruner's message has, in the last years, become increasingly more pointed. *He says... "ONLY* Our Lady can help us as She, Herself clearly emphasized at Fatima. Only when the Pope and the bishops obey the request given at Fatima by consecrating Russia to the Immaculate Heart of Mary at the same time in a solemn and public manner, can there be peace. There surely is no other solution whatsoever."

Father Gruner had charted a course for himself and the apostolate which would bring them within the ambit of the Vatican bureaucracy's radar. In fact, the surveillance had already begun.

PART TWO

POLITICS
VS
PRAYER

Chapter 9

The Network

In late July of 1989 Father Gruner received a most unusual letter from Cardinal Antonio Innocenti, Perfect of the Congregation for the Clergy. It was the ecclesiastical equivalent of a letter-bomb:

"This Congregation has been following for a long time your case which arouses serious preoccupation on the part of the Holy See. . . "

Case? *What* case? And why was the "Holy See"—that is, certain elements of the Vatican bureaucracy—"seriously preoccupied" with him? As Father Gruner read the rest of the "Innocenti intervention" he saw a pattern which would repeat itself over and over again in the years to come.

The letter did not bother to answer the questions it raised; it did not define its own terms. There was no explanation of what the "case" of Father Gruner consisted of, nor any reason given for the "serious preoccupation on the part of the Holy See." Instead, Cardinal Innocenti simply declared the result he desired, and Father Gruner was evidently expected to comply without benefit of due process of Canon Law: Father Gruner was to find another bishop by September 30 or else return to Avellino. Naturally, this would mean the end of the Apostolate.

A basic point of Canon Law occurred to Father Gruner as he read the "Innocenti intervention". The Bishop of Avellino had given no such order himself, and Cardinal Innocenti had no right to issue it in the bishop's stead. A bishop is the ruler of his own diocese, answerable only to the Pope, not to the Congregation for the Clergy. The intervention was, quite simply, void.

Father Gruner replied to the intervention in a letter which pointed out, among other things, that a Cardinal sitting in the office of a Vatican Congregation had no right to run the Diocese of Avellino. For good measure, Father Gruner placed a copy of a formal appeal against Cardinal Innocenti into the hands of the Pope himself at a general audience in January of the following year. Thereafter the "Innocenti intervention" vaporized. Cardinal Innocenti was never heard from again in the "case" of Father Gruner. It was later reported to Father Gruner by a friendly Vatican insider the Cardinal Innocenti had stated that the name of Father Nicholas Gruner was never to be mentioned again in his presence.

Although the "Innocenti intervention" went nowhere, it prefigured later developments in the "case" of Father Gruner. Many of those developments would be unprecedented in the annals of Canon Law, but they would not be without parallels in the prior abuse of priests and prelates who had posed an impediment to the executors of Ostpolitik.

To comprehend the suffering many priests endure today at the hands of the bureaucracy of the Church they have vowed to serve until death, we need look no further than Father Augustine Fuentes and Cardinal Mindzenty. Their history is useful to discuss here in an effort to appreciate the startling parallels with Father Gruner's case.

On December 26, 1957, Father Augustine Fuentes conducted a famous interview with Sister Lucy which was published in July, 1958, and reprinted thereafter by various magazines around the world.[1] A full year passed before anyone in "authority" suggested it was not authentic. On July 2, 1959, nine months after the death of Pope Pius XII, an anonymous chancery official (who has not been identified to this day) suddenly published in the Diocesan bulletin of Coimbra that Father Fuentes had lied and had made the interview up out of thin air.[2] He suggested that Sister Lucy did not say these things represented in the interview. Despite the fact that Father Fuentes' own Archbishop of Vera Cruz, and the Cardinal Primate of Mexico, publicly stated that Father Fuentes was an honest, good priest and did not merit the charges being leveled against him by the anonymous "news" bulletin.[3] Nevertheless, the anonymous bulletin of the Curia of Coimbra was successful in suppressing Sister Lucy's true statement and having Father Fuentes fired as vice-postulator for the cause of beatification and canonization of Jacinta and Francisco.[4] Interestingly, he was replaced by the very person that Frère François now accuses of being behind the bogus letters of Sister Lucy in 1989, Father Luis Kondor.[5]

As Father Paul Leonard points out: "Of course it is manifestly dishonest and unjust what was done to Father Fuentes. Obviously if that Curia official of Coimbra or anyone else is not willing to stand behind his words, if he won't even take responsibility for his own 'official' acts then clearly no one else should take his anonymous words and acts seriously either. This is clearly a case of some powerful figure who does not want anyone to question, rebuke, examine or subject his actions to judicial review but who wants to impose his opinion, judgment and decision. In other words, it is the action of a man who recognizes no authority over himself but who forces his will on others when he has no real authority to do so. All authority by men over other men comes from God, but God gives no one, not the President, not the Prime Minister, not the Pope nor the Supreme Court Judge any authority to command or judge unless the person in authority takes personal (and therefore not be anonymous) responsibility for his authoritative, official acts."

As Father Gruner notes: "The whole nature of law, which must be observed if a society is not going to be subverted by a secret society, is that those in authority must take *public responsibility* for their official acts. This posture is a fundamental requirement of the natural law."[6]

Incredibly, a similar attempt was made on no less a personage than a Cardinal of the Roman Catholic Church. In 1975, a statement was published declaring that Cardinal Mindzenty had resigned from being Archbishop of Esztergom, Primate of Hungary. The Cardinal issued an immediate rebuttal stating, "I have not resigned and I presently cannot resign because of all the things going on in Hungary today which endangers souls."[7] Here was a Cardinal, one of the electors of the Pope, a prince of the Church, but even this did not deter certain Vatican bureaucrats from removing him from office and, at the same time, giving the public the impression that he had left his post willingly.

Due to Cardinal Mindzenty's courageous stand, the truth won. He wrote:

> "On February 5, 1974, the announcement of my removal from the See of Esztergom was published. Next day, to my profound sorrow, I found myself forced to issue a correction through my office:
>
> "A number of news agencies have transmitted the Vatican decision in such a way as to imply that Jozsef Cardinal Mindzenty has voluntarily retired. The news agencies furthermore stressed that before the papal decision there was an intense exchange of letters between the Vatican and the Cardinal-Archbishop, who is living in Vienna. Some persons have therefore drawn the conclusion that an agreement concerning this decision had been reached between the Vatican and the Hungarian primate. In the interests of truth, Cardinal Mindzenty has authorized his office to issue the following statement:
>
> Cardinal Mindzenty has not abdicated his office as archbishop nor the dignity as primate of Hungary. The decision was taken by the Holy See alone.
>
> After long and conscientious consideration the Cardinal justified his attitude on this questions as follows:

1. Hungary and the Catholic Church of Hungary are not free.

2. The leadership of the Hungarian dioceses is in the hands of a church administration built and controlled by the communist regime.

3. Not a single archbishop or apostolic administrator is in a position to alter the composition or the functioning of the above-mentioned church administration.

4. The regime decides who is to occupy ecclesiastical positions and for how long. Furthermore, the regime also decides what persons the bishops will be allowed to consecrate as priests.

5. The freedom of conscience and religion guaranteed by the Constitution is in practice, suppressed. "Optional" religious instruction has been banned from the schools in the cities and the larger towns. At present, the struggle for optional religious instructions in the schools is continuing in the smaller communities. Young people, contrary to the will of their parents, are being educated exclusively in an atheistic spirit. Believers are discriminated against in many areas of daily life. Religious teachers have only recently been confronted with the alternative of choosing between their professions and their religion.

6. The appointment of bishops or apostolic administrators without the elimination of the above-mentioned abuses does not solve the problems of the Hungarian Church. The installation of "peace priests" in important ecclesiastical posts have shaken the confidence of loyal priests and lay Catholics in the highest administration of the Church. In these grave circumstances, Cardinal Mindzenty cannot abdicate.

This is the path I traveled to the end, and this is how I arrived at complete and total exile."[8]

Father Marcel Nault reflecting on the above experiences of Father Fuentes and Cardinal Mindzenty said:

"In Acts of the Apostles, Chapter 20 (Verse 28-31), St. Paul warns the bishops that, from among their own number, perverse men will arise to draw the faithful after them. And urges them to watch therefore and not be taken in. St. Jude, in verse 4 of his Epistle, says that infiltrators will enter the Church. In the Apocalypse we can read about the false lamb with two horns. This false lamb represents bad bishops. The two horns symbolize the two points on the miters of bishops who, while giving the appearance of a lamb, are actually false.[9] In fact, as we have learned from Frère Michel's painstaking research, the Third Secret clearly refers to the responsibility of a number of members of the hierarchy for the present state of apostasy within the Catholic Church today.[10] And as we have seen, this infiltration of the hierarchy has been predicted in Sacred Scripture.

"Thus, it seems we have here the terrible 'burden' of the Third Secret, namely, the infiltration of the upper hierarchy and their complicity in the apostasy sweeping across all Christendom. That would explain why a few members of the upper hierarchy seem to work so hard to discredit priests like Father Gruner. Simply stated, if Father Gruner succeeds in bringing to the attention of the Catholic faithful the existence of these false lambs and their plans, so that the faithful are able to protect themselves from these false prophets, and if he were to succeed in getting the Third Secret revealed, then, of course, their game would be up and Catholics everywhere would rise up to defend themselves against these interlopers.

"These same false shepherds are certainly going to do whatever they can to protect themselves from the exposure that revealing the Third Secret would bring."

Sister Lucy herself had been silenced since 1960. Would they attempt to silence Father Gruner? They certainly knew that he was not bound by obedience to remain silent about the Vatican-Moscow Agreement. The pretense that "Father Gruner must obey our commands" had not worked in the Innocenti intervention. But there were other ways of getting rid of an inconvenient cleric. The cases of Father Fuentes and Cardinal Mindzenty made that clear.

Father Gruner and Cardinal Mindzenty's case would prove to be strikingly similar, although Father Gruner would shrink from any comparison with the great prelate. By the manner of the trap set for them, by the type of isolation they suffer and by the intensity of their resistance to it, these two cases would illustrate what Father Paul Leonard calls "the decay of the moral leadership in the bureaucracy of the Catholic Church in this century."

The great St. Athanasius was exiled from his Diocese by the Conference of Bishops of Egypt five separate times. He spent at least 17 years in exile. He was even "excommunicated" by Pope Liberius, who ended up being the first Pope in the early Church not to be canonized. Athanasius continued to preach and ordain priests despite the "excommunication".

Another Saint, St. John Gualberto, went to the bureaucrats in Rome and complained to them regarding the Archbishop of Florence, who had actually bribed certain bureaucrats, to get himself appointed bishop. To this Saint the Vatican bureaucrats would not listen. So he took his case directly to the people and God worked a public miracle, at St. John Gualberto's request, to prove that what he was saying was true. The people drove the corrupt bishop out of town. What we learn here is that God expects clerics to go to the people to protect the Church when Vatican officials will not pay attention. "Front line" clerics must rally the Catholic faithful in this time of great confusion and deception. They must go to the people so the people can wake up to what they can do to resist and overcome the crisis.

There is also, of course, the example in Sacred Scripture of St. Peter being rebuked by St. Paul to protect the Faith and the Church. Saints and Doctors of the Church all concur that St. Paul was absolutely right.

What secret strengths sustain a priest when the bureaucracy of the Church for which he has laid down his life seeks to erase the good he has done, prevent the good his memory might yet do, and eradicate from the record any reference to the bureaucracy's part in the deed? Heaven alone knows.

It is a sad and oft-overlooked fact of Conciliar Church history that the two bishops "excommunicated" over their defense of the Mass of the Ages, Archbishop Lefebvre and Bishop de Castro Meyer, were also the two loudest voices, among the International Group of Bishops, raised in opposition to Vatican II's hush hush policy on Communism.[11] It cannot be mere coincidence.

The showdown between Father Gruner and the bureaucrats was inevitable. In view of the confusion deliberately generated by the anti-Fatima forces regarding the consecration, Father Gruner had gone directly to the world episcopacy in issue after issue of *The Fatima Crusader* during the late 80's and early 90's. The printed headlines sent again and again around the world had a much more long lasting effect than a television broadcast or radio could possibly have had. Statistics prove that the printed word receives eight times as many repeated viewings as any other form of media expression. *The Fatima Crusader* headlines continued to repeat the danger, "Lucy Silenced", "He (the Pope) Will Do It But It Will Be Late" " Make it Known to My ministers" "They Will Follow Him (the King of France) Into Misfortune".

Many predicted that the Vatican bureaucrats would step up their attack and take direct action to silence Father Gruner, to mute his insistence that the Consecration must be done, to prevent the public airing of his well founded perception of who was directly responsible for it not being done and, especially, to permanently prevent him , or anyone else from effectively obeying the command of Jesus to "Make it known to My ministers".

To those who might suggest that it was presumptuous of Father Gruner to undertake to obey the command "Make it known to My ministers", the reply ought to have been self evident:

First of all the command of Our Lord to Sister Lucy extended to all the ministers of the Church, including Father Gruner. What would be the point of making the message known to all the sacred ministers of the Church, if they were not to preach it.

Secondly, how could the message be preached effectively without including the bishops, whose pressing duties as heads of their dioceses might preclude a study of the message in all its implications.

Third, how could any of the sacred ministers remain silent in the face of Our Lord's command, merely because a few Vatican bureaucrats had deemed it inexpedient to speak any longer of the conversion of Russia as the only means to avoid annihilation of nations.

What is more, if these Vatican bureaucrats had undertaken a global campaign to bury the message of Fatima, did not the sacred ministers who had been ordered by Our Lord to preach it, have a sacred duty to mount an opposing campaign to keep the message alive?

The anti-Fatima bureaucrats in the Vatican had their work cut out for them. To destroy Father Gruner's Fatima Apostolate would be the objective. But that would mean silencing his continent-wide weekly television show, his daily radio broadcasts, and *The Fatima Crusader* magazine, of which he was the publisher. To eliminate all of them would be a formidable task. A much easier solution to the "Gruner problem" would be to take the outspoken priest out of contention with one simple masterstroke. The tactic chosen in the summer of 1989 would anticipate a more elaborate effort later on: The bureaucrats would make Father an offer he couldn't refuse. A new bishop in Canada would be offered on the condition of silence!

This ploy would involve the Secretary of State, Cardinal Cassaroli, the active participation of the Nuncio to Canada, Archbishop Palmas, Cardinal Innocenti from the Congregation of the Clergy and the current Bishop of Avellino, whose predecessor had ordained Father Gruner and given him written permission to reside outside the diocese of Avellino. Also drawn into the campaign was Bishop Fulton of St. Catharines, Ontario, Canada, in whose diocese the Pilgrim Virgin Apostolate was housed. For some years, Bishop Fulton had accommodated the Apostolate, at first by granting his permission to move the head office into his Diocese, and then by simply leaving it alone. Now, Bishop Fulton was to become a pawn in a game he did not initiate.

On August 9, 1989, a letter from Bishop Fulton arrived at the Fort Erie Fatima Center address.

"I have just received documentation from the present Bishop of Avellino, His Excellency Gerrardo Pierro," the letter read, " in which he raises the question of your possible incardination in the diocese of St. Catharines ...

As far as incardination is concerned, I would require ... that you would promise total obedience to me as Bishop and that you would accept an appointment at my bidding, which would require you to abandon the present apostolate which you have chosen for yourself."[12]

Pope John Paul II said "The Fatima Message is more relevant and urgent than ever. It is addressed to every human being. . . The Message of Fatima imposes an obligation on the Church".[13] Obviously it is not optional nor can priests take a vow of silence about it. It appeared that just as the Vatican-Moscow Agreement immorally and illegally but *de facto* imposes silence on priests, bishops and Cardinals, they would now pressure Father Gruner to make his own personal pact of silence regarding the full Fatima Message. The offer of incardination came with a string attached: "promise to keep silence about Fatima and all it implies."

It was clear as lightning in a Canadian sunset — we'll put up if you shut up! But such an agreement would be immoral. How could any priest in good conscience agree to be silent about a public revelation which the last five Popes have publicly promoted? How could any priest simply ignore the command of Our Lord Himself: "*Make it known* to My ministers." And why was this pact of silence not being demanded of Father Fox? It seems that the Fatima Message propagated by Father Fox had been "dumbed down".

The response to the offer was taken up, on Father Gruner's behalf, by one of the finest honed, and best aimed pens in the Catholic world, Father Paul Leonard.

"It would be the easiest thing in the world for Father Gruner to succumb to the machinations of Vatican bureaucrats and abandon the apostolate he has carried out for more than ten years. [Now in 1997, almost 20 years].

"How easy it would be to abandon Fatima to assume the much easier life of a small town curate, earning more pay for less work."[14]

"However, it is canonically illegal for Church authorities to attempt, in this manner to silence a priest from carrying out his priestly task of preaching the truth. In the Sacred Scriptures, St. Paul tells the bishop, St. Timothy, to impose silence on those false shepherds who depart from the teaching of the Church and thereby dissipate the Faith. (1 Tim. 1:3-7) It is high time that those clergy and laity, who are faithful to the Magisterium of the Church, resist the abuse of authority, whereby the holders of ecclesiastical office tolerate and permit the Faith to be dissipated, destroyed and expunged from the hearts of men by modernist priests, while they unlawfully attempt to impose silence on those who remain in steadfast conformity to the Gospel of Christ, the Magisterium of the Church, and the pontifically approved message of Our Lady of Fatima.

"The pressure applied by Cardinal Innocenti (the July 1989 intervention) is not merely against Father Gruner as a single individual, but is really against the Apostolate of *The Fatima Crusader*, *Heaven's Peace Plan* radio program and the TV program, *Fatima: "The Moment Has Come"*. All stressing the need for the Consecration."[15]

As Father Gruner had pointed out in his reply to the void intervention of Cardinal Innocenti, there was no need for him to obtain a new ordinary in Canada:

"There are many priests working in Canada who are not incardinated here, yet that does not appear to arouse any 'serious preoccupation on the part of the Holy See'. Canon Law does not *require* that all priests be incardinated in the diocese where they reside, and therefore, I would like to know what is the reason for this extra-legal requirement ...[16]

"If the Secretary of State and some bishops are displeased with my activity in promoting the Message of Our Lady of Fatima, then the burden of proof is on them to prove any wrongdoing on my part. I have sent my magazine to every bishop in the world for years. I have sent my book *World Enslavement or Peace, It's Up To The Pope*" to all the bishops of the world. No bishop, Cardinal, or any official of the Holy See has even suggested there is anything doctrinally wrong in anything that I have ever published.

"It is to silence us from denouncing the Vatican-Moscow Agreement that you unlawfully inflict this injustice."[17] Cardinal Innocenti never replied to these arguments. They were in fact unanswerable.

Sister Lucy herself gives us the key to understanding the persecutions of faithful priests while modernist wolves in shepherds' clothing roam at will: "The devil is in the mood for engaging in a decisive battle against the Blessed Virgin. And the devil knows what it is that most offends God and which in a short space of time will gain for him the greatest number of souls. Thus the devil does everything to overcome souls consecrated to God because, in this way, the devil will succeed in leaving the souls of the Faithful abandoned by their leaders, thereby the more easily will he seize them."

To those who suggest that the faithful should simply wait for the "competent authorities" to address the crisis, Sister Lucy had a pointed reply: "We should not wait for an appeal to the world to come from Rome on the part of the Holy Father, to do penance. Nor should we wait for the call to penance to come from our bishops in our diocese, nor from the religious congregations. No! Our Lord has already very often used these means and the world has not paid attention. That is why, now, it is necessary for each one of us to begin to reform himself spiritually. Each person must not only save his own soul but also all the souls that God has placed on our path."[18]

§

The Innocenti intervention and the "strings-attached" offer of a bishop for silence were the opening moves in a bureaucratic chess game which began after eleven years of dramatic growth for the Apostolate from 1978, when Father Gruner became its vice president, to 1989, when the first moves of the chess game were made in Rome.

Understanding the importance of the Fatima Message, despite all the controversy, Father Gruner's Apostolate had neither changed direction nor slowed down during that period. In 1985, Father Gruner had begun restoring a fast disappearing aspect of Catholic culture, a mission to India, with the Pilgrim Virgin Statue of Our Lady of Fatima. To the average Catholic, India represents a subcontinent of non-Christians, prone to hostile expressions regarding any missionary invasion ever since the time of St. Thomas the Apostle. In fact, the fervor for Catholicism sown by the Apostle was at a fever pitch in the mid-80's, far surpassing even the devotion expressed in the Western Canada tours of the late Seventies.

On May 13, 1985, having installed the Pilgrim Virgin Statue at the high altar built over the tomb of St. Thomas the Apostle, in the Cathedral of Madras, India, Father Gruner joined the Archbishop of Madras, His Grace Archbishop Rayappa Arulappa, to preach to the multitudes drawn by Her presence.[19]

The faith in Mary is still strong, beautiful and simple in India. Following this pilgrimage, Father Gruner supplied the newly opened International Fatima Crusade mission office in Madras with hundreds of thousands of scapulars, rosaries and holy cards.

By November 1985, he was in Rome to chair the first Symposium at the Vatican specifically on the Message of Fatima, "Is The 1985 Extraordinary Synod The Last Opportunity for World Peace?". This important meeting coincided with the opening of the Extraordinary Synod called by the Holy Father. The Apostolate hosted influential members of the clergy as well as such Fatima scholars as Frère Michel de la Sainte Trinité (France); Hamish Fraser (Scotland); Abbé Pierre Caillon (France); Professor Emilio Cristani (Italy).

There were also two bishops in attendance. The first was the Latin Patriarch of Jerusalem, His Beatitude Giacomo Beltriti, who was quite familiar with the consecration of Russia request and who acknowledged it had not been done properly by the time of the November 24, 1985 symposium. His Beatitude had publicly, at the Roman Synod of Bishops in October 1983, from the Synod floor asked the Pope and the bishops to consecrate Russia as Our Lady of Fatima requested. He agreed to be an honorary chairman of the Symposium. He told Father Gruner he would continue to work towards the consecration of Russia through diplomatic channels within the Church and he encouraged Father Gruner to continue to openly publicize the need for the consecration of Russia as Father Gruner had been doing for several years.

The second bishop present was Bishop Gabriel Ganaka, President of the Bishops' Conference of Nigeria. Bishop Ganaka was deeply impressed with the meeting and told Father Gruner that as a result of the presentation that he would talk to the Holy Father about the request for the consecration of Russia. A few days later, Bishop Ganaka arrived in the papal apartments for his appointed lunch with the Holy Father and a number of other bishops. He got there a few minutes early and in the sitting room on the coffee table was a magazine that headlined, "the consecration of Russia is already done." This confused the bishop who did not have enough background on the Fatima Message, and consequently felt it "prudent" not to bring it up with the Pope.

It became increasingly clear to Father Gruner, after Bishop Ganaka reported this experience to him, that a deliberate campaign of disinformation was preventing the consecration of Russia from being done. The Pope simply did not know just how many loyal bishops would obey him if he requested it.

In advance of a new pilgrimage to India, Issue 19 of *The Fatima Crusader* had drawn a letter of encouragement, support and prayers from Mother Theresa of Calcutta, April 7, 1986: " May Our Lord continue to bless your dedicated efforts to spread devotion to the Immaculate Heart of Mary." Her handwritten postscript, the cornerstone of her own apostolate, went straight to the heart of the India Pilgrimage, "Keep the joy of loving Jesus through Mary and share this joy with all you meet".

By May 1988, the International Fatima Rosary Crusade had expanded Father Gruner's radio program, begun in 1987, which was already reaching a potential 200 million people through 43 radio stations in the U.S. and Canada, via regular short-wave radio broadcasts to more than 40 nations overseas.[20]

By August of 1988, Father Gruner's book *World Enslavement or Peace, It's Up To The Pope,* a comprehensive analysis of the Fatima Message, had been published. It became a staple for Fatimologists, paving the way for the English translation of the three volumes of *The Whole Truth About Fatima*, the definitive examination of Fatima by Frère Michel de la Sainte Trinité which Father Gruner's own publishing house printed in the late 1980's and early 90's.

The explosive growth of the Apostolate from 1978 to 1989 had greatly alarmed the anti-Fatima establishment. Here was a genuine movement to keep alive a message most unpalatable for the executors of the new order — a message that Russia must be converted, and that locked in what had become known as the Third Secret were answers to the crisis which had spread throughout the Church since Vatican II. Clearly, something had to be done about the man leading the movement.

§

The pressure from various opponents of Father Gruner started to take on a frantic Keystone Cops pace. In *Soul Magazine*, the voice of the Blue Army, Bishop Luna declared that "The Holy Father is disturbed by the many letters being written demanding a consecration of Russia. The work in *The Fatima Crusader* by Fr. Nicholas Gruner is creating worldwide confusion. Pope Pius XII made a consecration of Russia; Pope Paul VI repeated the consecration when he went to Fatima in 1967 for the fiftieth anniversary. Pope John Paul II repeated the consecration in 1982 during his visit to Fatima and again when Our Lady's statue was brought from Fatima to St. Peter's Square in Rome in 1984." [21]

Then began the harassment that would continue for years. Bishop Luna wrote a letter to Bishop Legaspi, President of the Philippine Bishops' Conference, to which Father Gruner's Pilgrim Virgin tour was headed. In it, Bishop Luna lamented the fact that so many Blue Army members received *The Fatima Crusader*, because, he said, "its philosophy promotes ideas against the Holy Father and against the Holy See."[22]

Never has this claim of Bishop Luna been substantiated, nor could it be, as there is absolutely no evidence of any disloyalty or disrespect of the Pope in any of the Apostolate's activities or publications. Nevertheless, this letter was put to a very specific use in the city of Ilo Ilo in the Philippines. Father Gruner had been invited to bring the Pilgrim Virgin into the Cathedral of Ilo Ilo. Archbishop Piamonte, based on the Bishop Luna letter, informed the Faithful of his diocese that Father Gruner had canceled the visit and would not be arriving there with the statue.[23]

When the tour actually arrived at the Cathedral with the statue, the doors were closed. No official was on hand to welcome the Pilgrim Virgin as there had been at eight other cathedrals in the Philippines. Nevertheless, they entered the Cathedral and brought the statue into the nave. While the Cathedral was packed for Mass, the Archbishop and the vicar were out of town, and the two young priests left in charge did not bother to even acknowledge Our Lady's presence in their midst. The Vicar General refused to speak with the tour organizers.[24] At the end of Mass, their enthusiasm and devotion was not lost. The people crowded around Our Lady, paying homage to Her and enthusiastically demonstrated their appreciation to have Her in their midst.

The islands of the Philippines are half way around the world from that island of knowledge and inspiration wherein is deposited the key to the secrets of Fatima, one Carmelite nun in a convent of Coimbra. Yet it was in the Philippines that the long anticipated guerrilla-style harassment of Father Gruner's Fatima Apostolate first showed its face. The setting itself could only prompt one to wonder how much simpler life for the Church would be if only the Holy See's order of silence was lifted and the world could hear the truth from the voice of that one specially chosen woman a half a world away.

Meanwhile, the Apostolate continued its initiative in India. In October, 1991, Father Gruner had received a pressing letter from Victor Kulanday of the All India Laity Congress urging him to return to the subcontinent to meet with bishops and Catholic lay leaders to explain the urgent need to consecrate Russia in the manner Our Lady specified. Many of the 140 Indian bishops had already indicated their willingness to consecrate Russia as Our Lady asked.

Included in the pilgrimage were plans to meet with two Cardinals, two Archbishops, and the hope to meet again with Mother Teresa and that other legend of the Church in our time who had spent more than 60 years among the poor of Bombay, Father Maschio.[25]

According to Bishop Amalnather, 200,000 people welcomed the Pilgrim Virgin statue at Sacred Heart Cathedral in Tuticorin in mid November.[26] The November 24, 1991, edition of *Mid Day* also reported that more than 200,000 pilgrims welcomed the Pilgrim Virgin statue in Bombay, some several thousand miles away.

The fervor for, love of and devotion to the Mother of God evident in grassroots Catholic movements in India was of the type not seen in decades in North America or Europe. In city after city, tens of thousands came out bearing flowers and gifts for the Pilgrim Virgin, leaving forever impressed upon the mind's eye hundreds of thousands of outstretched hands reaching for scapulars and rosaries.

How much effect would this 'Garment of Grace' have on the Catholic culture of India? Bishops walked with thousands of their flock in procession to honor the Pilgrim Virgin. On at least one occasion, a bishop, after hearing Father Gruner's sermon on the message of Our Lady of Fatima, consecrated his Diocese to the Immaculate Heart of Mary.[27] One priest commented after Father Gruner had spoken to a rally of 60,000 people that the visit of the Pilgrim Virgin had revived the faith of hundreds of thousands.[28]

Father Marcel Nault, who had hosted the Pilgrim Virgin Statue at his parish of St. Stephen the Martyr in Dowling, Ontario, and who would later join forces with Father Gruner, accompanied him on that pilgrimage to India.

"In 1991, I went with him to India. I have never seen such poverty and yet so much modesty among the people. The Indian people are very pious, religious, peaceful, and dress with great decency.

"I was very much impressed by Father Gruner's extraordinary ability to preach for hours on the message of Fatima to millions. His is a marvelous holy work. He is a true crusader for Our Lady of Fatima.

"I stood alongside him for hours giving out Brown Scapulars."

The pilgrimage returned to Canada with the goal of providing in the first months of the following year one million Scapulars and scapular booklets to India's 25 million Catholics, with a special emphasis on Catholic school children.

At the end of 1991, the movement started by the apostolate showed no signs of distress, and its leader had so far fended off the first few thrusts of the bureaucratic forces which had yet to implement their definitive strategy.

In Portugal, in 1992, however, the effort to derail the apostolate and discredit Father Gruner would descend to the theater of the absurd.

Chapter 10

To Make The Guitars Laugh

Coimbra appears as if out of nowhere at a surprise turn in the road and the imagination instantly catapults back to the age of martyrs and saints. The incorrupt remains of St. Elizabeth of Portugal are preserved in the Basilica there on the hillside. Atop the hill, where the renowned fado festivals occur each spring, the University of Coimbra resonates like an exquisitely crafted guitar to the murmur of the heart of Portugal. Coimbra is proud. With good reason. Here in this fabled city rising upon the banks of the Mondego River is housed the Secret. The sole surviving seer from the Cova da Iria lives here behind very high walls.

The Carmel of Coimbra rests on the side of the hill, a massive white enclave with emerald green doors, a bejewelled rock on one finger of this historic mountain. Here where Rua Santa Teresa intersects with Avenida Dias da Silva, Lucy dos Santos has withstood the curiosity of the world through the second half of the most rapidly changing century in history.

Born seven months before Pius X published his condemnation of modernism, she has seen seven other popes take the Chair of Peter. Indeed, she has met several of them in person. Arriving here at this cloister shortly after the end of the Second World War, she has followed the Korean War, Vietnam, and the Persian Gulf conflict. She has watched Communism devour much of the world. She even now observes its supposed and much publicized 'collapse.'

Born before the birth of radio, she has lived to see pictures radioed back from Pluto. She has survived the countless tyrants, dictators and madmen who have promised the world thousand-year reichs, the burial of capitalism and the extermination of the Church. Of her life lived in private, away from the prying eyes of media entrepreneurs and religious fanatics, we know next to nothing. Time may bring us precise details of her hidden life in written accounts but of her actual life we can be sure of only one thing — she says her Rosary each day.

Photographs of this unique Carmelite taken in adult life reveal a dramatic face exuding confidence in the presence of popes and pilgrims — on occasion she has returned to the great monumental shrine now surrounding the azinhiera tree. There is in her face an obvious joy, the source of which must surely reach all the way back to that day in October, 1917, very near the Feast of Tabernacles that Jesus so loved, when the sun left its tent in the sky and educated the souls and hearts of 70,000 people in that famous Cova in Portugal.

There is in her countenance ample evidence of a lifetime of conscientious responsibility. But one special ingredient outshines all others. In her eyes there is freedom. Freedom born of the miniature winds that move the trees on the hills of Aljustrel, cool the rocks of the Cabeço, bend the flowers in the Cova da Iria. Freedom like the crafted winds spun by the flashing fingers of the fado players. Freedom from this world. It is the secret of the saints. It is this that makes the guitars laugh.

Upon beholding the Carmel of Coimbra one is reminded that God is the greatest of all storytellers. Behind these towering walls of Carmel, He put this specially chosen woman. And there He kept her very well. Like a princess in a castle keep, she grips our imagination, holds us in wonder, lest the rest of the story He is telling be tugged from our minds.

Many have tried to scale the heights of the Great Secret. None can prove they have succeeded. Many have tried to lure the keeper of the Secret into the light of day to unfurl those '24 lines on one lined sheet of paper' which contain the Secret. All have failed.

For 48 years, since departing her previous convent in Tuy to arrive here, she has been the focus of relentless scrutiny, outrageous speculation, misplaced devotion, political and ecclesiastical pressure. But at no time was her resolve more challenged, her personality more taxed, her very integrity more threatened, than in the year 1992, when it seemed all the world wanted to breach the white walls of this Carmel.

The concentration of pressure resulted from one reality; the fact that Sister Lucy has been silenced since 1960. Yet those who refuse to acknowledge that John Paul II has clearly and publicly said that the Consecration of Russia as requested by Our Lady of Fatima is not done, continue to try and bolster their position by fraudulently claiming that Sister Lucy agrees with them. They are only able to do this because she cannot respond and defend herself publicly without the permission of Cardinal Ratzinger himself.

As J. Kaess explains, "The Fatima establishment keeps" insisting that the consecration has been done. But "they cannot produce a single shred of evidence." First "Russia was not mentioned in the (1984) ceremony and they can't prove that any more than a few hundred bishops were involved." Second, "the 1984 Consecration was not a public act. Even though there was a public ceremony, not a single person in the world knew anything about it having anything to do with the Collegial Consecration until five years later when the 'writing was on the wall' in the Soviet Union."[1]

Alas for the establishment, the Catholic world has a longer memory than the establishment banked on. After waiting 40 years for the Consecration of Russia, Catholics were suddenly being told in the late 80's, "Oh, by the way, that was done back in '84." But, of course, the whole world knows that it was not done in '84. The most devout, attentive, loyal supporters of the Pope had not heard a thing about it. Suddenly, in 1989, pictures and articles appear in publications far and wide showing the consecration by John Paul II that took place in St. Peter's Square, March 25, 1984.

It was as if the FBI issued a news release in 1989 saying, "Oh, by the way, Walt Disney killed Kennedy. We proved it back in '84."

Cardinals, bishops and priests, and the faithful knew full well it had not been done. And as Father Gruner keeps saying, '... time is running out'.

Whoever the individual was behind that very transparent maneuver, he is a man never to be envied. In the circles where hoodwinking is a fine art, the supposed consecration whitewash was worse than a hoax, it was a *faux-pas*, a terrible mistake. By 1992, the establishment was dangling naked at the end of its tether. People wanted an explanation. The ruse of '89, designed to convince the faithful that the consecration was done, had exposed the Big Lie at home. By November of that year, the "Fatima Establishment" had been proclaiming that, in five letters supposedly written by Sister Lucy, the last living Fatima seer was confirming the Consecration of Russia had been done. The establishment now found that it had to scurry to provide more specific proofs that Fatima is finished.

March 21, 1992, the first incident. The chain of events this day triggered would turn 1992 into a rollercoaster ride for the establishment. That it was the direct result of the pressure applied relentlessly by Father Nicholas Gruner and his Apostolate was clearly confirmed from the onset by one of the most credible voices of the entire Fatima phenomenon.

Abbé Caillon writes, "The event was triggered off by a certain Father Gruner who *'runs a review on Fatima'* (author's emphasis) *in North America and who maintains that the consecration of Russia has not been made."*[2]

Father Messias Coelho explained (to Abbé Caillon), "This interview took place on the initiative of Doctor Lacerda, who was irritated with Father Gruner's campaigns."[3] In a letter dated December 20, 1991, addressed to Father Gruner's representative at Fatima, Doctor Lacerda stated, "Pope John Paul II effected this consecration on March 25, 1984. And what Gorbachev has done since 1985 can only be explained by this consecration".[4]

"It was necessary, therefore," says Abbé Caillon, "to go to the source."

On Saturday, March 21, 1992, a delegation of four people went to the Carmel of Coimbra to consult with the seer. It was the feast of St. Benedict, no longer much celebrated or even noted in the new liturgical calendar. But there was irony in the date. The obliteration of Monte Casino in World War II was nothing compared to what this meeting would do to the credibility of Fortress Lucy.

The group was comprised of the Apostolic Delegate to Portugal, Monsignor Luciano Angeloni; his secretary, Doctor Francis de Lacerda, and Father Messias Coelho, a longstanding Portuguese Fatimist who had, up until 1988, steadfastly maintained, along with Father Gruner and so many others, that the act of consecration of the world made on March 25, 1984, had not met the requirements given by Our Lady of Fatima.

Abbé Caillon reports, "The interview lasted one and a half hours. Sister Lucy declared that the consecration of Russia has been made."[5]

What? Sister Lucy says the consecration has been made? Even the most bold of the anti-Fatima forces hesitated crowing the news to the world at large. One would expect such world-shaking words to be immediately blasted from the housetops *ad mare usque ad mare*. They were not. Instead, a peculiar calm followed what should have been a grand victory for the anti-Fatima establishment. But an event was fast approaching that would provide a stage for the announcement.

Between May 8-12, 1992, an international congress on 'Fatima and Peace' took place in the Paul VI Center in Fatima as a build-up to the 75th anniversary of the first apparition in the Cova. About five hundred persons attended. It was the ideal setting for the great announcement.

Among those attending was Father Gruner, who was invited to endure hearing his entire life's work being dismissed by one particular speaker. Bishop Jose da Cruz Policarpo characterized those who still work for the consecration of Russia, (such as Father Gruner, although his name was not mentioned) as, "...inclined to a simplistic reading of history and with a taste for myth and the pseudo-eschatalogical ..." who accuse "... the popes and bishops of being responsible for the world's calamities through failing to accomplish the request of Our Lady of Fatima." (Bishop da Cruz Policarpo, formerly auxiliary bishop of Lisbon and now rector of the Portuguese Catholic University has been characterized as a '... man of the Left, known for his progressivist positions ...')[6]

But no great announcement of the supposed words of Sister Lucy of March 21 was made from the podium.

In an address on May 13, Cardinal Sodano, the newly appointed Secretary of State, mentioned the past consecration attempts of the Popes but did not mention that the only Pope to formulate an explicit (albeit incomplete) consecration of Russia was Pope Pius XII in 1952.

No great announcement of the words of March 21st followed this address either.

In a private conversation with Abbé Caillon, Father Messias Coelho reported part of the contents of the March 21st meeting: "Lucy said that the consecration had been made, that she has always said so, that she had never asked anything concerning Russia, but only concerning the union of the bishops. And since this union was imperfect, the fruits will not be as good as might have been imagined."[7]

Father Coelho added, "That there were things that Lucy said which he could not report because *the Nuncio had forbidden him.*"[8] So now there was a *fourth* secret of Fatima. No matter how strenuously the anti-Fatima forces tried to bend Sister Lucy to the shape demanded by their program, she would always say something which had to be hidden from the faithful. This would suggest, later on, that perhaps what was needed was a Sister Lucy whose words would be *entirely* theirs.

Entering into this debate was a brilliant young religious from France whose dramatic analysis on the people and events of the Fatima story reveals a talent that is part John le Carre and part G.K. Chesterton, Brother François de Marie des Anges of the Catholic Counter Reformation.

Brother François dissected Father Coelho's report with razor sharp precision.

"It is in fact unlikely that Sister Lucy declared on March 21, 1992, that she had always said that the consecration of Russia had been made when a series of concordant testimonies going back to 1984, 1986, 1987 and 1989, a good number of them collected by Abbé Caillon himself — shows that during those years she often stated that the consecration of Russia still had not been done as willed by Our Lady. Besides, how is it possible to believe Sister Lucy confided that she had never said anything about Russia? There we have travestied both the request made at Tuy and Our Lady's promise!

"We know, in fact, that on several occasions during the last decade she explained why the acts of offering of May 13, 1982, and of March 25, 1984, which were practically identical, do not correspond with Our Lady's request, at the same time affirming that 'God wants Russia to appear as the sole object of the consecration'. For the Divine plan to be fulfilled, the consecration of Russia alone is in fact necessary 'because Russia is an immense, well defined territory, and her conversion will be seen and will thus be proof of what can be obtained through consecration to the Immaculate Heart of Mary'"[9].

Then Brother François added his most convincing argument.

"Furthermore," he said, "if Sister Lucy had really said on March 21, 1992, that the consecration of Russia had been done, her declaration would not have remained secret, or 'hidden' to repeat the word used by Abbé Caillon. Firstly, the Apostolic Nuncio, Monsignor Luciano Angeloni, would have made it known on emerging from this parlor. Secondly, Father Messias Coelho would have published it in his review *Mensagem de Fatima*, and to be precise in his number which appeared a few weeks later for May (No. 189). Then Father Fox would not have failed to mention it in the July issue of his quarterly periodical, *Fatima Family Messenger*. Thirdly, Doctor Lacerda would have used this declaration of Lucy's as an unanswerable argument in his controversy with Father Gruner's representative at Fatima. Fourthly, the Rector of Fatima Sanctuary (Monsignor Guerra) would have referred to it when questioned by Abbé Laurentin.

"Fifthly, Abbé Caillon would have learned this news, not in the corridors of this Congress, but from the mouth of Monsignor Policarpo when he delivered his communication 'Fatima, Peace and Russia' mentioned previously."[10]

The accusation demanded a response. One came.

Monsignor Luciano Angeloni's letter to Brother François of August 4th, 1992, seems to let the steam out of the kettle: "On my last visit of this March 21st, I was accompanied by two specialists in Fatima affairs, who had asked me to provide them with the opportunity of returning to see Sister Lucy (whom they had not met since 1983). Without it being necessary to make known the news in question, I can tell you that there was no conversation. There were no special declarations. It was simply a visit on my part, during which those who had asked to accompany me wished to see Sister Lucy again. They spoke with her about various current matters — matters, for example, which have been published in her *Memoirs*."[11]

In other words, not the kind of exchange that would spawn a grand announcement at the Congress. In fact, nothing worth even a whisper. So — someone lied.

Ironically, at the same congress, Cardinal Casaroli admitted to the result of his 30 years of Ostpolitik. "The Church, who seemed to pay so much attention to the great questions of disarmament and tensions between the two blocs, now seems powerless before the mosaic of conflicts breaking out in the world. The fact that the highest international authorities prove to be equally powerless affords us no consolation."[12]

Brother François notes, regarding Cardinal Casaroli, that we have total collapse! but the former Secretary of State is not going to abjure his faith in Masonic humanism for all that.[13] Nor, we might add, his decades of faithful service to the Vatican-Moscow Agreement.

Who could have guessed that all that had transpired so far in this busiest of years was merely a prelude to the drama to unfold on the 75th anniversary of the Miracle of the Sun?

Chapter 11

Ambush In Fatima October 1992

The invitation to attend was simply worded: "The Fatima Crusader Magazine respectfully requests the honor of Your Excellency's attendance at an International Conference to publicly discuss the Collegial Consecration of Russia as requested by Our Lady of Fatima as a condition of World Peace."[1]

The note added, "As funds allow, accommodation and airfare will be provided through the generosity of thousands of supporters of Our Lady's Fatima Apostolate who have sacrificed for this intention, for those bishops from poorer dioceses who otherwise could not attend."

To bishops of the poorer nations who received this invitation in June of 1992, it was a generous offer. To those better off, who might be able to afford their own trip, it was a chance to mingle with brother bishops in the Cova da Iria on the 75th anniversary of the Miracle of the Sun. One hundred and ten bishops accepted the invitation.

Those returning to Fatima might well have anticipated the hospitality they would receive. Those coming for the first time must ready themselves for a warm surprise. The courtesy of the Portuguese people, specifically in the northern half of the country, may be one of the great mysteries of this century. How they have kept their sense of humor, their gentility, their irrepressible dignity in the wake of endless waves of humanity descending on the terrain of Our Lady is a question that was partially answered by Senor Vincente of the Virgin Maria Hotel where many of the bishops were billeted. When asked for the recipe to the justifiably famous soup he served to start each day's dinner Senor Vincente shook his head, admonishing the inquirer with a wagging finger.

"No, no, no," he warned. "That is the Fourth Secret of Fatima." Unwittingly, the genial proprietor had revealed the core of the

Portuguese character in the north — a reserve, prudence, confidence, pride, and humor that comes from living in a world completely mantled by the things of Heaven.

What occurred, then, upon the arrival in Fatima of the one hundred plus Bishops from 23 countries heading for the International Bishops Peace Conference, would shine a very stark light, indeed, on the Shrine management and on its rector, Msgr. Luciano Guerra himself. Shrine officials should have known better. But who, after all, had ever financed the gathering in Fatima of over one hundred bishops?

Bishop Alberto Cosme do Amaral of Leiria was hosting his own Pastoral Conference in the Paul VI Center for the laity, to which only a selected handful of bishops had been invited. The Fatima Peace Conference, to which all the bishops of the world were invited, in no way conflicted with Bishop Amaral's gathering. At most 50 bishops were in attendance at the Paul VI Center, most of which were drawn from those who had accepted the invitation of Father Gruner and whose passage to Fatima was paid for by *The Fatima Crusader*. More than one hundred bishops had come to meet at the Floresta Hotel which comprised the largest private gathering of bishops in the century. It was a veritable motherlode of Church Fathers that could hardly be ignored.

To assemble such a body of bishops had never been done before by any single organization. Its purpose was clear to all. The very words of the invitation contain the entire raison d'être of Father Gruner, 'Consecration...Russia...World Peace,' and his movement by now, one of the largest lay apostolates in the Church.

No one could claim ignorance of the motives for the gathering. It was, rather, because someone in a high place understood the purpose of it all too well that the opposition released its deadly whisper the moment the first plane touched down.

Last minute efforts to discredit the entire Conference included one of those bureaucratic gestures that reek of overconfidence and arrogance. Wednesday, October 7th, Cardinal Jose Sanchez, prefect of the Sacred Congregation for the Clergy, signed a declaration specifying that Father Gruner, "... does not have faculties from the Diocese of Leiria-Fatima to perform his ministerial acts ...' and '... his Congress has not been approved by competent ecclesiastical authorities."[2]

Yes, and so what? No "permission" or "faculties" were required under Canon Law, but the Cardinal neglected to mention this. The declaration was nothing but an imperious act of sabotage.

The sabotage continued at the airport. As the bishops arrived, they were intercepted by Shrine representatives attempting to hijack them to Bishop Alberto Cosme do Amaral's conference at the Paul VI Center and telling them that Father Gruner's conference at the Floresta Hotel was "cancelled" and "not authorized". Indeed, Shrine representatives were so brazen that they did this before the very eyes of the official welcome party of *The Fatima Crusader* who were on hand to greet the bishops and transport them back to Fatima.

The whisperers, however, did not include in their diversionary tactics the offer of accommodation and meals, for which Bishop Amaral had no intention of providing. Only when it came time to provide for the bishops they had diverted, did they send them back penniless, as bishops "without funds" were useless to them! A miscalculation that exposed the shrine officials for the cold and cunning pharisees they are. The assault on the dignity of these bishops, the majority of them from impoverished countries, was not considered, apparently, by the Shrine detractors. They had only one thing in mind, ambush the Reverend Father Nicholas Gruner.

The confusion generated in the local dailies and the publications of the International press by the movers and shakers of the Sanctuary had its effect. On Wednesday, October 7th, the day before the Conference opened, 25 of the bishops met with Father Gruner to have their questions and concerns answered. Having received frank replies, they then decided to send representatives to seek an audience with Bishop Amaral to, in effect, state their intention to proceed according to their original agendas.

That evening Archbishops Limon of the Philippines, Toppo of India and Cardoso Sobrinho of Recife, Brazil drove the 18 kilometers to meet with Bishop Amaral.[3]

The road to Leiria stretched out over the northern plain of Portugal beneath an autumn sun reddening the sky and turning the mind of October pilgrims back in time to the Miracle of the Sun 75 years earlier. Archbishops Limon, Toppo and Sobrinho were at that moment navigating their way through the thorn-ridden thicket of conflicting agendas that had separated the world famous apostolate of the Blue Army and *The Fatima Crusader* for over a decade, hurrying headlong toward that very seat of authority where the Great Secret had remained hidden from 1944 to 1957. In the beginning, the office was held by the friend of the seer of Coimbra, Bishop da Silva, ruling the diocese of Fatima from Leiria. Now it was Bishop Alberto Cosme do Amaral.

Shortly before 9:00 p.m., the three travellers were ushered into the Bishop's chamber. Also attending with Bishop Amaral was Coadjutor Bishop Serafim who would soon replace Bishop Amaral as Bishop and order that Msgr. Guerra be replaced as shrine rector one year and a half later. After the usual flurry of 'Brother Bishop' exchanges, the small assemblage got to the issue that had brought them to Leiria. The air needed to be cleared if only for the sake of the brother bishops. The actual facts facing Bishop Amaral were crystal clear. One hundred bishops whom he had not personally invited were, nevertheless, on his threshold. Among them were many with Canon Law expertise. The most knowledgeable among them had made it perfectly clear that, according to Canon Law they had no need of official recognition from Bishop Amaral or the Vatican to gather in private and confer, as they were doing. What could he do to them after all? Especially on the 75th Anniversary of the Miracle of the Sun? The events unfolding in Fatima would, for better or worse, become part of Church history before the sun set on October. Not surprisingly, Bishop Amaral agreed to make the Peace Conference an official part of his own Pastoral Conference on the provision that Father Gruner's Conference attend plenary sessions of Bishop Amaral's conference and the concelebrated Masses. It is important to note here that, obviously, Father Gruner was also invited to attend.

The return to Fatima along those 18 night-blackened kilometers provided an opportunity for the Archbishops to weigh the elements of the equation. They had come to Portugal with the best of intentions, to honor the Mother of God on this most meaningful of all anniversaries. They had been caught up in the vortex of lies and counter-lies that had long been multiplying over the crucial issue of the Consecration of Russia. They now found themselves on the soft shoulders of that very roadbed long ago sketched out by the designers of the Vatican-Moscow Agreement.

They arrived at midnight to announce an 'accord'. Come morning, Thursday, October 8, Archbishop Cardoso Sobrinho took to the podium and announced the meeting of the previous night, extending Bishop Amaral's welcome to all present, inviting everyone in the conference room at the Floresta to join in the Eucharistic celebrations of the next three days with the 50 bishops at Bishop Amaral's Pastoral Conferences and to attend, as a sign of unity, the primary sessions of the Pastoral Conference. With those provisos in place, the Peace Conference in the Floresta could proceed with Bishop Amaral's blessing. In short, they were to consider themselves Bishop Amaral's guests as well.

Father Gruner and the Apostolate immediately agreed to this proposal but not without grave inconvenience and upset to the schedules of speakers and events that had been months in preparation. Nevertheless, the Apostolate immediately proceeded to change the entire schedule of the conference (sometimes twice daily!) in order to work in Bishop Amaral's agenda.

Not too surprising, however, this gracious attempt by the apostolate was not reciprocated. The Apostolate had honored every one of the requests and more. In return every promise made to the Apostolate was broken. Amaral changed schedules at the last minute and created havoc for the Peace Conference. Deirdre Manifold, who came all the way from Ireland to speak, was on the podium only five minutes when a spokesman bishop from Bishop Amaral's court got up and announced that they had to all leave now for another "appointment" with Bishop Amaral, and this after they had returned one and a half hours late that very morning from another "unscheduled Bishop Amaral appointment".

Father Gruner's group did not give up. They responded graciously and went without sleep most nights to replan amidst the havoc caused by Shrine officials (in charge of Bishop Amaral's conference) to ensure the bishops' comfort and reasonable scheduling for the following day.

But the maneuvers of the Shrine official had their effect. By the time the first session opened, the number of bishops present was down to sixty. It would eventually dip to forty-five.[4]

Oh, unity, the things bishops do in thy name! Indeed, Father Gruner might well note, "Unity without truth is merely a compromise with sin."

Saturday, October 10, 1992

The esplanade of the Fatima Shrine is one of the great gathering places in the world. With as much love and care as the faithful could provide, the Cova da Iria has been paved over to provide for the millions who pray here in a gathering area four times the size of the Piazza of St. Peter's in Rome. Crowning the east end of the esplanade, with open arm colonnades extended to embrace the upper slope of the Cova, is the basilica containing the two precious jewels of Fatima, the bodies of Jacinta and Francisco. There, too, Lucy will rest when her mission ends.

To the west of the esplanade, reached by an underpass from the shrine enclosure, is the Paul VI Center. Architecturally, it is yet one more exercise in the dreariness the self proclaimed new "experts" have imposed on the Catholic world for thirty years. The quest for excellence in architecture had ever been a hallmark of the Roman Catholic Church until the "architects" of Vatican II unleashed on the Church a seemingly relentless pursuit of the mediocre.

No one looking at this bleak structure could possibly suspect that throughout history the Church has been the foremost patron of artists, architects and poets. It is a concrete container for bureaucrats. Nothing more. An edifice designed by accountants. Something every bureaucrat in the Church today would be comfortable entering, for there is absolutely nothing Catholic about its exterior.

To reach it from the esplanade, one must first bypass a mammoth statue of Paul VI, kneeling, hands posed in prayer, dwarfing much better and more artistic representations of Pius XII and Bishop da Silva of Leiria, he to whom was confided in writing the Third Secret.

To the north of the esplanade stands the tree under which the children stood in 1917 to await the warning flash in the heavens announcing the impending arrival of the Mother of God. Almost within the shadow of the tree is the miniature chapel, the Capelhina, so tiny one is tempted to tuck it inside the heart and make off with it. It marks the spot where the azinhiera stood. On its very leaves She to whom the Incarnation was made known by the Message of an Angel rested six times between May and October, 1917. She who received the Three Wise Kings, received here three peasant children. She Who said at Cana, "Do whatever He tells you,"[5] spoke equally specific words here. She Who stood 'by the Cross Her station keeping', here wept for all mankind. She Who at the age of 49, at the foot of the blood drenched Cross, received into Her arms the lifeless Body of the Son of God, came here for the sake of His Mystical Body, now afflicted with the neck-stiffening heresies of Modernism, and delivered the antidote for theological rigor mortis, a recipe for healing, namely the formula for an act of total unconditional faith in Her role as Mediatrix Of All Graces.

Here on the exact circle of earth on which the shadow of the azinhiera was drawn by the movement of the Fatima sun, a marble enclosure surrounds a table. On it the liturgy is said continually throughout each and every day. Marble benches allow concelebrants to sit in a circle around it, almost always dressed in white. Ironically, their circle sits atop the very circumference of earth that opened to reveal to the three children the vision of Hell that would haunt the Church for the rest of this century.

The Indians of New Mexico had a name for that opening into the earth through which evil spirits are supposed to enter the world. They called it Sipapu. On October 10, 1992, a Sipapu opened in front of the Capelhina.

On that day, and the previous one, the Conference had adjourned so the bishops could partake of the major public ceremonies preparing for the main anniversary celebrations of the 13th. On both days, the bishops vested for Mass in the vestry of the north colonnade. On both days, Father Gruner assisted the elderly Anthony Cardinal Padiyara of Ernakulam, India, and several other bishops in getting vested, and accompanied him from the main altar, at times, holding the Cardinal's arm to assist him as he walked.

On October 10th, after Mass ended at the Capelhina, Father Gruner walked alongside Cardinal Padiyara and was about to enter the sacristy when a layman, with no arm band or any other insignia of authority, blocked his way. In spite of him, Father Gruner managed to enter the sacristy, moving quickly indoors. There he was slowed by a gathering of bishops awaiting their turn to ascend the few stairs and narrow passageway into the larger room inside. In the meantime, the unidentified man, speaking Portuguese, ran in and blocked the stairway on the left side, in the process also momentarily obstructing the way of several bishops, among them, Maronite Archbishop Chucrallah Harb of Jounieh, Lebanon.[6]

Father Gruner, having dropped his sandals in the confusion, stepped up onto a chair. From there he spotted Bishop Amaral seven feet away. What happened next was one of those frequent, seemingly comic, moments in the career of Father Nicholas Gruner that are, in fact, all too often a prelude to something decidedly sobering. Here he was, a priest in the very prime of his Apostolate, standing in socks on a chair in Fatima, appealing for Christian charity from the Bishop of Leiria. He called out to Bishop Amaral, asking if this was how he treated his 'guests'.7

Bishop Amaral, who can speak English, did not respond, though he clearly saw and heard the priest on the chair. Turning his back, he hurried up the steps with the other bishops. The room emptied. When the stairs were clear of all bishops save one, Father Gruner, once more in his sandals, proceeded up the steps on the right side. The mysterious layman, who was talking to Archbishop Chucrallah Harb, left the Archbishop abruptly and flew after Father Gruner. Father Gruner had reached the first step when he was seized by his pursuer and thrown against the wall, the shocking sound of a ripping priestly cassock marking the moment. Then, a second assailant grabbed him, spun him around, and threw him against the wall again. [8] Witnesses recall that the second assailant disappeared almost as fast as he had appeared.

From behind, arriving at the top of the stairs, was Archbishop Cardoso Sobrinho and Father Francesco Pacheco, also from Brazil. They confronted the first attacker, in Portuguese. Later, Father Pacheco related that, incredibly, the attacker had openly admitted he was acting on *explicit directions from Msgr. Luciano Guerra*, who had ordered him to prevent Father Gruner from entering the sacristy.

Father Pacheco had demanded, "Why are you doing this? You know you cannot do this ... *this man is a priest!* Who told you to do this? Did the Rector tell you to do this?" To this the assailant nodded 'Yes'. It would emerge later that the attacker had been present at Bishop Amaral's residence in Leiria the night Archbishops Limon, Toppo and Cardoso Sobrinho met with Amaral.[9]

The bruises and abrasions resulting from the assault on Father Gruner were documented by Doctor Olinda Moura Almeida in the hospital at Ourem. Meanwhile, spin doctors at the sanctuary offices were fast denying that the assault had ever taken place. Once again, the Fatima faithful were subjected to the embarrassing display of power-proud Shrine bureaucrats surrendering to self-grown fantasies of their own importance. When they heard the attack had been witnessed and part of it video-taped, the shrine officials just as quickly dropped their denial. Their sad performance was not over, however. They limply claimed Father Gruner had staged it himself, "for publicity". No one wondered why when, within a year and a half of the supposedly choreographed spectacle, the new bishop of Leiria, Bishop Serafim, successor to Bishop Cosme do Amaral, insisted on a replacement for Msgr. Guerra as shrine Rector.

This was not, of course, the first time ecclesial bureaucrats had injected their venom into the life and apostolate of a faithful priest. Priests have been victimized over the centuries by appalling rumors planted and spread by bureaucrats jealous of the victim's following, support and personal appeal: Padre Pio, Father Gino, St. Maximilian Kolbe, the list goes on and on.

In Fatima and Portugal, the scuffle drew the attention of the faithful and the bishops mainly because of its profoundly sacrilegious nature. A priest had been manhandled on orders of a representative of honor of the Holy Father within a stone's throw of the very spot The Virgin had sanctified by Her presence. Shortly after the beating of Father Gruner, Cardinal Padiyara sent for him urgently, and when Father Gruner came, the Cardinal took him aside and warned him that his life was in danger as long as he was in Fatima. Father Gruner has not returned since.

The conflict between Father Gruner and the authorities of the Shrine had entered a new phase. What would happen next would challenge the imagination of the most daring of fiction writers.

An "Oscar" Winning Performance

The unthinkable began to take shape Saturday, October 10. Why not ask Sister Lucy herself, it was suggested, whether the consecration of Russia had been done according to the requests of Heaven. At first glance, it appeared that the bishops who had congregated in Fatima might actually produce something of value by this request. It was agreed that a delegation would be sent to Coimbra — Cardinal Padiyara, Bishop Michaelappa, and to ensure proper understanding, the Portuguese-speaking priest, Father Pacheco from Brazil.[10]

As a Cardinal, Padiyara needed no permission from either Cardinal Ratzinger, nor from the Bishop of Fatima, Cosme do Amaral, to request a meeting with the seer. It was agreed they would travel to Coimbra in the morning. Meanwhile, in advance of their visit, Father Kondor was presenting the Lusa news agency a communique announcing that Sister Lucy had declared the Consecration of Russia had been done.

While the communique was being published by the Portuguese dailies, Cardinal Padiyara, Archbishop Michaelappa and Father Pacheco were on their way to the Carmel of Coimbra, chauffeured there by a Carlos Evaristo.[11] Evaristo did some logistical works for the Apostolate in its Fatima office. He would prove to be an embarrassment of mammoth proportions.

Travelling the sloping streets of Coimbra to the Carmel that contains the most famous religious of the Twentieth Century must surely have a profound effect on Cardinals and Bishops as well as priests. This is no mere convent. This gleaming white building with emerald doors has the hand of the Mother of God holding fast its doors and its secrets.

Just before noon the high green portals of the Carmel of Coimbra opened to admit the travellers. They entered a stark, high ceilinged foyer, plain and unadorned, befitting Carmel. The doors to the cloister stand directly ahead. Immediately to the left, off the foyer, is the convent chapel.

The initial gloom of the chapel interior is soon pierced by threads of light where the chocolate brown interior is highlighted with gold trim. The high altar rising above the communion rail supports one of those stairways to heaven so common to the altars of Portugal on the top of which the ostensorium holds the Blessed Sacrament for adoration. Kneeling at the rail, one can look up, to the left, and see the second floor grille through which the Carmelites observe the Mass. Below and to the right of the grille is the breathtaking statue of the Immaculate Heart, specifically sculpted for this chapel. Facing it across the chapel is the equally awe-inspiring statue of the Sacred Heart as He appeared to Sister Lucy at Rianjo.

The certainty remains, that here, within these high walls, the voice of the Virgin remains inviolate in the memory of the last seer from the Cova. Here, at least, truth is protected, defended, and honored.

The Players:

Enter the "Oscar" nominee performers: Mother Superior and Carlos Evaristo. Enter a woman in a Carmelite habit who had the appearance of being Sister Lucy. Enter supreme guests of the command performance: Cardinal Padiyara, Bishop Michaelappa and Father Pacheco, allowed "on set".

The Play Begins:

"Sister Lucy will receive you," says an extern sister, returning from making the arrangements.

The doors open to the audience room. Two Carmelites are waiting just inside. On the left stands Mother Prioress. The nun on the right was presented as Lucy dos Santos, the most famous nun of the Twentieth Century. She turned ten years old seven months before the 1917 November Revolution in Russia. A tiny peasant child from Aljustrel. Now she is eighty-five. 'Much shorter' than was expected. She wears the habit of the Carmelites which, amazingly, does not properly fit her.

After initial introductions, the "players" move to an adjacent room where they sit down facing each other with no grille between them, totally contrary to the customary rule adhered to for the past 400 years both here and at all Discalced Carmelite Convents since their founding by St. Theresa in the 1560's.

Mother Prioress, according to her script, would begin, "Sister Lucy would you like me to leave you alone with the guests?" and on this cue, Sister Lucy would reply, "No, no, Mother, please stay here." And like any suspense novel cleverly planned to confuse the reader, the naive would be led to believe, why my goodness, this must mean Sister Lucy is not silenced! Mother Prioress, during the rest of the visit, would come and go throughout the interview that was to follow, although Sister Lucy had said she would like her to stay.

The Cardinal and the Bishop were 'very nervous' according to Evaristo.[12] And well they should have been. Unable to speak Portuguese, they were unknowingly about to participate in a great work of fiction, the likes of which had never been heard in the whole history of Fatima. It would be entitled *Two Hours With Sister Lucy*, the pamphlet Evaristo would fabricate claiming to be based on the "interview" with Sister Lucy. The answers to their questions, as reported by Evaristo, would go to the very roots of the azinhiera tree and tear them free of the millions of hearts from which they had drawn nourishment since first the Virgin stood upon it. The performance that would follow, the words about to be spoken, would starkly and cruelly suggest that Catholics who grew up believing in Fatima had been lied to at their mother's knee and been the victims of disinformation for 75 years.

But before we actually hear the words, the manner in which they were delivered must be addressed. By that is meant that the question of familiarity with this most unique and protected woman must be considered. For seven and a half decades this dear nun has been sheltered, shielded, protected by the Church. The labyrinth of authorities one must traverse to get permission to see her have not surrendered to any coherent mapping, but rather have become increasingly complex. So that anyone inquiring about seeing her is told first, "Oh, that is impossible." Then follows the long list of addresses and bishops and cardinals all standing in line to say 'No' to you, all, apparently on behalf of the man truly in charge of access to her, Cardinal Ratzinger. And, in spite of all that, the two hour interview about to take place occurs while this secluded nun, cloistered for all of her adult life, sits facing and holding hands with a man she has never laid eyes on before, who is neither Cardinal nor bishop, but rather one Evaristo, a minor employee of Father Gruner's Apostolate, who has chauffeured the dignitaries to Coimbra.

From the moment the group entered the audience chamber, the function of Evaristo as interpreter (he does speak Portuguese) and what we might, perhaps, call 'stage manager' of the event, emerged.

Arguing that it was indeed Sister Lucy they saw, Evaristo said to Brother François de Marie des Anges, "It was her. There is no doubt about it. I touched her face. I embraced her."[13] Touched her face? Embraced her? A Carmelite whom mere bishops and archbishops cannot approach without Vatican approval? A nun who was not able to see her own blood-sister Caroline for over forty years except through the grille and then only when surrounded by half the community. Embraced by a stranger?

Regarding Cardinal Padiyara, Evaristo reported to Brother François, "The Cardinal asked your questions (Brother François, upon being told of the impending visit, had sent two questions to be answered) and then seemed to be almost asleep."[14]

When Brother François challenged him, "You have no decisive proof that you were in the presence of Sister Lucy," Evaristo made the astounding reply, "She was sitting in front of me. She held my hand like this for two hours."[15]

For any cloistered nun to hold hands with a stranger for two hours is a curious business. For this particular cloistered nun it is unimaginable.

The Evaristo pamphlet presents a new Sister Lucy who serves as the pathetic ventriloquist's dummy of the anti-Fatima forces, obediently repudiating everything Sister Lucy of Fatima had said before. The pamphlet is a veritable cavalcade of capitulation in which the new Sister Lucy finds a way to consign to oblivion what the old Sister Lucy had told the entire world.

The old Sister Lucy had mentioned that Our Lady many times told her about the conversion of Russia as a nation and the old Sister Lucy had repeated this Divine requirement orally and in print over and over again to priests, historians, correspondents, and on the pages of L'Osservatore Romano during the previous 60 years and more.. Ah! But this was all a terrible misunderstanding, explained the new Sister Lucy! She had not been speaking of the nation of Russia at all!

Evaristo: "But didn't Our Lady want Russia to be specifically mentioned?"

New Sister Lucy: "Our Lady never requested that Russia be specifically mentioned by name. At the time I didn't even know what Russia was. We thought she was a very wicked woman."

So, there we have it: the three Fatima seers believed that Our Lady appeared at Fatima and God performed the miracle of the sun before

70,000 people simply in order to bring about the conversion of a very wicked woman who happened to be named "Russia". It was all a case of mistaken identity. Our Lady had neglected to inform them that Russia is a nation, not a lady by the same name!

The old Sister Lucy had told the world that Russia must convert according to the Virgin. Naturally, the world took conversion to mean the embrace of the Catholic faith. Not quite, says the new Lucy

Evaristo: "But is the conversion of Russia not interpreted as the conversion of the Russian people to Catholicism?"

New Sister Lucy: "Our Lady never said that. There are many misinterpretations around. The fact is that in Russia, the communist, atheist power, prevented the people from carrying out their faith. People now have an individual choice to remain as they are or to convert. This they are now free to do."

You see, Russia had already converted without becoming Catholic!

"Converted" really means that Russia is now free to choose the Catholic faith, therefore, Russia has "converted".

But one might consider that the Americans are free to choose the Catholic faith, yet none had ever suggested that the word "converted" applies to America, the land of "Roe vs Wade", abortion on demand, and partial birth infanticide.

Such considerations do not trouble the new Sister Lucy: her lower jaw moves up and down on its metal hinge as the ventriloquist throws his voice into the dummy, making it utter things unheard of in the history of Fatima, or indeed, the history of the Church.

A conversion without a conversion. Imagine that! All we needed was democracy, not a change of heart.

The old Sister Lucy had told the world again and again — in letters, interviews and other statements that Russia had not been consecrated in the manner prescribed by Our Lady and as a consequence, had not converted. But the new Sister Lucy has a surprise announcement:

Evaristo: "Has the conversion of Russia then taken place?"

New Sister Lucy: "Yes, news speaks for themselves."

So, the cloistered seer of Fatima reads the news! One could envision a surreal spectacle: the new Sister Lucy sipping her morning coffee and reading the headlines in *Diario de Coimbra*, which, of course, is delivered to her daily so that this consecrated soul, locked away from the world under a vow of enclosure, could keep abreast of current events! Or was this perhaps the case of a ventriloquist projecting his reading habits as well as his voice, into the dummy.

New Sister Lucy: "That man in Russia, unknowingly was an instrument of God in the conversion..."

Evaristo: "What man? Gorbachev?"

New Sister Lucy: "Yes when he visited the Holy Father in Rome, he knelt at his feet and asked pardon for all the crimes he had committed in his life."

The old Sister Lucy had spoken of the triumph of the Immaculate Heart of Mary bringing about the conversion of Russia and peace to mankind. But the new Sister Lucy has found a new instrument for the accomplishment of this miracle; Mikhail Gorbachev!!

But was not the new Sister Lucy aware that after Mikhail Gorbachev had knelt before the Pope in the Vatican, he returned to his chairmanship of the Gorbachev Foundation which promotes a New World Order of zero population growth and a New World Religion whose sacraments are contraception and abortion? To be fair to the new Sister Lucy, she could not possibly have been aware of the evil undertakings of "that man in Russia" because the new Sister Lucy is made of wood and has no brain, but only a jaw which mouths the words projected into her by others. That is, the new Sister Lucy is not Sister Lucy at all, but a new product to go along with "Fatima Lite": "Lucy Lite".

The other three witness to this "interview" of the new Sister Lucy knew a travesty when they saw one. Father Pacheco, the only Portuguese speaking witness besides Evaristo, fired off letters to Evaristo and to all concerned parties denouncing the pamphlet as "notorious", full of "gross lies" and "inventions".

Cardinal Padiyara made it clear that he could attest only to having been present during the "interview" but could not authenticate anything "Sister Lucy" had said since he did not speak Portuguese. Bishop Michaelappa went further: he ordered Evaristo not to publish the pamphlet. The fraud was summed up by Father Pacheco: "I categorically do affirm that the booklet, *Two Hours with Sister Lucy* published by Carlos Evaristo contains lies and half-truths and is not to be believed."

Brother François, unquestionably the most exacting investigator at work on the Fatima story today, summarizes the appalling possibility behind the catastrophic interview.

"In order to discredit the work of Father Gruner and to stop Pope John Paul being *'importuned'* with the request for the Consecration of Russia, did the authorities at Fatima, after circulating the apocryphal letters from Lucy, organize a parlor with a 'false Lucy' at the Coimbra Carmel on this 11th October 92? Until proof to the contrary, we are not rejecting such an hypothesis. For on this there is no possible doubt: if Cardinal Padiyara and his three companions actually met a person in the Carmel who spoke the words they have reported, then the person was not the seer of Fatima, Sister Maria-Lucy of the Immaculate Heart."[16]

So what did happen in the Carmel of Coimbra on the nearest Sunday to the 75th anniversary of the Miracle of the Sun? Did Sister Lucy make statements that completely and blatantly contradicted 75 years of previous statements? It is not merely a matter of Sister Lucy being out-of-character that day. To Lucy dos Santos was made the promise on June 13, 1917, by the Mother of God Herself, that the Immaculate Heart would never abandon her. The reportage as it stands is simply not believable. And the only other Portuguese-speaking witness present at the interview, Father Pacheco, has repudiated Evaristo's account.

Are there alternatives to the mendacity of Evaristo? Was there a deliberate mistranslation of her responses? Was Sister Lucy under duress to confirm the consecration? Surely, after a lifetime of fidelity to the Immaculate Heart, Sister Lucy would not suddenly resort to lying to cover up the failings of Vatican bureaucrats. The term 'mellowed' is used at the Fatima shrine to explain why Sister Lucy, in her eighth decade of life, is not pushing harder to make the truth known. Did Heaven leave the last Fatima seer alive all of this century so that she could 'mellow' picturesquely on the hillside of Coimbra? Perhaps many of these riddles could be put to rest if it was clearly understood how and why Carlos Evaristo managed to publish and distribute his booklets without any bureaucrat at the Shrine, or the Vatican, or any member of the Carmelites of Coimbra raising as much as a whisper of complaint or caution. Some light did filter onto the mystery when Evaristo, acting with more casual familiarity than members of her own blood family are allowed to, publicly interrupted Sister Lucy as she walked from the Carmel to cast her vote in the Portuguese elections, to introduce his wife and child and relatives. He claims also that he has returned to the Carmel to *interview her again*, without the benefit of a Cardinal on hand or the permission of the Holy Office. Someone, somewhere, has seen to it that this individual is allowed liberties. Why? Clearly the misinformation poured onto the unsuspecting faithful through this manipulated interview is satisfying someone's agenda.

Before the infamous October interview ended, nearing two o'clock in the afternoon, it was suggested that Father Gruner should come with Cardinal Padiyara, the next day, to hear these words for himself. Sister Lucy agreed. As did Mother Prioress.

The interview concluded. Cardinal Padiyara, Bishop Michaelappa, and Father Pacheco left the Carmel for the return drive to Fatima. After the meeting, as it is recorded in the *Diario de Coimbra*, the regional newspaper for Coimbra, Mother Prioress telephoned to Fatima for instructions.

Meanwhile, the Pastoral Conference at the Paul VI Center continued throughout the long afternoon of Sunday, October 11.

Brother François de Marie des Anges was present at this session. He brought into the midst of this high establishment occasion the accusation made in his book *Fatima Joie Intime Événement Mondial,* regarding the earlier "letters" of Sister Lucy. The accusation reads: "Under the authority of Bishop do Amaral, three ecclesiastics, residing in Portugal were directly implicated in the fabrication and spreading of these artificial letters — Father Luis Kondor, Father Messias Coelho and Monsignor Luciano Guerra. We think that Monsignor Guerra personally wrote several of these letters, including one dated November 21, 1989."[17]

At 5:30 p.m. Brother François, from the stage, addressed the head table at which sat Father Fox and Father Kondor. He denounced the five bogus letters supposedly written by Sister Lucy, the message of which Father Fox and the Blue Army had been propagating since the Fall of 1989, letters claiming the consecration of Russia had been done by Pope John Paul II, March 25, 1984.

"These letters are fake," said Brother François. "I have already published the demonstration of it and my demonstration has not been refuted. I am ready to justify my actions and if necessary to retract them if my criticisms are refuted in a decisive manner."[18]

Neither Father Fox nor Father Kondor gave a reply. Instead the session was swiftly closed. The following day, Abbé Laurentin expressed surprise when he learned that both Father Fox and Father Kondor failed to give any response to these serious allegations against them.

§

Evening. One of those blissful October Sundays when it seems the whole world is either gathered in or headed to the esplanade to have one last look at the Capelhina before sundown. Cardinal Padiyara must have wondered how he came to play the role thrust upon him that day. He expected no such chore when he boarded the plane for Portugal a few short days before. Now he was preparing to announce tomorrow to the gathered bishops what he had been led to believe had transpired in the Portuguese language during the interview — namely that Sister Lucy had apparently confirmed that the consecration of Russia was done, that the Third Secret was intended exclusively for the Pope. The announcement would, without doubt, add yet another layer of confusion to those already accumulated throughout the 80's regarding the Fatima Message. Clearly, he could be relieved of the onerous task once Father Gruner met with Sister Lucy in person the following day. That would provide a solution.

Alas, Cardinal Padiyara would be granted no such reprieve.

Early Monday morning, October 12, 1992.

Seventy-five years ago this morning, all over Portugal, people were rising and gathering belongings for the trip to a shepherd's field near Aljustrel, where the Voice of the Virgin, repeated by three peasant children, promised a great miracle. It was one of the truly great spontaneous movements of a people in all of recorded history. Seventy thousand people on the move.

That morning, 75 years ago, Portugal was on the alert. To those who fear God, there was no doubt He was going to do something never before done in all of salvation history. To the godless, there was no doubt the Church was about to try to manipulate away from the Masonically controlled state the uneducated masses of people.

It was the fear of God in those 70,000 that drew down from Heaven the unparalleled blessing of the Miracle of the Sun. To the innocent hearts of Portugal, God showed a sign which He had refused to the haughty Pharisees. To the latter, none but the sign of Jonah. Truly, the very willingness of the Son of God to die at the hands of men was sign enough of what was in His Heart. Raising Himself from beyond death to, among other things, confirm the forgiveness He offered them from His Cross, was more than the human mind could script. Certainly a dance of the sun was more than man's imagination could entertain.

Seven and a half decades later the day began, as it does in most hotels and hostels of Fatima, with early risers, almost always American, looking for a waitress, a coffee pot and an ashtray for that all important first cigarette. For the hour preceding the customary 7:30 breakfast serving, line-ups form in lobbies and hallways throughout this one-of-a-kind hamlet. Non-muttering line-ups. Not even hungry tourists would dare to complain in Fatima.

In the rooms above the foyer of the Virgin Maria Hotel, bishops prepare for the descent to breakfast. Is it true, they wonder, are they all being encouraged to travel to Coimbra for a visit en masse with Lucy? They will find out more at breakfast.

Breakfast ends. Time speeds past. Watches are wound furtively. 'Is the appointment not for 10 o'clock? When do we leave?'

Corazon Aquino is in Fatima. The former president of the Philippines is going to Coimbra. Her appointment is for 11 o'clock. Two of the most remarkable women of the century will be meeting immediately after Sister Lucy grants her audience to Father Gruner. The solution to the mysteries that have spurred on *The Fatima Crusader* Apostolate for fifteen years are to be sandwiched into what communication can be exchanged within one short hour.

Aquino is on everyone's tongue. Few women in the 20th Century can command such heartfelt approval. It is akin to heresy to detract in any way from the legend she has become in the short few years since her husband was shot to death on the tarmac of a Philippines airport.

On any other occasion, her presence in Portugal would bring the press to a standstill. But this is the 75th anniversary of the Miracle of the Sun. Fatima is crowded with legends and legendaries.

10:05 a.m. Outside the entrance to the Carmel of Coimbra, journalists and photographers await the arrival of Corazon Aquino.

10:10 a.m. A bus holding fifty bishops from the International Peace Conference makes its way down the slope of Coimbra toward the Carmel.

10:25 a.m. Twenty-five minutes of the precious time allotted to meet with Sister Lucy have ticked by before a taxi carrying Father Gruner, Father Paul Leonard Kramer, Archbishop Michaelappa and Cardinal Padiyara pulls to a stop below the high doors of Carmel.

10:28 a.m. The car driven by Evaristo veers into a parking space in front of the Carmel. He had been an hour and a half late arriving to pick up his intended passengers. What happens next makes nonsense of the centuries of protocol and security for which the very word 'Carmel' is justifiably famous. Kings, Emperors, Popes, have had their footsteps chosen for them by the precise and well thought-out design of Carmel entrances. In this case, the large square foyer previously described as having three doors, determines what anyone entering must do. The high green entrance door admits the visitor. The door to the left looks in at the chapel. The door to the wall immediately ahead leads to the enclave. History itself takes off its hat in this precious space. It is impossible to stand in such an intersection of pathways and not be moved to silence by thoughts of the countless gifted women who have chosen to live out their lives completely shielded from outside interference by the very specific blueprint of their convent fortress.

Nevertheless, Evaristo, having rushed past the delegation, strides across the foyer, past the chapel entrance to his left, and, unbelievably, swings open the door to the enclave. Totally unchallenged, he proceeds to the door in the far wall of the next room. He is now directly adjacent to the parlor in which the most protected woman of the 20th Century has met with a thoroughly screened select few over the decades. Not until he is about to throw open the door in front of him does a voice call out to stop him. Two men dressed in lay clothes have appeared. One refers to himself as the chaplain of the Carmel, even though he wears a shirt and tie. The other layman is a doctor. Words are exchanged. Evaristo returns and immediately begins to usher from the foyer back into the street those who had followed in his wake. The meeting, he announces, has been cancelled.

During these bewildering moments, Father Paul Kramer had been assisting Cardinal Padiyara through the doorway. Suddenly, a layman grabbed the Cardinal's arm in what was perceived by onlookers as a threatening gesture intended to prevent him from entering. The only words to accompany this manhandling of a prince of the Church were that, 'Sister Lucy was not feeling well', and is unable to receive visitors.

The acts of Evaristo secure him a unique place in Church history. For the greater part of this century the words, actions and security of Sister Lucy have been treasured by Catholics. This gifted woman, grown from an illiterate peasant child into the most sought after woman religious in the Church, is practically a member of each and every Catholic family. She has been with us for so long, her life recognized as so humble and admirable, that she is, to Catholics the world over, simply 'Lucy'.

She is one of the most precious ingredients of the Catholic legacy the next century will inherit. To understand the real import of what was permitted to happen that morning in Coimbra, one must contemplate a tragic fact — namely, that not even the Immemorial Mass, the Mass of the Ages, the Gregorian Carlovingian Mass was spared in the attack upon the Catholic Faith this last half century. Debilitating the status of Sister Lucy, demonstrating her new insignificance, was what Evaristo's walk into the enclave was all about. And make no mistake about it — every reader of these words is familiar with the hush that consumes even the most aggressive rock fan when he finds himself outside the dressing room of his favorite musician. In the history of human behavior there is no precedent that can explain Evaristo's charade other than this — the mastermind, working overtime to devalue anything Catholic in this world, orchestrated the vulgarization of chivalry displayed that morning. The sensation remaining explains the degree of their success: someone just wiped his shoes on your heart.

Despite the visit being officially agreed to by Mother Prioress, Father Gruner and Cardinal Padiyara were refused entry into the Carmel of Coimbra. And despite the chaplain of the convent saying that the last surviving seer of Fatima was ill, a half hour later Corazon Aquino and her party of nine met with Sister Lucy.

The chaplain added another ring to the circus of confusion by telling the daily newspaper *Journal de Noticias* that "He (Father Gruner) came to Coimbra to provoke this scene and nothing more." But he did not. The facts are clear. The agreement for this visit was given to Cardinal Padiyara, Bishop Michaelappa and Father Pacheco the day before. This is all witnessed by at least six people and cannot be denied.

Evaristo's sabotage of Father Gruner's interview with Sister Lucy is recalled by Mairead Clarke, an apostolate employee who dealt with Carlos. She recounts that frustrating morning:

"I was present for the sequence of events. Carlos was to arrive early at our hotel at 7:00 a.m. so that the tail pipe of the car purchased for this apostolate by a supporter could be repaired. A minor job of replacing a few brackets, which Carlos was aware of, but refused to do anything about, claiming that it was extremely difficult to get parts for foreign cars, which he had insisted we purchased as the only car worth having in Europe.

A supporter who was with us at the hotel had asked that the car be brought over early so that the exhaust could cool before using a wire hanger to effect the temporary repair. Any repairs were the responsibility of this apostolate as we were the owners. (I say "were" as Carlos refused to turn the car over to us at the termination of his employment. He had changed the registration to his mother's name.)

However that Monday morning, Mina, Carlos' mother refused to wake him as "the boy needs his sleep". Yes I can quote her because I was the person who telephoned three times to his home to find out what was causing the delay. I finally told her that if Carlos did not arrive within the next few minutes I would personally come and get him out of bed. That last call was no more than an hour before the time of the meeting. Bishop Michaelappa had telephoned from his hotel to find out why Carlos had not already picked up Cardinal Padiyara and himself.

Father Gruner was very anxious to meet Sister Lucy. Finally Evaristo condescended to come to the phone and was strongly ordered to get the Apostolate vehicle over to the hotel immediately. He arrived at the hotel more than two hours late, with a dragging muffler that could not be repaired until the car cooled down.

The most dramatic meeting imaginable between two of the world's most devoted Fatima names never happened because a non-entity named Evaristo claimed to be "tired" and had a punctured muffler which he repeatedly avoided repairing. Father Gruner and the Cardinal had been forced to call a cab!Yet Evaristo would dare to claim that Father Gruner missed his interview because he, not Evaristo, was late! Nevertheless, Evaristo miraculously was able to get to Coimbra himself via his "broken down" vehicle.

A few minutes after Father Gruner and the Cardinal had left the Convent, President Aquino and her entourage would arrive and immediately be escorted in to be received by Sister Lucy, who had miraculously recovered in a few minutes time. So much for the excuse offered by the Convent officials that Sister Lucy was unable to meet the Cardinal on this day because she was sick. Obviously they did not feel the charade of the previous day would stand the scrutiny of Father Kramer and Father Gruner together with the Cardinal.

§

Noon, Monday, October 12, 1992. The Paul VI Center in Fatima: At the end of the closing sessions of the First International Pastoral Conference at the Paul VI Center, Brother François de Marie des Anges confronts Monsignor Luciano Guerra regarding the apocryphal letters written on a word processor supposedly by Sister Lucy:

Brother François: Monsignor Rector, can you swear on the Gospel that you have not written the apocryphal letters of Sister Lucy?

Msgr. Guerra: No, I do not want to. I cannot do it now in these conditions ...

Brother François: Internal criticism of these letters show that they are fake.

Msgr. Guerra: I will not discuss with you. You have no heart ... you have no heart.

Brother François's trust in Sister Lucy stems from his simple faith in her upbringing: "Her sixty-five years of religious life and the many divine communications with which she has been favored can only give her a greater taste and esteem for the virtue and wisdom of her mother, Maria Rosa, who 'had never tolerated a lie from her children.'"

Furthermore, Heaven has prolonged the life of the eldest of the Fatima seers in the Carmel of Coimbra to the ripe age of 90, doubtless "... to repeat the message and doubtless to prevent it being stifled or falsified."

Furthermore, "When God has a great mission of charismatic order to be accomplished in history, He is wise and prudent enough to choose and prepare adequate instruments, and, without violating their freedom, to enable them to fulfill with His grace the essential mission for which He has destined them from all eternity."[19]

The undermining of the credibility of the last living Fatima seer and of the Fatima Apostolate other than the "official" Blue Army was just one in a series of steps seemingly aimed at relegating the Message of Fatima to that same dumping ground where so many treasures of the authentic Catholic Church had been discarded. Poorly trained clergy now in control of some Church bureaucracies feel obliged to constantly reinforce the myth that the Church began with Vatican II and that anything that came before is a cause for Catholics to apologize to the world at large.

Father Nicholas Gruner unmasks the salesmen of this new attitude with clear, concise accuracy:

"When it comes to Fatima, we have been sold a bill of goods, namely that Fatima is a private revelation and is not that important. But Fatima is a *public prophetic revelation*, not simply a private revelation.

"If one has a vision of Our Lady, in which Our Lady said, 'In order for you to save your soul you must say 15 decades of the Rosary every day', that would be a private revelation, and it would be imprudent for the individual not to pay attention to it.

"But any other person wouldn't have to believe it. Such a revelation is private to the one who receives it. It places no obligation on anyone else.

"But, at Fatima, Our Lady gave a message to the world and confirmed it by a public miracle before 70,000 people. That's not a private revelation. That's a public, prophetic message. It cannot be lumped in with private revelations.

"Saint Paul says in First Thessalonians, Chap. 5:19,20: 'Do not extinguish the spirit. Do not despise prophecy'. If we represent a certain public, prophetic revelation as something to which we need pay no attention then we can make the very serious mistake of despising prophecy.

"Miracles prove revelations. If God takes the trouble, by working the great Miracle of the sun with first class miracles of cures, to make it evident that He has sent the Blessed Virgin Mary to give a message to mankind, then one does not have the option of despising that prophecy by terming it a private revelation to which we need give no attention.

"The second part of the passage in Colossians 2:20 says the Church is founded upon the foundation of the Apostles together with the prophets. The Holy Spirit spoke through a prophet of the Catholic Church and said, 'I want Saul set aside'. To set someone aside is to consecrate them to the service of God. The Holy Spirit said He wanted Saul set aside. The bishops understood and obeyed. They prayed, they fasted. Then they made Saul a bishop.

Father Gruner then said "The hierarchy has the obligation to test if the message comes from God. They have the right to test. They have an obligation to test. In fact, in that same passage of Sacred Scripture (1 Thess. 5:20,21) St. Paul says, "Test all things and hold fast to that which is good." If it passes the test, then no one any longer has the right to say it is optional. They no longer can say I can ignore that. That is despising prophecy.

"We have a prophet in Sister Lucy, though she denies being a prophet out of humility. But God, through Our Lady, chose Lucy and this message cannot be despised. We despise it at the peril of our spiritual lives, of our eternal souls, even at risk of our physical lives.

"For priests to despise Fatima would be to do so at the peril of those lives and the souls entrusted to us priests. Maybe priests can be excused for mixing up their own lives, but ruining the lives of the faithful is not excusable. Priests must realize that Fatima imposes an obligation on them.

"However, any priest who tries to fulfill the demands placed on all of us by Our Lady of Fatima to work for the consecration of Russia becomes a target of that very bureaucracy that should be supporting priests in their work. Why? Once again we are brought back to the infamous Vatican-Moscow Agreement of 1962 when the Vatican made an agreement with Moscow to not denounce communism. Besides being morally wrong, this is a fundamental error in geo-political strategy and bad for all of us.

Fingering his Rosary beads Father Gruner continues: "I have denounced the Agreement as criminal, as being morally corrupt. It must not be sustained. Now I am even going so far to say that the people who made the agreement back in '62 did it with good intentions. But it has been a disaster for the Church. Time has proven that I'm right. I'm prepared to say that in an open court of the Church."

"I do not stand alone in seeing the danger of dealing with Communists. Pope Pius XI and Pope Pius XII both saw the very real dangers that it poses to the world and to the Church.

"To be perfectly clear, Pope Pius XI, in his encyclical *The Divine Redeemer,* clearly taught 'Communism is intrinsically evil and no one who would save Christian civilization may collaborate with it in any undertaking whatsoever.'"[20]

Touching the Miraculous Medal around his neck, Father Gruner concluded: "The people responsible for the agreement are operating under the illusion that diplomacy can correct the errors of Russia. The Mother of God in Her messages at Fatima explicitly told us the only solution to avoiding the errors of Russia and not being a spiritual and physical victim of their killing errors, is exact obedience to Her message at Fatima. Does any faithful Catholic truly think that Her advice can be ignored?"

After the Sister Lucy "interview" there would surface a photo of Evaristo in Fatima proudly standing with Cardinal Casaroli, the Vatican Secretary of State, the "Great Architect" of Ostpolitik. Evaristo explained that Cardinal Casaroli had shown great interest in him. Might this interest explain his betrayal of the Apostolate and, indeed, Sister Lucy? One could hear the sound of certain pieces of a great puzzle snapping into place.

Yet Evaristo had become an even bigger embarrassment to the anti-Fatima forces than he had been to the Apostolate. The Evaristo pamphlet was a manifest absurdity which only helped the cause of Father Gruner's Apostolate by demonstrating the mendacity of its opponents. The anti-Fatima forces needed a definitive strategy for dealing with the "Gruner problem" in a way that would not explode in their faces. Soon they would reveal their new device.

Chapter 12

The Incardination Game

In his opening speech to the Second Vatican Council, Pope John XXIII made the momentous announcement that with the advent of the Council the Church would cease dispensing Her traditional remedy for heresy, the anathema, because "[S]he prefers today to make use of the medicine of mercy, rather than of the arms of severity".[1] Henceforth the Church would merely *explain* her doctrine in an amiable conversation with the world, "showing the validity of her teaching, rather than ... issuing condemnations."

This new approach to error could be viewed as an implicit criticism of Pope John's 259 predecessors on the Chair of Peter. In any case, His Holiness did not explain in this unprecedented speech how could it be an act of mercy to avoid condemning errors which lead souls into the eternal abyss of Hell.

Thus officially began the astounding process by which the Holy Catholic Church would be converted almost overnight from an impenetrable fortress against error into a veritable infirmary for the doctrinally diseased, who would soon be queuing up in large numbers to demand their daily dose of this new medicine of mercy, dispensed in a candy coating of "dialogue".

Within a few years of the Council's close the Church would throw down her "arms of severity": the Index of forbidden books would be abolished, along with the Oath Against Modernism prescribed by Pope St. Pius X. Gone would be the Councils of Vigilance that sainted Pope had ordered to be erected in every diocese in the world, as he had decreed in his monumental encyclical against the modernists, *Pascendi.*

Invigorated and emboldened by Pope John's amnesty, the heresiarchs who had been expelled from the seminaries and chanceries in keeping with the mandate of Pope St. Pius X's *Pascendi* would soon return in triumph, as prodigal sons who had *not* repented. Indeed, some had already returned in their new guise as *periti* —experts!—at Vatican

II. Yesterday's heresy or proximate heresy would become today's "problem in theology", while the clear propositions of the past would soon recede in the endless palaver of the very modernists of whom St. Pius X had written in *Pascendi*:

> "They bowed their head for a moment, but it was soon uplifted more arrogantly than ever."[2]

Only this time, the head of modernism would be uplifted with the official toleration of many of the highest authorities in the Church.

The resulting resurgence of modernism, condemned by Pius X as "the synthesis of all heresies", would make the revolt of Henry VIII seem like a Catholic Restoration by comparison, as the perennial liturgy, priestly formation and catechesis of the Church were swept aside in a neo-modernist debacle of unthinkable magnitude. Soon the toleration of error would lead to the persecution of Truth by the very neo-modernists who would gain sway in the hierarchy, and strict adherence to Tradition would become the only condemned doctrine.

Yes, the Deposit of the Faith would remain intact through it all, as Our Lord had promised; but only a very diligent student of Tradition would be able to find it in the midst of the reigning confusion. For the rest of the faithful there was only a datum of daily experience in the light of which it would be difficult to disprove, to the average Catholic in the pew; the thesis that the Catholic Church had changed in substantial matters. No less than Cardinal Ratzinger himself would be forced to admit years later in his memoirs that the loss of appearances would make it impossible for many to find the substance of the Faith.

> "But if in the liturgy the communion of faith no longer appears, nor the universal unity of the Church and of her history, nor the mystery of the living Christ, where is it that the Church still appears in her spiritual substance?"[3]

In a Church which no longer wishes to condemn anyone or anything, but merely to explain itself to the world, how would it be possible to silence Father Nicholas Gruner? That he would have to be silenced was a foregone conclusion; his teaching and preaching of the undiluted message of Fatima had for too long been an intolerable irritant to the executors of Ostpolitik and the new ecumenism in the Vatican.

The mild mannered priest from Canada was spoiling the global party by constantly pointing out in his vexatious magazine that the Pope is not the mascot of a New World Order of ecumenical brotherhood, but the Vicar of Christ, empowered by God Almighty to bring about the Kingship of Christ through the Reign of Mary, and with it *the end of all heresy*, by the means She had revealed at Fatima:

> "In the end My Immaculate Heart will triumph. The Holy Father

will consecrate Russia to Me. Russia will be converted, and a period of peace will be given to mankind ... If My requests are granted, many souls will be saved and there will be peace."

Such antiquated triumphalism was an embarrassing eyesore in the new post-conciliar landscape of religious liberty and world ecumenism. Who could speak seriously any longer of the Kingship of Christ and the Queenship of Mary, at a time when the Vatican was dispatching Cardinals to attend the gala opening of the first mosque in the city of Rome?[4]

But on what *grounds* could this meddlesome priest be silenced? After nearly 20 years of apostolic work, no Church authority had even suggested that Father Gruner had taught or believed anything contrary to faith and morals, much less that he had been guilty of immorality. It was certainly no canonical crime to do what Catholics had always done and to believe precisely what they had always believed. As for the Apostolate, there could be no question that under the 1983 Code of Canon Law, promulgated by Pope John Paul II himself, its activities were entirely permissible, indeed encouraged, and certainly in no need of any official "ecclesiastical approval" which could now conveniently be withdrawn.[5]

Besides, now that the Church had become thoroughly infested with openly heretical priests and laity and their innumerable heterodox associations, all of them operating with impunity under the same Code of Canon Law, any attempt to silence Father Gruner and his Marian Apostolate on doctrinal grounds would make the bureaucrats look ridiculous—they would lose their *bella figura*. What is worse, they would have to *prove* something in a canonical proceeding involving witnesses and documents, with a right of defense afforded to Father Gruner.

No, that would not do. Yet there was one seemingly foolproof stratagem at the bureaucrats' disposal, and they would seize upon it with a vengeance: They would invoke the so-called "administrative law" of the Church, which regulates the status of priests through "extra-judicial" administrative "decrees" of bishops on such matters as where a priest will reside, what faculties he will be able to exercise in a given diocese, and what sort of "canonical mission" he will be given. In Father Gruner's case the ensuing administrative battle would revolve around a single word: incardination.

Canon 265 of the 1983 Code of Canon Law provides that:

> "Every cleric must be *incardinated* in a particular Church [the post-Vatican II term for diocese] ... unattached clergy are by no means to be allowed."

"Incardination" is a word derived from the Latin and literally means to be hinged or attached to something. As the Canon states, every priest must be "hinged" to a bishop so that there would be no unattached or "vagus" priests in the Church.

Father Gruner had never been a "vagus", of course. Like many other priests in the Church today, he had been given the right to live and work outside the diocese of his incardination. In fact, his permission had been given in the form of a binding, written decree, signed and sealed by the Bishop of Avellino. There was certainly no need for his services in the Diocese of Avellino, where his inability to speak the obscure local dialect precluded any parish assignment or other canonical mission. Thus, since 1978 Father Gruner had been conducting the Apostolate in Canada under the written permission to be outside the Diocese of Avellino, which permission was expressly to continue until such time as another bishop invited him to transfer to his diocese. At least three bishops would extend such an invitation to Father Gruner, but certain Vatican bureaucrats were not about to let a few benevolent bishops stand in their way.

For Father Gruner, a rather commonplace and perfectly legal arrangement with his bishop had become an Achilles' heel. *The Plan* to exploit it was quite simple: First, Father Gruner would be ordered to find another bishop to incardinate him; then the bureaucrats would block all offers of incardination by benevolent bishops in other dioceses; then they would cause the Bishop of Avellino to revoke the permission to live outside the Diocese and order Father Gruner to return to Avellino, on grounds that he had "failed" to find another bishop.

If Father Gruner would not submit to exile in a foreign diocese, then he would be subjected to the ultimate penalties: suspension from the priesthood, followed by reduction to the lay state[6] -- penalties which not even raving heretic priests are threatened with in the Church today. The destruction of Father Nicholas Gruner could thus be accomplished entirely in the realm of "administrative" decrees, without the slightest proof of any offense against faith or morals or any opportunity for Father Gruner to mount a defense. To be sure, *The Plan* would require the cooperation of the Bishop of Avellino, whose jurisdiction over a priest of his own diocese could not simply be usurped by Vatican bureaucrats. No matter: By judicious application of pressure from above, the bishop could be persuaded to go limp like a marionette and allow the bureaucrats to pull his strings. And while even an "administrative" decree must be founded on just cause and respect the natural rights of the priest, who would be looking over the bureaucrats' shoulders to make sure they had acted justly?

In fact, the first attempt to implement *The Plan* had occurred back in

May of 1989, when Father Gruner received a letter from the Bishop of Avellino warning of the "worried signals" he had been receiving from the Vatican "Secretary of State" and the "Congregation for the Clergy."[7] Thus the bishop was already being remote-controlled by "signals" from Vatican bureaucrats, broadcast on secret wavelengths to which Father Gruner would never be a party. Cardinal Innocenti would soon admit as much in his extraordinary July 1989 "intervention" referring to the secret "case" of Father Gruner which "arouses serious preoccupation on the part of the Holy See". (See Chapter 9)

By November 1989 the bishop had responded to the "worried signals" of the bureaucrats by writing Father Gruner in badly translated Italian in broken English as follows: "In the meantime decide what to do: or you make you hing (i.e. "hinge" or incardinate elsewhere) or you come back to Avellino."[8] But the bishop did not seem to have his heart in *The Plan*; he could not bring himself to carry out the unjust execution of his own priest.

In subsequent meetings and correspondence with Father Gruner and his friend, Father Paul Kramer, the bishop repeatedly reaffirmed Father Gruner's longstanding right to reside outside the diocese while seeking another bishop.[9] During one of those meetings, just before cooking a steak dinner for his guest from Canada, the bishop had declared: "Father Gruner, to suspend you would be a mortal sin. But if the Vatican tells me to do it, I will do it."[10]

He was never put to that test. In February 1993 a new bishop was installed in the Diocese of Avellino. Now *here* was a man who would quite eagerly play the marionette. This became apparent almost immediately: In July of 1993 Father Gruner received a written offer of incardination from the Bishop of the Diocese of Simla-Chandigarh, India, who was only too happy to sponsor Father Gruner and the Apostolate in his diocese.[11] It would have seemed to any objective observer that Father Gruner's administrative problem was over: He had been directed to find another bishop, so he had found another bishop. *Arrivederci* Avellino.

But the new Bishop of Avellino promptly took the unprecedented step of turning the offer of incardination over to the Congregation for the Clergy, waiting several months to advise Father Gruner that "the request for incardination has been passed to the Congregation and has (sic) put me in the condition of not being able to act. I await the instructions of Mons. Sepe [Secretary of the Congregation for the Clergy]."[12]

In other words, the new bishop had simply surrendered his jurisdiction over a priest of his own diocese to a Vatican Secretary who would now dispose of Father Gruner outside the proper channels of

Canon Law.[13] While Father Gruner waited months to hear from the Bishop of Avellino, the Bishop of Simla-Chandigarh was reached in his remote diocese and "informed" by the bureaucrats of Father Gruner's "situation", and the offer of incardination was suddenly withdrawn. *The Plan* was proceeding to perfection.

On January 31, 1994, just as *The Plan* required, the Bishop of Avellino issued an "administrative decree" ordering Father Gruner to return to the Diocese of Avellino in 30 days, after an approved absence of more than *sixteen years.*[14] Father Gruner was evidently expected to abandon his life's work, close up his residence, leave his personal affairs in disarray and immediately enter lifetime exile in a remote foreign diocese which had never supported him nor required his services since 1976!

The pretext for the decree was, of course, Father Gruner's pre-arranged "failure" to be incardinated in another diocese. But Father Gruner had met with the Bishop of Avellino only 18 days before to discuss, among other things, the offer of incardination from the Diocese of Simla-Chandigarh which the bishop *admitted* had been blocked by the bureaucrats. How in conscience could the bishop issue a decree only days later pretending that Father Gruner had culpably "failed" to find another diocese to accept him?

The bishop seemed to recognize that he needed a fig leaf to cover this atrocious fraud, as well as some pretext for the canonical "warning" contained in his January 31 decree. So he made reference also to unspecified "complaints" against Father Gruner. Yet during the meeting only 18 days before, the bishop had also admitted that *there were no complaints* against Father Gruner in his files, that Father Gruner was certainly a priest in good standing, and that it was only pressure from Vatican bureaucrats which was forcing the bishop's hand.[15] How in conscience could the bishop now issue a decree pretending there were "complaints" against Father Gruner?

And what was the evidence of these "complaints"? The decree mentioned nothing but an anonymous letter from 1978, regarding an unspecified complaint, *not from any Church authority*, but from someone within the Apostolate itself. The anonymous complaint apparently claimed that Father Gruner had somehow injured the Apostolate. Injured? Since 1978, the Apostolate had grown fifty-fold under Father Gruner's leadership, from a fledgling group of a few laypeople to one of the largest Fatima apostolates in the world.

During those sixteen years, the Apostolate had produced and distributed around the world several million books, magazines, pamphlets and tracts on the Message of Fatima; had broadcast thousands of hours of radio and television programs in North America; had sent over 20 mailings to every bishop in the world, including six books; and had staged a conference in *Vatican City itself,* and another conference in Fatima to which the entire world episcopate was invited. Yet in this vast record of teaching and preaching, in the entire life's work of Father Nicholas Gruner, the current Bishop of Avellino could dredge up only a *sixteen-year-old anonymous letter* containing unspecified charges as "grounds" for the recall to Avellino!

This lack of evidence was a major embarrassment to *The Plan.* Father Gruner had been conducting the Apostolate for the past 16 years without the slightest objection by three successive Bishops of Avellino. Apparently *The Plan* had no statute of limitations!

It was obvious that the strings of the marionette were being jerked very violently indeed, for *The Plan* needed to be accomplished, and quickly. Since the result was predetermined, the quality of the evidence hardly mattered—anything at all would do, even a sixteen-year-old complaint about nothing in particular. Curiously enough, never once in the working out of *The Plan* would the bureaucrats ever make reference to Father Gruner's preaching and teaching on the Message of Fatima. It was as if they were deathly afraid to mention the true objective of their actions.

Yet there remained a few more impediments to the destruction of Father Gruner and his work: there were other benevolent bishops willing to offer him sanctuary in their dioceses. On May 29, 1994 the bishop of the Diocese of Anapolis, Brazil, offered Father Gruner incardination in his diocese, commencing July 16, 1994.[16]

Being mindful of the hostility of the bureaucrats, the bishop cautioned in his written offer that the incardination must remain confidential until its effective date. But it was not confidential enough. The bureaucrats soon contacted the bishop to "advise" him about Father Gruner's "case". After receiving this "advice", the bishop hastily withdrew his offer without explanation, telling Father Gruner only that he must "accept the decisions of the Congregation". Decisions? *What* decisions?

As Cardinal Innocenti had made clear in his 1989 intervention, a whole new mode of canonical procedure had been devised especially for Father Gruner: a secret "case" in the Congregation for the Clergy, culminating in secret "decisions" barring his incardination by benevolent bishops who would otherwise be happy to incardinate him in their dioceses.

The 1983 Code of Canon Law specifically guarantees the *right* of a priest to transfer to another diocese should he find a bishop who would make better use of his priestly services.[17] Yet Father Gruner would never be given even a glimpse of the secret proceedings by which this right was being denied him without due process. No mere law of the Church would take precedence over execution of *The Plan.*

Meanwhile, Father Gruner had made a canonical appeal from the Bishop of Avellino's order to return. *The Plan* had taken account of this contingency as well, however, for the appeal would have to pass before the Congregation for the Clergy, where the judges would be none other than two of the same bureaucrats who had been orchestrating *The Plan,* Cardinal Sanchez and Archbishop Sepe.

It was they, of course, who had issued "declarations" in the Vatican media urging the entire Church to shun the Apostolate's conference at Fatima, thereby effectively interdicting Father Gruner and the Apostolate without even a semblance of canonical due process. At the same time, of course, heretical associations were staging conferences and issuing impudent manifestos throughout the world without a peep from the Congregation for the Clergy.

It hardly required the gift of prophecy to predict that the same two bureaucrats would uphold the order to return to Avellino. In a perfunctory decree issued only days after Father Gruner's appeal was filed, they declared that the Bishop of Avellino had acted correctly in ordering his return—after all, Father Gruner had "failed" to find another bishop, had he not? *They* had seen to that. Thus was on display the marvel of "administrative law" in the Vatican bureaucracy: bureaucrats who had publicly condemned the accused without grounds or a hearing and had improperly interfered in his rights, were allowed to sit as judges on an appeal *from their own actions.*

On June 7, 1994 Father Gruner made further appeal to the Apostolic Signatura, the highest court in the Catholic Church, next to the Pope himself. Here the Incardination Game would continue, as the Prefect of the Signatura, Cardinal Agustoni, would issue a decree which teemed with factual and legal errors and embarrassingly strained to reach the desired result: permanent exile of Father Nicholas Gruner to a place where, it was hoped, he would never be heard from again.

More than two years would pass before Father Gruner received an official copy of the decree—he was literally the last to know. In the meantime, the Providential discovery of a "smoking gun" would ultimately force *The Plan* into the light of day. The canonical appeal process would reach a new level of complexity as the Incardination Game moved into its end-game sequence. But this is to anticipate. Only a few months after Father Gruner's appeal to the Signatura, there would be another Fatima conference: Mexico City, November 1994. What would the bureaucrats do about a second gathering of bishops to discuss the "forbidden" Message of Fatima?

Chapter 13

The Balamand Connection

In the offices of the Vatican Secretary of State there are exquisitely sensitive diplomatic alarms, attuned not to heresy, scandal or other threats to the Faith, but to the slightest breach at the perimeters of Ostpolitik and world ecumenism. In the spring of 1993, some 18 months before Father Gruner and the Apostolate would stage a second Fatima Conference in Mexico City, those alarms were tripped by an emergent situation in Romania and the Ukraine.

Now that the "former Soviet Union" had been "liberated", it seemed likely that a significant number of Russian and Romanian Orthodox clergy and laity would commit the diplomatic gaffe of simply resuming the practice of the Catholic Faith, picking up where their forebears had left off when the Communists seized their "uniate" Catholic parishes, arrested their priests and bishops and installed Orthodox clerics in their places, most of them KGB operatives.

In Russia, it was not an easy matter for the Soviets to create an Orthodox Church consisting essentially of KGB spies. It took awhile to wean the Russian Orthodox Hierarchy of 50,000 priests down to a manageable 500 Soviet agents in clerical garb.[1] The Metropolitan of the newly constituted spy-church, Sergei Stragodorsky, was mysteriously released from prison in 1927 and announced to the world that the Russian Orthodox Church had not been persecuted.[2] He had apparently been persuaded to overlook the disappearance of 49,500 Orthodox priests.

The imminent recrudescence of Eastern Rite Catholicism should have been an occasion of great joy in the objective order of things, but for the schismatic Orthodox hierarchy, which had for so long enjoyed the use of Communist plunder, it was a grave emergency: several cathedrals and some 2,000 parish properties were already in dispute in Romania and the Ukraine, not to mention a potentially vast loss of forcibly acquired adherents. The resulting hue and cry clearly posed a threat to the progress of Ostpolitik and world ecumenism in "the former Soviet Union."

A "fix" was not long in coming. In June 1993 Vatican representatives and representatives of the Russian and Romanian Orthodox Churches (among others) met in Balamand, Lebanon, to discuss the "crisis" at the "VIIth Plenary Session" of the "Joint International Commission for the Theological Dialogue between the Roman Catholic Church and the Orthodox Church." The chief Vatican representative, from the Second Section of the Vatican Secretariat of State, was Edward Cardinal Cassidy, who also carried the title, President of the Pontifical Council for the Promotion of Christian Unity. The result of the meeting was "The Balamand Statement". In this astounding document Cardinal Cassidy and the other Catholic representatives agreed that the Catholic Church would no longer seek either the conversion of the Orthodox or even their simple return to the Catholic faith of their forefathers:

> "[I]n the search for re-establishing unity there *is no question of conversion of people from one Church to the other in order to insure their savlation*." (¶15)
>
> "Pastoral activity in the Catholic Church, Latin as well as Eastern, *no longer aims at having the faithful of one Church pass over to the other*; that is to say, *it no longer aims at proselytizing among the Orthodox*. It aims at answering the spiritual needs of its own faithful and it has *no desire for expansion at the expense of the Orthodox Church*. (¶22)
>
> "To pave the way for future relations between the two Churches, passing beyond *the out-dated ecclesiology of return to the Catholic Church connected with the problem which is the object of this document* [i.e. the "threat" of a mass return of Orthodox to Rome!], special attention will be given to the preparation of future priests . . ." (¶30)
>
> "By excluding for the future *all proselytization and all desire by Catholics for expansion at the expense of the Orthodox Church,* the commission hopes it has overcome the obstacles which impelled certain autocephalous Churches to suspend their participation in the theological dialogue . . ." (¶35)[3]

At Fatima, Our Lady had prophesied that "In the end, My Immaculate Heart will triumph. The Holy Father will consecrate Russia to Me. *Russia will be converted,* and a period of peace will be given to mankind." Not if the Second Section[4] of the Vatican Secretariat of State had anything to say about it! After all, what did the Blessed Virgin Mary know about the exigencies of Ostpolitik and world ecumenism?

Consider: The Balamand Statement implicitly claims that when Our Lady spoke of the conversion of Russia, She, *and therefore Her Divine Son*, were espousing an "out-dated ecclesiology of return to the Catholic Church". Contrary to Our Lord and Our Lady, Balamand teaches that "in the search for re-establishing unity there is no question of *conversion* of people from one Church to the other in order to insure their salvation." Yet Our Lady of Fatima did speak unambiguously of the *conversion* of Russia to the Catholic faith, did She not? Was it therefore the position of Cardinal Cassidy and the Vatican Secretariat of State that Our Lord had allowed Our Lady to use the *wrong word* in the Message of Fatima? Did they suppose that Our Lady had not been advised by Her Son of future developments in the field of ecumenical relations which would render the term "conversion" rather quaint, and quite obsolete when applied to the adherents of Orthodoxy?

At Balamand, the bureaucrats had brought out a large rubber stamp and slammed it down on the Message of Fatima. And when the stamp was lifted the word "OVERRULED" appeared across the words of the Message. The Balamand Statement can only be seen as an insult to Our Lady of Fatima, and thus an infinitely graver insult to Her Divine Son, Whose message She had conveyed.

Yet one might at least find some solace in the fact that this arrant repudiation of the Message of Fatima lacked, and still lacks, formal papal approval. But this would be to ignore the reality of Church governance since the Second Vatican Council. Cardinal Cassidy's masterpiece of capitulation was promptly delivered to the Eastern Catholic primates by the Papal Nuncios, whose ascendancy as the Vatican's semi-secret diplomatic representatives began with the disastrous concordats of the Napoleonic era. With the Nuncial package came the implicit understanding that Balamand's "ecclesiological principles" and "practical rules" would, naturally, be implemented immediately—even though the Pope himself had not actually given such an order. Of course, a papal order was a mere formality. After all, Cardinal Cassidy was head of a Pontifical Council; therefore he acted with Papal authority, did he not? Not only that, the document had been delivered by a Papal Nuncio. Thus, it gave every *appearance* of being a Papal order, even if it contained no actual order from the Pope.

One of the prelates who received the Balamand Statement *via* Nuncio was the Cardinal Archbishop of Lviv in the Ukraine, His Eminence Myroslav Lubachivsky. Cardinal Lubachivsky wrote to Cardinal Cassidy to assure him that:

> "I commit myself, my brother bishops, clergy and faithful, to applying the practical rules of the Balamand Document to the best

of our ability. These include . . . *not to seek the passage of faithful from one Church to another* . . ."[5]

How distressing to note that on April 24, 1990, Cardinal Lubachivsky had written to Father Gruner to encourage his work in spreading awareness of the need for the Collegial Consecration of Russia, which he clearly agreed had not been effected in 1984 as the anti-Fatima forces were now claiming:

> "I want to thank you for all that you do for the Church and for continuing to spread *the full Fatima Message*; in particular for insisting on *the urgent need to have Russia consecrated by all the bishops of the Church in union with the Holy Father*. Be assured of my prayers and the prayers of the Ukrainian people *for all that you are doing to save Russia*."[6]

Only three years later, this same prelate would feel obliged to forget the conversion of Russia—on the strength of a non-binding statement by a theological commission meeting in Lebanon, negotiated by a Vatican bureaucrat of no greater hierarchical status than his own. And this despite the fact that it was atheistic Russia which had committed the genocide of 20 million of his own people and stolen their priests, bishops and churches from them. *Simply because a Nuncio had delivered a document from the Vatican apparatus*, this prince of the Church would immediately abandon any effort to exercise his Divine commission of promoting the return—yes, the *return*—of the Ukrainian Orthodox to the one true Church of Christ. Instead, he would now agree to view the perennial teaching of the Magisterium on the spiritual state of schismatics just as the Balamand document said it should be viewed: "the outdated ecclesiology of a return to the Catholic Church."

And so a mere bureaucratic decree would become the policy of the Holy Catholic Church in Eastern Europe. It would soon come to pass that entire villages seeking to return to Rome would be told by Catholic bishops that a return was no longer necessary. No, they were to *remain* in the schismatic church in which their forefathers had been forcibly transplanted by Communist barbarians. The crisis was over. Mission accomplished. The world was safe for Ostpolitik and world ecumenism. Without the Collegial Consecration which would have made the conversion of Russia a certainty, the Balamand Document was all that was needed to keep it from happening.

The Balamand Statement recalls another tragic blunder of Vatican diplomacy in which defeat was snatched from the jaws of victory: Just as the *Cristeros* in the mid 1920's seemed to be turning the tide against the Masonic revolutionaries who were ravaging Mexico, U.S. Ambassador Morrow and Vatican representatives negotiated an agreement under which they would lay down their arms in exchange for paper promises of amnesty and respect for the religious liberty of Catholics.[7] Following the orders of the Vatican, the *Cristeros* laid down their arms, only to be hunted down and butchered by the Masons.[8] The corpses of faithful priests and laity would festoon trees and telephone poles in Mexico for many years to come.

The Balamand debacle, like the betrayal in Mexico, shows how the Mystical Body has been pulled to the ground and immobilized by a thousand Lilliputian strings emanating from Vatican secretariats, councils and commissions which form no part of the divine constitution of the Church. It typifies the *modus operandi* by which the virtue of obedience in faithful clerics like Cardinal Lubachivsky is exploited by bureaucrats issuing documents which have the *appearance* of a command, but which in reality command nothing. These vaporous non-orders have acquired the power to negate Tradition, and even to overrule the plain words of the Mother of God.

It would be Father Gruner himself who unearthed another spectacular example of this phenomenon in May of 1995, at a public address by Alfons Cardinal Stickler on the subject of the Traditional Latin Mass. In response to Father Gruner's written question, the Cardinal revealed to the audience that in 1986 a group of nine Curial Cardinals assembled by Pope John Paul II himself, all with doctorates in Canon Law, had voted 8-1 in closed session that Pope Paul VI had never actually ordered the suppression of the Traditional Mass, and that its celebration *had never ceased to be entirely permissible* under Church law.[9] Incredibly, the Pope had been unable to determine just what his predecessor had ordered in promulgating the New Mass. In fact, the actual suppression of the Traditional Mass had been accomplished entirely through the decrees of Vatican congregations and commissions, and not by any explicit Magisterial act of Paul VI. As the vote of the Cardinals made clear, *bureaucrats* had obliterated the entire liturgical tradition of the Roman Rite without a single actual order of the Pope suppressing it!

Thus has the Catholic Church been governed for the past 30 years.

§

In the early summer of 1994, a year after Balamand, news of the Apostolate's plan for a Mexico conference on the Message of Fatima reached the bureaucrats of the Secretary of State, and the alarm bells rang once again: *What?*—a gathering of bishops to discuss the "conversion of Russia", after Vatican representatives had just negotiated an agreement promising not to convert the Russians? This was intolerable.

The first employees of the Secretary of State to be mobilized in any crisis are the Nuncios. Should the Nuncios be mobilized on a global scale against a lone Canadian priest and his Marian apostolate, they could present a formidable force which might well annihilate plans for the Mexican conference. Unthinkable? It should have been. Yet that is exactly what happened in the summer and autumn months of 1994.

PART THREE

A FATIMA SPIRITUALITY FOR THE 21ST CENTURY

Chapter 14

Terrible Words

The events which had unfolded since the Fatima conference of 1992, by any reckoning, would have annihilated most priests — especially one who was now being pressed in the vice of "administrative decrees" intended to crush the life out of his Apostolate by removing him from it, and who wished to speak with bishops in Mexico about the conversion of Russia which had just been bartered away at Balamand.

Nevertheless, while the Balamand Statement was being implemented, and the bizarre "Sister Lucy Interview" publicized by Carlos Evaristo was being taken as gospel by those who wanted apparitions with more ecumenical messages to replace Fatima's stern warnings, Father Gruner coolly moved forward to appeal once more to the bishops in the cause of Fatima.

The decision to hold a Second International Peace Conference in Mexico might seem like a suicide mission to most. But Father Nicholas Gruner saw it as providing a golden opportunity to penetrate even deeper into the compelling reasons for the collegial consecration of Russia. He could not forget that Our Lord's words to Sister Lucy at Rianjo conveyed one of the most terrifying prophecies and rebukes in a century of Marian apparitions:

In the August 1931 message, Our Lord in Rianjo, Spain, gave Sister Lucy of Fatima a very stern warning to pass on to the hierarchy when He said: "Make it known to My ministers, given that they follow the example of the King of France in delaying the execution of My command, they will follow him into misfortune".[1]

Our Lord is referring to the misfortune of King Louis XVI, who was the third king to reject Our Lord's plan given through St. Margaret Mary for the consecration of France to the Sacred Heart. Having failed to effect the consecration, Louis XVI was guillotined in 1793, by the

French revolutionaries. Through Sister Lucy, Our Lord admonished the Pope and the bishops about the fate which awaits those who refuse to carry out the Divinely mandated consecration of a nation.

The old "krock" on Father Gruner is that he is "disloyal" to the Pope. His critics have never bothered to explain how it could be loyalty for a subject to ignore a grave warning from a Divine messenger that the life of his sovereign was in jeopardy. Our Lord had not predicted a great tea party when He told Sister Lucy at Rianjo that His ministers would follow in the footsteps of the beheaded Louis XVI should they fail to heed His commands at Fatima. If loyalty was lacking, it had to be on the part of the critics who continue to hide the warning of Our Lord from the Pope and the bishops.

What better place to remind the bishops than in the fast-beating heart of a country that has been the center of persecution of the Church throughout her long, tortured history -Mexico?

It is said that thirty million people live within whispering distance of one another in Mexico City. To descend by plane into the ocean of light this population generates at night is to experience the shock Cortes must have felt when he came through the high mountain pass of Popacatapetl and saw Montezuma's capital at his feet. Mexico is the center of a world apart. It was at the fast-pulsating heart of this endangered world that the Second International Peace Conference for Bishops was scheduled for November of 1994.

In the months leading up to the Conference, invitations went out to the bishops of the world, announcements were sent to interested Church associations, 150,000 posters promoting the Conference were distributed and over 500,000 copies of a special issue of *The Fatima Crusader* were mailed to supporters.

To prepare for the Conference, the first undertaking in the spring of '94 was for Father Gruner to meet with Bishop Fuentes, the bishop of a small diocese in Mexico, whom he had met in Fatima in 1992. At first Bishop Fuentes appeared delighted with the proposal for a conference and most co-operative, going so far as to make introductions to the Mexican Bishops Conference, the CEM. Abbot Schullenberg, Rector of the Shrine of Guadalupe, encouraged Father Gruner to use the Aula Magna, the Great Hall at Lago de Guadalupe, which is owned by the CEM.

On May 2, the Secretary-General of the CEM, Bishop Ramon Godinez Flores, agreed to the rental of the Aula Magna conference facility[2], the same facility where the Mexican Bishops hold their annual meetings. On May 5, the CEM accepted and deposited the check which had an endorsement clause typed on the back of the check indicating that endorsement and deposit of the check constituted an agreement to rent the Aula Magna conference facility. Everything seemed to be proceeding smoothly — too smoothly.

Under the relentless demands of producing the Conference, it was natural that the signs and signals of a determined opposition might slip by unnoticed or without being afforded the attention that may have been due. In the offices of the Vatican Secretary of State the opposition was forming its battalions, and they were ready to move into action.

October 2nd: A letter from Bishop Flores, dated a month earlier, arrived at Father Gruner's Canadian office. It contained the second of the checks initially sent to reserve additional rooms for the event, the text of the letter announcing that the reservations of the Aula Magna facilities had been canceled. The stunning words used were:

> "... this terminates the possibility of effecting the above-mentioned meeting."[3]

Not quite. Only five weeks remained to the opening speeches of the Conference, to which considerably over 100 bishops had committed to being present. Even so, no one panicked. After the letter of cancellation arrived, the immediate need was to find alternative facilities in Mexico City. It was done: God willing, the Second Fatima Peace Conference would take place instead at the Sheraton Maria Isabela Hotel on Paseo de la Reforma.

It was then that the Apostolate heard about the Big Lie. All the way from Rome to Mexico. At first it was just a whisper. Then a letter surfaced that had been sent to every bishop in the world *via* the global network of Papal Nuncios. Father Gruner began receiving notes from bishops who had been advised by the head of the Conference of Bishops in their own countries not to attend, on the strength of advice reaching them through the Apostolic Nunciature in each country. The letter from the Vatican was a recycled version of the same "declaration" published in *L'Osservatore Romano* and elsewhere by Cardinal Sanchez and Archbishop Sepe to derail the 1992 Conference in Fatima.[4]

The letter referred once again to the old canard that Father Gruner did not have "permission of ecclesiastical authority" to hold the Conference in Mexico City. This in spite of the fact that it was manifest that Bishops of the Catholic Church do not require the "permission" of Vatican bureaucrats to attend a private religious conference. To add to the absurdity, no official Vatican mechanism even exists for the "official authorization" of such private events. The "declaration" was demeaning, insulting to the bishops, and (as expected by its issuers) the cause of mass confusion and upset.

The letter was a prime specimen of the literally truthful lie: yes, there was no "ecclesiastical permission" for the conference, but *none was required in the first place.* By use of this literally truthful lie, the bureaucrats had hoped to create the impression that bishops — who by virtue of the divine constitution of the Church are the rulers of their own dioceses and answerable only to the Pope — were somehow subject to travel restrictions imposed by a pair of Vatican bureaucrats sitting in the Congregation for the Clergy!

The law of the Church is clear, and the law had not changed since the first Conference, when canon lawyers had emphatically stated what should have been a matter of common sense: Absolutely no "permission of ecclesiastical authority" is needed for any member of the faithful, much less a bishop, to be present at a private Marian conference. On the contrary, it would be a violation of the law of the Church to *require* such permission. The bureaucrats were in fact openly defying the present Code of Canon Law promulgated by Pope John Paul II — a Code which had by Providence made explicit the always — existent natural right of the faithful to form associations, conduct meetings and present their concerns about Church affairs to the sacred pastors.* The modernists had been abusing this same natural right for thirty years, staging their motley assemblies and issuing their heretical manifestos with total impunity. Oddly enough, the bureaucrats had never seen fit to interdict any of these modernist gatherings with letters dispatched to the entire world episcopate through the Nuncios.

To give one example among many, in August 1995, the 25th Anniversary of the leftist *Campaign for Human Development* (CHD) was held in Chicago. At this event, twenty-five bishops, including three Cardinals gathered with priests, nuns, ex-nuns, and laity. The conference promoted left-wing political actions, it sneered at "the religious right", promoted "anti-patriarchy" feminism and called for improvement for the lives of such "minorities" as gays and lesbians.

The Saturday afternoon CHD liturgy included pagan dance at the offertory by dancing girls in leotards and low-cut tops, and scandalous irreverence of the Blessed Sacrament after Communion when about ten lay "extraordinary ministers" gathered around the altar irreverently gulping down the consecrated Bread and Wine as if they were at a cocktail party, talking and chatting out loud with each other and friends all within arms reach of the 25 bishops who simply sat and watched.[4B]

Yet *not one* of the bishops participating in this event received even a slap on the wrist from Roman authorities for attending. But then, the

*The detailed case against these illegal maneuvers by a very small number of Vatican based bureaucrats has been officially lodged with His Holiness Pope John Paul II, on November 20, 1996, in exact accordance with the provisions of Canon Law for cases like this one where a Church official grossly abuses his position of authority. Read this detailed case in Appendix VII.

modernists were not gathering to discuss and promote the "intolerable" Message of Fatima.

Although the Mexico Conference in no way offended Canon Law or general ecclesiastical practice, nevertheless a majority of the bishops who had planned to attend cancelled after receipt of the Nuncial missive. Why the high casualty list? Because, without ever telling an explicit lie, the letter clearly implied two very false things:that Father Gruner was under some sort of ecclesiastical penalty, an outlaw, and that any bishop who attended the Conference would be engaging in an act of disobedience. This was all couched in *studied ambiguity.* No specific offense was attributed to Father Gruner, nor any specific prohibition on attendance at the Conference — because there *was* no offense, and no prohibition. In the 18 years of his priesthood and work in the Apostolate, Father Gruner had never been charged with an offense whatever against the good of the Church, and neither had the Apostolate. The "declaration" was pure vapor. But the vapor had its effect.

To the outsider, the political maneuver from the clique of bureaucrats was nothing less than bizarre, and, with no little hangover from the '92 Conference, outright vindictive. Most priests would have been intimidated into abandoning the undertaking and seeking new winds to fill the mainsail. Yet that did not happen. Despite the withdrawal of many bishops, and the continuing interference of the same Vatican bureaucrats, Father Gruner persisted in completing plans for the Conference. His fixity of purpose was, as many watchers of his Apostolate now recognize, pure vintage Gruner.

Publicly, Bishop Flores made use of the Nuncios' letter to "justify" his cancellation of the Conference at the CEM facilities. As Bishop Flores proceeded to go about sweeping the whole thing under the carpet, and Father Gruner kept moving forward to meet his deadline, the serpent of old extended a second suffocating coil around the Conference plans.

From the Middle East came news that a bishop had been denied a visa on the grounds that the Conference was not approved by the Mexican Government. Incredibly, the Mexican government had indeed announced that they had not "authorized" the gathering.

October 21: An official communiqué from the Mexican Government revealed it was Bishop Flores himself who had gone to the Ministry of the Interior in Mexico City and condemned the Conference. On that same day, further confirmation of Bishop Flores' interference was received from the Consulate General of Mexico, in Toronto.

Officials of the Mexican Government found their hands tied. Under orders from the Ministry of the Interior they could not issue visas for people from other countries who wished to attend the Conference. Around the world, Mexican Consulates had been informed that those applying for visas for this purpose were not to receive them because the Secretary-General of the Bishops Conference in Mexico, Bishop Flores, had not given his *completely unnecessary* "authorization" for the Conference.

There were both physical and logistical hardships for the bishops who had seen through the vaporous letter from the Nuncios and managed to obtain visas (in most cases by not disclosing the exact purpose of their trip). Arrangements in some cases had been made many months in advance. Worse still, inconvenience to the guest lecturers scheduled to speak at the Conference mounted. Remunerative engagements turned down for the chance to address the bishops were lost.

All these obstacles caused Father Gruner to pause and consider whether there was really a way around the multiplying problems. But he remained convinced that he had a duty to proceed. Nor could he live with the pain of knowing that souls were being lost because the requests of Our Lady had been buried and forgotten in so many quarters of the Church:

> "I believe in conscience that each day the Consecration of Russia as requested by Our Lady of Fatima is delayed, many, many people die in the state of unbelief and other mortal sins. Unless they miraculously convert on their deathbed, they will go to hell. Thus, due to each day's delay, many souls are lost for all eternity, and wars continue to erupt without abatement around the globe. Since 1984 alone, when the Consecration was supposedly done according to the conjecture of the ill-informed, over 10 million people have died in new wars. If you consider the undeclared but very real war upon the unborn, since 1984 there have been, around the world, at least 600 million victims. Russia, since her supposed Consecration in 1984, has become the place where Polish Catholics go for their abortions. Is *this* the fruit of the Consecration which Our Lady promised would bring peace to the world? Please! Every day that we delay there are over 100,000 innocent victims in this war. It is a tragedy that the bishops of the world have the truth about Fatima hidden from them. Yet it is only through them that the wars and violence will stop as Our Lady of Fatima said 'If My requests are granted many souls will be saved and there will be peace'. This, after all, is why we work so hard at getting the consecration done.

"If I, like anyone else, do not do what I can to make the truth known, however small my effort, then each of us doing nothing will have complicity in this debacle, because we knew and did nothing."

And so the Conference would proceed. New arrangements to meet the bureaucratic offensive were being worked out in round-the-clock planning sessions back at the Apostolate. Coralie Graham recalls: "We were determined to provide in a dignified and gracious manner for the bishops who would attend. Thank God for the help of friends of the apostolate like Ray Flores and Louis Acosta, whose fluency in Spanish was crucial to undoing the damage that had been done in Mexico City and to putting the Conference back on track."

November 8: Translators at the back of the Conference Hall in the Maria Isabela Hotel began their simultaneous translation of the opening speeches of the Second International Bishops' Conference. A moment of triumph for the cause of Our Lady of Fatima — and a day for savoring the irony in the October letter from Bishop Flores in which he had so confidently declared:

"...this terminates the possibility of effecting the above-mentioned meeting."

The damage had been severe, but not terminal: Out of the 100-plus bishops who had committed to attending the Conference before the nunciatures applied their pressure, only a fraction would arrive in Mexico City. But their arrival was a testament to the inability of a few Vatican bureaucrats negate to entirely the divine constitution of the Church and the natural rights of the faithful. The curtain had been drawn back for a moment, and at least a few of the bishops had realized that like the Wizard of Oz, the bureaucrats were mere men, actuating the levers of a great machine which generated a lot of intimidating noise and smoke, but had no legitimate power over them. They realized that the only power these men exercised with their great apparatus was the power of fear; and they had overcome that fear.

Father Gruner felt deep sorrow that so many bishops were intimidated by the clique of bureaucrats in the Vatican, and did not attend. Father reflected on this tragedy.

"Although we very carefully conformed to all of the laws that the Church prescribes governing conferences, which are given in the 1983 Code of Canon Law, promulgated by His Holiness, Pope John Paul II, the clique of Vatican bureaucrats still worked to prevent the conference. These officials were in clear defiance of the Code set up by His Holiness.

"Unfortunately, because of the vicious attacks by these bureaucrats, I have been made to look as though I am disloyal to His Holiness.

"On the contrary, I have a deep love and affection for His Holiness, and I regard myself as a 'loyal son of the Pope'. I am in opposition to some people around him today, because I am trying to warn the Pope that he is in grave danger. I cannot forget the dire warning directed to the hierarchy that Jesus gave Sister Lucy at Rianjo."

Father Gruner goes on "As of yet, almost every prophecy given at Fatima has come to pass. The few that are left will happen in the near future. Francisco and Jacinta were both prophesied to die shortly after the apparitions, and they did die. Our Lady prophesied World War II, which would begin during the Pontificate of Pope Pius XI, and it happened as She said. Our Lady of Fatima prophesied a number of other world events which have also come to pass. Clearly, then, this prophecy which warns that the very lives of our Holy Father and the world's bishops are in danger, must be taken very seriously."

§

The Sheraton Maria Isabela on Paseo de la Reforma, in the very center of Mexico City, perfectly befitted the hosting of the Fathers of the Church. Throughout her history, the Church has never let danger or controversy intimidate it. The symbolism of veils, crosses, mitres could not possibly go unrecorded in Mexico. Not too long ago, Catholic clergy could be shot for wearing clerical garb in this city, the way Father Pro and the *Cristeros* were shot during the Mexican Revolution — suddenly, without fanfare. International Masonry had tried awfully hard in the last two centuries to keep the Church out of Mexico. Now, under the mask of modernism, certain malevolent forces came close to succeeding once again, this time maneuvering from inside the Vatican itself.

The lesson was not lost on the bishops who appeared in the hotel lobby in the vestments of their office. In a country where pectoral crosses are rarer than passenger pigeons, the hotel employees, taxi drivers, street vendors, and passers-by stared awestruck at the colors of faith exposed so openly. They had reason to be awestruck — outside the hotel a statue of Gloria Liberty reminds anyone gazing out the Conference window that power in Mexico is in the same hands that once 'tilted the plank' on altar and crown in the France of Robespierre and Fouquier-Tinville.

The presence of these bishops in Mexico City was an eloquent gesture of licit resistance to Church bureaucrats who seem determined to suppress every element of Catholic Tradition. It seems that any bishop today is free to waltz with heretics and polka with infidels, flatter bizarre creeds, grovel before dissidents and allow a homosexual theologians' mafia to deform and disinform his seminaries. Yet bishops had to struggle against fierce Vatican opposition to attend a conference devoted to Our Lady of Fatima. Had it been a conference of heretics, the journey to Mexico would have been unopposed.

For gatherings with heretics, there is freedom of speech and assembly. For conferences on the full message of Fatima, there is bureaucratic repression on a global scale. The disparity is a stunning example of how Ostpolitik is the one "dogma" that certain Vatican bureaucrats are willing to defend with stern measures.

In making the journey to Mexico, these bishops had reflected the fierce yet humble Catholic spirit of Mexico itself. Mexico is a culture and a world unique even among the many countries where the Church has suffered throughout the ages. For 100 years, priests and bishops in this profoundly Catholic nation had been at the head of an endangered species list. The survival of the Church in Mexico is the *history* of Mexico. Bishop Clement Kelly, one of the foremost historians on Mexico, wrote from the Mexican perspective on this ability of the Church always somehow to *survive*:

> "The historian is ever on the watch for Her (the Church's) entrance upon any scene, always certain that, if She is not on the stage where the human drama of life is being played, She is somewhere in the wings, or perhaps, raising or dropping the curtain. She loves the peaceful and quiet parts, does not disdain even comedy, but tragedy is Her very life."[5]

Next door to the Maria Isabela Hotel stands the American Embassy. For days to come, riot police would come and go from the streets, hoping to contain massive protests against California's Proposition 187. This too was fitting — Proposition 187 is all about keeping Mexican Catholics out of the United States. Mexico is peculiar that way. It is both a place from which Catholics seek to escape, and a haven in which the Catholic Faith has survived, despite the depredations of the Masons. Thus it seems that someone is always trying either to keep Catholics out of Mexico or forcibly to return them there.

Father Gruner believed the Conference had to proceed because the tragedy of Mexico's past could well mirror the tragedy awaiting the Church Universal if Our Lady of Fatima were not obeyed. A suggestion of the import of the meeting came at the air terminal in Mexico City when Father Marcel Nault, a priest who always wears his cassock, was confronted by a man wanting to know if priests were now allowed to be seen in public in cassocks in Mexico. When Father Nault answered that yes, they were, the man asking the question gave him a look, which brought to mind the sight of dead *Cristeros* hanging from trees during the Mexican Revolution. Of course, the Revolution against the Church continues in every country in the world. That is why Our Lady came to Fatima. And that is why the bishops had come to Mexico City.

The opening Mass for the Conference started on time at the Shrine of Our Lady of Guadalupe. Ten million pilgrims a year come to pray before the Tilma of Our Lady on which Her miraculous image appears. All of the conflicts, crises, and struggles of the Church fade from mind as that small assembly of bishops lined up to concelebrate Mass. Then something happened. The bishops, upon entering, passed in single file before the image on the Tilma. Anyone who has seen it, passed by it, stood under it, gazed upon it, prayed before it, will tell you: *the image is alive.*

One looks upon it. It looks back. And the world changes. Those bishops who insisted on attending, gathered upon arrival to look up into the living eyes of God's Mother. She looked back at them. Millions have experienced Her glance. A living person looks out from the holy Tilma, subjecting Herself to the scrutiny of the curious for the sake of Her Son. She is indeed alive.

Perhaps it was there at the Shrine, before the Tilma, that the determination was made to go forward with the Conference as if numbers did not matter. From that moment on, the Conference unfolded with ease. As they concelebrated Mass before the Tilma, the bishops were serenaded by specially assembled Mexican musicians, the music of the Mexican people was a reminder that they were at the foot of Tepeyac Hill, the very spot where Our Lady expressed to Juan Diego the will of Heaven itself with such eloquence She caused the great nation of Mexico to resound with Her praises throughout the centuries, regardless of opposition.

Not even the dreadful architecture of the new Shrine of Our Lady of Guadalupe could diminish the unquenchable Marian devotion of the Mexicans who flock there. Like much of the post-conciliar Church architecture, the new shrine is an incomprehensible clash of styles reflecting the conflict of ideologies clawing for supremacy in the Church today. It offers not one reflection of the glories of the Faith, the traditions of the past, the authority of the Church. Not even an echo of the glorious cathedral that was originally the home of the Holy Tilma is represented in the new shrine. It stands, a hollow, empty drum of cement, an appalling concrete tent pitched over the miraculous portrait of Guadalupe.

To the people of Mexico, the mammoth empty shell reflects none of their culture nor their faith which, from its inception, was nurtured by the Tabernacle of the Living Lord. As for the Tabernacle in the shrine, merely to locate it in this architectural wasteland could consume an entire Mexican holiday. Who could have been surprised, therefore, when Rector Schullenberg, who directed and oversaw its construction, was widely reported to have recently declared that Our Lady had never even appeared at Guadalupe.[6] The resulting public outcry would force his removal as Rector — proving once again that sometimes the duty of maintaining the integrity of the Faith devolves to an angry laity, rising in righteous opposition to feckless clerics.

Nevertheless, amidst the coldness of the place, Bishop Salazar's warm words of gratitude and recognition during his first Mass at the Guadalupe Basilica touched the hearts of Father Gruner and his group: "I am here precisely because Our Lady called me through the continual invitation of Father Gruner and his group accompanying him. There is something precious here because what we are seeking is peace."

But no one gathered in the Shrine that day for the opening of the Conference could have foreseen that the Vatican bureaucracy's poison-pen letter was to bring to the floor of the Conference a voice that would cut like a two-edged sword, ripping apart the curtain concealing the forces which had tried to crush the Conference.

The dramatic moment came with the arrival on the Conference floor of the Vatican-based Archbishop Emmanuel Milingo. From this brother of Peter, Cardinal Sanchez and Archbishop Sepe received a fiery public reprimand. Also reprimanded was the Vatican Secretary of State's office, for its heavy-handed use of the Nuncios to browbeat bishops into shunning the conference. Archbishop Milingo issued a powerful testament that Truth cannot be imprisoned in a Nuncio's briefcase.

The deliberate undermining of his own personal and unshakeable loyalty to the Holy Father implied in the letter to the bishops triggered his dramatic statement to the stunned assembly. His ringing commentary was in the form of an authoritatively worded protest delivered not to the Conference but from him as a consecrated bishop of the Church of Rome to those forces that had tried to prevent him from attending.

Brandishing a letter from the Nuncio in Nigeria telling bishops not to attend the Conference, Archbishop Milingo electrified the delegates with an eloquent defense of the prerogatives of the episcopacy, which the bureaucrats seemed to have overlooked. He denounced the letter from the Nuncio as an illicit attempt to take away his freedom of conscience and his freedom to act on his own recognizance. He blasted the letter as an abuse of authority, an insult and a humiliation to all the bishops who received it, and he noted, just for the record, the empty seats reflecting the number of less courageous prelates who had been intimidated into staying away.

Apparently, the much touted 'religious liberty' of Vatican II had been suspended at the hotel Maria Isabela, denied to the consecrated leaders of their own Church. The laity who had been preparing to speak to their pastors were to be denied freedom of speech on the very spot where Our Lady of Guadalupe had expressed the will of Heaven. To all this, Archbishop Milingo, a Church Father with six million followers, brought a crystal clear focus. Holding up the letter for all to see, he zeroed on a major failing of the pastors and laity of the Church today with a litany for the episcopacy in our time: Why are we not making new disciples for Christ? Because the bishops are " ... shaking in their trousers!" he cried. Why are they shaking in their trousers? Because they don't have real authority.

Why don't they have real authority if they are consecrated bishops? Because a clique of bureaucrats in the Vatican, trading on the Church mystique, can, with unjustified letters, completely unchallenged and unchecked, dictate to bishops what they can and cannot do.

How can they get away with it?

Because bishops who resist them can find themselves removed to the backwoods, removed from benefits, reduced in every way imaginable! They are living on suspended authority, he proclaimed angrily. If the certain Vatican officials pull the plug then the bishop is retired. Under such conditions the episcopacy is merely a front for the games of unnamed and unseen bureaucrats.

The bureaucratization of the Holy See was harming the divine constitution of the Church, preventing the bishops from acting according to their conscience and denying the faithful their God-given right to petition the Holy Father for the Consecration of Russia:

> "I also have received thousands of letters that were addressed to the Pope for the Consecration of Russia to the Immaculate Heart of Mary. I myself have brought from my office directly to the Secretariat of State many, many, many of these letters since 1991 ... *I am quite certain that is where they stopped.* I really do not blame the bishops. If some resist, they are just a few. And letters like this will make some of the bishops have no courage."

But what of "obedience" to the "Holy See"? Should not the bishops comply with directives from the Secretariat of State? Archbishop Milingo reminded his brother bishops that Our Lord did not establish Vatican Secretariats to rule over the descendants of His Apostles, and that it was a false obedience which the anti-Fatima bureaucrats were promoting:

> "[T]his letter from the Nuncio telling us not to come to this Conference shows, as a matter of fact, how one can misunderstand

obedience. This [letter] says to those who came here, you were disobedient because an official letter told you not to come. *Then people tremble in their trousers.* What a pity. It [The letter] is a humiliation to a human being who is an apostle—a humiliation intended to prevent him from fulfilling his duties according to his own personality and character... [Y]ou have got someone *suspending your authority* in carrying out your duties and fulfilling your responsibilities ... I am not one whose authority is suspended. Not at all. *I am an apostle...* If this letter represents their way to control us, it means that they don't trust the people to whom they have given authority. And that doesn't do it at all. That is not at all correct. Therefore I am very happy to take this letter signed by the Papal Nuncio to the Holy Father ... I will explain about this, that I have been there [Mexico City], but I take full responsibility for coming here and I accept the consequences. *And I can assure you there will be no consequences.*"[7]

Of course, Archbishop Milingo was right: There would be no consequences for his coming to Mexico City because, in truth, the Vatican bureaucrats had no authority to forbid or to punish his appearance. Where the descendants of the Apostles were concerned, the bureaucrats were in truth as powerless as the Wizard of Oz behind his flimsy curtain. If only his brother bishops would understand this, they could shake off the paralysis of fear which had gripped the Mystical Body of Christ since the Council:

"Not one of us will go to Heaven without holding a brother, a sister. Each and every one of us must step out of the crowd and stand on one's own feet strong enough to be a Christian ... We are acting as if the Catholic Faith were a private affair. That is not true at all. There is still a lot to be done even if the opening for the Consecration is not yet there ... The world must be saved and it must be saved through each one of us."[8]

The scenario Archbishop Milingo depicted in his fiery oration was indeed a bleak one. The Pope is dependent on his bishops. But the bishops have become subservient to the bureaucrats, whose agenda does not include the Message of Fatima. The Pope is therefore at the mercy of those same bureaucrats regarding the Collegial Consecration. The bureaucrats had decreed in Balamand that there would be no conversion of Russia, and the prelates who had endured Communist persecution in Eastern Europe obediently fell into line, somehow failing to notice that the piece of paper which commanded them to forget the Message of Fatima was in reality no command at all, but simply a piece of paper. It could not overrule the decree of Heaven at Fatima.

At the service of the bureaucrats are the Nuncios, transporting their demands and instructions from country to country, to the bishops of the world, as they had after Balamand. The Nuncio has become the henchman of the clique—thus have the words 'diplomacy' and 'diplomat' become ghosts of their former meaning, and the Nuncios mere couriers of an earthly enterprise.

The effect can be deep and long lasting. Consider that it is one thing for officials in Rome to pull the plug on a bishop, but how are they to dispense with priests? Simple. Even unsubstantiated fluff, passed from the hand of a Nuncio to a bishop has the potential to irreparably damage a priest.

How then, in Archbishop Milingo's terms, can bishops make disciples of priests if the Nuncios have them 'shaking in their boots'? How then can priests make disciples out of the people if the priests are "shaking in their boots"?

Is it any wonder the Church is wounded and limping? Under these conditions, a small, privileged clique, completely unthreatened by anyone in the Vatican regardless of what they do, can destroy anyone who stands in their way.[9]

This time, however, Father Gruner's refusal to cancel the conference had uncovered the less than savory practices of intimidation and coercion the Nuncios and their bosses around the world had been practicing. Their purpose being, in the words of Bishop Flores, to "terminate the possibility of effecting the above-mentioned meeting."

In mid-week of the Conference, the bishops concelebrated Mass in the Cathedral of Mexico, which once enshrined the image of Our Lady of Guadalupe. Few locations on earth more aptly mirror the state of the Church today. The building is propped up by scaffolding indicating a much-touted "restoration" and "renewal" that is supposedly under way. But anyone who understands scaffolding can tell at a glance that the cobwebs which cover it mean that the scaffolding is here to stay. The man-made structure it supports has already crumbled into dust; only the falling down remains. It would take a supernatural Hand to restore this once magnificent structure and remove the endless layers of artificial support.

To appreciate the reality of its decay, the bishops had only to walk to the center of the interior and see the pendulum hanging there. It is surely a most fitting symbol of the Church in our time. A gigantic plumb bob, suspended from the ceiling, hangs off kilter, pointing away from the perfect center of gravity. The Church is off her axis.

Yet, even in this collapsing Cathedral, nothing can prevent the faithful from adoring the Blessed Sacrament or walking on their knees to petition for favors. Confessions, a marriage, and baptism were occurring simultaneously amid huge crowds as the bishops entered and departed the Cathedral.

The power of Our Lady is demonstrated with overwhelming force just outside and behind the Cathedral walls. Here stand the fabled 'Halls of Montezuma', on the site of Montezuma's Great Temple where as many as 8,000 human victims a day had their hearts ripped out while they were still alive to appease a demonic force that had seized control of Aztec culture.

On this spot, where the tortured cultures victimized by the Aztecs may well have despaired of rescue, Cortes put an end to human sacrifice. Shortly after, in 1531, Our Lady appeared at Guadalupe. Within a few short years of Her appearance, nine million Mexicans were baptized into the Catholic Faith, replacing within the Church the number of Catholics the arch-heretic Luther had led out of it, in Europe. But the intersecting lessons of Fatima and Mexico do not end there.

Thirty miles north of the city, the pyramids of Teotihuacan stand, as they have since long before those same Aztecs came to central Mexico. History has allotted these structures the names of the Pyramid of the Sun, the Pyramid of the Moon, and joining them, the Avenue of the Dead. It was indeed a sobering moment when the bishops were guided toward a ledge from which they could look down into the enclosure where the demonic priests of that bloodthirsty culture performed human sacrifices.

This is a city of death. It is also a metaphor in stone for our own times, when the ravenous god of progress demands daily flesh and blood from once-Catholic cultures. Suzanne M. Rini, in writing on current-day eugenic experimentation, states the parallel with horrifying clarity:

> "... the human preborn baby, (especially prized by eugenics researchers) is, through the power, will and imagination of the scientist, 'elevated' to the status of a live human sacrifice in return for the demonic reward of the secret knowledge regarding human life itself."[10]

We ought to take a moment to allow the overwhelming nature of this parallel to impress itself upon our hearts. Can there be a more poignant example in the whole history of this century of the effect of the errors of atheistic Russia than the way that evil empire's "legalized" sacrifice of the unborn has spread, as Mary predicted at Fatima, throughout the world—all the more so since the alleged "consecration" of 1984? The Aztec warrior-priest at least indulged in his sacrifice to appease the demands of an imaginary god. Today, the innocent child is slaughtered to appease the demands of a credit-card vacation or a car payment.

The whole truth about Fatima is that Our Lady promised to turn all this around. She laid out simply and clearly how it would be done. The conversion of Russia would come when the Pope and the bishops of the world together consecrated Russia — Russia! — to Her Immaculate Heart. Yet that is the only thing that has *not* been done in the era of Ostpolitik and world ecumenism.

So much for pretending Fatima is over and done with. So much for the word-processed "letters of Sister Lucy", proclaiming the very opposite of what she had said in her own handwriting so many times before. So much for creating the illusion that the consecration of Russia has been done and there remains nothing more at stake in the Fatima story. Clearly the stakes are as high as ever. The few bishops who had attended the Conference in Mexico City knew this well.

In reality, it appears as if the Mexico agenda had proven to be the greatest challenge to the Vatican bureaucracy since the Vatican-Moscow Agreement and the Balamand Agreement provided the Russian Orthodox hierarchy and the KGB a foolproof impediment to the Consecration of Russia.

§

It is one of the trademarks of secret societies is that nobody knows where the order comes from. This time, however, an Archbishop had dragged into the light of day in Mexico City the men behind the campaign to silence one lone priest — a priest who in himself could not have caused them the slightest concern, if not for the content of his message.

Within the closeted precincts where appalling agreements have been forged which betray the mission of the Church, there lays an offspring coiled and ready to poison any movement toward fulfillment of the Fatima requests. It was spawned from the illicit union of atheistic communism and the chaperones of the Bride of Christ. Nothing reveals its character more than the tactics it employed in attempting to derail the Mexico Conference: Intimidation. Denial of the freedoms to assemble and to speak openly without fear. Humiliation of the rightful heirs of authority. And always the veiled threat of reprisal.

We have seen these tactics before. They are the currency of the Communist State, whose crown jewel is Russia, where the citizens of Poland today take weekend sojourns to obtain their abortions — 13 years after the supposed "consecration" of Russia in 1984.

Communism was founded on lies. It was coached by the "father of lies". It lied its way into the Vatican just before the Second Council. And it cannot stop lying.

On a trip to the Pyramid of the Sun during the Conference, so near to one of the greatest victories of Our Lady in history, Her conquest of the hearts of Mexico, a reprise of the Fatima Message was inevitable. It was to Louis XIV, who called himself The Sun King, that Our Lord sent Margaret Mary Alacoque June 17, 1689, with the request that France be consecrated to the Sacred Heart, with the promise that He would save France by this means. The Sun King did not fulfill the request. One hundred years later to the day, his grandson, Louis XVI, was stripped of power and France convulsed under the forces that brought about the French Revolution.

Louis XVI studied clocks. His hobby was assembling them. Louis might be called the Time King. The sound of his clockwork ticking in the old Templar Fortress as he awaited his coach ride to the guillotine must surely be one of the most horrifying sounds in history. The ticking clock of history could be heard again when Our Lord said to Sister Lucy at Rianjo that the Ministers of the Church are following the example of the King of France in delaying the execution of Heaven's command, and that "they will also follow him to misfortune."

Watching these brave bishops from around the world contemplate the pyramids with this message in mind, one thought of Bishop Clement Kelly's great work on the conversion of Mexico, *Blood Drenched Altars*, which enshrines the words of Christopher Hollis on the faith of Saint Thomas More:

> "It is the mark of a Christian ... that he possesses the imagination to jump back across a thousand or two thousand years of history. His whole life is lived under an excitement similar to that of the first disciples when they heard the tomb was empty. To him the news is so amazing that he never forgets to be surprised at it. And ... the news, if true, is so important, that it is mere madness to give one's mind to any other business ..."[11]

Today, certain bureaucrats in Rome are telling us that Catholics must apologize for their past, their present, their future. This means apologizing also for the Message of Fatima, because the Message of Fatima tells us that Christ must be King and Mary His Queen. The world will not tolerate this Message today; we must, therefore, stop proclaiming it, and start apologizing for it. That is why the Message of Fatima must be suppressed wherever it might be spoken loudly enough for the world to hear.

Chapter 15

Fourteen Fabulous Footsteps Forward To Our Lady

When we opened our eyes in the 20th Century to the horror of war, the war that killed St. Pius X, the war throughout which Benedict XV struggled so hard to keep the Church neutral, we were opening our eyes to the horrors of which man is really capable. Our Lady of Fatima imprinted on our souls the words reparation, consecration, and the word "Russia". Is this consecration done? Is it not done? If it is done or not done, what do we do about it? If the Holy Father in 1984, and on a previous occasion, chose to omit the word "Russia", what does that mean? A Canadian teenager who wishes to remain anonymous, in a Wednesday evening study class on encyclicals came to a conclusion.

"I have a solution", he said. "In *Quas Primus*, Pius XI reviewed why specific and great devotions had been inaugurated throughout Church history. When Pius XI discussed the Sacred Heart, he said, "The feast of the burning love of the Sacred Heart was inaugurated to warm men's hearts that had grown cold for lack of love, lack of faith. And he instituted the Feast of Christ the King and the processional of Christ the King, so that Christ would get the acknowledgement of His Divine Kingship as He deserves."

So this teenager said, "The solution is simple — institute a feast of the Immaculate Heart."

He had to be told that Pius XII had instituted a feast to the Immaculate Heart and that Paul VI instituted a Feast to Our Lady of Fatima.

The teenager did not give up. He said, "Well, why don't they make an act of gratitude for all that Our Lady has done for us, every year, on this same day. Consecrate Russia every year on that day. Sooner or later, every bishop in the world will take part as Our Lady wants."

In his fiery address, Archbishop Milingo emphasized that the bishops would co-operate if the Pope made specific demands of them. So far that has not been done.

There could be no doubt, among those watching the progress of the Mexico Conference, that Father Nicholas Gruner has access to some hidden reserve of energy and determination. He, himself, merely refers to his uncanny resiliency as the result of 'undeserved grace'. Knowing the obstacles that had to be overcome to launch this week of bishops' talks, one would have expected him to be sidelined by the need for some peace and quiet, even perhaps to take the first day as one of rest and allow someone else to open that day's sessions. But he was at the helm from the first moment to the last never at a loss for co-ordinating the interests of the bishops on hand. It was a member of the laity who placed the whole conference in perspective for the average Catholic in pews around the globe.

"Since Vatican II, the modern Church has been playing down the Message of Fatima," said New York delegate Jean Fioretti. "When I was in school, I had 12 years of Dominican teachers. Every year we heard the Message of Fatima. The Message of Fatima through the 50's was very important. We spent the '50's waiting for the Secret to be opened in 1960. Then it never happened.

"There's been a great loss of faith since then. Catholicism is 'easy' now. People have become, in fact, lazy. We don't hear anything anymore about sacrifice, only about celebration and mercy. Of course, the mercy of God is ever available, but you no longer hear about the penance God asks for to win His mercy.

"My generation was raised to listen to the priest and the nuns, to listen to the Church. After Vatican II we were told we had to 'start thinking for ourselves', as if we hadn't been doing that all along. It became very hard to disregard what the priest was saying.

"Our church with its modern look is very sterile. They forget that we're human and humans have to have things appeal to their senses — music, flowers, candles. One can pray anywhere but oh, how helpful it is to have the beautiful."

One of the great sources of beauty for the faithful in this century was the whole Fatima story, from beginning to end it had beauty, warmth, love, hope, and it was peopled by characters whose personalities stayed with you all your life.

Regarding the conference, Jean Fioretti remarked, "The first few days, there was a natural reticence — nobody wanted to say too much or make any waves. But all were very receptive to the Fatima focus. It was successful because we don't have these things being said anywhere else in the establishment Church. Being human, we know all these things but we forget them.

"It's so important to know there are others out there who believe as we do. Again, being human, it's a kind of fearful thing to feel so alone. You think, is there something wrong with me? Why am I the only one who still says my Rosary?"

The opportunity to answer that need for the laity worldwide was at hand, front and center of the conference hall. Father Gruner took full advantage of it. It was his skill in drawing upon the best in all the personalities present in the room that allowed this small beleaguered representation of the world's episcopacy to hammer out a veritable catechism of Fatima. Under his chairmanship, the bishops crafted 'fourteen' unique resolutions for the purpose of advancing the cause of Our Lady of Fatima. These Fourteen Resolutions, represent a new treasure for Our Lady, diamonds for Her crown, crystallized under colossal pressure. They read as follows:

The 14 Fatima Resolutions

I/We hereby agree to the Resolutions drafted and agreed to by the bishops, priests and laypeople at the Second Bishops Conference for World Peace held in Mexico City on November 8-14, 1994 as indicated below. I, the undersigned, in my personal capacity, responding to the inspiration of Our Lady of Fatima to work for peace, have read the resolutions that I have signed and agree with each one's doctrinal content and personally undertake to see that truth contained in each resolution be lived and any undertaking stated therein I shall personally do.

In order to bring about peace and proper ordering of man to God as individuals, in society and in the Church, I hereby make the following resolutions and encourage men and women of good will around the world to join us.

1. We the undersigned individual laypeople, priests, bishops, in our personal capacity, hereby profess our loyalty to the Holy Roman Catholic Magisterium and the august person of His Holiness Pope John Paul II and above all to the Catholic Faith as handed down by the dogmatic councils, tradition, and the approved creeds, not limited to but including the Apostle's Creed, the Nicene Creed, the Athanasian Creed, the Creed of the First Vatican Council and the Credo of the people of God of Pope Paul VI and those doctrines taught Magisterially by the Second Vatican Council.

"Magisterially" — That is, those doctrines that are taught infallibly by the Ordinary and Universal Magisterium of the Church in Vatican II documents.

2. We, as loyal Roman Catholics, as expressed above in resolution number one, also believe that world peace will not be brought about except through obedience to the full meaning and message of Our Lady of Fatima.

3. We undertake to do what we can and we believe it is part of our duty of state to bring about the Triumph of the Immaculate Heart through the specific plans and requests She made to us in the public and prophetic Message of Fatima.

4. It is our duty according to our state to do all we can and tell those we can to thereby make the full message of Our Lady of Fatima known as Jesus Himself has commanded, despite any difficulties.

5. We the undersigned, mindful of Our Lady of Fatima's request, undertake to personally pray the Rosary every day and to strongly promote this devotion to Our Lady, to those around us.

6. We the undersigned, mindful of Our Lady of Fatima's request that we, each of us, wear the Brown Scapular of Mount Carmel, undertake to personally wear the Scapular and to promote the Brown Scapular among the faithful and men of goodwill that God puts on our path.

7. We the undersigned, recognizing that Our Lady of Fatima and God Himself want to establish devotion in the world to the Immaculate Heart of Mary; and further recognizing that Our Lady and Our Lord especially want us to embrace this devotion; we therefore, personally undertake to make the personal act of consecration to Our Lady's Immaculate Heart. We will also promote it to those God puts on our path.

8. Since Jesus and Mary have so ardently desired the practice of the 5 First Saturdays and Communions of Reparation to the Immaculate Heart of Mary, we personally undertake to do these Five First Saturdays as requested and explained by Our Lady of Fatima and Jesus Himself. We also undertake to promote the Five First Saturdays to the faithful Catholics God puts on our path.

9. Since Our Lady of Fatima wants the Third Secret to be published to the world, we the undersigned, until it is officially revealed, will endeavor to read, study and distribute knowledge of the Third Secret — from the best sources available.

10. We also respectfully petition for the release of the actual words of Our Lady's Third Secret according to Her instructions.

11. Since Jesus and Mary in the Fatima Message make it clear that it is only by means of the solemn and public Consecration of specifically RUSSIA, RUSSIA to the Immaculate Heart of Mary by all the Catholic bishops together with the Holy Father on the same day at the same hour, that true peace will be given to the world: we the undersigned undertake to bring about the long desired Act of Consecration. Such actions (to cause this Act of Consecration) are not limited to, but may include: Prayers; Rosaries; Sacrifices offered to Jesus and Mary for this intention; to attend seminars, symposiums, conferences; to hold such conferences to promote this Consecration; to circulate books, videos, audio tapes to laypeople, priests and bishops to promote this Consecration.

12. We the undersigned, will strive to make known those prophecies that as far as we can ascertain, contain parts of the 3rd Secret which are found in Sacred Scripture and in Church approved apparitions, as Cardinal Ratzinger indicated in his interview with Vittorio Messori, published in November 1984 *Jesus* Magazine.

13. Inasmuch as God wants all men to be saved and come to the knowledge of the truth, and inasmuch as in an approved apparition of Our Lady of 1838 — Our Lady revealed the Green Scapular of the Immaculate Heart of Mary — especially for the preservation among Catholics and the spread of the Catholic Faith to non-Catholics; and inasmuch as God wants to establish devotion to the Immaculate Heart throughout the world; we the undersigned resolve when opportune to propagate as widely as possible among men, women and children of the world, the Green Scapular and encourage others to do the same and to pray the prayer indicated therein for the conversion of all non-Catholics and the preservation of all Catholics in the Catholic Faith which is so necessary in order to save one's soul.

14. That in the light of our desire to please Our Lady, that the Consecration of Russia be renewed on the Feast of the Immaculate Conception — December 8th, each year by the Pope and all the Catholic Bishops of the world; we the undersigned, respectfully ask for this Consecration of Russia to be done on the above date.

§

On the final day of the Conference, as its Fourteen Resolutions were printed up and distributed for all to see, there was a trace in the air of music—festive, familiar, a sound the bishops had encountered after leaving the shrine of Guadalupe to climb Tepeyac Hill—a mariachi marimba band, from somewhere within the hotel. The Virgin of Guadalupe, it seemed, was coming to them.

Before the closing of the Conference, Father Gruner was presented with a life-sized crucifix purchased on the Shrine grounds. Looking up into Christ's eyes on this crucifix gave one a small taste of His Agony and Passion: exquisitely painted, not skimping on the Blood as most modern day artists do; transparent tears fill His eyes and spill over down His cheek; His eyes conveying an intense plea for our repentance.

The magnificent Crucifix was presented to Father Gruner with few but very meaningful words: "You have carried many crosses, Father; we felt you would not mind one more." Perhaps Father Gruner and the Apostolate had participated in some small way in the Passion of Christ, as all Catholics are called upon to do. When he returned to Canada, Father Gruner had the Crucifix erected in the Fatima Center Chapel, literally cutting a hole in the roof to accommodate its magnificent presence.

Opposition to Our Lady throughout the Church today is formidable; but the Virgin's defenders deflect the blows gladly, because they know the blows are really aimed at Her. Yet always the question remains—how much punishment can a man absorb? Surely after Mexico anyone would decamp and rest. Take a strategic retreat. Yes, Father Gruner and the members of the Apostolate would do that. And when they were rested, then what? Surely not another campaign ...

Chapter 16

Window On The Arena

Rome. July 3. 1995. 6:30 a.m. The Bridge of Angels has carried countless armies across the Tiber over the centuries. They have strolled, strutted and goose-stepped onto the cobblestones before Castel St. Angelo with remarkable frequency, carrying onto the north bank of the river all manner of ferocious determination. But it is doubtful if even one of their number did not sense a dent in his resolve when the ancient street beneath his feet deposited him on the edge of St. Peter's Square. The vision in marble staring back at him represents the most awesome power on earth, the dome of the Fisherman, the incomparable St. Peter's, the earthly intersection of Time and Eternity.

To comprehend the character of Father Nicholas Gruner, one can do no better than to see him, alone, an army of one, stepping off the Bridge of Angels, and contemplating the dome before him. It cannot be said that he too is not intimidated. No one born of woman could resist recognizing his smallness before this treasured dome rising above the very center of all Christendom. The old Borgo that once obliterated the view of the dome from the Bridge of Angels is no longer there. Today the Via Della Conciliazione, designed at Mussolini's request in response to Pius XI signing the Lateran Pact of 1929, gives a clear view of the breathtaking outline of the historical center of Christianity. Bramanti, Michelangelo, Della Porta knew how to intimidate.

Rome has been civilization's center of gravity for so long that, should it cease to exist, civilization would be knocked off its axis. Countless intersecting prophecies of the end times do predict the earth being knocked off its axis. Some interpreters of the Fatima phenomenon read the Miracle of the Sun as a depiction of that coming catastrophe, when order will be restored to the globe through the intercession of the Virgin.

This July morning, the rising sun warms the dome with a golden stroke of the brush. In ancient days, the Romans watched the sun pass overhead on its way to slumbering the night away in Lusitania. Today, the sun watches Romans pass from Christianity back to a long-slumbering paganism. The Church has been knocked off its axis and is rolling crazily out of orbit. Only Christ can save her. When He comes to do so, as He promised He would, He will come from the East, like a flash of sunlight. That is why throughout its history, churches were built facing eastward, for Christ was their hope. Then modern liturgists turned everything around. Now, when Christ returns, the priests will not see Him coming. They will have their backs turned, paying tribute to "the dignity of man"; for according to what can be glimpsed through the modernist theologians' fantasy threshold, man, not God, is the new hope.

The neo-modernist debacle of the past 35 years reminds us of the warning given by Pope Pius XII in light of the Message of Fatima:

> "Suppose, dear friend, that Communism (Russia and Russia's errors, in Fatima terms) was only the most visible of the instruments of subversion to be used against the Church and the traditions of Divine Revelation. *I am worried by the Blessed Virgin's messages to Lucy of Fatima* ... A day will come when the civilized world will deny its God, when the Church will doubt as Peter doubted. She will be tempted to believe that man has become God."[1]

Father Nicholas Gruner is not shaken at the prospect of being in this city of cities. He lived here during his early seminary days and afterward, and knows the sounds, the smells, the pace of the streets. He knows also that the Church was put in the hands of Italians, among other reasons, because of their unrelenting ability to endure the vicissitudes of time.

This day Father Gruner shares a goodly portion of that patience. He has come to Rome on a mission as bold as any he has ever pursued since the day he first offered himself to Our Lady of Fatima. He moves through the streets as one who knows he has no time to lose. That, of course, is the ultimate reality — there is no time left. Not for the world, not for Rome itself.

Christ promised that when He returned, it would be terrible, with all the power and might of Heaven armed for battle, more terrifying than the sun falling from the sky at the Cova da Iria. Mankind has this escape — the Virgin. Just as at Fatima, when the sun obeyed Her command, the Virgin in the end will bring us to safety. For She and She alone is our threshold to Christ.

All of Father Gruner's efforts over the years in promoting the consecration of Russia had brought to bear on his life and his Apostolate the full weight of the bureaucracy that plans and labors in the offices and corridors and meeting rooms circling the great piazza of St. Peter's. For centuries the famous obelisk now standing in the center of that piazza marked the spot where St. Peter was crucified upside down in A.D. 67 in the area where now stands the sacristy. Then it was moved to center stage of the new St. Peter's landscape, carved out of Vatican Hill in the 16th Century.

Today the obelisk makes of the cobblestone surface of the piazza a great sundial. Upon the rising of the sun, the shadow of the obelisk points directly at the balcony from which the reigning Pontiff has delivered his New Year's blessing *Urbi et Orbi* for the last four hundred years. Atop the obelisk stands a cross which contains a sizable portion of the True Cross brought back from Jerusalem by St. Helena. Each day, the shadow of the True Cross is drawn over the cobblestones by the passing overhead of the sun. Many a penitent pilgrim has deliberately positioned himself motionless in prayer in the piazza where the shadow of the True Cross would roll ever-so-slowly over his legs, arms, shoulders, bowed head.

When the shadow of the True Cross leans exactly north-northwest it points directly at the window of the Papal apartment, known simply as "the Pope's window"—second from the end on the top floor. Each Sunday, the Holy Father stands in full view of the pilgrims gathered below and leads them in the Angelus from that window. The daily shadow on the window reminds us that inside is a man to whom Christ said: "Whatsoever you bind on earth shall be bound in Heaven; whatsoever you loose on earth shall be loosed in Heaven."[2] For, yes, that man is Peter.

If the man behind that window were the only man on earth who could bind and loose, all men who understood the nature of sin would come to this piazza and never again leave it. Alas, in today's Church the true nature of sin is scarcely understood by a large number of its members. Still, the man who resides behind the window remains the earthly head of legions of men to whom Christ, through Holy Orders, extended the same power to bind and loose in the Confessional that He had given to Peter. Father Nicholas Gruner is but one of them; but there in the shadow of the obelisk, he is as much at home as any priest who has walked these cobblestones over the centuries, looking up at the window.

During World War II, Pius XII looked out the window at a city in the grip of Nazi rule. On February 11, 1929, Pius XI looked out the window on the anniversary of the first appearance of the Immaculate

Conception at Lourdes, toward the Lateran Palace where Mussolini and the Pope's envoy, Cardinal Gaspari, were signing the Lateran Pact which ended the Roman Question, the relationship between the government of Italy and the Holy See, and sixty years of the Pope being a "prisoner of the Vatican". But that piece of paper did not end the phenomenon of the Pope as prisoner.

Many Catholics today believe that the current Pope is a "prisoner of Vatican II". The commitments made to Ostpolitik and world ecumenism by his predecessors and their bureaucrats have trapped him in a never ending round of concession-making to non-Catholic and non-Christian peoples. Catholics may differ in their view of the ecumenical venture of John Paul II, but what is not in dispute is the present day crisis of faith around the world.

This much was admitted without ambiguity by the Cardinal Prefect of the Holy Office, which is now called the Congregation for the Doctrine of the Faith. In 1985, for the first time in the history of the Church, the man in charge of defending Her doctrine for the Pope published a book explicitly and repeatedly stating that the faith of Catholics is under severe attack and is weakening around the world. *The Ratzinger Report* was published in a number of languages and sold over 1 million copies. No one in the know has refuted Ratzinger's thesis. According to Father Alonso and Frère Michel this crisis of faith is the main subject of the Third Secret of Fatima. It is certain that many Catholics agree that the looming crisis in the Church and the world is the direct result of not fulfilling the precise requirements of Our Lady.

Even so, for Father Nicholas Gruner, there has always been hope that his efforts on Her behalf, however small, will help bring the desperately needed about — face. After all, Our Lord did not say His Church would last until the Age of Aquarius and then be given away by resident aquarians. He said it would last until the end of time.

It was directly below the Pope's window, on May 13, 1981, just a little east of north by northwest, that John Paul II felt Mehmet Ali Agca's bullet tear into his body. That bullet, taken from the abdomen of John Paul II, now rests in the crown of the statue of Our Lady of Fatima standing at the capelhina in the Cova da Iria on the exact spot She hallowed with Her presence in 1917. What greater verification could the faithful need that the Message of Fatima and the crisis in the Church intersect in time and space?

On July 3, 1995, as Father Nicholas Gruner moves through Rome on a private mission, the shadow of the True Cross on the obelisk in the piazza pointed at the Pope's window: 12:30 noon. Father Gruner is very aware on this day that the Congregation for the Clergy in the Vatican, a few paces from the obelisk, has been charged with the duty to uphold the rights of priests against the abuse of ecclesiastical power. And yet an abuse of power had emanated from that very Congregation against him. Not once, but at least six times. What are Diocesan priests to do when it is the bureaucrats in that same Congregation who persecute them? It is in the defense of priests whose rights are not defended, that Father Gruner goes on this mission.

A brisk fifteen minutes' walk from the obelisk, across the Bridge joining Via St. Pius X, down the Corso Vittorio, is the Piazza della Cancelleria. There, the Apostolic Signatura meets to consider appeals from the Congregation for the Clergy. There Father Gruner had made his appeal from the self-affirming decree of Cardinal Sanchez and Archbishop Sepe. What he did not know on that day in July, 1995, was that the Signatura had already implemented the next phase of *The Plan* for his destruction; the punishment for his proclamation of the Heavenly Message which had been "overruled" by the theological negotiators at Balamand.

The decree of the Apostolic Signatura, dated May 15, 1995, would soon be leaked to the anti-Fatima forces. It would appear in *Soul* magazine, the publication of an organization once known as The Blue Army, but which had recently taken to calling itself "The World Apostolate of Fatima", as if to hide its embarrassment over once having been a part of the outdated Church Militant. *Soul,* now duly "approved" by "ecclesiastical authority", had become the mouthpiece of the forces which had produced the Vatican-Moscow Agreement and the sell-out at Balamand. *Soul* was delighted to announce that the Signatura had agreed with Cardinal Sanchez and Archbishop Sepe: there was indeed "just cause" to consign Father Gruner to oblivion in the Diocese of Avellino. He had, after all, "failed" to find another bishop to accept him. No matter that the "failure" had been orchestrated by Cardinal Sanchez and Archbishop Sepe themselves, in an arrogant suspension of proper canonical procedure. *Soul* was not interested in the justice of the matter. The important thing was to declare Father Gruner a non-person, so that the New Fatima, the "Fatima Lite" of the Carlos Evaristo pamphlet, could be peddled to a narcotized public in place of the real thing.

The decree of the Signatura would not be the end of Father Gruner—not yet. His case would return to the Signatura on new grounds.

And there would be further complications to *The Plan.* Those complications would lead to further canonical appeals which could not be so easily disposed of. It would seem as though Our Lady were politely tripping Father Gruner's pursuers, sending them sprawling to the ground each time they were about to lay hold of their prey.

Long ago, at the crossroads in old Jerusalem where the thoroughfare coming in through the Damascus gate goes toward the market place, and intersects with the Via Dolorosa, Our Lord met His Mother. There Mary gave the future priesthood of the Church a gift of Her own will and action to keep them free of doubt for all time. She went up the hill to Calvary after Him. There's only one way for today's priest to know for sure which way to go in today's Church. Stay with Mary. She has no doubts about which way to go. And stay close to those priests who visibly and openly serve Her. Father Gruner was in Rome in Her service.

On the lower floors below the Pope's window, behind the Bronze Doors, lay the Vatican Secretariat of State which had long ago taken notice of the Canadian priest with the worldwide following. This day its power seemed even more overwhelming, because on this day the Pope was out of town. It is always unsettling to know that the Pope is out of town. There is about the papacy a sense that Peter should always be here, where the Church of Christ on Vatican Hill rises from the spot where the blood of Peter soaked the soil of Nero's Circus. The Pontiff will return for the Wednesday General Audience, but his momentary absence prompts the question, "What is a Pontiff?"

"A bridge builder," wrote Anne O'Hare McCormick in her *Vatican Journals*. "For he comes from farther back in time and sees farther into the future than other leaders", at the service of what she calls, "...the only unbroken tradition left in the world."

This bridge builder, John Paul II, knows that he has not yet fulfilled the command to consecrate Russia. On March 25, 1984, after he consecrated the world to the Immaculate Heart, the Holy Father said twice to Our Lady and to thousands of the Faithful that, *although* he had consecrated the world, still he had not done what Our Lady of Fatima commanded to be done. This was openly repeated on the 26th of March in the official Vatican newspaper, *L'Osservatore Romano**. It was this fact, more than the injustice of his particular case, which had brought Father Gruner to Rome for the job he had to do:

Not only by personal observation and reflection, but also by reliable reports of the Pope's own words, Father Gruner is convinced that the Pope feels he needs more support from the Catholic bishops of the world before he can actually consecrate Russia as Our Lady asked at Fatima. For this reason, Father Gruner had sought and received confirmations from more than 1500 bishops that they supported Our Lady's command. If the Pope gave the order to consecrate Russia, these bishops would

* (See photograph of this article in the photo section.)

obey, of that Father Gruner was certain. It was the bureaucrats, the technicians of Balamand and the Vatican-Moscow Agreement, who were striving to keep from the bishops the whole truth about Fatima; it was they who had convinced the Holy Father that his bishops would not obey. How does one penetrate this phalanx of bureaucrats to tell the Pope that his bishops will obey him?

Father Gruner reached a print shop within walking distance of the Vatican and made his way to the back rooms where layout and design are finalized. He spread out, before the workers, the text of the letter he had carried to Rome. He had picked them especially for their skill and professionalism, and their ability with languages, for this letter was intended for His Holiness, John Paul II himself. It was not intended for mailing. It would appear as "An Open Letter To The Pope" in a two-page spread in Rome's largest daily newspaper, *Il Messaggero.* And the deadline was fast approaching.

To catapult over the heads of the bureaucracy surrounding the Pope has been a fantasy engaged in by many a priest over the centuries. Few have ever succeeded. Father Nicholas Gruner knew that he must, for he was all too aware that he represented not only the membership in his Apostolate, but the entire beleaguered priesthood of the Catholic Church. The Open Letter would serve not only his mission, but countless priests who were being ground up in the bureaucrats' inexorable machinery of intimidation and reprisal.

Father Gruner was not daunted by the gamble. A priest, he always insists, is within his rights to demand that the law be upheld. So too are the laity. Two ecumenical councils of the Church have indeed defined as a doctrine of the Faith-namely, the right to petition the Pope for redress of just grievances in the Church.[2] But how does one exercise this God-given right when the Pope is immured in layers of bureaucracy which filter out the pleas of the faithful? The Open Letter seems the only way.

And so, on a hot July day in Rome, the leverage of the press is about to be employed to plead a case to "the final judge". No one, not even His Holiness, could overlook a request so public, though the format of the appeal was bound to trod on the feet of nearly everyone in the Secretariat of State, the Congregation for the Clergy and the Apostolic Signatura.

Father Gruner's right to do so has never been in doubt. "It is Catholic dogma that Catholic priests are members of the hierarchy and our God-given rights in the Natural Law cannot be morally or legally taken away by anyone, not even by a bishop's decree."

Nor would the false "obedience" to ecclesial bureaucrats which had surrendered Romania and the Ukraine to the dictates of the Balamand Statement prevent Father Gruner from petitioning his Pope in this way. He would later explain that his belief in the right, and duty, of licit resistance to abuse of authority in the Church had been formed in him during his days at seminary:

> "A Monsignor doing his doctorate in philosophy talked about how the situation in the Church could be turned around. 'All it would take,' he said, 'is one medium sized diocese, five pastors or so, to say: "We will not go along. We will not have Communion in the hand. We're going to preach Catholic doctrine." If just *five* of them took a united stand the bishop would find it very hard to touch them. He could move one around, punish him, but *five* of them standing united?' The persecution of five parish priests who are standing up for the Magisterium would be manifested very clearly. If several dioceses did the same thing, there would build a will to resist corruption. But too many priests today make a virtue out of weakness, citing 'obedience','humility' and 'docility' as excuses for not standing up for God and His truth. David, in the Scriptures, says: *'be angry* and sin not'. There is a time for holy anger. Anger not for ourselves but for God. If priests realized that, they would stand up and do their duty..."
>
> "...Their duty to the common good is greater than the average person. They are members of the hierarchy and have an obligation to not be silent like dogs, an obligation to speak out and not worry that certain people find it politically incorrect."

Throughout the day Father Gruner comes and goes from the back room, studying proofs, giving them a meticulous scanning. A day is consumed by attention to minuscule details: translating, re-translating, spell-checks, leaving not one punctuation mark to chance. The Open Letter is finally put to bed. It is late evening. Daylight lingers late in the sky over Rome. Time to walk where saints and apostles have walked.

§

St. Paul's Outside the Walls, Rome. Midnight. For centuries this location defended Rome from attacks from the sea. It perfectly befits, therefore, the site for the massive enclosure named after the Apostle to the Gentiles. In the distinctive Roman moonlight, the hooded statue of St. Paul stares directly at the silhouette of a cassocked priest at the gate. Slivers of moonglow outline the two edges of St Paul's upright broadsword.

Two thousand years of efforts by dissenters from the True Faith have failed to imprint on mens' minds the image of St. Paul as an opponent of Peter's. Other religions have tried to adopt Paul as their very own; Protestant efforts to make him their Peter have consistently come to naught. The unshakable integrity of Saul of Tarsus resists all attempts to paint him as disloyal. When he challenged Peter, it was out of love for the purity of the faith, not in opposition to it.

St. Paul's Outside the Walls is a fitting place for Father Nicholas Gruner to contemplate his priesthood, his past as a seminarian, his present as a promoter of the Fatima Message, and the future that he will have to endure, now that the 'Open Letter to the Pope' has gone to press. He, too, has had his loyalty to the Pope impugned by his critics. He directs those critics to examine his record. He readily admits that, so long as God permits, there will be one unalterable purpose to his Apostolate—the collegial consecration of Russia to the Immaculate Heart of Mary. In spite of endless criticism, and the risk of losing his audience, he has continued for two decades his repetition of the words "the consecration of Russia", hoping to keep that divine imperative before the minds of the faithful and the hierarchy.

His choice of approach has been misconstrued as an "attack" on the Holy Father. There are reasons to believe that John Paul II does not see it that way at all. There are reasons to believe that Father Gruner has been surreptitiously targeted by the bureaucracy for extinction *precisely because* the Holy Father harbors sympathy for the work of Father Nicholas Gruner. Father Gruner explained it this way :

> "We are on a collision course, the Apostolate of Our Lady of Fatima and the bureaucracy. Either the Apostolate will back down and cease proclaiming the Fatima Message or the Secretary of State will stop promoting the Vatican-Moscow Agreement and the betrayal at Balamand."

The Vatican-Moscow Agreement and the Balamand Statement have given the most voracious hunter in history an open field in which to pursue the hunted. Men of blood, atheistic power mongers, seek to victimize and control the whole of the world. Abortion, socialism, liquidation of the middle class, God excluded from public affairs, immorality, immodesty.

A new world order with a one world religion is the goal of these internationalists. They are dead of soul, and work to impose their godlessness, their coldness, their emptiness on all of us. In their language, they want to proclaim the world "God-free". What they really want is to tyrannize the rest of us, but as long as we have God, we have our God-given rights. If they succeed in taking faith in God away from us, then they succeed in enslaving us. The number one bastion of defense, the Catholic Church, has suffered insidious attacks by infiltrators as St. Jude warns in his Epistle. Those interlopers have lowered the drawbridges, drained the moats and left the flock very vulnerable.

Whether the hunter will succeed in capturing and killing all but a remnant of the prey will, of course, depend finally upon the correspondence of the man in the pew with the graces he is given. In any other century but this one, perhaps, that might have been a reliable ingredient in the equation. But the man in the pew is no longer encouraged to be Roman Catholic. He is being told that he must apologize for 2,000 years of Catholic history, learn to have more respect for Martin Luther, forget his liturgical heritage, assume personal responsibility for the holocausts of madmen, and stop speaking of conversion to the one true religion. That he is expected to continue to believe in and remain loyal to a Church which could have insisted upon such disastrous reversals as these, surely ranks as one of the great enigmas in recorded time.

As Sister Lucy said, "The devil is in the mood for engaging in a decisive battle against the Virgin. And a decisive battle is the final battle where one side will be victorious and the other side will suffer defeat." Each man must choose sides. If he chooses the side of God, his weapons have already been issued to him. The Rosary, The Scapular of Mt. Carmel. Daily sacrifices. The Five First Saturdays. But the climate in today's Church is not conducive to the promotion of devotions such as these. Some Cardinals, bishops, priests shun anything that smacks of pre-1960 piety. That the Rosary, daily sacrifices and the Five First Saturdays are uniquely Roman Catholic practices makes them totally unwelcome in certain quarters of the Church. In today's ecumenical Disney park, anything goes as long as it is not Roman Catholic.

Bureaucratic anger at the placing of the ad in *Il Messaggero* would be ignited because it had provided John Paul II with an opportunity to intervene and settle one of the most contentious battles raging in the Church today. And therein lies the cause of so much of the bureaucratic opposition to Father Nicholas Gruner: such a show of authority by John Paul II would cure, at one stroke, the ecclesiastical paralysis resulting from the fatally flawed principle of collegiality operating through bureaucracy.

Retaliation for the printing of the Open Letter will surely be aimed hot and heavy at Father Gruner by the unseen bureaucrats in the Vatican. They will go as far as they can, as long as they don't risk losing their anonymity.

"In the end Our Lady will triumph," Father Nicholas Gruner repeats again and again. "But enough people must be on the right side. If you are not on Jesus and Mary's side, you are on the side of the Evil One and his earthly allies."

Down along the embankment from the grilled entrance to the courtyard of St. Paul's Outside the Walls, several cars of midnight revelers enjoy the late night and one another's company. As Father Gruner walks back to his car, eyes pick up his cassocked figure walking through the moonlight. For a brief moment he stands motionless, an icon of the besieged priesthood of Our Lady in today's tormented Church. The cassock bridges the centuries linking together those countless men who have exhausted their lives in the order of Melchisedech. He is just one in the long line of those who undertook untold risks to serve their Master, and spread His precious Word.

Saint Isaac Jogues, a veritable mirror reflecting the daring character of St. Paul himself, gave his life for the baptism of native Americans. Nothing could deter him from returning to his Indians again and again, even though they despised him so much that he was made to curl up and sleep with their dogs. Even while Father Jogues was in North America, it was known throughout Europe that his captors had chewed his fingers off. They would chew down to one knuckle, let it heal, then chew down to another. Rescued by Protestant Dutch merchants, he made his way back to France. Upon being received in the foyer of his former Jesuit residence, he was bundled up against the cold, arms held tight undercover for warmth. Upon hearing that a missionary had returned from America and was in the foyer, the Superior came running into the room and cried aloud asking if the stranger had any news to relate about Isaac Jogues. Father Jogues did not answer. He merely unfolded his arms and extended toward the Superior the stumps of his fingers. The Superior fell on his knees, kissing the mangled hands, and showered the priest with his tears. Shortly after, Father Jogues returned to his Indians and to his martyrdom.

There is no happiness in today's world for the priests of Mary. She did not promise them any. Bitten off little by little each day in this era of the "dignity of man" is the dignity of God's ordained. Nowhere in today's world can the Marian priest be sure of a welcome. Not even in the Church they serve. That is all part of the "persecution of the Church" that was spoken of at Fatima in 1917. No one who truly understands the Fatima Message should be surprised at it. Persecution from within would not have occurred to anyone before 1960. But after the last thirty-five years of turmoil, lies and betrayal, no one any longer looks exclusively outside the Church for the enemy.

From St. Paul's Outside the Walls to St. Cecilia's in Trastevere is a short drive that leads through the ruins left behind when the Church of

Christ conquered pagan Rome. Outside the gate of St. Cecilia's, the sounds of Trastevere remind the tourist that there is a Left Bank in every city that has a "soul". How perfect that the great Saint who was martyred here should be the Church's patron of music.

Here in this church is where it really all began for Father Nicholas Gruner. It was here that his father, Malcolm, was instantly converted to Catholicism so many decades ago, and it was here that St. Cecilia was sealed inside a steam room to suffocate, or so the persecutors of the faithful virgin hoped. When the door was unsealed to ascertain her fate, there she sat, breathing freely, a mystery memorialized by artists who so often place a calliope in her hands. So she was beheaded. But she survived the first two strokes of the axe, living for two days during which she dictated her spiritual and legal legacy. Then she died. Sculptors depict her prone, offering her throat to the blade yet one more time.

For nearly six years, Father Gruner had survived the steam room which the bureaucrats had placed him in. Now that the Open Letter was about to be published, the question remained, would he be able to survive the axe blade that the anti-Fatima bureaucrats were sharpening for him?

Chapter 17

The Letter

On the morning of July 12, 1995, readers in Italy of *Il Messaggero*, the largest daily in Rome, are stunned to open their newspaper and see:

OPEN LETTER TO POPE JOHN PAUL II
and to all Catholics and to all peace-loving men

Most Holy Father . . .

One year ago, planning began for a great Conference of Catholic bishops to be held in November 1994 in Mexico City, Mexico. The purpose of this Conference was to privately bring together our Church leaders to discuss the Message of Our Lady of Fatima and its unique Heaven-ordained role in the search for peace in our troubled world. As Our Lady said at Fatima, "If My requests are granted many souls will be saved and there will be peace."

As organizers of this Conference, we were guided first and foremost by the teachings of our Holy Mother, the Church, especially those contained in documents of the Second Vatican Council pertaining to the rights and obligations of the laity. As Your Holiness knows, the Dogmatic Constitution on the Church enjoins the Faithful to "disclose their needs and desires" to their pastors and states that "by reason of the knowledge, competence or pre-eminence which they have, the laity are empowered — indeed sometimes obliged — to manifest their opinion on those things which pertain to the good of the Church." (*Lumen Gentium* IV.37; See also the New Code of Canon Law 212.

Your Own Advice, Holy Father

Moreover, in all our planning, Holiness, we were constantly mindful of the advice you yourself had offered in the presence of Cardinal Wyszynski in 1980 that those seeking the fulfillment of Our Lady's Fatima requests (especially the Consecration of Russia as a condition of world peace) should go to the bishops first and seek their support and assistance. From 1983 to 1993 we have written all the Catholic bishops numerous times about this matter, as well, we called and met with a number of bishops, particularly at our first Bishops Conference at Fatima in 1992.

As a result of all these efforts we have obtained the support of 700 Catholic bishops from every part of the world for the consecration of specifically Russia to the Immaculate Heart of Mary. But still it seemed we had not done enough.

And so, in the spring and early summer of 1994, in a pious and humble spirit, we wrote again to all the bishops of the world and invited them to come together in a private setting near the Shrine of Our Lady of Guadalupe in Mexico to openly and freely discuss the Message of Fatima. Through the generosity of many thousands of Faithful souls committed to the goals of this Conference, we were also able to offer the bishops the full financial assistance they needed to travel and stay in Mexico.

Your Holiness should know that, prior to sending this invitation, we had consulted in person with His Excellency, Bishop Ramon Godinez-Flores, Secretary-General of the Mexican Conference of Bishops, and informed him of our intentions. In May 1994, Bishop Flores gave his enthusiastic approval to the Conference and went so far as to offer us the rental of the Mexican Bishops' own official headquarters as a site for the Conference. We gladly accepted and provided His Excellency with an immediate deposit for the facility.

The Bishops Respond Enthusiastically!

Over the course of the next few months, we received many cordial replies from bishops around the world, indicating their intention to attend the Conference and warmly commending the notion of such an event. It is clear that the bishops have both an obligation and a right to know (as completely as possible) the full Message of Fatima, and they rejoiced at the opportunity. From the early and enthusiastic responses we received, we estimated that as many as 300 bishops would attend the Conference, representing close to *10 percent* of the entire Catholic Episcopate worldwide! A tremendous accomplishment considering the private nature of the gathering and the logistical and travel difficulties involved.

It was at this time, Holy Father, that we began to receive disturbing reports of letters and phone calls being made by some few bureaucrats of the Holy See to various bishops and nuncios in a direct effort to discourage and even forbid participation in our Conference. At first, we could hardly believe these reports, not understanding why Vatican bureaucrats would or could object to a private gathering of Catholic bishops and priests whose *only* purpose was to freely discuss the plan for peace that God's Mother gave the world at Fatima!

A Campaign of Deception and Lies

Sadly, upon further investigation and with the assistance of sympathetic bishops, we discovered that indeed such letters had been sent from a few Vatican bureaucrats to chancelleries around the world. Incredibly, at a time when you yourself were forcefully speaking out publicly on the need for peace, these letters from your own subordinates suggested that our Conference was somehow inappropriate or out-of-order. To make matters worse, these letters contained outright lies and egregious libels concerning the prime organizer of the gathering, Father Nicholas Gruner. With no regard for the truth, Father

Gruner's status as a priest-in-good-standing was called into serious question as well as his proven loyalty and dedication to Your Holiness' person and high office.

These unfounded charges and outrageous accusations were especially painful in the face of Father Gruner's long and tireless efforts (even at the expense of his own health) on behalf of Our Lady and Her Fatima Message. In the last 20 years, despite constant opposition from radical modernists and anti-Marian forces within the Church, he has succeeded in creating one of the largest lay Apostolates in the world, bringing together nearly 500,000 individuals in a community of prayer and sacrifice dedicated to promoting the full and complete Message of Fatima. Through magazines, radio and television programs and in public appearances in many countries, Father Gruner has brought the Mother of God's Fatima words to tens of millions of souls around the world ... and all in perfect accordance with the teaching and traditions of the Holy Magisterium. Father Nicholas Gruner's current status as priest-in-good-standing is unquestionable and dramatically verified by the testimonial you yourself issued on February 1, 1993, honoring his 16 years of priestly service and personally congratulating him on his work for Our Lady of Fatima.

No Word of Warning or Protest

Your Holiness, it is an understatement to say that we were dumbfounded when we first read the outrageous statement contained in these "official" letters. The Conference had been public news for many months, yet in all that time not a single Church official had even once contacted us with objections. More than 4,000 formal invitations had been sent to bishops, *including yourself*, and not a single word of protest had been received from any ecclesiastical authority. Now, only weeks before the Conference was due to commence, we found ourselves fighting against unseen enemies spreading false information and outright lies.

Despite our best efforts to counter this campaign of deception and lies by providing the true facts of the case, many bishops felt obliged to withdraw their support of the Conference out of fear and simple confusion. It soon became plainly obvious to us that spreading just this kind of dissension and confusion amongst the bishops was the underlying intention of this campaign in the first place! Adding insult to injury, not long before the event, we received a letter from Bishop Flores canceling our agreement for accommodation and withdrawing his official sanction. His Excellency cited comments made by an official of the Secretariat of State as being responsible for his decision.

Holy Father, we are sure you will understand that we were deeply discouraged and disheartened by these events. We debated long and hard whether we should move, postpone or cancel the Conference outright. In the end, we turned to Our Lord and Our Lady in prayer and, confident of Their guidance and protection, chose to continue our plans as originally announced. Even though time was critically short, by God's Grace, we were successful in obtaining (albeit at considerable financial cost) new meeting facilities and sleeping accommodations for the bishops. Through His Mercy, we were also able to overcome the last-minute legal and political impediments that Bishop Flores had engineered through the Mexican government (in clear violation of both God's law and Civil law) to prevent the issuance of travel visas to bishops who wished to attend our Conference. *Blessed be God. Blessed be His Holy Name!*

The Conference is Held!

On November 8, 1994, "the Conference on World Peace and the Immaculate Heart of Mary" was formally convened in Mexico City in the presence of bishops from every continent in the world as well as honored guests and members of the Catholic and secular press.

Over the next week, in a series of plenary sessions that were extraordinary for their seriousness and piety, the participants freely and openly discussed Our Lady's Fatima Message and its special role in the Church's effort to bring peace to our nations, to our families and to the world.

Your Holiness, while the number of bishops in attendance was far short of our original expectations, we were nevertheless deeply gratified that those who did attend represented so diverse and honored a cross-section of the Episcopacy. In prelates like Archbishop Accogli, Archbishop Capucci and Archbishop Milingo, we truly witnessed men who were worthy and noble successors to the Apostles themselves! We will forever be thankful for the courage and dedication that they and their colleagues showed in attending our Conference.

In the end, despite the sinister machinations of Our Lady's enemies, the assembled delegates came together to produce an historic document that we believe represents a new treasure for the Church. Consisting of 14 Resolutions, this document reaffirms Our Lady of Fatima's crucial role in the process towards true peace and in the mystery of our salvation itself.

Archbishop Milingo Accuses the Bureaucrats!

Holy Father, it was left to a member of your own sacred Curia to deliver the most dramatic address of the Conference. Archbishop Emmanuel Milingo, formerly Ordinary of Lusaka and now Special Delegate of the Pontifical Council for the Pastoral Care of Migrants and Itinerants, rose and delivered an electrifying condemnation of those who had attempted to prevent this gathering of bishops from occurring.

Speaking to his fellow bishops and to the entire Catholic world, His Excellency deplored the efforts of a few Vatican bureaucrats to suspend the lawful authority of the Episcopacy and prevent the bishops from carrying out their duties and fulfilling their responsibilities. Holding a copy of the letter that had been sent to the bishops of Nigeria, Archbishop Milingo stated:

"What a pity! It is a humiliation to a human being, who is an apostle, a humiliation — intended to prevent him from fulfilling his duties according to his own personality and character ... It is sad. It is humiliating. It lowers the dignity of a human being to have a letter like this going around that actually prevents someone from coming to a conference for Our Lady. ... If this letter represents their way to control us, it means that they don't trust the people to

whom they have given authority."

Archbishop Milingo concluded his address by forcefully encouraging all those who truly believe in peace to persevere in our efforts to bring the *full* Fatima Message to the Faithful and to the world. As His Excellency said, "I think we can go very, very far if we can make each and every one of our Catholics concerned with the whole welfare of the world." And, indeed, it is just in that spirit of Christian charity and with utmost respect and humility that we are publishing this Open Letter.

Holy Father, World Peace is in Your Hands!

The Blessed Mother of God came to Fatima to give the world the way to achieve true and lasting peace. She entrusted the means to this end to the Church, through you, the Vicar of Christ, in union with the bishops of the world. It has now been 78 years since Our Lady first appeared at Fatima. In that time, we have witnessed millions of lives destroyed through violence and war. Today, we continue to watch as millions of children are murdered in their own mothers' wombs and tens of thousands of more lives are lost each year in bloody conflicts around the globe. The Queen of Peace has offered us an end to this tragic cycle of death and misery *if* we will but obey Her requests for prayer, reparation and consecration.

Your Holiness, we intend to continue to do our part to encourage all Catholics and others of good will to place their trust in the Sacred and Immaculate Hearts of Jesus and Mary. With all respect and love, we also intend to continue our efforts to bring Our Lady's *full* Fatima Message to the Church, particularly to you and your fellow bishops. Our campaign for the Consecration of Russia to the Immaculate Heart (as commanded at Fatima) will continue unimpeded. We and the other 5,000,000 souls who have signed petitions to you asking for this act to be accomplished (and the millions more who await it) shall not be frightened or intimidated into silence by mere bureaucrats in pursuit of a private agenda.

The history of our Holy Church and the lives of our holy saints teaches us that we must resist evil from wherever it arises. Our hearts remain indissolubly united with yours, Holy Father, but we fear that you are being deceived and misled by those in whom you have placed your trust. The facts we have presented in this Open Letter combined with private information from Episcopal sources lead us inevitably to the conclusion that a small handful of Vatican bureaucrats are *deliberately* and *maliciously* withholding information from you and acting without proper authority in your august name. We respectfully urge you to take this opportunity to investigate the actions of those officials who — in clear violation of Canon Law and the Constitution of the Church — attempted to sabotage our recent Conference and blacken the name of a pious and humble priest who has sacrificed so greatly for the sake of Our Lady and the glory of Holy Mother Church.

We Appeal to You, Holy Father!

Your Holiness, at the time of our first Bishops' Conference in Fatima in 1992, we were appalled by the manifestly unjust statements made by certain

Vatican bureaucrats who opposed the gathering. Nevertheless, we held our tongues, hoping and praying for Christian charity to prevail. We fully expected that, following the event, the magnitude of their error would be so obvious that these officials would publish an immediate retraction. At worst, we assumed that these illegal and unjust efforts to prevent us from promoting the Fatima Message would stop.

Now, following the events described in this Open Letter, it is manifestly clear that our patience and silence was taken by these individuals as a license for even more bold and unjust action against our attempts to bring Our Lady's Message to the bishops and to the world. After the bitter experiences of the last two Conferences, it now seems undeniable that there exists a small group of Vatican officials who have become so confident of their unbridled power that they will use *any* means (including lies, slander and libel) to silence anyone promoting the *full* Fatima Message. Thus, Holy Father, we are obliged to appeal to you directly in this public letter, trusting as always in your probity and fairness.

A New Conference is Announced!

At the Mexico City Conference in November, we were encouraged by the bishops and others in attendance to undertake yet another meeting of bishops to discuss the Message of Fatima and its role in the peace of the world. Several bishops specifically urged us to hold this next conference in Rome under your protection and guidance.

Lest we be accused of planning in secret or not seeking proper authorization, we here and now — in this public forum — announce that we shall yet for a 3RD *time invite* every *bishop in the world (whether friend or foe of Fatima) to join together* in Rome *for a Conference on Peace and the Immaculate Heart of Mary, dates and times to be announced by formal letter and publication.*

Holy Father, we pray that you will bestow your Papal Blessing on this meeting and, if possible, attend one or more of its sessions. No Pope has ever spoken as movingly as you have of the urgent need for peace nor given so much respect to the Message of Fatima. We believe it is therefore most fitting and proper that your name come first in the list of those in support of this historic event.

Submitted in all respect and love to Your Holiness and in the names of Our Lord and Savior, Jesus Christ and His Blessed Mother, Mary.

§

The Open Letter was signed by an archbishop, a bishop, many priests and religous as well as more than 9,000 lay supporters.

Spread across two full pages of the largest daily in Rome, the ad was a calm and articulate presentation to His Holiness John Paul II of everything that Father Gruner and the members of the Apostolate had yearned to say to their Pope over the past three years. The Open Letter was both a plea and chronicle: In tones both reverent and frank, a plea for the Collegial Consecration, and a chronicle of the systematic abuse of power by the anti-Fatima forces in the Vatican bureaucracy, who had acted as if they thought themselves above reproach and beyond the strictures of Canon Law.

Avoiding harsh polemics, while according the bureaucrats in question the dignity of anonymity, the Open Letter had vaulted the concerns of the 9,000 faithful Catholics who had signed it over a phalanx of papal advisors and into the full view of His Holiness.

Opponents of the Apostolate would call it a "scandal", but the careful reader could see that the signatories of the Open Letter believed they were expressing true loyalty to the Pope in this, the Age of Fatima. They had launched a respectful but fearless entreaty to the Vicar of Christ—precisely because he *is* the Vicar of Christ—to bring about the triumph of the Immaculate Heart of Mary, and with it world peace and the Reign of Christ the King, by the means entrusted exclusively to the Pope at Fatima. Not the peace of an earthly Utopia, but the Reign of Christ the King, and Mary His Queen Mother. Not the grotesque accommodation of an ecumenical brotherhood between the adherents of contradictory and warring creeds, but the unity of *one Lord, one Faith, one Baptism* in a Catholic social order embracing the globe. The very globe beneath Our Lady's feet, as depicted in the Miraculous Medal whose design She, Herself had specified in Her apparition to St. Catharine Labore.

Yes, the signers of the Open Letter had advocated triumphalism, pure and simple. For triumph is the destiny of Christ from all Eternity, and the mission of His Holy Catholic Church is to secure that Triumph and nothing less than that Triumph, or we should be unfaithful to His unalterable commission: "Make disciples *of all nations*, baptizing them in the name of the Father, the Son and the Holy Ghost; teaching them to observe all things whatsoever I have commanded you." *All things whatsoever,* including teaching the necessity of joining the one true Church, the Catholic Church, and obeying the Message of Fatima, which "imposes an *obligation on the Church*" as the Holy Father himself had declared at Fatima on May 13, 1982.

In a Church which had been seething with open heresy and scandal for the past 35 years, the bureaucrats' global campaign against a cassock-wearing Marian priest from small-town Canada had been without precedent. Fittingly, so was this response by the thousands of rank-and-file Catholics who had supported Father Gruner's work over the years. To be sure, since the issuance of *Humanae Vitae* dissidents of all stripes had resorted to the forums of public opinion, even open letters in newspapers, to vent their splenetic fury against some detested article of the Faith. But never had loyal Catholics so clearly in awe of the power of the Papacy ever ventured to approach the Holy Father in this way: "Our hearts remain indissolubly united with yours, Holy Father, but we fear that you are being deceived and misled by those in whom you have placed your trust." The Open Letter was an act of love, born of necessity. There was nothing else to do.

§

Alberto Carosa writing from Rome: — "'No comment' was the Vatican's official reaction to the two-page 'Open Letter' to the Pope which appeared in Rome's largest daily paper *Il Messaggero* on July 12, 1995. The ad, entitled an Open Letter to His Holiness, Pope John Paul II, was paid for by the free-will offerings of nearly 10,000 Catholics from around the world."

The Italian news media, including the major news agencies, devoted extensive coverage to the Open Letter after it appeared in Rome. The Venice-based *Il Gazzettino* spoke slightingly of "hardened traditionalists who do not realize that Russia has changed" and erroneously noted that "it is not the first time that Catholic groups from America buy full pages of European papers to publicize ideas and initiatives." *L'Indipendente* described the ad as an "awkward form of correspondence," whereas Milan's *Il Giorno* report called it "articulate" and an "unusual initiative from which the Vatican distances itself by saying 'there is nothing to say'." This was followed, several days later, with a full-page interview with the Papal advisor and Fatima expert, the Slovak bishop Pavao Maria Hnilica, who described the Open Letter as "undoubtedly significant" since it was published by a Marian movement that is "widespread throughout the world."

There would soon be a talk show, the staple of Italian television, revolving around the "Open Letter". In the crossfire of the participants, Father Rene Laurentin would finally be forced to admit, despite everything he had said before, that the Collegial Consecration of Russia requested by Our Lady of Fatima had never actually been done in the manner requested.[1]

Completely overlooked by the media was the appearance of another (this time, anonymous) ad in *Il Giornale* on July 14, headlined "July 13, 1917: Third Meeting with Our Lady". July 13 is the anniversary of the third apparition of Fatima, a date scarcely noted by the media in their coverage of the Open Letter's publication. This anniversary coincided with one of the most horrific events in the ongoing Balkan conflict: the fall of Sbrenicia. The ensuing massacres, rapes and mass displacements featured prominently on the front pages of all the newspapers, were a terrible (if unconscious) reminder of the great chastisement of war that forms so integral a part of the Fatima Message.

At offices of *Il Messaggero* itself, which curiously ran no story about the Open Letter, the phones rang incessantly the day after publication, until they were taken off the hook. It was reported that more than one of the callers was a furious Vatican bureaucrat demanding to know how this could have happened. One can well imagine the commotion in the Vatican offices of those who had devoted their ecclesiastical careers to such "triumphs" as the Vatican-Moscow Agreement and the surrender at Balamand. Above all else, the Open Letter was a reminder that Heaven has ordained that real, lasting peace will never come through negotiations with the powers of the world. It will come through the Mother of God, mediating to men the non-negotiable and irresistible *fiat* of Christ the King.

The Mother of God does not lie. It is *only* through Her that Russia will be converted—*converted*— and peace granted to the world. The Open Letter had pleaded with the Pope and the world to address what is manifest: that the Consecration has not been done. Certainly the errors of Russia have spread across the planet. No one with eyes to see could genuinely claim that those errors have undergone a contraction since the putative consecration of 1984. Rather, they have only deepened and intensified, finding new and more evil ramifications by the day. Unless the Holy Father commands all the bishops of the world to join him in the act of consecration, the errors of Russia will most certainly enslave the world.

Hence the Open Letter, whatever the consequences it might bring to Father Gruner and the Apostolate.

§

St. Peter's Square, evening: Father Gruner responds to a request to bless a rosary. It is for a grandmother who is a "fervent Catholic". The young California woman holding the rosary out to be blessed is well spoken, beautifully respectful and totally self-composed. She volunteers that she herself is not a Catholic. She listens courteously and with genuine interest as Father Gruner commences with ease to instruct her and her companion. She could have had no way of knowing that the priest leading her into considerations of the Faith is arguably the most controversial priest in the Church today.

Father Nicholas Gruner has been at the center of one controversy or another his entire priestly life. But he has never claimed to be anything other than a priest promoting the Message of Our Lady of Fatima. As such, he has attracted the animosity, envy, and hatred of his adversaries, plus the regular censorship of those "Untouchables" in the Catholic Press who feign righteous horror at his tactics. What he is and what he does is known worldwide. Yet there is about his priesthood an aspect that draws intense fire from those who would like to see his traditional style of priesthood vanish.

In conjunction with the Open Letter, Father Gruner brought 40,000 petitions from Catholics around the world, in addition to the hundreds of thousands of petitions he had already delivered. All of the petitions pleaded with the Holy Father to consecrate Russia according to the exact specifications of the Virgin—pleaded with His Holiness because it is manifest that something is wrong. In the nine years which followed the apparition of Our Lady of Guadalupe, nine million souls, an entire nation, climbed out of the abyss of pagan idolatry and human sacrifice and into the sanctuaries of Catholic churches, baptized and converted. But now it is 13 years since the putative consecration of Russia in 1984—in which the bishops had not participated and only the world, not Russia, had been mentioned. In those 13 years, the most optimistic reports indicated around two hundred thousand conversions in a nation of two hundred and fifty million people, including the Ukraine.

Indeed, the conversion of Russia had incredibly, been *forbidden* by the Vatican bureaucrats whose capitulation at Balamand would bar as "outdated" the the return of the Russian Orthodox to the Holy Catholic Church.

Russia having been forbidden to convert, had become even more corrupted by her errors while the world had continued its ever-accelerating descent down that declivity whose terminus is Hell. None of this could have come to pass if Our Lady's Message had been fulfilled. For Our Lady does not lie. Her designs of peace had been thwarted by men.

The size of the constituency represented in the Open Letter is staggering for those who have not followed the Apostolate's ups and downs. But would that constituency and the Apostolate remain intact during the events of the coming year, as the conference in Rome approached and the bureaucratic thrusts aimed at the heart of Father Gruner's priesthood seemed near to striking the mark? Perhaps the answer would lie in the decree of yet another benevolent prelate who would come forward in the cause of Our Lady of Fatima.

Chapter 18

End Game

"*Remember, O Most Gracious Virgin Mary, that* **never** *was it known that anyone who implored Thy help or sought Thy intercession was left unaided.*"

Some four months after publication of the Open Letter, Father Nicholas Gruner knew that he had not been left unaided by Her to Whom he had devoted his entire priesthood. On November 4, 1995, His Excellency Saminini Arulappa, the Archbishop of Hyderabad, India, handed Father Gruner a formal decree incardinating him into his Archdiocese.[1] The two men were standing in St. Mary's Church. It was the First Saturday of the month. And not ten feet away was the Apostolate's Pilgrim Virgin statue, blessed by Pope Paul VI, of which Father Gruner had been the curator for nearly 20 years of travels in the cause of Our Lady of Fatima.

It was, appropriately, a Marian pilgrimage which had brought Father Gruner on this day to the teeming precincts of Hyderabad and St. Mary's Church. Over the years Father Gruner had made several pilgrimages to India, where hundreds of thousands of the Indian faithful had gathered to see the Statue, to receive Rosaries and Scapulars and to hear Father Gruner preach in his quiet way on the Message of Fatima.

In Hyderabad, the Apostolate supports an orphanage which has the care of fifty little souls. The welfare of these children is one of the many things at stake in the canonical struggle which began when the bureaucrats pulled the strings of their marionette, and the Bishop of Avellino suddenly recalled Father Gruner after an approved absence of more than 16 years.

The Plan for Father Gruner's virtual imprisonment in Avellino had depended, of course, entirely on the pretense that since Father Gruner had "failed" to find another diocese to accept him, he must return to the Diocese of Avellino. Yet here was the *third* benevolent bishop in succession to offer Father Gruner incardination outside Avellino. The bureaucrats had "persuaded" the first two bishops to withdraw their offers easily enough; the Nuncios had done their job of back-channel influence. This time, however, no less than an Archbishop of 25 years standing, had gone so far as to issue a formal decree of incardination to Father Gruner, on the record, before the bureaucrats had been able to get to him.

But the Archbishop had done more than simply incardinate Father Gruner in his Archdiocese. With the full authority of his office, the prelate had extended his protection to the whole Apostolate and had condemned the bureaucrats who were trying to destroy it:

> "I grant you all the faculties you need for continuing your God-given mission on earth. *Evil forces have conspired to destroy your work of love.* But you go ahead trusting in the Lord. His love is steadfast and He will never fail, though you may be subject to many a trial and even persecution ... *Bureaucratic forces cannot stifle God's work.* It is my prayer that you continue in your God-given mission in spite of great opposition."[2]

The Archbishop's decree was a canonical bombshell. At the very moment their carefully prepared circumvention of the Code of Canon Law had nearly succeeded in neutralizing its target, the Archbishop had rescued him with the stroke of a pen. To make matters worse, the Archbishop had just provided objective confirmation in an official ecclesiastical document that "bureaucratic forces" were engaging in illicit maneuvers against Father Gruner.

The Plan was at a standstill. Father Gruner could not very well be ordered back to Avellino for having "failed" to find another bishop, when an Archbishop had just incardinated him with a formal decree the bureaucrats would not be able to countermand. They had absolutely no power under the Code of Canon Law, much less the divine constitution of the Church, to dictate an Archbishop's decision about whom he could incardinate in his own Archdiocese; and they knew it. But they did have one tool at their disposal: fear.

The unexpected visit of a Papal Nuncio can intimidate even an Archbishop. When the clasps on a nuncial briefcase snap open, it would only be natural to cringe in apprehension over what might be inside. Sometime in January 1996 the Papal Nuncio to India, Archbishop Zur Giorgio, got aboard an airplane and flew from Delhi to Hyderabad—a most unusual expenditure of time and money for a Vatican ambassador with many pressing duties of state. The Nuncio's only purpose in making this extraordinary trip was to meet with Archbishop Arulappa concerning Father Nicholas Gruner. This was a most urgent meeting—so urgent it could not even wait for the Archbishop to recover from the heart surgery he had just undergone. When the meeting was over the Archbishop had begun to view the matter of Father Gruner's incardination somewhat differently. He was afraid. And who could blame him? He had not seen behind the curtain of the Wizard of Oz.

On January 31, 1996, Father Gruner received a letter from the Archbishop: Did Father Gruner have a decree of "excardination" from the Diocese of Avellino, releasing him from the jurisdiction of its bishop?[3] This was indeed a technical requirement for the transfer. But as providence would have it, the Bishop of Avellino had issued just such a decree to Father Gruner in 1989, before the bureaucrats began tugging on the strings of his more compliant successor. Father Gruner still had the document in his files. He had the decree of excardination hand delivered to Hyderabad. The technical requirements were complete. He was now a priest of the Archdiocese of Hyderabad—or at least, according to the Code of Canon Law. For any other priest in the world, the matter would have been ended there. But for Father Nicholas Gruner, the Code of Canon Law was no longer operative. The bureaucrats had suspended it, in his case.

The Open Letter to the Pope and the benevolent intervention of the Archbishop of Hyderabad had shown the hunters that their prey was not without resources. Father Gruner would not simply lie down and die. Something was keeping this priest on his feet and moving forward. The prey, then, would simply have to be crushed to death, rather less elegantly than anticipated, by the vast apparatus at their command. Of course, this would require further actions outside the normal channels of Canon Law, but *The Plan* could not otherwise be fulfilled. The law of the Church would not serve the hunters, so it would have to be discarded. Nevertheless, the appearance of following the law would be maintained as the "front end" of their operation. They must maintain their *bella figura*.

What followed over the next six months was a coordinated international campaign of punitive actions the like of which no priest in living memory had ever been subjected to-including the heretics and homosexuals who contentedly infest seminaries and parishes of North America without the slightest disturbance from Rome.

January 1996. The Papal Nuncios carry a new "declaration" from Archbishop Sepe, Secretary of the Congregation for the Clergy, to every bishop in the world. It concerns the Apostolate's upcoming Fatima Conference in Rome, which had been announced in the Open Letter. Sepe's decree is an incredible travesty of Canon Law: the interdiction throughout the entire Catholic Church of a priest who had done nothing wrong:

> *"The Gruner case has a long history and consequently there are volumes of dossiers in the archives of this Congregation."*

What exactly was "the Gruner case"? And what was contained in the "volumes of dossiers" at the Congregation for the Clergy? Sepe does not say. Better to create the false impression that there must be *something* pretty terrible in those records.

> *"Also this conference [in Rome] includes plans for a number of activities which the Reverend Gruner has developed without any ecclesiastical permission ..."*

What "ecclesiastical permission" is needed to hold a conference on Fatima? None, of course, but Sepe does not mention this. The Literally Truthful Lie is launched around the world again. In a Church teeming with conferences and workshops —none of them with "ecclesiastical permission", and many conducted by fulminating heretics—only one gathering consumes the attention of Archbishop Sepe and his fellow Vatican bureaucrats: a conference in Rome devoted to the Message of Fatima.

> *"So that this priest might not continue his harmful activities, the Bishop of Avellino, on January 31, 1994, called upon him to return to the diocese within one month."*

What "harmful activities" was Father Gruner guilty of? Archbishop Sepe has no particulars to offer. And neither did the Bishop of Avellino in his order recalling Father Gruner—the very order Archbishop Sepe himself had orchestrated by blocking Father Gruner's incardination in any other diocese but Avellino.

> *"At this point in time there is nothing to do but to ask ... the bishops of your country not to accept the invitation of Father Gruner, and to avoid doing anything in this regrettable situation to make matters worse."*[4]

Why exactly is the situation "regrettable"? What would happen to any bishop who made "matters worse" by showing support for Father Gruner? Better to leave that threat *sub rosa.* End of letter.

What had Father Nicholas Gruner actually *done* to merit this unprecedented communication to every Catholic bishop in the world? Even a cursory reading of Archbishop Sepe's letter would reveal the answer: *nothing; absolutely nothing*. That is, nothing which he could safely mention. For it simply would not do to admit that the "harmful activity" in which Father Gruner had been engaged for his entire priestly life was nothing more or less than teaching and preaching the Heaven-sent Message of Fatima—especially its now-intolerable claim that Russia must be consecrated to the Immaculate Heart and *converted* to the one true religion, so that the world would be saved from Russia's errors.

January 26, 1996. The Bishop of Avellino issues an "admonition" to Father Gruner that he must return there because "idle had been the various written interventions of my predecessors ... with which you were invited to look for another bishop."[5] Father Gruner sends two letters in February, pointing out that he has been incardinated in the Archdiocese of Hyderabad, has therefore *found* another bishop, and is no longer bound to return to Avellino. The Bishop offers no reply. He is clearly awaiting further orders about what to say regarding Hyderabad.

February 1996. A copy of the decree of the Apostolic Signatura upholding the first order to return to Avellino is published in *Soul* magazine, organ of the "World Apostolate of Fatima"—the new "Fatima Lite" version of the once-militant Blue Army, which now has direct ties to the Vatican anti-Fatima bureaucrats. Oddly enough, Father Gruner himself had not yet received a copy of the decree, although the "World Apostolate of Fatima" has obtained it from the Canadian Bishops' Conference. The decree is accompanied by a libelous error-filled "exposé" by E. William Sockey III, which portrays Father Gruner as a disobedient, schismatic cleric without priestly faculties.[6] In the same month, a local affiliate of the "World Apostolate of Fatima" publishes the same decree, but includes a fabricated paragraph condemning Father Gruner which is nowhere to be found in the original document.[7]

March 1996. The bureaucrats attack the Hyderabad problem: Archbishop Arulappa receives a letter from Cardinal Sanchez advising him not to incardinate Father Gruner, even though he has already done so. The letter mysteriously lacks a protocol number which would place it in numerical sequence with the official documents of the Congregation[8]—evidently because it is *unofficial* and quite outside the proper channels of Canon Law. Cardinal Sanchez has absolutely no authority to forbid an Archbishop to incardinate a validly ordained priest. He does so anyway. Who will stop him? Three months later the beleaguered Archbishop would write to Father Gruner: "I request you to understand my predicament in the present circumstances. I do hope, God willing, a satisfactory solution will be found."[9] He would also disclose through his assistant that he had been placed in fear of reprisals against his whole Archdiocese because of his support of Father Gruner.[10] Still, the Archbishop would never actually withdraw the decree of incardination. There would have to be grounds to do so, and a hearing at which Father Gruner could present a defense.

§

By mid-spring of 1996, with the Rome Conference only six months away, the bureaucrats were ready to implement the final phase of *The Plan*. It commenced on May 16, 1996. On that date the Bishop of Avellino issued a further decree advising Father Gruner that unless he returned to the Diocese of Avellino in 29 days he would be suspended from the sacred priesthood.[11] The decree claimed that the matter been decided the day before at a "hearing" to which Father Gruner had not been invited. Actually, it had been decided *years* before in the offices of certain Vatican bureaucrats.

Yes, but what about Father Gruner's incardination in the Archdiocese of Hyderabad? Did it not place him beyond the jurisdiction of the Bishop of Avellino? The May 16 decree revealed the stratagem on which the bureaucrats had settled to deal with that particular problem: the incardination in Hyderabad was declared *tanquam non existens*—it was non-existent! Poof.

But on what basis had the incardination in Hyderabad been declared non-existent? According to the May 16 decree, Father Gruner was not "canonically set free" to be incardinated there. And why was he not "canonically set free"? Because he had been ordered to return to Avellino. But why had he been ordered to return to Avellino? Because he had not found another bishop. But was not the Archbishop of Hyderabad another bishop? Yes, but his incardination of Father Gruner was non-existent. The classic circular argument. Crude. Ridiculous. But it would do until something better came along. The main thing was to achieve, at last, the objective of *The Plan*: the exile or defrocking of Father Nicholas Gruner, preacher of the unacceptable Message of Fatima.

Father Gruner would appeal the preposterous decree of May 16 to the Congregation for the Clergy. There, once again, Cardinal Sanchez and Archbishop Sepe, his executioners, would also be his judges. This time, however, Father Gruner would request their recusal. Perhaps even they would recognize the absurdity, if not the injustice, of sitting as judges in a case they had been stage-managing behind the scenes for years. To Father Gruner's request for recusal, the judges had a ready reply: "The request for disqualification cannot be taken into consideration because it is not foreseen in the legislation."[12] In other words, Father Gruner had no right to an impartial judge! But the right to an impartial judge *is* foreseen in "the legislation", namely, Canon 1449. Also, natural law, common sense and basic decency all dictate that a man cannot judge a case in which he is an adverse party. But Canon 1449, natural law, common sense and basic decency were impediments to *The Plan*. The bureaucrats simply heaved them overboard.

On September 20, 1996, with the Rome Conference two months away, Cardinal Sanchez and Archbishop Sepe upheld the May 16 decree of the Bishop of Avellino. That is, they upheld their own manipulation of the marionette whose strings they had been pulling since at least January 1994.

The End Game was now down to a few rooks and pawns on the board, and the pieces left were heavily weighted in favor of his opponents. The remaining moves seemed few, and too easily calculable for the other side, but Father Gruner would force them to make every move until checkmate. He would do so not out of any perverse stubbornness, but for the cause of Our Lady of Fatima, and because it was not in his nature to allow the truth to be subjugated to the crooked rules of a rigged game. He would later explain:

> "If it were merely the question of my own personal ruin, there might be no need for such resistance. But they are not interested in ruining me for its own sake. What they really seek is to silence a message they do not want to hear, and do not want others to hear: the Message of Fatima in all of its political incorrectness. *The truth.* That is the only reason they are interested in me. In the entire record of the so-called 'Father Gruner case' referred to by Archbishop Sepe in his letter to every bishop in the world, you will find *nothing* which states exactly what it is I am supposed to have done to justify actions against me which not even the worst heretics in the Church today are subjected to. How can they mention that it is the *truth* which so offends them? It is the truth which is at stake. And so I must resist, with all the means the law of the Church gives to me."

On November 15, 1996, the very day he boarded the plane for Rome, Father Gruner would appeal the Congregation's decision to the Apostolic Signatura. Not even the bureaucrats could do anything to alter the basic norm of Canon Law that the appeal prevented the operation of all threatened penalties. Thus, there would be no suspension from the priesthood, nor any obligation to return to Avellino. When he arrived in Rome to address the Apostolate's Third Fatima Conference, Father Nicholas Gruner would be, as he had always been, a priest in good standing.

And when he arrived he would have with him a document as unprecedented as the illicit global campaign against him by the bureaucrats, yet a document expressly authorized by the Code of Canon Law Pope John Paul II himself had promulgated. That document, together with the appeal to the Signatura, would bring new complications to the End Game, prolonging it in ways his opponents had never anticipated.

§

November 18, 1996. Rome. The Apostolate's Third Fatima Conference begins. Across Piazza Euclide from the hotel where the Conference is being held is an impressive parish church in the Greco-Roman style. On its curved stone facade is an inscription in Latin: *In Honorem Immaculati Cordis B. V. Mariae Reginae Pacis* — "In Honor of the Immaculate Heart of Mary, Queen of Peace." At a conference entitled "World Peace and the Immaculate Heart of Mary", the inscription is one of those signposts on the byways of Providence which encourage a weary traveler.

By now the bureaucrats' strange preoccupation with the Canadian priest and his Marian apostolate had become almost laughable. Ten months earlier the Nuncios had delivered the urgent missive of Archbishop Sepe to every bishop in the world, stating that the Conference was "without permission of ecclesiastical authority." A week before the Conference began the Nuncios delivered yet another priority bulletin to the entire world episcopate. This one was from Cardinal Gantin, Prefect of the Congregation for the Bishops, who conveyed the alarming news that:

> "Father Gruner has convened the Third International Conference on 'World Peace and the Immaculate Heart of Mary' to be held in Rome 18-23 November 1996; it is absolutely without approval of ecclesiastical authority."

The Literally Truthful Lie had been given added emphasis in the latest communique: the Conference was *absolutely* without the "approval of ecclesiastical authority". Since it was *absolutely* without approval, no bishop should go to Rome to discuss World Peace and the Immaculate Heart of Mary. But since no ecclesiastical approval was required in the first place, why *exactly* should the bishops stay away? Why, because of Father Gruner's "situation" and "activities", the communique suggested. *What* "situation", and *what* "activities"?

The bureaucrats had already seen what happens to bishops who are provided with the full Message of Fatima: *they listen.* And once they listen, they tend to become supporters of the Apostolate's work in making known to all the faithful the urgent nature of the Message in its entirety, despite the negative implications of that Message for the grand human scheme embraced by the Vatican-Moscow Agreement, Ostpolitik and the Balamand Statement.

At the 1992 Conference in Fatima 60 bishops had politely insisted that the Bishop of Fatima give his approval to the conference. After Father Gruner was assaulted in the sacristy of the Fatima Shrine by thugs in the employ of its rector, two prelates who had attended the

Conference vowed to petition the Pope for the retirement of the bishop of Fatima, who had clearly lost control of the Shrine. Three months later the Bishop of Fatima was retired. Had the Apostolate been heard, with sympathy, by the Pope?

At the Mexico conference in 1994, the assembled bishops had drafted and approved 14 Resolutions which constitute a veritable charter for promulgation of the Fatima Message in its entirety, including the Consecration of Russia and disclosure of the Third Secret. The Resolutions were a statement of uncompromising Catholic militancy in an era of ecclesial accommodation and retreat. These 14 Resolutions were published in Rome on July 12, 1995, as part of the Open Letter to the Pope. Had not the Holy Father become aware of the consensus of these bishops?

By Autumn of 1996 the bureaucrats could not have failed to notice that the Conferences and related activities of the Apostolate had marshaled the support of some 1200 bishops, about 30% of the total world episcopate, for the collegial Consecration of Russia. The Conference in Rome could not be interdicted by any *legitimate* means, because nothing about it was doctrinally, canonically or morally objectionable — nor could the bureaucrats credibly claim otherwise. But it would not do to have an end run of bishops, priests and laity around the Vatican-Moscow Agreement, Ostpolitik and the Balamand Statements which the bureaucrats evidently considered better policies than the words of the Queen of Heaven. Thus, the Third Bishops' Conference obviously loomed large in the bureaucratic radar: the full Message of Fatima was going to be discussed again. *With bishops*. Once again, therefore, measures had to be taken.

As with the Mexico conference, the nuncial apparatus had managed to block the issuance of visas to many of the bishops who had committed to being in Rome. But, as in Mexico, a few determined prelates avoided diplomatic confinement and made their way to the Conference. One of these was His Excellency Benedict To Varpin, Archbishop of Madang, Papua New Guinea. He had made the journey despite a seemingly endless series of phone calls, faxes and letters from the Nuncio pressuring him not to go.[13] On the ride from Leonardo da Vinci Airport to Piazza Euclide, Archbishop To Varpin explained that he had seen enough carnage among the warring factions of his own island nation to recognize that the promises of Our Lady of Fatima could not possibly have been fulfilled. He had come to Rome to find out why. Over the next few days he would know the answer.

And so they came for a third time: bishops, priests and laity from around the world. A modest group, really, but large enough to cause the mobilization of a worldwide apparatus against the gathering. Most curious. Or rather not so curious when one considered that the list of topics to be covered by the speakers at the Conference read like an Index of Forbidden Subjects in the Church today:

"Heaven's Request for the Consecration of Russia to the Immaculate Heart"
"The Fatima Message Imposes an Obligation on the Church"
"The Third Secret of Fatima and the War Against the Church"
"Has Russia Been Converted?"
"The World As It Will Look Under the Reign of Mary"
"Outside the Church there is no Salvation."
"The Plot to Silence Our Lady"
"Divine Impatience"
"The Five First Saturdays"
"How to Avoid Hell and Shorten Purgatory"
"The New Paganism and Globalism versus the Principles of a Catholic Nation"
"One World Church Expected Next Year"
"The Perestroika Deception"

Throughout the world today conferences, congresses and "workshops" devoted to undermining the Holy Catholic Church convene and spread their errors with impunity: women priests, the end of priestly celibacy, the 'coming out' of homosexual clergy, changes in the teaching on marriage and procreation, celebration of the 'gay and lesbian communities', inclusive language, goddess worship, Wicca, popular election of the Pope, use of polls and petitions to determine Catholic doctrine—the heresies and absurdities freely discussed, diffused and demanded are uncountable.

This unprecedented situation in the Church suggested a thought-experiment to more than one of those who had come to Piazza Euclide that week in November: Suppose they had gathered, not to discuss the Message of Fatima, but to revel at yet another festival of heretics. What would the world's Nuncios have done to stop them? The results of the experiment registered almost instantly in the mind: Why, the Nuncios would have done nothing. For there would have been no communiqués from the Vatican Congregations to deliver to every bishop in the world; nor would the Nuncios have been ordered to engage in the arduous work of denying travel visas to descendants of the Apostles. The slumber of the bureaucrats in the face of ecclesial chaos would have continued serenely.

Since 1965 exactly *one* Catholic has been excommunicated by the Vatican for heresy: an obscure and laughably clumsy "theologian" in

Sri Lanka. The *subtle* heretics, who pose the real threat to the faith, have remained ensconced in seminaries and universities throughout the Church. Meanwhile, at a bookstore only a few paces from the perimeter of Vatican City, one can purchase theological texts propounding any number of propositions that were once condemned. Adoring crowds wave to the Pope on his various motorcades, but when they go home they ignore his teaching on contraception or divorce and remarriage. The pollsters who interview papal fans when the outdoor Masses in the football stadiums are over, find that most of them "disagree" with the Pope on other matters of the Faith as well.

In the 32 years since the Bronze Doors closed on Vatican II the clamor of dissent from both clergy and laity has become the baseline; a constant "white noise" like static on a television set when a station has gone off the air. As anyone who has fallen asleep with that noise in the background would know, it is a very soothing noise to sleep by. Today it would seem that only a confluence of the zealously orthodox is capable of producing a sound to rise above the static and waken a bureaucrat or two in the Vatican. For a *zealous* orthodoxy is not content to attribute the crisis in the Church merely to Original Sin, and to inquire no further. Those who love their Church with a fierce love will tend to ask questions about what has gone wrong; and those questions will invariably lead them to Fatima, and then to Rome.

The clergy and laity assembling at Piazza Euclide had come, therefore, to ponder embarrassing questions: *Why* had the Church descended into this fugue state of chaos? *Why*, eighty years after the Virgin appeared at Cova da Iria, had the promises of Our Lady of Fatima not been realized? Why had those promises instead been allowed by the sacred pastors to recede beyond the memory of nearly everyone, while the world succumbed to an ever-expanding holocaust of the unborn and a violent disintegration of nations which the Church seems powerless to arrest—no matter how many papal trips are made to the areas of distress.

There was something else these Catholics had come to Rome to consider; a matter which caused perhaps the greatest agitation among the bureaucrats who had tried to keep the bishops from attending:

Some forty years ago the auxiliary bishop of Fatima held a sealed envelope up to the light and tried to discern the writing inside. He counted 24 handwritten lines on a piece of paper which he could not read: the Third Secret of Fatima. Those 24 lines had been written by Sister Lucy after three months of being terrified to commit them to paper. Only after January 2, 1944, when the Virgin had appeared again to tell her that it was Heaven's will, was Sister Lucy finally able to write the Secret down and deliver it in a sealed envelope to the Bishop of Fatima.

The Third Secret was to have been revealed to the world not later than 1960. Sister Lucy had explained that by then the meaning of the Secret "would be more clear." The Secret was delivered to the Vatican under seal in April, 1957, and the faithful of the world waited. In February, 1960, Pope John XXIII, having read the Secret, caused worldwide dismay by announcing through an anonymous press release, which no one took responsibility for, that the Secret would not be released that year and possibly not ever. Pope John Paul II and Cardinal Ratzinger have since read the Secret, along with several other current members of the hierarchy, but none of them has divulged its contents.

By those who have read the Secret we have been told, in turns, that it is not sensational, and that is sensational; that it is not apocalyptic, and that it concerns what is already revealed in the Book of the Apocalypse; that it does not predict a world catastrophe, and that it predicts the sudden loss of millions of lives. The one thing we have not been told—as we have in the case of every other Marian warning of the past century, no matter how dire—is what the Third Secret actually *says.*

It is a common perception among Catholics that the world began to come apart in earnest around 1960. It is the year that seems in retrospect to mark a great divide beyond which the exhausted remnants of Christendom lost their remaining power to restrain evil, and all that had been unthinkable quickly became commonplace. The year before, Pope John had convened his Council with the promise that it would mark the opening of the Church to the "modern world". He illustrated his intention in a famous incident: a reporter had asked what His Holiness hoped to accomplish at the Council, whereupon the Pontiff strode across the room and threw open a window. Yes, that musty old Catholic Church needed some fresh air.

On June 30, 1972, thirteen years after Pope John opened his window, Pope Paul VI would lament that "from somewhere or other the smoke of Satan has entered the Church."[14] Pope Paul too had read the Third Secret. He would die wearing a hair shirt, it is said, having wept over the establishment of an abortion mill in Rome. Like the others who have read the Secret, Pope Paul would not disclose its contents; but who could doubt that his terrifying and wholly unprecedented remark about the state of the Church reflected something in those 24 lines in the handwriting of Sister Lucy. Sister Lucy had said that the meaning of the Secret would be clearer in 1960. Many Catholics who attended the Conference, and millions more around the world, had long suspected that they knew why: *Because the Secret predicted an unprecedented debacle in the Catholic Church beginning around that year.*

In the decades before the Council a line of Popes Pius had warned us of the shoals ahead which threatened the bark of Peter. After 1960 every one of those warnings would be forgotten:

• In his encyclical *Quanta Cura* and his *Syllabus of the Errors of the Modern World,* Pius IX had condemned the modern notion of "religious liberty" as a right proper to every man and essential to a just society. After the Council that very notion would be embraced by much of the Vatican hierarchy.

• In *Pascendi,* Pius X condemned modernism as "the synthesis of all heresies", prescribing the Oath Against Modernism for all priests and theologians. After the Council the Oath was abandoned and modernists took key positions throughout the Church.

• In *Mortalium animos,* Pius XI condemned the fledgling "ecumenical movement" as a threat to the very foundations of the Catholic faith, and forbade any Catholic participation in it. After the Council many Vatican bureaucrats would embrace the ecumenical movement.

• In *Mediator Dei,* Pius XII condemned the innovators who sought to revise drastically and render in the vernacular, the "august Sacrifice of the Mass." After the Council the ancient Latin liturgy of the Roman Rite was abandoned overnight in favor of an unprecedented new rite of Mass—entirely in the vernacular.

• In his Christmas message for 1957 Pius XII had repeated the constant teaching of the Church that dialogue with communism is impossible because it does not share a common language with Christianity, and he maintained the excommunication for any Catholic voting for or joining the communist party. In 1962 Cardinal Tisserant dialogued with communist prelate Nikodim of the Orthodox Church, a KGB agent, and committed the Catholic Church to the Vatican-Moscow Agreement, promising that at the upcoming Council there would be no denunciation of Communism. After the Council began, Pope John XXIII, in *Pacem in Terris,* suggested that one could be a member of the communist *movement* as an evolving historical phenomenon without necessarily embracing condemned principles.

While none of these reversals of Church policy compromised directly the deposit of the Faith or negated the charism of papal infallibility, never had the constant judgement of so many popes in so many matters been in practise, so completely reversed. *Every reversal occurred within a few years of 1960.*

If the Third Secret of Fatima does indeed speak to post-Conciliar period—to the unprecedented destruction of the Roman liturgy, the universal collapse of Church discipline, the pandemic of dissent, the softening of the Church's obdurate opposition to communism—then its disclosure would be nothing less than the unsealing of a Heavenly indictment of the governance of the Church since Vatican II. That indictment would implicate some of the very bureaucrats who had tried to interdict the Conference. It would condemn what had been wrought by the architects of the Vatican-Moscow Agreement, Ostpolitik, and Balamand who still walk the corridors of the Vatican. Those implicated in the indictment would naturally do everything in their power to prevent it from being unsealed.

Here, then, lies the beating heart of the bureaucrats' constant opposition to the work of Father Nicholas Gruner; for nothing else about this mild-mannered priest could explain the concentration of forces against him. The heart of the matter is simply this: *To view the crisis in the Church from the perspective of Fatima is inevitably to realize that the crisis is a failure of the upper hierarchy.*[15] To stand in Cova da Iria and look toward Rome in 1996 is to see that the premonition of Pius XII, spoken at the edge of that great divide of 1960, was a true prophecy:

> "I am worried by the Blessed Virgin's messages to Lucy of Fatima ... A day will come when the civilized world will deny its God, *when the Church will doubt as Peter doubted.* She will be tempted to believe that man has become God."[16]

November 20, 1996. Paul VI Audience Hall. If one walks down the Via Aurelia, along the south wall of Vatican City, one will see something quite startling jutting above the wall: a huge concrete shell with a drooping roof line, and set in its wall a great squashed ovoid of a window, the modern notion of a clerestory, its concrete muntins describing counterpoised ripples which meet in the center and cancel out. You will have found Nervi's Paul VI Audience Hall, a Vatican tribute to that great age of architectural renewal: the Sixties.

The participants in the Conference would go to the audience hall on this day to see their Pope. Once they were inside they would be appalled; because the place is indeed appalling. The vast sterile space is oriented *downward* toward the stage on which the Vicar of Christ appears for his Wednesday general audience. The holder of the Keys to the Kingdom of Heaven will be looking up at the spectators as they look down upon him. The enormous expanse of concrete floor is studded with thousands of steel pedestals on which thousands of small, armless seats are perched like mushrooms. Beneath each seat is something very curious: a metal drain grate. Is the Papal audience hall *hosed* clean?

After the hall was completed in 1971 papal audiences would no longer be held in St. Peter's Basilica. The audience hall of the Vicar of Christ in this post-conciliar era is devoid of any sign of the Catholic Faith. It is a sparsely furnished living room for a conversation with the world, designed neither to offend nor to awe any non-Catholic guest.

And then there is The Thing. At the rear of the audience hall's enormous stage, spanning most of its great width, sits a mass of twisted shards of metal, resembling a giant thorn bush; and in the midst of the thorn bush, the huge figure of an emaciated man, limbs and torso grotesquely attenuated, hair gathered in an undulating rope which streams off to its left, as if the figure were being sucked into a vacuum located offstage. The Thing is horrifying. The Thing is Pericle Fazzini's "Resurrection of Christ."

Soon the Pope will enter from stage right, sit in front of this embarrassing monstrosity, and deliver his weekly audience talk. But first the prelates who have come to see the Pope will be given seats on the stage. Among them are two attending the Conference at Piazza Euclide: Archbishop To Varpin and Bishop José Alfonso Ribeiro.

The Pope arrives on the stage, and it is clear that the Holy Father is terribly ill. He shuffles when he walks, and his posture is severely stooped. His face shows little expression. His limbs appear rigid, so much so that he must fall backward into the papal chair. His left hand trembles uncontrollably, and his speech is slurred. One can barely make out the words of his brief address. The Vatican has ceased denying that the Pope has Parkinson's disease, and indeed the standard medical description of the progress of the disease is a description of the man on the stage:

> The disease begins with a 4-to-8-hz 'pill rolling tremor' of one hand. The tremor is maximal at rest ... The hands, arms and legs usually are most affected, in that order. Progressive rigidity, slowness and poverty of movement and difficulty in initiating movement follow ... The face becomes mask-like and open-mouthed, with diminished blinking ... The posture becomes stooped ... Patients find it difficult to start walking; the gait becomes shuffling with short steps, and the arms are held flexed to the waist and fail to swing with the stride ... [*Merck Manual*, 16th Edition, p. 1496]

Throughout 1996 the Pope had seemed to be moving in his audience addresses toward an infallible definition of Mary as Mediatrix of All Graces and Coredemptrix. In audience address after audience address the Holy Father had been explaining the virtues of Mary, as if to instruct the faithful in preparation for a definitive pronouncement on Her role in the economy of salvation. The preparation would have to be extensive indeed, for the infallible definition of this Marian dogma might trigger a storm of protest from the forces of world ecumenism which would make the worldwide dissent from *Humanae Vitae* seem like papal allegiance by comparison.

Were the Pope to proclaim that Mary is Mediatrix and Coredemptrix he would remind the world that the Catholic Church is different in *essence*, not merely in appearance, from any other organization on earth which calls itself a church. No human institution could possess such countercultural audacity. Ironically, he would also be bringing to a screeching halt the very "ecumenical venture" to which he had wedded his pontificate.

But such surprises are not uncommon in the history of the Church, given the influence of the Holy Spirit on her course. The world was surprised and outraged when Pope Paul VI, acting against his own advisors, affirmed the constant teaching of the Magisterium against the contraceptive act. Similar outrage greeted Pius IX's *Syllabus of Errors,* written by the once-liberal pontiff after he had been driven from the Quirinal palace in 1848 by Mazzini's Masonic army, fleeing for his life in disguise after his personal secretary had been shot to death. Through such surprises does the Holy Spirit govern the Church in times of gravest crisis.

There are no doubt bureaucrats in the Pope's retinue of advisors who vigorously oppose the Marian definition: "Holy Father, it would not be opportune. The consequences for ecumenism would be disastrous. We urge you to wait, Holy Father." Many of those who were attending the conference, including Father Gruner himself, could well envision the same advice being given by the same advisors regarding the Collegial Consecration of Russia. On May 18, 1936, Sister Lucy related to Father José Bernardo Gonçalves, S.J., her spiritual advisor, an intimate conversation with Our Lord in which He had said: "Pray very much for the Holy Father. He will do it (the Collegial Consecration of Russia) but it will be late." On November 20, 1996, in the Paul VI Audience Hall, it was very late indeed, yet still not too late.

Were the Pope to proclaim this Marian dogma infallibly he would surely roll back many of the gains of the post-conciliar revolutionaries. But if he were to insist upon the Consecration of Russia as well, he would annihilate the Revolution completely and bring on the Reign of Mary, as She had promised at Fatima on the authority of Her Divine Son. He would put to an end the dark time prophesied by Pius XII and likely also predicted in the Third Secret; the time when "the Church herself would doubt as Peter had doubted." The consecration of Russia was the fervent hope of those who had come to Rome for the Third International Fatima Conference; it was their prayer for an ailing Pope.

The papal audience moved toward its conclusion, with various groups, including some Texas Baptists, leaping to their feet and waving, singing or whooping when their names were read from a list of attendees. In an age when the Pope is viewed as a celebrity, rather than the anointed Vicar of the King of the Universe, papal audiences had come to resemble high-school pep-rallies. But then, what would one expect to see in a place that resembled nothing so much as an outsize high school auditorium?

As the audience concluded, however, something happened which reminded the spectators at the pep rally, for a moment at least, of that ancient unity of divine worship which had been destroyed by the post-conciliar "reforms": the Our Father was prayed in Latin. Many in the vast crowd still remembered, and the majestic words rose up into the hall and toward Heaven: *advéniat regnum tuum: fiat voluntas tua, sicut in caelo, et in terra.*[17] There would be no Hail Mary, lest the Protestants in the audience be offended, but for that moment there was *Catholic* worship in the unity of Faith. There was also a sense of loss for what had been toppled over and shattered by the violent winds blowing into the Church through Pope John's open window.

The members of the Conference had come to see their Pope, but they had come to do something else. They had come to exercise a God-given right, infallibly defined as such by two Ecumenical Councils: the right of the faithful to petition the Supreme Pontiff for redress of just grievances in the Church.

At the end of the audience a line of prelates and disabled people moved past the Pope on the stage to receive his personal greeting. When Archbishop To Varpin and Bishop Ribeiro reached the Pope they each handed him a document. A companion document was handed to the Pope by Joseph Cain, a worker for the Apostolate who was pushing Ed Reczak, a disabled lay member of the Conference confined to a wheelchair.

The document the Pope had just received was specifically authorized by Canons 1389 and 1405 of the 1983 Code of Canon Law, promulgated by John Paul II himself. The document was a *libellus*, a canonical lawsuit. The defendants were Cardinal Sanchez, Archbishop Sepe and all those who had collaborated with them in the attempted destruction of Father Nicholas Gruner and the Apostolate. The plaintiffs were Father Gruner and several lay directors of the Apostolate, who had devoted their lives to its work.

The *libellus* set forth in painstaking detail the proof of what Canon

1389, enacted by their Pope, was designed to punish: the abuse of ecclesiastical power by high-ranking prelates in the Church. It detailed the illicit execution of *The Plan*; the unprecedented interference with the rights and jurisdiction of the benevolent bishops who had wished to incardinate Father Gruner or attend the Fatima Conferences; the outrageous attempt to interdict throughout the entire Church a Marian priest, and a Marian apostolate of faithful clergy and laity, who had done nothing wrong. And, finally, the *libellus* pleaded for relief from all the actions of those who had abused the authority of their high ecclesiastical offices to crush that priest and that Apostolate, while heresy and scandal run riot in the Church.

Under Canon 1405 this case was reserved exclusively to the Roman Pontiff. Only Pope John Paul II could hear it. And now the Pontiff had received the case from the hands of an Archbishop, a bishop and a humble young man pushing a wheelchair. The case was before the First See; there would be no biased judges passing judgment upon the validity of their own illicit acts. The judge would be the Pope—judge of the judges in the Church. In a most righteous sense, then, the hunters had become the hunted.

Before the Pope received it, Father Gruner presented a copy of the *libellus* to a distinguished Monsignor residing in Rome, a holy cleric of great learning who had found a niche in which to weather the post-conciliar storm. The Monsignor had been involved in the drafting of Canon 1405. As he read the *libellus* he smiled. Yes, it was for the redress of grievances such as these that Canon 1405 had been written, he confirmed. Father Gruner had understood well, and had proceeded correctly.

§

In three days the Third International Fatima Conference would end with a blessing by the bishops in attendance. Replicas of the Pilgrim statue would be distributed and the *Memorare* recited. The participants in the Conference would return to their homes and their dioceses around the world, renewed in their commitment to keep alive the Message of Fatima. The Message would not die with them.

Father Gruner would return twice more to Rome in the next six months to search for canon lawyers who were not afraid to assist him in resisting *The Plan*. Several had seemed interested but had hastily backed away after consulting with certain bureaucrats at the Vatican tribunals. Father Gruner would invoke the intercession of St. Anthony of Padua. The distinguished advocate of the Apostolic Signatura who would ultimately accept his case is a professor at a university—the University of Padua. Another signpost on the byways of Providence to gladden a weary traveler.

Before Father Gruner returned to Canada to await the outcome of the End Game he would have another surprise for his opponents across the board. He had found the proverbial "smoking gun". Civil litigation in Canada had uncovered in the files of the Archbishop of Toronto a most interesting letter, dated October 27, 1989, from Cardinal Agustoni, Prefect of the Apostolic Signatura, who, in 1989 was Secretary of the Congregation for the Clergy. The letter was addressed to the Bishop of Avellino. Entirely in Italian the letter secretly instructed the Bishop to revoke Father Gruner's permission to live outside the diocese, recall him to Avellino, threaten him with suspension, and if necessary to silence him, reduce him to the lay state. The letter cautioned that the bishop was to act as though these measures had been his own idea and not the Cardinal's. *The very judge who was about to decide Father Gruner's case in the Apostolic Signatura had been the one to devise The Plan.*

The Code of Canon law requires that any request for recusal of a Cardinal from judging a matter in a Church tribunal be made directly to the Pope.[18] Father Gruner would dispatch to the Pope from a Roman post office a copy of Cardinal Agustoni's 1989 letter and implore His Holiness to remove the Cardinal from his case. The smell was too putrid for even the bureaucrats to hide. It was announced several days later that Cardinal Agustoni had stepped down, marking the first time in the history of the Apostolic Signatura that its Cardinal Prefect had been recused. Another unprecedented turn in the unprecedented case of Father Nicholas Gruner.

The Signatura, minus Cardinal Agustoni, would now decide the two appeals which Father Gruner had placed before it: The first was an appeal from the original decree of the Signatura upholding the 1994 order to return to Avellino, which decree Father Gruner had finally received. The second was an appeal from the 1996 order to return to Avellino, which order had simply ignored Father Gruner's incardination by the Archbishop of Hyderabad. And then there was the canonical lawsuit now before the Pope. The End Game had become vastly more complicated than the opponents had imagined it would be. One could hope that Our Lady of Fatima was smiling down upon the chess board.

Father Gruner had done all that was humanly possible within the law of the Church. It was time for him to go home. To wait. To work. Above all, to pray.

CHAPTER 19

Epilogue

CATHOLICS IN CHINA, FACING CRACKDOWN, RETURN TO THE UNDERGROUND

The New York Times—January 27, 1997

"The new wave of religious repression [of Catholics] in China seems in largest measure the product of President Jiang Zemin's policy to shore up 'the socialist spiritual civilization'..."

LEFT WINS STRONG MANDATE AS VOTERS IN FRANCE REJECT AUSTERITY IN FAVOR OF JOBS

Socialists Are Expected to Form a Coalition with Communists

The New York Times—June 2, 1997

"French voters on Sunday gave the Socialist Party and its Communist allies a mandate ..."

CATHOLICS BARRED FROM CHURCH NEAR MOSCOW

Keston News Service—May 28, 1997

"[L]ocal authorities...continue to withhold registration of the Catholic Church on the pretext that the parish is a 'foreign' religious organization...[T]he authorities plan to turn the Church building, now under repair, into a Russian Orthodox museum..."

POLISH EX-COMMUNISTS BLASTED BY CARDINAL

CWN—May 30, 1997

"Cardinal Josef Glemp told 20,000 worshipers in a Corpus Christi procession that although Communism ended in 1989, the same people remain in power...'[T]he spirit of Marxism is rising over different fields of endeavor'."

June 6, 1997 — Feast of the Sacred Heart; Fort Erie, Ontario. Eighty years ago, Our Lady of Fatima appeared in Cova da Iria to deliver a message from God, authenticated by a public miracle the like of which has never been seen in the history of the world:

> "The Holy Father will consecrate Russia to Me and she will be converted, and a period of peace will be granted to the world...If people do what I ask, many souls will be saved and there will be peace."[1]

To read the headlines from the perspective of Fatima is to recognize that a Heavenly promise has not yet been fulfilled. The lack of fulfillment is not, of course, the fault of Heaven: "Russia will be converted" the Virgin had said at Fatima, and the Virgin does not lie. The fault can only be with men. The earthly plans of men militate against the Message of Fatima.

The Message of Fatima is not only a promise, but a warning. The promise has not been fulfilled because the warning has not been heeded:

> "If My requests are not granted, Russia will spread its errors throughout the world, raising up wars and persecutions against the Church, the good will be martyred, the Holy Father will have much to suffer and various nations will be annihilated."[2]

In Canada, Father Gruner reads of the Holy Father's trip to Poland which many say will be his last. In Poland, the earthly plans of men are proceeding apace. Over the past few years the Pope has addressed his people repeatedly as an anguished father addresses his errant children, pleading with them to turn away from the materialism they have embraced since "the fall of communism". Poland has recently enacted a liberal abortion law.

Only days before the Pope's arrival, the "ex-communists" now ruling the Pope's homeland had removed religious instruction from kindergarten classes and replaced it with sex-education. In response, Cardinal Glemp had asked: "Who can be opposed to little children's natural inclination towards God?" The answer is that men who hate God can be and are opposed to it.

Poland is ruled today by atheists. They are Communists by a different name. Catholics in China have been driven underground. France has given a mandate to socialists and Communists, as the European nations are integrated into a "European Union" of abortion, contraception and divorce. Abortion has been "legalized" in all the nations of the world, with "legalized" euthanasia following closely behind. In Russia, the Russian Orthodox are told by Catholic bishops that they need no longer return to Rome, and a Catholic parish church becomes a Russian Orthodox museum. Russia has not converted.

At Fatima, Our Lady informed us that "Russia is the instrument of chastisement chosen by Heaven to punish the whole world (for its sins) if we do not obtain beforehand, the conversion of that poor nation."[3] But Russia's conversion can only come about "by this means"; that is, by the consecration of Russia to the Immaculate Heart of Mary by the Pope and all the Catholic bishops on the same day at the same hour.[4] Failing the conversion of Russia in time, "various nations will be annihilated"[5] and "Russia will overcome the whole world."[6] Yet, Russia has not converted.

The purveyors of "Fatima Lite", now allied with the anti-Fatima forces in the Vatican, have been telling the world that the Pope consecrated Russia to the Immaculate Heart of Mary in the Orwellian year of 1984. Oddly enough, the Pope himself has never said so, although they constantly invoke his authority for their claim. Indeed, the Pope has said quite the opposite on the front page of *L'Osservatore Romano.*[7] Yet thirteen years after the alleged consecration of Russia, the anti-Fatima forces persist in their claim that Fatima is finished. As they peddle a "Fatima Lite", stripped of its Divine warnings and reduced to generic pietism, the world moves ever closer to that great chastisement of which the Virgin has warned us again and again in this age of apostasy.

In 1951, Pope Pius XII said, "the world today is worse than before the flood."[8] But in 1951, abortion had not even been legalized, except, of course, in the Soviet Union and Red China. Since then, Russia has spread her errors, including abortion, throughout the world, just as Our Lady had warned at Fatima. Since 1984 alone, over 600,000,000 children have been murdered in the womb.

In that very year, the marketers of "Fatima Lite" introduced their new product: "Consecration Lite". The blood of every child aborted since the introduction of "Consecration Lite" cries out to Heaven for vengeance, as Sacred Scripture confirms. Still, the merchants of "Fatima Lite" continue to purvey their fraudulent products, ignoring the warning that stares them in the face.

It is the warning of Fatima which most concerns Father Gruner today. The time for conversion and repentance promised by the Virgin if men cooperated with Her requests must nearly have expired, and the annihilation of nations must nearly be upon us. For many Catholics, there is a palpable sense that this is true. But for too many others, there is denial. "To whom shall I speak? And to whom shall I testify that he may hear? Their ears are uncircumcised and they cannot hear...And they healed the breach of the daughter of my people disgracefully, *saying 'Peace, peace', when there is no peace...*"[9] Thus declared the prophet Jeremiah against the false prophets of Jerusalem, who had made themselves deaf to the warnings of Heaven. In 1997 the false prophets have made their ears deaf to the Message of Fatima. "Peace, peace", they say, when there is no peace.

Father Nicholas Gruner does not claim to be a Jeremiah. He has never claimed to be anything but a Catholic priest who can see what is manifest: that the promises of Our Lady have not come to pass, and that the fault cannot be Hers. He will not say peace, peace, when he can see there is no peace. He will not commit that sin. He resolves to go on with what he is doing until God no longer permits it. He will pray for the strength to do so.

Introibo ad altare Dei. I will go in to the altar of God. The prayer of the Mass ascends to Heaven in the private chapel of Father Gruner's modest dwelling. Anyone who has seen Father Gruner offer Mass will be reminded that he is, before all things, a priest. He offers Mass as he always does, in the ancient Latin rite of the Catholic Church. Here, too, the words of Jeremiah may be recalled: "Stand ye on the ways, and see, and ask for the *old* paths, which is the good way, and walk ye in it, and you will find refreshment for your souls..."[10]

A few months earlier, during Father Gruner's last trip to Rome, Cardinal Ratzinger gave a press conference in which he introduced his newly-published memoirs. In those memoirs, the Cardinal concedes what had been obvious all along: The drastic reforms of the Mass in 1969 had caused "extremely serious damage to the Church".[11] The suppression of the "old Mass" was a "break in the history of the liturgy, the consequences of which could only be tragic".[12] And most significant in light of the Third Secret, which the Cardinal has read: "The ecclesial crisis in which we find ourselves today depends in great part on the collapse of the liturgy".[13]

For nearly 30 years the post-conciliarist revolutionaries and their active and passive collaborators had mocked and marginalized "traditionalist" Catholics as "disobedient" and "disloyal" to the Pope, for saying the very things now being said by the Prefect of the Congregation for the Doctrine of the Faith. Cardinal Ratzinger is known to be the closest advisor to the Pope — the Pope, in whose hands Father Gruner's *libellus*[14] had been placed only six months before by two prelates and a young man. For Father Gruner, there was some small measure of relief and hope in what the Cardinal had said in his memoirs. The tide was perhaps beginning to turn, not merely for him but for the whole Church. The Message of Fatima might yet be heeded; the new Jerusalem might yet avoid the fate of the old.[15]

After Mass in the private chapel, there would, as always, be many prayers at the altar. Father Gruner would kneel serenely for nearly half an hour on a solid wood kneeler which would cause many others to squirm in pain in a few moments. Later there would be the Divine Office and always the Rosary. Some three hours that day, and every day, would be consumed by prayer. Mass after Mass, Rosary after Rosary, would be offered for the Consecration of Russia and the Apostolate devoted to its promulgation.

As the priest prays, his prayers are joined by those of bishops, priests, religious and laity around the world who have stood by him and supported his work despite all the controversy it has engendered. Why do they do so? The answer to that question cannot be found in any mere attachment to the man. The man is no more important than other men. The answer is found in what he *says*. For what he says is nothing more, *or less,* than what Our Lady said at Fatima.

The priest on his knees in the little chapel understands that the Message of Fatima is the urgent plea of a Mother to Her children, at a time of unprecedented peril for a world which grows more rebellious by the hour: "Only I can help you," She said at Fatima. By the grace of God obtained through the intercession of the Blessed Virgin Mary, the priest believes this as a child believes it — literally, and with his whole heart. So, by that same grace, do many others. But not enough.

The sun descends beneath the edge of the Niagara escarpment as Father Gruner prays the Divine Office, fulfilling one of the duties of the state to which God has called him. Those who have opposed Father Gruner's work for so long know that the grace of his priesthood sustains him. When the sun that has descended on Niagara rises in Rome, the battle over Father Gruner's priesthood will continue.

On a stage far vaster than the distance between Canada and Rome, the drama of Fatima moves toward its conclusion. In the fading light of a secluded chapel, Father Gruner prays. To the right of the altar where he has just offered the Holy Sacrifice of the Mass is a statue of the Pilgrim Virgin which had been blessed at Fatima by the very Pope who had proclaimed Mary, Mother of the Church as well as Mother of God. The Pilgrim Virgin smiles down upon the kneeling priest, as She has throughout the twenty years of their travels together.

The Apostolate goes on, and the man they call "*the Fatima Priest*" continues to guide the dissemination of the Message of Fatima to millions. To the bewilderment of the anti-Fatima forces, the Apostolate continues to gather support for the cause of Our Lady of Fatima from Catholics around the world.

In the end, it can only be explained by the priest's unwavering adherence to a Message which is not his, or any man's, but Hers. The many Catholics who support Father Gruner and his work, have provided unanimous testimony that his survival despite all opposition, is owing to nothing more or less than this: "He tells the truth."

BOOK II

IN HIS OWN WORDS

Chapter 1

Schism And The Common Good

Ten years of serving Our Lady of Fatima had made Father Nicholas Gruner a household word around the world by the mid '80's. His *Fatima Crusader* now had a readership of over one million souls. He had logged months touring with the Pilgrim Virgin Statue. Hundreds of thousands of rosaries, scapulars and devotional booklets were in the hands of the needy, and the poor were having the Gospel preached to them through these instruments his work had generated. But the shadows of Church and State politics that had been deepening all round his Apostolate seemed suddenly ever more charged and dark. Yet nothing in the Apostolate's history so far even suggested that a rest or a lull in its agenda was in the offing. What would the trajectory of the Apostolate be in the next few years?

Recently, on a May 13th anniversary of the first Fatima apparition, Father Gruner sat in the living room of his modest quarters in Fort Erie, Ontario, Canada, and looked back over those crucial years. To best underscore the reason and the need for his Apostolate's continued drive, he verbally scanned the state of the Church in our day. With the comforting rays of a classical Canadian sunset warming the library titles, he addressed the issue at the heart of the consecration dilemma — the question of the actual influence John Paul II has on his bishops.

> "If the Pope needs to order the bishops to consecrate Russia with him on the same day in their own cathedrals around the world, what kind of motivation is he going to provide them. What kind of co-operation will he receive from some of his bureaucrats in the Vatican?"

Father Gruner examined the quandary through the prism of salvation history.

"Before original sin Adam had perfect control of his faculties. One can say Adam was not tempted to over-eat because his appetite was so subject to his reason. It was obedient to his reason, as were all his faculties. Thus, after he ate enough, the appetite simply turned off until it was needed again. If he needed sleep, he didn't say wait, I've got to do this last job and stay up three more hours. His every faculty was so obedient that it was not a question of his members saying but I want to go this direction, I want to go that direction.

"Today, after original sin, without grace and without mortification, none of us would have any control. We see the case of people who drink too much, who are not faithful to their wives or husbands, not because they don't realize there's something wrong, but because of original sin their appetites have not been reined in by their reason. But Adam initially did not have that struggle. What happened after original sin? He no longer obeyed his reason. His eyes wanted to see what they should not see, his ears to hear what they should not hear, and his wife did not want to obey him either. Her own faculties did not want to obey her. These are the effects of original sin.

"Sickness comes about because of disorder, because the agent of sickness does not obey the higher faculty. Ultimately, this is what is happening in the Church. The disobedient bureaucrats have not obeyed God, so they are reaping the reward.

"They tell God, 'This is our church now. You're up in Heaven, we're going to do things our way. We're not going to listen to the voice of prophecy, we're not going to reveal the Third Secret, we're not going to consecrate Russia, we're just going to do our own thing.' At the same time, they say to their inferiors, 'you down there, you must obey me.'

"Since Our Lady's message, which is obligatory to obey, has been largely ignored by those in authority, the Church is suffering diabolical disorientation. People may do their best resisting the disorientation but they don't have the specifics, they're not canonists, they're not theologians, they simply intuit that something is wrong.

"Let me share with you a key to understanding much of the disunity and division that has invaded the Church since 1960. I was in the seminary in Montreal when I made one of my biggest discoveries during my theological training.

"In January of 1967, the Vicar General of the diocese of Montreal put out a statement in which the basic impression created in the mind of the reader was that priests and lay people were forbidden to promote the message of Garabandal."

Nicholas Gruner, like thousands of other people read that letter and understood that it was his obligation under obedience to not promote Garabandal in the diocese. Then he read it a second time.

"I realized that no order was contained in it whatsoever. In my thorough Germanic nature, I went to the Vice Chancellor of the diocese of Montreal and I said, 'Do I understand this letter correctly or not?' I told him it appears to give an order, but upon careful reading it is clear that no order is given. His answer was extremely enlightening. He said, 'Yes, we wrote it that way on purpose.'

"It took me some time to think about it but I finally realized the implication of such a diabolical technique. I realized I was not bound to obey such an order 'not given'. In Canon Law a person in authority has to give an order and not simply imply he has given one. Second, the person giving an order has to take personal responsibility for giving the order. In this case it was obvious, by the Msgr.'s own admission, that they had purposely written the letter in such a way as to give the appearance of an order, without having actually given it, so when proven wrong they can state they never said that."

The library interior altered as the sunset darkened. Father Gruner thought aloud about the whole nature of subversion.

"Jesus tells us in St. John's gospel that the shepherd is the one that comes through the gate, but the thief climbs up another way.[1]

"In Isaias, God, speaking to the prophet says, 'I have not spoken in secret, in a dark place of the earth.' In other words, God, and those who act authoritatively in God's stead, must be willing to publicly take responsibility for what they say.[2]

"Whereas a subversive, whether in the Church or the State, such as Masons, do not give their orders in the open and they do not take personal responsibility for the orders they give.

"To this day, some bureaucrats, even in the Vatican, craft a document to give the impression of issuing an order without any order actually being given. This is not an accident or sloppiness but it is a subversive technique. It doesn't look like it at first. The technique is diabolical. This is also a schismatic practice. Schism in Greek means 'to tear apart'. Today it means to tear apart the unity of the Church. When authority gives such non-orders, the faithful are divided. Those faithful who think they must be obedient to the 'non-order' frequently misjudge the other faithful who are astute enough to not fall for the 'non-order'. Thus many good priests and faithful in the Church are forced to work against faithful who, out of misguided loyalty to the 'non-order', put obstacles in their way. 'The same technique was used regarding the Novus Ordo.

"In 1969, the New Mass was 'promulgated' in such a way as to give the impression that the New Mass was what priests must now say and that the old Mass was forbidden.

"But look closely and you will find that there was no order given, that no law was passed and that it is not binding.

"Nevertheless, you now have people saying, 'I will not attend the Tridentine Mass', and they say to those on the other side, 'You are disobedient. How can you call yourself Catholic and disobey the order of the Pope?' The confusion was deliberately caused."

One week after making this statement, Father Gruner's opinion regarding the legality of the old Mass received forceful support from a high-profile Vatican official. On May 20, 1995, Alfons Cardinal Stickler, speaking before several hundred lay people, canon lawyers and priests at Fort Lee, New Jersey, confirmed that in 1986, a papal commission of nine Cardinals appointed by Pope John Paul II found that the Tridentine Mass was perfectly legal and in force and that no Pope or any other competent authority had forbidden it from being said by any Catholic priest.

"The technique is diabolical," Father Gruner continued, "and has set up within the Body of the Church, two opposing factions. There is a battle within the Body of the Church because of the technique. The members of the Mystical Body are warring against one another because of it. You cannot give two contradictory orders and expect the body politic to live in peace as God intended them to. Let me explain:

"If a father tells his two oldest sons to paint the living room green and then outside their hearing tells the next two sons to paint it red and then hides himself so that neither the first sons nor the second sons can find him, you have massive confusion.

"Both sets go off and paint the same living room, each one fights against the other because each is being obedient to the father. But the father gave contradictory orders which causes in turn the sons to fight, to break up, to tear apart unity which should be in the family. The father's orders would be causing a schism in the family. Such orders are wrong. If done deliberately by the father, they are sinful. It is clearly an abuse of authority.

"You still get the same result if, instead of giving directly contradictory orders, he spoke in such a way as to deliberately mislead his sons into thinking he gave orders binding them to do a certain thing, but some sons were astute enough to realize he had not actually given an order and these sons were actually able to realize that the 'implied' order was sinfully imprudent and were able to realize that their father did not have authority for such orders, and that is why he spoke that way, whereas, on the other side, there were other sons who were not so astute and felt bound to obey this 'implied' order. Then the sons would still be at loggerheads. Still a schism is caused by the deliberately schismatic command and the father would be guilty of sin for doing such a thing to his children. This is what is happening in the Church today. Let me give an example to illustrate what is happening:

"My mother judged me for years as not being obedient because I ignored that bogus Chancery letter in Montreal. She did not tell me of her judgment but held it against me for several years. It only came up when we were discussing something else and I explained. She became angry with the Chancery officials for having perpetrated this lie upon her."

Gradually the weight of the chaos in the Church seemed to bear down on the darkening evening itself, as it had on the very Faith through heresy, apostasy, schism.

"Schism," Father Gruner explained "means to tear apart and usually schism is understood that someone does not recognize legitimate Church authority. But authority can also be guilty of schism by giving orders that are illegal or given in such a way as to cause division among the faithful, as I explained above. St. Augustine says, 'In essentials we must have unity, in non-essentials we have liberty, and in all things have charity.' Garabandal is not an essential. I had the right to promote it and my mother had the right not to do so if she chose. This deceiving letter caused a division between a son and his mother. This technique is immoral, yet it is too widely used by some Churchmen in authority.

"Who's at fault? God does not contradict in dogma. He cannot contradict a truth, neither can God contradict in orders. God is not at fault in this but those who abuse their positions of authority clearly are at fault.

"God the Sanctifier does not contradict God the Creator. There is only one God. God is the author of nature and grace builds on nature.

"The true Church cannot give contradictory orders. This technique has been used to destroy the Church from within. The individuals who have been employing this technique consider themselves more intelligent than the average guy. But they are working for the devil. The Church is not the bureaucrats' plaything. These bureaucrats have caused a virtual schism. They are tearing apart the Body of the Church by this technique of giving the impression of issuing an order but not issuing it.

"God, the Creator, God, the Sanctifier, created the Church. He did not make the laws of the Church in contradiction to the natural law. All public authority in Church or State in promulgating law must respect the natural law governing men. Grace builds on nature, as St. Thomas teaches.

"It is a principle of natural law that no Catholic philosopher, no Catholic Theologian would deny — that for a law, any kind of a law, to be truly law it must be promulgated; if a law is not promulgated[3] then it does not bind in conscience, and we need not obey it.

"Thus, in the example given above about the Montreal chancery, I was totally not bound by that 'non-order'. I was free to disobey. Similarly, I am not bound by the non-command which passes for a law — to not say the Tridentine Mass.

"Such orders are clearly causing division in the body of the faithful. Such divisions are obviously and clearly against the common good and it is clearly the abuse of authority by those in authority which is causing these divisions.

"Our Lord said, 'Let your words be yes for yes and no for no, anything else comes from the evil one.' (Cf. Matt 5:37, James 5:12)

"This is particularly true in the office of a public authority whether it be the pope or the governor or a judge or a legislator. This seems to be a terrible persecution for the Church, this double talk that's going on. With this persecution of the Church, you are being persecuted, I am being persecuted."

Thirty years after Vatican II ended, one of its most vital decisions was shaping the possible destiny of this Fatima Apostolate.

"When Vatican II refused to invoke its authority to teach infallibly, it was not being fully magisterial, plain and simple. In short, it was not accepting full responsibility. As a result, there are people in the Church who feel Vatican II is the only definitive Council despite the fact that the Council Fathers themselves clearly pointed out that it is not infallible in many things. As a matter of fact, some Vatican II interpretations are clearly heretical. Post-Vatican II Catholics, because of their own ignorance of the facts, erroneously think that the Catholic faithful who hold closely to the infallible definitions of Trent and Vatican I are somehow 'outside the Church' and accuse them of being against the Pope. They even go so far as to 'self-righteously' punish those Catholics who are faithful to the infallible Magisterium. All this would not be taking place had the teaching authority of Vatican II taken full responsibility and taught only those things it was certain of, in clear language, and invoked its infallible authority.

"The Vatican-Moscow Agreement, concocted in secret, is another example of them refusing to take public responsibility. Part of the Agreement is not to talk about it. What government has the authority to make something binding on the members of an institution without it being public? This secret agreement which attempts to bind the Church into silence before grave moral evil is clearly against the Common Good, the Natural Law, and the Divine Positive Law.

"What is missing is the responsibility to the Common Good. Even a Pope, if he were to give an order contradicting the Common Good of the Church, then that order would not be binding. St. Paul makes it clear. No Pope has the right to be silent or to command silence in face of apostasy, schism or heresy against God, Christ and the Church.[4]

"A good Catholic philosopher could prove by the light of reason alone that each of us is obliged to help the Common Good, or the Common Wealth as it is sometimes called, by our work, actions, and words and by avoiding anything that would harm it.

"First, it should be obvious that each member of a city, a family, a country, should not do anything that will harm the Common Good.

"Second, he should also do all he can to help the Common Good to the extent his other duties to God and neighbor allow.

"To prove this, at least in part, what would happen to our society if people were allowed to act in such a way as to harm public good — so long as their lying or cheating did not harm identifiable individuals alone, but only a group?

"If God made individuals, He also made society. Man is meant to live in society. God did not want us to live all alone. Society, to survive, needs certain rules to be obeyed by all, even when they are sometimes inconvenient, even costly, to some individuals who practice them.

"Society cannot exist if all members only look out for their own interests, and take advantage of all the rest of the members of society.

"Such an attitude cannot be justified on the grounds of taking care of a family, or an exclusive group of friends, when it causes the rest of society to lose their wealth, their freedom, their lives, and most important, their souls.

"We are our brother's keeper. We must respect his freedom and independence but we must also look out for his interests if Providence puts events, people or things in our path that impact on our neighbor's good.

"It is not only true for my neighbor whom I know or meet

occasionaly, but for all my fellow men in my community, country, world, and especially, as St. Paul admonishes, for all who belong to the household of the Faith.[5]

"By the light of revelation, we know that God the Father appointed God the Son, Redeemer of all mankind, as King of kings and Lord of lords.[6] Thus all presidents, kings, lords, judges, legislators, officials and bureaucrats must obey the King of kings, Christ the Lord, in Church matters and in civil matters, upholding the right to property, life, and freedom in general, and also in particular instances.

"Thus the common citizen must vote for those legislators and presidents and Prime Ministers that uphold the law of God and vote against those that would attack the law of God.

"It is what we pray for every day when we say the Rosary. Every day we say, 'Thy Kingdom come.' If we really mean this, that we pray for the coming of Christ's Kingdom on earth, we must work and speak and pray for the Common Good.

"We are not only praying for the coming of mankind into Christ's kingdom in Heaven. We are also praying for His kingdom here on earth, because Jesus taught us to pray 'Thy will be done on earth as it is in Heaven.'

"On the contrary, a subversive group attacks the very basis of authority. The very nature of a secret society is you don't know who the authority is, what doctrine it is upholding. In the Natural Law, which God has instilled into the very fabric of society authority, responsibility and accountability go together. A person can't have authority without responsibility. That's in the Natural Law. This is how God created public authority to operate both in the Church and in the State. By 'giving orders without giving them', in the short term, the public authority seems to get the benefit of giving an order without taking responsibility for it. In the long term, such governance is destructive of authority and divides members of the Church. 'A house divided against itself cannot stand.'...Jesus said.

"Our duty is to build up the House of the Faith, not tear it down. Our duty is to build up the welfare of society as well. The directives of Our Lady of Fatima are the most perfect means of doing both."

THE COMMON GOOD

"In continuing to promote the full message of Fatima, I am only fulfilling my obligation to the Common Good. Yet I am not the only one who has this duty. Everyone is bound to contribute to the Common Good. If this was more generally understood, then many more people would promote the Fatima message, perhaps not to the extent that I am, but in whatever capacity they were able.

"The issue of the Common Good is a vital subject that is much neglected these days. It needs to be more widely known in order to correct a multitude of false ideas that work toward the detriment of public welfare, the de-Christianization of society, and prevent Our Lady's requests from being fulfilled.

"This is not just a particular fancy of mine. The Common Good is of such significance that it actually is a vital component to what makes a just law. So it is necessary to address the issue of the Common Good first in regard to law, our obligation to it, and especially how it relates to Fatima.

"Catholic moral theology of all time teaches that there are four components to a just law.

"A just law is:

1) a principle of reason,

2) for the Common Good,

3) promulgated,

4) by the person who has care of the community.[7]

"If any one of these four 'ingredients' is missing, then there is no true law and we are free to disregard it.

"So we can see how important is the Common Good. Any act of legislation that is not for the Common Good is not a genuine law. So as I mentioned before, even if a Pope were to give an order which went against the Common Good of the Church, then that order would not be binding.

"So then, not only is the Common Good a constitutive part of law and society, but it is something to which *everyone* must contribute, be they those who govern, or those who are governed.

"Our obligation to the Common Good is twofold. Not only may we *not do* anything that *hinders* the Common Good, but we must do all we can to *advance* the Common Good.

"Of course, in order to keep our balance, we must point out that there is a hierarchy of personal responsibility which includes the Common Good. One has one's duty to God first of all; duty to one's soul second of all; duty to one's own personal well-being and after one's soul and the soul of one's neighbor, particularly one's family and friends. Finally, there is the duty to the Common Good.[8]

"The Common Good actively involves our neighbor, those men or women and children who in some way or other God puts on our path, whether they live next door to us, whether they work at the same job as we do, or whether we sit on the same bus with them going to work, or whether we see them at church on Sunday. Somewhere or other we are in contact with them; somehow or other because of physical location or because of the kind of work we do, some specific person is a neighbor to us. Most important, our duty to the Common Good not only involves the neighbor whom we meet, but the neighbor whom we shall never meet.

"For example, if I am preparing to vote in an election, I cannot vote for a pro-abortionist. A certain pro-abortionist may have a great plan for saving employment, but I cannot vote for a pro-abortionist because he is doing something that is intrinsically evil, i.e., using the position of legislator to do evil to thousands of babies. My obligation to the Common Good requires that even though my neighbor, my co-worker, my brother, sister, aunt or cousin might be puzzled by my choice in voting, I still am bound to do the right thing in the fear of God for the sake of the natural and supernatural welfare of individuals and society.

"It does not matter that I probably will never meet the children I save by voting pro-life. I am still responsible before God to protect them by whatever actions I take, however small, in the public domain.

"Most of us fail in our obligation to the Common Good of both the Church and the State because we falsely believe that public welfare is solely a matter for the authorities. In the State, there is the notion that only rulers and politicians are responsible for the Common Good. In the Church, there is the idea that only the Pope, Cardinals, bishops and priests are responsible for the Common Good. In both cases, the average layman operates on the premise that because he cannot do a lot, therefore he may do nothing. Sometimes this incorrect notion is the result of misinformation, sometimes it is due to disinformation (that is the deliberate efforts of enemies to spread falsehood under the guise of information). Whatever its cause, this false mind-set must be fought against. In the case of Fatima, it has disastrous consequences.

"Of course, more is expected of those who have wealth, power, influence, prestige, to uphold the Common Good. But because we may not be in positions of authority, power or influence, that does not mean we can do nothing. It does not mean we have nothing to contribute. We are never excused from working toward the Common Good.

"Moreover, this duty does not only extend to our peers and those over whom we have authority, but we must even rebuke our superiors if necessary, if our superiors are acting to the detriment of the Common Good, providing it is done with due regard for persons and positions. St. Paul had to rebuke St. Peter, the first Pope, when he 'walked not in truth'.[9] And Saint Thomas Aquinas teaches that it is sometimes to the duty of the inferior to either disobey or correct the superior[10] if the Common Good calls for it.

"St. Robert Belarmine says that we must positively resist those policies of people in authority which go against the Common Good.[11]

"All this, of course, must be done in charity, since knowledge and action without charity is destructive.

"On the other hand, charity, to be effective, must be based on truth. Without the truth in the mind of the charitable person, his efforts to build up the Church are often doomed to failure because of his lack of knowledge. Much destruction has come to the Church and world because of 'misdirected charity', i.e., the toleration of behaviors and principles that are destructive to the Church and society. Often, this misdirected charity is the fruit of ignorance. Does not Scripture teach 'My people perish for lack of knowledge'?[12]

"Now, charity and truth must be lived out. Charity and truth impose certain duties upon us, and sometimes these duties are difficult.

"Therefore, we must not stand by idly when a lie is told that affects the Common Good or even the good of a smaller segment of society. Also, if we know the truth that will signifcantly help our fellow man, we must proclaim it, because by our silence, the good may be lost.

"This is especially true for Catholics living in the 20th Century since we now have the spiritual weapons God has given us that will infallibly bring about His kingdom on earth.

Because in our time, God has revealed in a public, prophetic revelation His plan for world peace and the establishment of His kingdom on earth. This plan was established from all eternity, but was made clearer in our day through the message of Fatima.

"Never before in history, I think, has an apparition of Our Lady been so identified with Sacred Scripture. Pope Paul VI clearly indicated his thought that Our Lady's appearance and message of Fatima is a fulfillment of biblical prophecy, namely Apocalypse, Chapter 12. He believed that Our Lady of Fatima is what Saint John the Apostle saw in a prophetic vision 2000 years ago.[13] Sister Lucy tells us the Third Secret is in the Apocalypse, Chapters 7 to 13.[14] Cardinal Ratzinger tells us he has read the Third Secret and that it refers to the last times and that it is contained in Sacred Scripture.[15]

"Clearly, if the message of Fatima is part of Biblical prophecy it is not simply a private revelation that can be ignored without sin."

In his book *World Enslavement or Peace, It's Up to the Pope,* Father

Gruner spent 50 pages demonstrating that even if Fatima is not contained in Sacred Scripture, we are still bound under pain of sin to listen to and obey Our Lady of Fatima's message and requests. This obligation, he explained, extends to all of us: layperson, religious, priests, bishops and the Pope.

"If I were to deny or put into doubt this truth, I myself would not be serving the Common Good. I would sin.

"Nor am I the only one bound to uphold this truth. Anyone who knows Fatima and its message cannot escape this obligation. If anyone thinks I am incorrect, then I believe they must at least examine my theological reasons before they conclude the contrary position, since we all have the obligation to seek the truth.

"Imagine the glorious consequences if enough people understood their duty to the Common Good. Just think if every layperson, man, woman and child were aware of Fatima and the crucial role the consecration of Russia has for their faith, family, freedom and that of all their loved ones. Imagine if every man, woman and child in the entire world phoned their bishop, their pastor, and the Pope, to ask him to do the consecration of Russia. If this was done, you can be sure the Pope would do it.

"Because he would have all the moral support he needs to enact it. He would be able to command any recalcitrant prelate, he would have no fear of any disobedient bishop leading a revolt against his Papacy.

"Let no one say the laity have no place in dealing with the consecration. It is true that in this matter they do not have the power to command. It is true laypeople are not bishops, they have not been called upon to directly make the act of consecration. Only the bishops together with the Pope can do that. But laypeople certainly have the power to inform the bishops, they have the power to influence public opinion inside and outside the Church. They have the power to invoke their God-given rights to ask for responsible government and to hold their superiors accountable to the public promises their pastors made in taking on their job as pastors.

"There is much they can do. They can pray for it as Jesus and Mary have told us to. They can sacrifice for it. They can tell all persons they meet about it. Because God wants this consecration and its resultant conversion of Russia to be known and seen as a victory to the Immaculate Heart of Mary.[16] This will only be known if those who know the Fatima prophecies about Russia pass this on to their fellow man.

"The false theology and mind-set that 'the laity can do nothing' must be overcome so as to create a groundswell of support for the consecration of Russia. This widespread public show of support could happen, but to achieve it we need more priests, more laypeople and more bishops coming out in favor of the collegial consecration of Russia as requested by Our Lady of Fatima.

"We certainly have not been left without guidance and directives in this area.

"Sister Lucy indirectly addressed the issue of the lay - Catholic's duty to the Common Good when she said 'do not wait for the call of penance to come from the hierarchy'.[17] It is obvious, then, that Sister Lucy is encouraging personal initiative. On another occasion when asked about insisting on the consecration, She answered by clearly pointing out the necessity of the Consecration of Russia as commanded at Fatima.[18]

"Another great Catholic of our time, Hamish Fraser, pointed out that lay-Catholics have a duty to act as apostles in their own milieux without waiting for orders from the hierarchy. He castigated those Catholics who simply lament the deplorable condition of Church and State today but took no action to restore order.[19]

"Canons 208-223 of the New Code of Canon Law, which deal with the rights and obligations of Christ's Faithful, support this position in various places. I am especially impressed with Canon 212, No. 2 which states that 'Christ's faithful are at liberty to make known their needs, especially their spiritual needs, and their wishes to the Pastors of the Church.' That is a direct quote from Canon Law. Yet, when we respectfully exercise this liberty in petitioning for the consecration of Russia, we are falsely accused as inciting 'bitterness toward the Holy Father.'

"I am also very much struck by Canon 225, No. 2 which states that 'each lay person in accord with his or her condition is bound by a special duty to imbue and perfect the order of temporal affairs with the spirit of the Gospel'. What better way to permeate the 'order of temporal affairs' with 'the spirit of the Gospel', than to work toward the collegial consecration of Russia, which is Our Lord's plan for perfecting society according to His Divine Law through Our Lady's Immaculate Heart?

"So, while it may be said that working for the Common Good in this manner is 'politically incorrect', especially in ecclesiastical circles, it cannot be said that it is against Canon Law, Church teaching and practice.

"Therefore, let no one say the laity have no place in dealing with the consecration. It is wrong and against our prayer 'Thy kingdom come, Thy will be done on earth' and our Faith to say that the layman can do nothing about bringing the reign of Christ on earth. As I mentioned before, this is especially true for Catholics living in the 20th Century because now we have the spiritual weapons God has given us that will infallibly bring about His kingdom on earth. First, we must make our Eucharistic reparation, pray Rosaries, wear the Brown Scapular, make the Five First Saturdays and bring about the Consecration of Russia. In our time, God has revealed in the public, prophetic revelation of Fatima, His plan for world peace and the establishment of His kingdom on earth.

Remember, God wants this consecration and its resultant conversion of Russia to be known and seen as a victory of the Immaculate Heart of Mary. This will only be known if those who are aware of the Fatima prophecies about Russia pass this on to their fellow man.

"Laypeople and priests can support those who are promoting it among the laity, priests and bishops by their prayers, sacrifices and financial contributions. They can let the truth be known by opposing and silencing those ignorant of Her message, who fight against the collegial consecration and who seek to discredit those who promote the consecration of Russia.

"If they have been guilty in the past of sowing confusion of mind, or dissipation of energy, or division of hearts over this issue, they should make reparation by reversing their previous sins of word and actions, and work as hard or harder to promote union of minds, hearts and energy toward this great moment of Triumph of Our Lady.

"All those in whatever walk of life, who could help promote the consecration of Russia and do not, have only themselves to blame if the threatened chastisement of being enslaved by atheistic Russia takes place. They, and their families, can expect in justice that they, first of all, will fall victims of their sins of omission.

"Perhaps they actually would be second to fall victim. The first place is reserved for those who, while claiming the laypeople can do nothing in this regard, make it their business to print and promote lies among members of the Church against this most crucial request of Our Lady regarding the necessity of consecrating Russia.

"Today, we need to pray for protection from those people who work against the Fatima message. I am referring to those who do nothing to promote this absolutely essential condition for world peace (because of their ignorance of the true Fatima requests). These same people spend a great deal of energy, like the Pharisees of old, pretending to be scandalized at those who promote the truth. Further, just like the Pharisees of old, they seek to destroy the reputation of those good people who refuse to be hypocrites like themselves. It is similar to what the Pharisees did to Our Lord.

"In their spiritual jealousy, they become guilty of fighting against God and the known truth. This is a weighty offense and may even be a sin against the Holy Ghost.[20] Such as these are in grave danger of losing their souls, and it may take a special grace to save them from hellfire.

"We must pray for the weak souls who labor under the burden that these hypocrites place on them through their lies and libel.

"We must be on our guard against them.

"We must avoid people and directives that tell us:

1) That we have no obligation to the Common Good

2) That the individual can do nothing to effect the consecration of Russia.

3) That Fatima is not morally binding on us.

"If they really believed those three statements, why do they seek to dissuade us? If it really makes no difference, why don't they just leave all of us in peace?

"Secondly, why do they profess love, devotion and obedience to Our Lady of Fatima, while all the while they work to destroy people's belief, adherence and support of Her full message and request. Our Lady came for a purpose. She told us the truth and She expects us to believe and obey Her. These people claim Our Lady for themselves, but they lie. Do not follow them.

"No matter what anyone may say to the contrary, it is a fact that we all have an obligation to the Common Good. We must tell the truth in public and private. Therefore, we must publish and promote the truth, the whole truth about Fatima. We must pray and work for the will of God to be done on earth as it is in Heaven.

"None of us are excused from this obligation. None of us may hinder those who truly work for the Common Good. To the extent that we are able, we must do what we can now because none of us have a guarantee that we will be here tomorrow.

"We have to pray our Rosary each day, make sacrifices, wear our scapular, consecrate ourselves to Our Lady and make the Five First Saturdays. These are things we can do as Catholics. It's *everybody's* job, not just the Pope and the bishops. Heaven did not give the great grace of the Fatima Message in order for us to yawn toward it with indifference. Responding to Fatima is a duty to which each and every one of us will have to render an account before God."

Father Gruner's whole life and apostolate have been lived in the conviction that, in spite of what the media says, Communism's struggle against religion has never been more alive or active. He makes no apologies for his conviction that Our Lady of Fatima and *only* Our Lady of Fatima has the antidote to the poison that, in spite of Vatican bureaucrats insisting upon the opposite, simply will not vacate the veins and arteries of the Church.

In the last 20 years, thousands of priests have left the priesthood. Why does Father Gruner continue to soldier-on in the face of almost unprecedented opposition from within his own Church? In reply, Father Gruner says, "I believe Our Lady means it absolutely and literally when She says 'If My requests are granted, many souls will be saved and there will be peace. If My requests are not granted, Russia will raise up wars and persecutions against the Church, the good will be martyred, the Holy Father will have much to suffer, various nations will be annihilated.'[21] I don't think we have any other choice *but* to continue to promote Our Lady's full Message with all our strength. What else can we do?"

The source of his determination in the face of seemingly insurmountable odds was, after all, discovered early in life:

"Never was it known that any who implored Thy help and sought Thy intercession were left unaided ..."[22]

Chapter 2

Why The Open Letter?

Father Gruner, do you think the Open Letter to the Pope of July 12, 1995 brought you any closer to your life's goal?

"Yes. I think it has already. But will it actually succeed? That still depends. Let me explain.

"First let me note that we are not here to blame the Pope or the bishops for not doing that act as commanded by Our Lady of Fatima. Nor is it our purpose to pass the buck, the responsibility, to everyone else so we can feel good about ourselves. We all, lay people, priests, bishops, Cardinals and even the Pope must realize that we are in this together.

"In fact, the repercussions for good or evil do not only affect Catholics, but every man, woman and child on the face of the earth today and for generations to come. All of us, saint and sinner together, priests and bishops and laymen, will be either annihilated or enslaved unless this Fatima command is obeyed.

"Time is of the essence to realize that we are like the people of God standing on the banks of the Red Sea[1] and the army of God-hating militant atheists, secular humanists, new age fanatics, Masons, Marxists, just to name a few, are joined together to either kill or enslave anyone who doesn't go along with their agenda.

"There is no hope, no human solution, no escape from their clutches except through obedience to Our Lady of Fatima's requests; in particular, the widespread praying of the daily Rosary, the practice of the Five First Saturdays, the conversion of hearts of enough people away from sin to the fervent practice of the Catholic Faith and above all and especially and necessarily, the obedience of the Pope and the bishops to consecrate Russia to the Immaculate Heart of Mary.

"If we do not achieve this goal in time then we shall be enslaved, imprisoned, impoverished, tortured, killed and entire nations annihilated. Until we become aware of the solution and the urgency that time is running out, humanity could just slide into this disastrous punishment and still not know why it all happened.

"Thus it is crucial to continue to talk about it, publish it and insist upon it; in public and private; in season and out of season; in the hope, prayer and expectation that finally enough people will eventually pick up the ball and run with it.

"Again I must insist; we are not here to blame anyone, but we must draw upon the lessons of history so that we are not condemned to repeating the same errors. Already since 1917, we have had the Spanish Civil War with 1.5 million dead, World War II with 50 million dead, the Korean War, Vietnam, Afghanistan, the Persian Gulf conflict, Palestine, Bosnia, Somalia and many more too numerous to mention here; all because the solemn request for the consecration of Russia has not been effected since Our Lady's request on June 13, 1929.

"Conceivably, we could have World War III, and even more local, regional and global wars and still, people would not know why it happened, nor would they know wherein lies the solution.

"In the last 80 years, there were those who fought in the First World War on the promise that by joining in the battle they would end all wars, but obviously the secular solution to obtain world peace did not come out of WWI or from the League of Nations that followed World War I.

"There are those in Germany who were terribly treated by the Treaty of Versailles in 1919 following WWI and were essentially driven into the arms of Hitler and his brand of saving the German nation. That also ended in disaster, not only for the world but for them as well.

"Then there are the idealists as well as the greedy who have rallied to the Communist solution which is essentially to inflict war on everyone and hate everyone who is not part of this Communist alliance.

"This 'solution' of Marx, Lenin, Stalin, Gorbachev, etc. to obtain world peace has been the greatest and the worst disaster mankind has ever faced and endured with more than 150,000,000 violent deaths perpetrated and justified in the name of helping the poor, world peace and prosperity.

"Neither peace nor prosperity has resulted from this enormous human cost and billions and trillions of dollars spent by Russia for promoting their war against God and man, which, despite current propaganda, still enslaves over one billion people in China, North Korea and other places.

"Then, there are those who put all their hope and faith in the democracies and trusted their secular political leaders, meanwhile the Christian citizens of the west have acquiesed in the handing over of Christian Eastern Europe into the hands of the God-hating, Christian-hating Communists between 1945 and 1956, as well as handing China over to the Communists in 1949.[2]

"Defending Eastern Europe and particularly Poland, was the reason given for opposing Hitler in 1939, at the cost of 50 million dead. Yet, by the Yalta Treaty of 1945, Poland and Eastern Europe were handed into the power of the Soviets with not so much as a vote by the people of either Poland or of the Western democracies. Thus the secular, democratic "statesmen" and diplomats called us in to war to save Poland from Hitler, to only turn around and give Poland to Stalin who was just as bad as Hitler, if not worse.

"After World War II, undaunted in this betrayal, the peoples of the world have been and continue to be sold the idea that peace can be achieved and maintained by the United Nations despite its sad history of leaving its fruits of war, destruction and disaster. This fact has already been demonstrated in various books.

"Then there is the secularist ideal of bringing peace to the world by opposing Communists by simply economic and military means. Billions and trillions of dollars have been spent in this endeavor and millions of lives have been lost in this ongoing warfare which seems at times to be somewhat successful and other times to be a losing battle. But while the Western democracies and the Western secular idealists claim victory, these same secular forces ignore the fact that whereas Communism could not kill the majority of citizens of the U.S. on the battlefield, it has achieved their aim by the cultural warfare of spreading the error of abortion so successfully that today more than 30 million citizens are dead because "in the land of the free and the home of the brave", where no one should be deprived of life, without due process of law, more than 30 million Americans have in fact been murdered in their mother's wombs without due process of law protecting them. And the slaughter goes on and on and on.

"And other Western democracies, Canada, Britain, France, Germany, Italy, etc., also have succumbed to the cultural warfare and the militant atheists who started this war and continue to wage it against us all so mercilessly. This war of ideas and social practices against God and man was perpetrated first of all by Russia and this war continues to spread out from Russia. At our present rate of success against these errors we, in our old age in the Western democracies will be telling the world how free we are now that our children and grandchildren are free to murder us through euthanasia instead of dying at the time, place and moment that God has appointed for us.

"No doubt, the devil and foolish human beings can persuade themselves with another 5, 10, 100 or 1000 solutions to the problem of bringing about world peace, and will spend billions and trillions of dollars proposing and imposing their ridiculous secularist solutions while the one and only way to world peace is unknown, or, if known, is ignored.

"If one or two voices pop up and say, 'Look at the Fatima solutions', 'At least try it', the anti-God forces and secular humanists can depend upon the Pharisees in the Church and in the Vatican bureaucracy as well as Pharisees like certain people we hear from who claim to love Our Lady of Fatima, cry out: 'Shame, shame, you are wasting money'; 'Shame, shame, you are divisive, you lessen the prestige of the Holy See'; 'Shame, shame, you are fighting against another Marian Apostolate'; 'Shame, shame, you do not obey your bishop.' They continue to shout: 'Shame, shame,' with all the other foolish reasons they give us for not insisting upon, broadcasting and propagating the *only* solution for world peace. Also, mankind might be condemned to a hundred years of being enslaved by militant atheists, limited in giving birth to only one child per family as in China and to becoming simply cattle to serve the greedy and power-hungry rulers of the world in the New World Order, United Nations, One World Church and the Global Government.

"People of various parts of the world, at various times in the past eighty years have looked to the United Nations, the United States of America, Hitlerism, Communism, the New World Order, New Agers; all promising their own peculiar brand of 'world peace' through the secular means of: spending billions of dollars, managing armies consisting of millions of soldiers; and hiring and paying for countless bureaucrats, politicians and diplomats who are in the service of National and International bodies around the world. They undertake merely human plans for peace, or oppose the totalitarian solutions offered by other human solutions often inspired directly by the devil himself.

"Let me repeat, in all this, unless the only solution is announced, republicized, explained, urged and implemented, the whole of the human race is in grave danger. So, if we really love our fellow man, if we realize our obligation to the Common Good, if we truly love God Who commands us to love our neighbor, not in words only, but in deeds, then how can we not cry out, explain, and insist upon the only solution, both in public and private.

"This applies not only to myself and those officially associated with our apostolate, but to all men, women and children who have been graced to hear, to know, and to understand the full Fatima message. When enough people actually obey and pass on as far as possible all of Our Lady's urgent requests, then Our Lady will triumph.

"So in this context, any reasonable public and private promotion of the Fatima message will bring us at least a little closer to the goal of world peace, the salvation of millions of souls and the magnificent triumph of the Holy, Maternal, loving, Immaculate Heart of Mary.

"To explain further, I will use the Biblical example of the chosen people of God of the Old Covenant to describe the situation of the chosen people of God of the New and Everlasting Covenant.

"The Old Covenant was truly of God, but it is not an everlasting covenant. Moses said that those physical decendants of Abraham would be cut off from the chosen people and the promises who did not accept the Prophet to come, that is Jesus Christ. If they did accept Him they would become inheritors of the New and Everlasting Testament. Since Jesus has come into the world, born, lived, died and rose again; the Old Testament is over. But the examples given in the Old Testament were given for our edification and education and were also meant as the preparation for the New Testament.

"Thus the example of the people of God on the banks of the Red Sea is most appropriate for our instruction and also for our consolation. As you recall, the Israelites were defenseless against the Egyptian army bearing down upon them in their chariots, with swords drawn ready to slaughter God's people.[3]

"They had nowhere to go and no defense at all when God gave the order to Moses to extend his arm over the Red Sea. The whole people of God were dependent upon the faith and obedience of one man, Moses. If he had not believed, or if he had not obeyed, the whole nation of Israel would have been wiped out then and there.

"What took place on that day is an accurate picture of what the people of God in the New and Everlasting Testament (Covenant) are facing. We are defenseless. We are surrounded and our enemies are close to moving in for the kill. Many have not been watching and find it hard to see how close to slaughter, true believers in Jesus Christ are — around the world.

"But if you carefully read the propaganda of the New World Order, the One World Religion, the New Agers, the Secular Humanists; not to mention the still-powerful hard line Communists; they are openly calling for death to all resisters to their 'utopia'.

"Under the guise of 'ecological reasons' they are openly calling for the elimination of 4.5 billion people; that is nine-tenths of the present day world's population. This is so incredible that I plan to print in an upcoming Fatima Crusader, a photograph of the obelisk with their above-mentioned intent inscribed in stone which stands today in Elberton, Georgia. (See photo section)

"Once the larger picture is seen, once the full message of Fatima is understood, we cannot think anyone would not do their part — or at least within the measure that human weakness allows each of them to try to do their part to promote knowledge of and obedience to the precise requests of Our Lady of Fatima.

"It does not require the whole of humanity to understand and obey at first. It does not even require the whole membership of the Catholic Church to do so immediately, although their obedience is eventually expected after the initial triumph of Our Lady for the conversion of Russia.

"So what is it that this sufficient number of people must obey, and what must they do? Let us examine this because it indicates how we should use our limited resources of time, energy, money and positions of influence.

"In one sense, all that is needed is for the Pope, one man, to obey. Uniquely and ultimately it depends on the Pope, just as it depended on Moses in the Old Testament, by his unique, personal, and official obedience, to deliver the people of God.

"If our Open Letter had convinced the Pope to obey, it would have been enough. The Holy Father wants to obey but feels he cannot obey until his bishops at first indicate their willingness to join him when he finally gives the command to consecrate Russia together with him.

"Thus we sent the Open Letter to all the Catholic bishops of the world in six different languages. We also sent it to 85,000 English-speaking Catholic Priests.

"We must note here that there are those who claim there are other considerations which seem also to obstruct the Pope's fulfillment of Our Lady's requests. Ultimately, the Pope needs our prayers. Jesus said, 'Pray a great deal for the Holy Father, he will do it (the consecration of Russia as requested by Our Lady of Fatima) but it will be late.'

"We must pray that the political pressures within and outside the Church change so the Pope feels free to do the consecration. Or we could simply pray that he overcomes his fearful perceptions and trusts in God and Our Lady that they will take care of the small details that now obstruct his path. To God all things are possible.

"But you may ask, if the Pope only needs prayers, he knows that better than you — why does he not say anything? Sister Lucy, on December 26, 1957, gave us the answer;

> 'Do not await for the call to (prayer and) penance to come from the Vatican on the part of the Holy Father, it will not come.
>
> 'Do not await for the call for penance to come from the chancery offices on the part of the bishops, it will not come.
>
> 'Do not await for the call to penance to come from the religious

orders, it will not come.'

"That is why it is so necessary that each one take care of his own soul and all souls that God has put on our path. (See Father Fuentes' interview in Appendix III.)

"Our Open Letter was a call for all men of good will to do that; it was not only addressed to the Pope. Our Lady's message would go much further if it was not simply dependent on one or two small voices of priests like myself to be heard.

"So our Open Letter is an appeal to everyone; priests, bishops and laypeople, to accept the call and add their voice of support, or at least to do what they can in their own area.

"But the Open Letter was also necessary to expose what certain Vatican bureaucrats were doing to obstruct our legitimate efforts and to prevent them from further fooling the public with their lies, slander and pressure tactics. We had hoped they would, at the very least, cease and desist. But they did not, as is evidenced by their immoral and illegal tricks they pulled against our 1996 Congress of Bishops held in Rome, November 18-24. At least now they cannot say they weren't warned and the Holy Father and others know we tried to correct our brothers as Christ advised us to do, (Mt. 18:15) before going to lodge formal legal complaints against them in Church courts.

"We take no pleasure in doing this. Frankly, I would prefer to live my life free from such struggles and in peace, but since every other avenue we have pursued has been blocked, we are left with no choice.

"Since the Open Letter did not succeed in the short run against this persecution, it at least set the stage for going to the next step in the formal legal procedures against the Vatican bureaucrats who are enemies of Our Lady of Fatima.

"A number of members and supporters of the apostolate have filed a formal legal brief (Libellus)* to the Pope as is our guaranteed right defined as Catholic Dogma by the Second Council of Lyons in 1274 and the First Vatican Council in 1870 and as codified in the New Code, (e.g. Canon 1405, 1406).

"Will that at least open the doors for the full Fatima message being given the hearing, the attention, the obedience that Our Lady deserves? Time will tell!

"Like the blind man who was cured because he kept crying out 'Jesus, Son of David, have mercy on me' even though he was told by others to be quiet. (Luke 18:38-43) Similarly, we must cry out to the Pope despite the fact that those around him tell us to be silent."

* See Appendix VII *A Canonical Petition to John Paul II* by Coralie Graham, Mairead Clarke and Mary Sedore.

Chapter 3

The Truth Will Make You Free

I have talked to a number of your critics and they say, "You are divisive, you are scandalous, you lessen the prestige of the Holy See, you are against the Holy Father, you have a false idea of the role of the laity and hierarchy, you are wasting your time and resources; by insisting on propagating the full Fatima message and in particular on insisting about the consecration of Russia?"

What do you reply to these criticisms?

"These remarks are all so general, it would require a separate book just to answer them but obviously we haven't time here to do that.

"I would first point out that I have already answered some of these criticisms at greater length in *The Fatima Crusader* and some as well are answered in my book *World Enslavement or Peace.*

"Secondly, to limit my reply to a manageable size, I will not explain here the 'Catholic terms'. For those outside the household of the Catholic Faith I will be happy to explain further if they wish to contact me. For agnostics and atheists who deny any common premise from which we can build an understanding, my answer will never satisfy them other than to say to them that it costs really nothing to do the consecration. If nothing happens, nothing really is lost. If the great good of world peace follows then they should realize that it is only by the Divine intervention of God that it has come about.

"To people of good will whose background I have not included above, who cannot follow the truth and proof of what I say, I invite them to write to me, so we can address their concerns.

"Since Pope John Paul II has said that the Message of Fatima is addressed to every human being, and since we are the only worldwide Apostolate of Our Lady of Fatima that daily reaches out by Radio, TV, books, magazines and World Wide Web site (see address at Appendix

I) to countless people with the full message, we try to answer any genuine questions by giving them an honest complete answer. There is no question on Fatima and our Apostolate that cannot be answered. The truth is on our side or more exactly, we are on the side of truth.

"To all those questions, I say, if you know the whole truth about Fatima, then you should understand that we have no other choice but to proclaim the truth, to insist upon the truth being proclaimed and to defend our right and the right of every one to hear the truth, know the truth, repeatedly proclaim the truth and live by the truth.

"Our Lord said 'The truth will make you free' (Jn. 8:32). The new Code of Canon Law also says that everyone has the right to seek the truth. It is not the Church that gives that right, nor the Pope, the bishop, the president, the Prime Minister, but it is God Himself who gives us the right to seek, know, and live by the truth. God also demands that we seek, know, and live by the truth because it is our solemn obligation.

"To those who claim knowledge of Fatima, but who still question our insistance upon its proclamation, even if they are of good will it seems to me that despite what they think about their knowledge of Fatima, they are in fact ignorant. They are all the more dangerous because they think they know, they will claim sincerity of intention while they go about (in their ignorance) attacking those who are serving God, Our Lady and the truth.

"If their ignorance is only pretended, and not real then they are malicious. If their ignorance is in some way due to their own fault, for example, by refusing to apply themselves to learn when they could; by relying on obviously false 'experts'; by refusing to see the other point of view because it is inconvenient to their lifestyle or the demands of their confused friends, then their ignorance would be guilty ignorance and would not excuse them on judgment day. To the extent that their ignorance is their own fault, will be the extent God will hold them responsible for all the harm they do for opposing Fatima.

"Only God can judge whether the actions of some bureaucratic authorities in the Church is due to malice or ignorance. God will judge all those, who behind closed doors, in whispers tell others in power, authority and influence — to not help the cause of Our Lady of Fatima and Father Gruner, who is trying to promote Fatima. They accuse me of being divisive even though they know (or should know) that such a question is to be judged by the Congregation for the Doctrine of the Faith. Insiders in the Vatican who are opponents of my Apostolate and of Our Lady of Fatima know that they do not like what I say so they want me silenced. Yet there is nothing illegal or immoral about what I say so they seek to silence me by attacking me indirectly.

"As Chris Ferrara pointed out in his speech at Fatima 2000, (See Fatima Crusader Issue No. 54) my enemies have imposed a totally unjust legal proceeding against me. The very same bureaucrats who want me silenced but have no legal grounds for demanding it, have themselves broken the law by: 1) Persecuting me by, among other things, libelous statements against me in the press; 2) Then pretended to be impartial judges after manipulating that the case came before them; 3) Then ruling that I am disobedient when it is they themselves who have made it physically and morally impossible to obey their order to find a new bishop to incardinate me; 4) They therefore rule on the basis of my 'failure to obey' this first order that now I am to be silenced, to amend for my first disobedience.

"There are officials who claim jurisdiction that is not theirs to have. They claim knowledge and they profess to be 'judges in Israel' yet they will not follow procedures that protect them from making errors against the defendant. They are guilty like the Pharisees of old who were guilty for not following the procedures designed to prevent them from passing sentence on the 'Innocent one of the Lord,' the Messiah.

"But to come back to the main point —

"If people knew Fatima, then they would know that only through Our Lady and obedience to Her formal solemn request that the Pope and the bishops consecrate Russia, and only through this obedience to Her request, that Russia be solemnly, publicly, explicitly, exclusively, on the same day, at the same hour, consecrated by the Pope and all the Catholic bishops will there be peace throughout the world and there would be the salvation of millions and millions of souls.

"And if there is not this obedience then wars will continue, both large and small around the world. Also, millions of souls who otherwise would be saved will continue to fall into hell for all eternity through their own individual lack of cooperation with grace. And some of those going there may well be those who oppose Fatima in their ignorance or their malice.

"If this obedience is not done in time then 'various (entire) nations will be annihilated'[1] and the rest of the world will be enslaved by militant atheists.

"With such a great good to be achieved and such a great evil to be avoided, how can we, and for that matter everyone else too, not continue to insist, publish, petition, promote and persuade others to work with all legitimate means to bring about the Consecration of Russia as commanded by Our Heavenly Mother, Our Heavenly Queen who has the right and the power to command us to work, pray, sacrifice towards this end.

"All those who still protest seem to have forgotten the Pharisees. They fall into pharasaical scandal. In essence they say, 'Since what you do scandalized us, you must stop because we are scandalized.' To them I reply like Jesus did, 'Ignore them; they are blind and leaders of the blind and both of them will fall into the pit.' (Mt. 15:13)

These are strong words. How can you justify them?

"Remember I started off by pointing out that we are talking about people who know, claim to know, or who should know the full Fatima message. If they don't know it, then they owe it to their eternal salvation to learn it before they sit in judgment on those who promote it vigorously.

"To explain further, there are three kinds of scandal.[2] Each kind is very different from the other, and what we must do in the face of the third kind is also different from what we must do in the face of the first two kinds.

"The first kind is 'scandal in itself', the second kind is 'scandal of the little ones', and the third kind is 'Pharisaical scandal'.

It is important to have a clear understanding and description of each kind. It is especially important to know the essential difference between 'pharisaical scandal' and the 'scandal of the little ones', because there are Pharisees who sometimes call themselves 'little ones' and we must not be fooled by this sinister maneuver.

"Before I go on, I wish to reassure you that everything I am saying about the three kinds of scandal directly relates to the question I have been asked and the criticisms about lessening the prestige of the Holy Father.

"The first kind, 'scandal in itself,' is when a person does something against the law of God, and another person seeing him do it follows the bad example. For example, if the first person steals goods from a store, the second person following his example is guilty of the sin of theft, but the first person is guilty of the sin of theft and also guilty of scandal. Also, if a third person should steal because of the bad example of the second person, the second person too would then be guilty of the sin of scandal. This is 'scandal in itself'.

"The second kind is 'the scandal of the little ones'. This is different from the first kind, because the person committing this scandal does not break the law of God in what he did in itself, but only because a little one who misunderstands his action goes out and actually does commit a sin that he thought he saw the first person do.

"This sounds complicated but it is really quite simple.

"St. Paul in Sacred Scripture explains it with this example.[3] A Catholic, who knew his Faith very well, and therefore knew that 'idols are not gods,' and that meat sacrificed to idols hasn't really changed at all, and that all meat exists because the one true God created it for the nourishment of man as Genesis says, would realize that he would not sin if he bought meat sacrificed to idols in pagan Greece or Rome.

"St. Paul confirmed that in itself, this would not be a sin for that well informed Catholic.

"However, if this action was *seen* by a little one and this little one, a poorly educated Catholic, were to draw the false conclusion that the educated Catholic was now offering sacrifice to idols, and thus this poor little one, this uneducated Catholic were to go and actually offer sacrifice to idols himself, then a little one would have been scandalized.

"This is 'the scandal of the little ones,' and although the act of buying and eating meat sacrificed to idols was not in itself wrong to one who can make all the proper distinctions — it was nevertheless wrong because a little one who witnessed this was led into sin. So, this first person in this example was guilty of sin for misleading a little one.

"It is important to note that the good to be achieved by the first act, eating of meat, was very small in comparison to the evil effect. That little one was led into losing his soul. This limited good of eating meat could have been achieved in other ways such as going to another butcher shop that didn't sell the meat offered to idols. We must look out for the little ones, who are poorly educated, who have feeble minds, who cannot see the real distinction between two acts that look so similar.

"But that does not mean we always stop doing anything just because someone shrieks 'I am scandalized by what you do, by what you say.' There are times when we must go on despite their scandal, because they are acting like the Pharisees. We must, in those cases, say with Jesus, 'Blessed is the man who is not scandalized in what I do' (Mt. 11:6).

"You see, the first moral law is stated clearly in the principle Do good, avoid evil. We are not only commanded to avoid evil, but we are also commanded to do good. It is precisely because of this first principle that we must do the good that is set before us even if the Pharisees cry out to us to stop and tell us they are scandalized. Even if the Pharisees drag us before the State or Church courts, and pronounce a sentence of 'justice' on us, as was done to St. Joan of Arc. She was condemned by a Church court, but she is a canonized Saint today, because despite those Pharisees, she insisted on doing good.

"What then is pharasaical scandal? It is when a person does an important good deed, that the Pharisee wants to stop because he does not agree with it, either at that time, or at that place, or in the manner, or some other pretext he offers for obstructing the good deed.

"Our Lord healed on the Sabbath. The Pharisees claiming the law, told him to stop, to not do the good of healing on the Sabbath. Our Lord went on anyway and did the good. He also pointed out to the Pharisees that they were using a double standard of weighing His good deeds against the deeds they *did* allow by their human traditions, such as allowing a man to work very hard to pull his donkey out of a pit on the Sabbath. If this was lawful to do, as Our Lord Himself did not dispute, then it is obvious that the good He achieved on the Sabbath, namely pulling a man out of the pit of illness, blindness, crippledness was a much greater good and therefore also allowable on the Sabbath. The Pharisees' bad will was evident by their refusing to answer Our Lord's honest question. If they did answer, they would have to acknowledge the truth of what He said and the intrinsic goodness of what He did, and that He broke no law by doing that good deed on the Sabbath.

"So the lesson here is that we must do all the good we can despite all the Pharisees who tell us they are scandalized. Despite the garb these Pharisees clothe themselves in, be it the garb of 'little ones' who feign scandal, or be it the garb of an Archbishop in the Vatican who tells canon lawyers not to defend me in the Apostolic Signatura because what Father Gruner says is 'divisive'. I am 'guilty of being divisive' because what I do separates the followers of Our Lady from those of the devil."

Father Gruner, do you think that everyone who opposes the publication of the full Fatima message, especially the command to consecrate Russia, is a follower of the devil?

"I must insist, I do not judge people's hearts or intentions unless people explicitly declare them. Not every opponent and quite possibly not even the majority of those who oppose Our Lady's most solemn request do it because they are satanists or devil worshipers, but all who oppose the Mother of God's command by their actions, words or omissions are to that extent helping the devil, following him, because they do what the devil wants them to do, since satan knows that when Our Lady's command is obeyed, the devil's empire on earth will be finished, utterly destroyed by Our Lady's triumph, which will only come through the Pope's fulfilling Her command to consecrate Russia in the manner specified.

"There are many shallow criticisms, spoken by some priests or prominent laypeople who you would think know better. Perhaps I give them too much credit for intelligence or maybe they are just overworked and fatigued but their remarks need to be answered lest their errors ensnare little ones because of the prestige of those opponents of Fatima.

"And those who claim I lessen the prestige of the Holy Father, of the Holy See, of wasting time and money etc., are really telling me: 'Let the whole world be enslaved. Let the ministers of Christ and the Church be led to the guillotine like Jesus warned would happen if they disobeyed and delayed. Let entire nations be annihilated, wiped off the face of the earth. Let millions of souls be lost forever in Hell who could otherwise be easily saved. Let your mother, father, sister, brother, wife, husband, child, be tortured, raped, imprisoned, enslaved, murdered' rather than let a few people be slightly embarrased ever so briefly.

"The difference is clear — the good to be achieved by crying out the louder, the longer and the clearer is infinitely important. The evil that they say I do is non-existent. I must follow Our Lord's words and ignore them because they are blind and leaders of the blind.

"Also, as St. Paul says to the blind of heart '... seeing you shall see and shall not perceive'." (Acts 28:26)

"Now if they are not blind, but only ignorant I remind them of their own obligation to know the whole truth about Fatima. Let them read Frère Michel, Frère François or my book.

"If they are still not convinced then let us defend our intellectual positions before impartial judges, with the impartial rules of debate being followed to the letter. Anyone of good will can come to know the whole truth about Fatima and our mutual obligation to promote this great good without ceasing and without hinderence of Pharisees at whatever level in the Church — from layman to the Holy See itself."

Chapter 4

Historic Crossroads

Father Gruner tell us why this work you do is so important at this time.

"You see we are at an historic crossroads. Most people do not realize it, nevertheless, it is where we are.

"This is not simply my view but that of Pope John Paul II as well. Our present Holy Father, before his election to the papacy, went to the Eucharistic Congress in USA in 1976. There in his formal address he said:

> 'We are now standing in the face of the greatest historical confrontation humanity has gone through. I do not think the wide circle of the Christian community realizes this fully. We are now facing the final confrontation between the Church and the anti-Church, between the Gospel and the anti-Gospel, between Christ and the anti-Christ. This confrontation lies within the plans of Divine providence: it is a trial which the whole Church must take up.'[1]

"Today more than ever we face a most grave crisis. Before humanity lies apostasy and annihilation, or peace and salvation. How can I, in a few words, clearly show you this reality and demonstrate that mankind today really has only one way to achieve peace and salvation?

"First of all, God has made men to live in society. By his very nature, man is meant to live together in houses, villages, cities, cultures and civilizations. He has done so for all history. Man is born into a family, lives with his parents, brothers and sisters, and works with his colleagues and continues through life, living, working, recreating and learning; always in the company of friends and associates. There are times when he is alone, but not for long, except in the rare case of less than 1% of men who are hermits.

"Secondly, men live and work together because they share common goals. Their goals define their society. It is the very nature of men to share not only each others' company, but each others' purposes.

"Thirdly, St. Augustine points out that there are really only two cities or civilizations of men. There is the city of God, that is human society built upon the ideal, the purpose of loving God and keeping His law. And there is the city of man, which puts seeking man's happiness on earth as its primary purpose, even to the point of excluding God and His laws.[2]

"The city of God has Jesus Christ as the King and Mary as its Queen. The city of man, built upon the love of man, and the hatred of God has the devil as its master. Satan is the prince of this world, as Jesus said.[3]

"Now these two cities, or civilizations, are at war, and have been at war, hot or cold, throughout human history. In fact, the enmity of the children of Mary against the children of the devil goes back to the first book of the Bible. In Genesis God speaks and says:

> 'I will put enmity between thee and the Woman, between thy seed and Her seed, and She shall crush thy head.'[4]

"Now this enmity between the followers of Mary and the followers of the devil has continued through the centuries and is vigorously playing itself out in our time.

"There are various levels of commitment by the followers of either side to their own leader, but all people sooner or later have to choose sides. Each side has those who see the battle lines more clearly and what must be done to advance their cause. Also, each side has written and published their battle plans and strategies extensively, and has left a record of previous skirmishes and battles, won and lost.

"As Pope Pius XII pointed out; in 1517, Luther said Yes to God, Yes to Christ, No to His Church.

In 1717, the Masons said Yes to God, No to Christ, No to His Church.

In 1917, Marx and Lenin said No to God.

"Now the 'No' to the Church leads eventually to 'No' to Christ. Because if you truly love Christ you will love His Spotless Bride, the Church. If you reject His Church you will eventually end up rejecting Christ. Similarly, if you reject Christ, you will also end up eventually rejecting God.

"Now it is in 1917 that Our Lady promises to reverse all the above 'No's' when Her requests are granted. Russia will be converted and peace will come to the world. But the peace can only come to the whole world when the anti-God, anti-Christ, anti-Church forces are converted away from their sin to be pro-God, pro-Christ, pro-His Church.

"Certainly, down to our times, there are secret and open societies who have declared war on Christ, Mary, the Catholic Church, Christian civilization and the Catholic soul, conscience and heart. Two of the most famous to openly declare this warfare against the Church and its members is Masonry and communism, in all their colors and forms, shapes and sizes.

"Furthermore, not one of these anti-God, anti-Christ, anti-Church movements has ever publicly repented of its goals. To do so, they would have to truly convert and become Catholic, and that, everyone knows has not happened.

"I hope that this bare outline is enough for you to understand the truth that each man, and by extension each society, is either for Christ or against Him. There is no middle ground. 'He that is not with Me, is against Me'.[5] 'He who is not against you is for you'.[6]

"As men became more organized in society they gathered together with others of like mind and purpose and thus there emerges those fervently committed to God, His Revelation, His Sacraments and His law; and there are those who are militantly against Christ and His Church.

"These forces have come to a decisive battle in the 20th Century. It was easier for the common man to see the battle before the recent smoke screen of Perestroika.[7] However, despite the smoke screen, the hearts and intentions of both sides remain the same; to be intensely for God first and above all or to be against God and for the establishment of the kingdom of man under the leadership of satan who promises paradise on earth, and 'man will be as gods.'

"This decisive battle is taking place in our time and it is why Our Lady came with such power, and such tears and love and warning. It is why She said to us in this time 'Only I can help you.'

"In the light of this background we need to clearly see and survey the only three strategies open to us at this time. We need to consider the example of Mr. Evil Hunter and Mr. Intended Victim. Mr. Hunter is a man who, together with his friends, has previously killed 160,000,000 'Victims' and he has sworn with the most solemn oaths that his purpose is to wipe out Mr. Victim and all his friends and relatives.

"So Mr. Hunter tells Mr. Victim, 'I am going to kill you'.

"Mr. Victim basically has three choices. It could be said that he has a fourth choice, which is to give up and let himself be killed. But he cannot do this in conscience since God expects him to pass on his sacred heritage of the Faith and civilization to the new generation.

"So Mr. Victim really only has three choices. He can run away, hoping to avoid ever meeting Mr. Hunter; He can stay and fight hoping to overpower Hunter and win and thereby survive Mr. Hunter's attack; or he can negotiate. He would hope to persuade Mr. Hunter to change his mind and decide to not kill Mr. Victim. Run, fight, negotiate. There are no other choices.

"This picture of Hunter and Victim is an image of militant anti-God forces against the Catholic Church. The Church can hope to survive by either fleeing the battlefield, fighting, or negotiating with the enemy in the hope of persuading them.

"Now, at this juncture of history, Our Lady appears at Fatima to tell the Pope, the Cardinals and the bishops that they only really have one choice and that nothing else will work.

"Obviously, the Church can't run, since both the anti-God forces and the Catholic Church are worldwide and there is no place to run to. So that leaves two choices. Fight or negotiate.

"Some bureaucrats in the Vatican have decided they do not have the firepower to win in a fight so they must negotiate. Here we have the Vatican-Moscow Agreement,[8] to *not* denounce the errors of Communism. The guarantee of silence by the Vatican and all its Nuncios in the face of the greatest social crime of Godless Communism imposed on nearly one-third the world's population was exacted as the price Russia demanded of the Vatican before negotiations would continue.

"It is specifically this silence, the wrongful putting away of the moral authority to speak out against the organized enemies of the Church, the State and salvation of souls, that has spiritually and temporally disarmed the Church. It cannot fight; at least not directed from headquarters because headquarters has agreed to lay down the sword of truth against these adversaries. This first round of negotiating has already made the Church a sure loser in this battle of wits because the publishing of the truth about Communism, militant atheism, and satanism is a necessary weapon, in the natural order that the Church has in this war to death with its mortal enemies.

"Mr. Hunter is analogous to the anti-God forces which have sworn enmity to Christ, His Church and His followers. The anti-God forces have openly made Russia their headquarters in their fight against God and His Church.

"The Church cannot give up the weapon of truth. But that weapon alone is not enough to win this fight. It also needs the supernatural help of Heaven, more exactly the help of Our Lady Herself. This is in fact the explicit teaching of Our Lady of Fatima. She says 'Only I can help you'.[9]

"She warned that in this battle with the mortal enemies of Christianity, we are bound to lose unless we use the specific means She offered in Her Fatima message. 'Russia is the instrument of chastisement chosen by Heaven to punish the whole world if we do not beforehand obtain the conversion of that poor nation'.[10] But the only way to convert Russia is 'by this means'; that is the Consecration of Russia in the explicit manner Our Lady of Fatima commanded.

"Professor William Thomas Walsh reports 'Sister Lucy made it plain that Our Lady did not ask for the consecration of the *world* to Her Immaculate Heart. What She demanded specifically was the consecration of *Russia* ... She said more than once and with deliberate emphasis: 'What Our Lady wants is that the Pope and all the bishops in the world shall consecrate Russia to Her Immaculate Heart on one special day. If this is done, She will convert Russia and there will be peace. If it is not done the errors of Russia will spread through every country in the world.'

"Professor Walsh asked through his interpreter Father Manuel Rocha, 'Does this mean in your opinion that every country without exception will be overcome by communism?' Sister Lucy answered 'Yes.' Father Rocha continues, 'Mr. Walsh wanted to be positive about the answer and therefore repeated the question adding 'and does that mean the United States of America too?' Sister Lucy answered 'Yes'.

"I must repeat, the only way to convert Russia is the consecration of Russia by the Pope and the Bishops. Our Lady said most solemnly, 'The moment has come in which God asks the Holy Father to make together with all the Catholic Bishops of the world the consecration of Russia to My Immaculate Heart, promising to save it, *by this means*.'[11]

"There is no other means to save Russia. When Sister Lucy asked Jesus to explain why He would not convert Russia except through that consecration, Jesus replied, 'Because I want My whole Church to acknowledge that consecration as a triumph of the Immaculate Heart of Mary, so that it may extend its cult later on, and put the devotion to this Immaculate Heart beside the devotion to My Sacred Heart.'[12]

"After a great struggle, we know Our Lady's children will be on the winning side because Our Lady said 'In the end, My Immaculate Heart will triumph. The Holy Father will consecrate Russia to Me. Russia will be converted and a period of peace will be given to the world.'[13]

"But the victory will only come when we take Our Lady's advice. Instead of negotiating, we must fight our mortal enemies, not only with the sword of truth but above all with the one weapon that Our Lady gives us that promises ultimate victory. Without it we shall lose the battle. That weapon is the consecration of specifically Russia to the Immaculate Heart of Mary by the Pope and the bishops in a solemn, public way, on the same day at the same hour.

"It is not through negotiating. The weapon is not to kill but to convert the anti-God forces in Russia away from the devil to the cause of Christ and His Church.

"There is no other strategy that will win for us. Every other strategy will lose. We must 'pray a great deal for the Holy Father'[14] as Jesus told us to in the Fatima message. We have His assurance 'He (the Holy Father) will do it (the consecration) but it will be late.'[15] (Not "too" late as some have misstated.)

"We must never lose hope in the dark hours ahead while our leaders seem oblivious to the only solution, the full Fatima message, or they seem to think it is optional. It is not. Or that it is unimportant. Nothing is more important. Or that it is not binding upon them. It is most solemnly binding upon peril of their souls and lives. Or that they think they have fulfilled their obligation to this request. They most certainly have not. All these things we can prove in our public writings if we have not already done so.

"But in the meantime, while we await our opportunity to do our duty and explain in depth in person to the bishops and Cardinals why we have no other choice; we, while we wait and work very ineffectively, must, above all, hope and pray. As Jesus said. 'It is never too late to have recourse to Jesus and Mary.'[16]

"You ask: 'What is your opponents' position regarding the consecration of Russia, what do they say?' The only opponents there are who have professed any position at all is that the consecration of Russia was done March 25, 1984.

"Unbelievably, they expect the whole Catholic Faithful to believe this when it is obviously not true. Our Lady promised the conversion of Russia. She was not talking about Perestroika but conversion to the Catholic Faith. Today we have the perversion of Russia even worse than before with their introduction of Western-style prostitution and pornography. That was not there before except for tourists.

"Russia certainly is not Catholic today. The present day Administrator of the Latin Rite Diocese of Moscow will not accept converts from the Russian Orthodox Church. It is his policy, (thanks to the Balamand Agreement), so as to not disturb the Russian Orthodox Church leaders. Surely, as long as that Latin Rite Bishop Tadeusz Kondrusiewicz and his policy are there, we will never have the conversion of Russia.

"The fact is that 13 years after the supposed Consecration, there are still no fruits of world peace. There are still 10 million victims of wars, not counting the 650 million victims of the war upon the unborn in the past 13 years alone. Certainly, this is not the peace Our Lady promised.

"When Our Lady appeared at Fatima, Portugal was under a Godless government — the openly Masonic government. Within two years of Our Lady's appearance at Fatima, the Masonic anti-Church laws and policies were repealed. Within nine years, the government was replaced by a pro-Catholic government. When Our Lady appeared in Mexico on Dec 12, 1531, there were almost no Catholics, zero among the natives. Ten years later, the whole Mexican nation of natives was practically all Catholic. Now after 13 years the hidden hand of the Communist party, the KGB or whatever its new name is, and the Red Army are still obviously very much in control.

"The two books by Anatoliy Golitsyn, *New Lies for Old* and *The Perestroika Deception*, published in 1984 and 1995, proves this to any serious scholar of the Moscow scene. Russia has not changed its goal of world domination. If we need to, we can demonstrate that with hundreds of significant facts, except to those who prefer not to see. Presently, the Communist Party USA reports its best years of recruitment among the American people.

"Apart from the fact that the fruits promised by Our Lady of Fatima and by Jesus Himself are not achieved, it is also easy to demonstrate that the consecration of March 25, 1984, did not fulfill the commands of Our Lady. To do this, let me leave Father Paul Leonard, who publicly disputed this subject with Father Fox, point out the obvious.

"Both in 1990 and in 1992 Father Paul challenged Father Fox to answer the following nine points. To date, seven years later, Father Fox still has not answered. Here we quote Father Paul Leonard at length.

> 'What can be said about a person who ignores the argument and the evidence that proves his position to be erroneous? It is difficult to believe how such a person can be honest. Such a person appears to wilfully resist the truth, or at least remains wilfully blind to the truth. This appears to me to be the state of mind of Father Fox.
>
> 'It may appear at first to some that I judge Father Fox harshly, but I believe that the facts speak for themselves, and the material that Father Fox publishes presents a strong case against himself.
>
> 'Father Fox has made no attempt to answer the serious arguments and evidence that *The Fatima Crusader* has presented, which demonstrate beyond reasonable doubt that the consecration of Russia requested by Our Lady of Fatima has not yet been done.
>
> ## Facts Father Fox Chooses To Ignore
>
> 'Here is some of that evidence:
>
> *Fact #1* Sister Lucy gives two versions of the words that Our Lady of Fatima spoke to her in the apparition of June 13, 1929:
>
> a) The moment has come in which God asks the Holy Father, in union with all the bishops of the world, to consecrate Russia to My Immaculate Heart, promising to save it by this means".
>
> b) The moment has come in which God asks the Holy Father to

make, and to order that in union with him and at the same time, all the bishops of the world make the consecration of Russia to My Immaculate Heart..."

Fact #2 Sister Lucy wrote in a text she gave to Father Gonçalves in 1930:

> 'The Good God promises to make an end of the persecution in Russia if the Holy Father deigns to make, and orders to be made, by all the bishops of the Catholic World, a solemn and public act of reparation and consecration of Russia to the Most Sacred Hearts of Jesus and Mary and if in return for the end of this persecution His Holiness promises to approve and recommend the practice of reparatory devotion (the Five First Saturdays).'

Fact #3 She wrote in a letter dated June 12, 1930:

> 'If the Holy Father will himself make a solemn act of reparation and consecration of Russia ... as well as ordering all the bishops of the Catholic world to do the same.'

Fact #4 On March 21, 1982, Sister Lucy declared in the presence of the Apostolic Nuncio to Lisbon, Archbishop Portalupi, the Bishop of Leiria and Dr. Lacerda that the Pope must select a date on which to order the bishops of the whole world to make a public and solemn act of reparation and consecration of Russia to the most Sacred Hearts of Jesus and Mary, each in his own cathedral and at the same time as performed by the Pope.

Fact #5 On the afternoon of March 19, 1983, the Apostolic Nuncio, Archbishop Portalupi met with Sister Lucy in order to establish precisely what Sister Lucy had to say concerning the consecration of the world that the Pope had performed on May 13, 1982. Besides the Nuncio, two other witnesses were present, Dr. Lacerda and Father Messias Coelho. Sister Lucy declared that "the consecration of Russia has not been made as Our Lady has demanded" and she added,

> 'I could not say so because I did not have the permission of the Holy See.'

In that same interview, Sister Lucy explained the reasons why the Holy Father's 1982 consecration did not fulfill Our Lady of Fatima's request:

a) Russia had not clearly been indicated as the object of the consecration.

b) Each bishop had not made a public and solemn ceremony in his own cathedral.

Fact #6 The Pope's March 25, 1984 consecration of the *world* did not clearly indicate Russia as its object and each bishop did not participate by making a public and solemn ceremony in his own cathedral. Sister Lucy, therefore, has already stated in 1983 the reasons why the 1984 consecration does not fulfill Our Lady's request for the consecration of Russia.

Fact #7 On July 20, 1987, Sister Lucy stated to Enrique Romero in a subsequently published interview that the consecration of Russia requested by Our Lady of Fatima is not yet done.

Fact #8 In an interview which appeared in the September 1985 issue of *Sol de Fatima*, Sister Lucy was asked if the Pope fulfilled the request made by Our Lady at Tuy when he consecrated the world on March 25, 1984. Sister Lucy answered: "There was no participation of all the bishops, and there was no mention of Russia." The interviewer then asked, "So the consecration was not done as requested by Our Lady?" Sister Lucy answered: *"No. Many bishops attached no importance to this act."*

Fact #9 Pope John Paul II on March 25, 1984, *after* he had consecrated the world, twice addressed words to Our Lady of Fatima which contained a clear admission that the Consecration that She requested still remained to be done. His words, published in the Vatican Newspaper, *L'Osservatore Romano*, were: "Enlighten especially the peoples of which You Yourself *are awaiting* our consecration and confiding". Several hours later the Holy Father again addressed Our Lady of Fatima in St. Peter's Basilica with these words:

> 'We wished to choose this Sunday for the act of entrusting and consecration of the world ... of all peoples especially those who have a very great need of this consecration and entrustment, *of those peoples for whom You Yourself ARE AWAITING our act of consecration.'*

Our Reflections On These Facts

'These public utterances of the Holy Father clearly demonstrate that the Pope is himself aware of the fact that Our Lady of Fatima is still waiting for the consecration of Russia to be performed.

'In fact #1 we have the Blessed Virgin's own words explaining that God asks that the Pope *order all* the Catholic Bishops of the world to consecrate *Russia* to the Immaculate Heart of Mary. In facts #2 and #3 we have Sister Lucy's hand written text specifying precisely the same thing as the Blessed Virgin, namely that the Pope must *order all* the Catholic bishops of the world to consecrate *Russia*.

'In fact #4, we have Sister Lucy's *official and public statement* explicitly setting forth the very same conditions that she has been consistently stating for more than fifty years, namely that Our Lady requires that the Pope *order all* of the Catholic bishops of the world to consecrate *Russia* to the Immaculate Heart of Mary.

'On May 13, 1982, the Pope consecrated the *world* to the Immaculate Heart of Mary. The evidence in fact #5 establishes the fact that Sister Lucy, carrying out her God-given mission to make known to God's ministers His (and Our Lady's) request, states that the 1982 consecration *did not fulfill* Our Lady's request for *two reasons:*

1. Russia was not clearly indicated as the object of the consecration.

2. Each bishop did not participate in a solemn and public manner.

"In 1985 Sister Lucy says that the March 25, 1984 consecration did NOT fulfill Our Lady's request for the same two reasons. (Fact #8.)

'In fact #9 we have the Pope's own *public acknowledgment* that the consecration of Russia requested by Our Lady of Fatima has not yet been done. It is very strange indeed that Father Fox, when he reproduced the formula of consecration recited by the Pope on March 25, 1984, deleted this critical passage from the text.

This Evidence Cannot Be Dismissed

'Until now Father Fox has not given clear and direct answers to the evidence presented in all of the above points (Let the reader bear in mind that all of this evidence has already been published in past issues of *The Fatima Crusader*). The evidence that I have presented may not be dismissed or ignored: It is the words of Sister Lucy, the Pope and the Blessed Virgin Herself.

'It certainly appears that Father Fox thus far has desperately avoided any confrontation with the already published evidence when he presents his reasons for believing that the consecration of Russia requested by Our Lady of Fatima has already been done. Father Fox's pronouncements do exhibit an immense degree of confusion and a gullibility that almost defies belief; but his utter refusal to give serious response to the evidence and the arguments that we have published in issue after issue suggests something other than mere stupidity.

'It was back in 1990 when the above-quoted text was published in *The Fatima Crusader.* Father Fox has had ample opportunity to answer the nine points that I raised nearly a year and a half ago. Clearly we are not dealing with mere stupidity, but with a lack of honesty on Father Fox's part, since to date Father Fox persists in his obstinate refusal to answer to the facts and arguments presented a year and a half ago in my article, *The Fatima Consecration Hoax*, which appeared in the Winter 1990 issue of *The Fatima Crusader.*'

"I think Father Paul Leonard has done a great service to the Church by clearly pointing out that the position of Father Fox is completely untenable.

"Father Fox, despite being challenged to respond twice by Father Paul and *The Fatima Crusader*, never did reply because there is no answer except to acknowledge that the consecration of Russia was never done.

"Apart from Father Fox, his imitators and teachers, there is no other official position.

"The Church has never pronounced that the consecration is done. In fact, on two separate occasions, Pope John Paul II has publicly acknowledged that the consecration of the world on March 25, 1984 did not fulfill Our Lady of Fatima's request. (See the news clippings of *L'Osservatore Romano* on March 26, 1984 in the photo section).

"No one in authority has, in any official way, stated that Our Lady never asked for the consecration of Russia. No one in authority has ever officially stated that the Church, the Pope and the bishops, are not bound to obey.

"On the contrary, on May 13, 1982, Pope John Paul II stated publicly 'The Message of Fatima imposes an obligation on the Church'.[17] Pope Pius XII said, 'Now, the time for doubting Fatima has passed, the hour for action has arrived..'[18]

"All we are doing is simply stating, repeating, explaining what the Popes and Our Lady and Our Lord said through the Fatima Message. Our enemies call this divisive because it goes against their own private plans which are in opposition to Our Lord and Our Lady's publicly pronounced and approved plans for the Church and world peace. In the light of the strong opposition of a few but well-organized opponents of Fatima in the Vatican, Pope John Paul II feels his hands are tied until he gets more support.

"Many do not come on the side of Fatima because they do not know of it at all or they are confused by the deceptive propaganda put out by the anti-Fatima forces. I am very sorry that Our Lady has not yet found someone who is willing and capable enough to demonstrate to the world and the Church membership and hierarchy the only solution there is to the otherwise certain disaster of war, annihilation, torture, enslavement and apostasy. Please pray that Our Lady gets this message effectively out so that people of good will everywhere will act on it before it is too late.

"Getting back to your question as to why our work, the promotion of the full Fatima Message is of such importance, it is because we are living at an historic crossroads, 'the final confrontation between the

Church and the anti-Church, between the Gospel and the anti-Gospel, between Christ and the anti-Christ'. Fatima, is our only hope.

"I conclude with two statements of Jesus given through the Fatima message. 'Pray a great deal for the Holy Father, he will do it but it will be late.' It is already very late. We must pray, and remember Jesus also said to Sister Lucy 'It is never too late to have recourse to Jesus and Mary'."

Chapter 5

The Most Grave Obligation

Father Gruner, does God oblige the Pope and the bishops to obey Our Lady of Fatima?

"Yes. Certainly!"

Are you aware that not many theologians say what you have just said?

"I very well know that to say such a thing is not popular, nor is it prudent if you wish to live in peace. Obviously, I am attacked by powerful Vatican bureaucrats and have been for years. You notice, however, they never argue with me or point out in open discussion where I am wrong in my dogmatic or moral theology. Nor where I am wrong in this theological conclusion, arrived at after many years of prayer, reflection and study."

Are you saying then, despite the fact that what you say is uncommon, th*at it is nevertheless certain that the Pope and the bishops are bound under pain of sin to obey the solemn command to consecrate Russia to the Immaculate Heart of Mary, in the manner specified by Our Lady of Fatima?*

"To be very exact, I say that in the objective moral order, to disobey, to not fulfill this command of the Queen of Heaven, in such a most serious matter, where the salvation of millions, if not billions of souls, hangs in the balance, where the very existence of various entire nations hangs in the balance, where many other disasters of grave magnitude in the temporal order (such as the enslavement of the whole world under atheistic rulers, widespread famine, open persecution of the Church spread over many more nations of the earth, etc.) then how can anyone not agree that the Pope and the bishops are bound, under pain of mortal sin, to do their duty and obey. This has to be so since only they can deliver us by using the power and authority they have from God.

Are you saying, then, that the Pope is now in a state of mortal sin because he has not obeyed Our Lady?

"I most certainly am not. Please notice that I insist on the phrase *'in the objective moral order'*. In other words, in the subjective moral order—that is, is the Pope, are the bishops, actually guilty of sin by not obeying Our Lady of Fatima's most solemn command, given explicitly in the name of God? To that question, I must reply, I do not know. I am not their confessor so I cannot determine if in their own minds and hearts they realize this command binds them under pain of mortal sin.

"As you know, in the subjective moral order, all theologians and the Church herself teaches that for a subject, a person, to commit a mortal sin, three conditions are necessary:

1) It must be a serious matter, or at least be considered a serious matter.

2) There must be sufficient reflection by the person who commits this act, (or omission) in other words the person must be aware that what he does is gravely, seriously wrong.

3) The person committing the act (or the omission) must fully consent to this act.

"Since I am not in the position to know the state of mind and will of the Pope and bishops, of course I cannot say they are subjectively guilty of sin."

Father Gruner, St. Augustine says that God does not command the impossible. Hence, it is privately said that Pope John Paul II knows that he as Pope is obliged to obey, but he finds it impossible at the present time, thus the Pope holds that for him he is not obliged to obey. What do you reply to this moral teaching?

"Of course I agree with St. Augustine; God does not command the impossible. If He did, we would fall into the blasphemous and monstrous teaching of some of the Protestant leaders of the 16th Century, that God positively wills the damnation of souls. Because if God commanded the impossible under pain of mortal sin, then it would be impossible for those so commanded to avoid going to hell. Such an idea is blasphemous and totally against the love of Christ Who died on the cross for love of each and every human being, in order to deliver them from sin and hell.

"Nevertheless, I must insist that in the objective moral order, under pain of mortal sin, the Pope and the bishops are bound to consecrate Russia to the Immaculate Heart of Mary.

"If the Pope, today cannot obey Our Lady's command that does not exclude him from doing what he can to bring about conditions whereby tomorrow he can do the consecration in the exact proper manner. What is needed above all is a widespread public campaign for the Rosary.

"The Council of Trent, commenting on St. Augustine's statement 'God does not command the impossible' tells us to do by our own strength what we can, and to draw upon the power of God by asking for His help through prayer. Certainly, by himself, the Pope cannot do it. Jesus said, 'Without Me you can do nothing, with Me you can do all things.'

"So by prayer, what the Pope cannot do on his own, he can do, if he and we pray. Jesus tells us in the Fatima message, 'Pray a great deal for the Holy Father, he will do it (the consecration of Russia in the manner specified) but it will be late.'

"Besides prayer, which the Holy Father could foster by writing Rosary encyclicals like Leo XIII did at the end of the 19th Century; Leo XIII wrote 17 Rosary Encyclicals encouraging the Faithful to pray the Rosary every day. Today we need the Rosary more than ever. Every Pope of the 20th Century up to the time of Vatican II and beyond, wrote encyclicals on the Rosary. Pope Paul VI and Pope John XXIII also exhorted the faithful to pray the Rosary. It seems to me, today we hardly hear about the Rosary from the Vatican.

"Besides calling for millions of Rosaries and other supernatural acts of prayer and reparation by the faithful the world over, the Pope can do many things to set the stage for his eventual obedience of Our Lady's command to consecrate Russia together with all the Catholic Bishops.

"If I am strictly obliged under pain of mortal sin, to go to the next city 100 miles away, to fulfill some act of justice or charity, I cannot simply say: 'I am not an angel, I cannot this instant be in that next city; therefore I am not obliged to do anything.' On the contrary, I am still obliged to be there, but that also implies I am obliged to take the means necessary to get there. So I must take a car or get a ride, or take a bus or start walking. Just because I cannot fulfill my obligation in one instant, does not take away my obligation to fulfill my duty.

"Similarly, just because the Pope at this instant cannot fulfill his obligation to command all the Catholic Bishops to join him in consecrating Russia does not mean he is not obliged. He is most definitely obliged to take the means necessary to fulfill this obligation. And if he cannot do it in his lifetime he at least must work towards making it possible for his successor to fulfill this most solemn obligation.

"One of the means the Pope, in the objective moral order must take, is to properly inform himself about this question. He cannot plead ignorance of what is going on in the Church. He is the supreme shepherd and he personally must be informed about the most important item in the Church's agenda. He cannot rely on dubious information or gossip.

"There is nothing more important for the Church or the world, for peace, for solidarity, for fostering true religious unity, for any and all good things that all men, women and children hold to be of value in this world, and for the salvation of millions of souls in the next world, than the consecration of Russia. He personally is commanded by Jesus and Mary, to do this act. It is not something he can delegate to another. He personally must be informed of the actual situation and the prevailing conditions in the world and the Church preventing him.

"Up to now, without any merit of my own, I and the apostolate I lead, is by far the largest worldwide apostolate promoting this aspect of the Fatima message. We have written to all the bishops of the world 35 times and almost every time we have spoken about the solemn request and command of Jesus and Mary to consecrate Russia. We are perhaps the best informed of anyone in the world about the actual, real support the Pope has from the bishops to obey today.

"I mention this point because it is often said that the Pope wants to obey but he feels he does not have the support of the bishops. I think the Pope has certainly been told this by his advisors but he needs to inform himself in this crucial point by asking others outside the Vatican bureaucracy. It is clear that the vast majority, over 80% of the bishops who write us, positively support our endeavors. We have had over 1700 bishops write to us. The slight opposition among the bishops to the consecration is less than 2%. The militant opposition is less than 1/2 of 1%.

"But I have never been able to inform the Pope directly. I have never been asked to inform him. Yet, of all individuals on this planet, I perhaps have more information on this point that the Pope needs to know to be accurately informed. At the very least, he needs to obtain this information which will contradict the misinformation his advisors are feeding him so as to at least have a better perspective of where the truth lies.

"Besides informing himself, the Pope must, (again in the objective moral order) exercise his authority and powerfully rebuke those bureaucrats, including Cardinal Sanchez and Archbishop Sepe who are abusing their authority by preventing the bishops from hearing the truth about the obligation to consecrate Russia.

"Pope John Paul II has received, from the hands of several bishops and from the hands of a layman (see photo section) formal canonical complaints (Libelli) against the above-mentioned Vatican bureaucrats who have grievously broken Canon Law in their ongoing continual operations to impede the truth about Fatima from reaching the Catholic

Bishops of the world.

"It seems to me that as long as Pope John Paul II tolerates these illegal and gravely immoral acts by his own Vatican bureaucrats, he cannot, in the objective moral order, claim that he has done all he can to bring about conditions whereby he or his successor could finally do the consecration.

"About the only excuse the Pope might have for the present state of affairs of allowing his bureaucrats to rule in his name but against his will, is that he is so ill with Parkinson's disease, that he is physically incapable of asserting his papal will. In the Old Testament, King David, in his old age, while still on the throne, actually had one of his sons usurp his royal prerogatives.

"So I wish to be perfectly clear. First of all, you asked me if the Pope and the bishops are obliged under pain of mortal sin to obey this command to consecrate Russia. I answered that in the objective moral order, 'Yes they are.' But this does not mean I am hereby judging the Pope. Only God, the Pope and his confessor can do that. I am not the confessor of the Pope so I cannot judge his subjective state of guilt or innocence. I have confined my answers to what the Pope is bound to do in the objective moral order."

Then Father Gruner, why do you say such things, when you know they might be published? Are you not then guilty of the charge you are against the Pope? Should you not maintain silence in face of these questions?

"No, I am not guilty. No, I should not remain silent. I think I have already distinguished between scandal of the little ones and pharisaical scandal. Because the truth needs to be known, because there is a great deal of good, world peace and salvation of millions of souls, then I cannot omit to do the good. I must let the truth be known. I must proclaim that the Fatima consecration binds under pain of mortal sin. I do this even if I must stand alone, because there seems to be no one else who will. I owe it to the Common Good to do what I can to ensure this most important truth is known.

"St. Alphonsus teaches that we must make known moral obligations, even to people who will not accept our teaching, if our silence would scandalize the rest of the flock or if an injustice were about to be inflicted or has been inflicted on a third party.

"In other words, if leaving a parishioner in ignorance about his duty only causes the parishioner/penitent to harm himself and no one else, then a confessor or a pastor of souls could choose to leave the person in ignorance if he prudently foresaw that the offered correction would be rejected thereby making that person guilty of sin by knowingly refusing to do his duty in a serious matter.

"But if the ignorant person, performing some act or omitting some act, not only hurt himself by committing a sin in the objective moral order, but also harmed another person in his rights, then the confessor, the pastor of souls could not in good conscience leave the ignorant person in his ignorance, even if he prudently foresees that that person will refuse the correction and not amend his ways.

"That is because the confessor, the pastor of souls owes it to the Common Good of all men, or simply to the good of these other person(s) wronged by the ignorant person's objective sins.

"So, even if the Pope or the Pope's confessor were not to accept the clear teaching of the Natural Law and Divine Revelation as applied to this moral obligation to obey Our Lady of Fatima under pain of mortal sin, I am still bound to proclaim it, lest I myself become guilty of sin in the objective moral order by my silence.

"The Pope's confessor has a strict obligation to bring this matter to the Pope's attention. Just as the bishops' confessors have this strict obligation before God. We are not allowed to leave our penitent in ignorance about this matter, no matter how inconvenient we find it to bring it up, explain it and insist upon it.

"I am not the Pope's confessor but if I were, knowing all I know about this consecration of Russia's request, I would be duty bound to insist with the Pope that he do all he can to bring it about. Of course, I would have to listen to whatever difficulties he perceives in doing this, but unless there is some really new significant factor I do not know, then I would still have to insist on his serious moral obligation to solemnly undertake to do what he could to obey Our Lady of Fatima's command that the Pope consecrate Russia.

You are very strong on this point. Are you saying that you would be duty bound before God to insist with the Pope?

"Yes, and so is anyone else who knows Fatima like I do. Let me explain. You know that the Pope, the bishops and parish priests have received a canonical mission to save the souls entrusted to their care. Each pastor of souls, (each cleric noted above, pastor, Pope, Bishop-Ordinary) then has a solemn obligation to feed his flock the Sacraments and do his other duties to those souls which are necessary for salvation of his flock's soul, even at the risk of losing his life.

"For example, if a pastor of the parish has a parishioner who has been partially buried alive, but who can still speak and confess his sins, the pastor is bound to go down to hear his confession if the entrapped man asks for him, even if there is proximate danger that the pastor would be buried alive by a second collapse of the ground above. Even though it is perilous, the pastor must go down in that dangerous spot if he physically is able to, and give the parishioner the last sacraments in order to save his soul."

I didn't know that.

"Yes. Each and every pastor receives from God Himself a most serious charge, the salvation of the souls entrusted into his care. The pastor, for the eternal life of each and every member of his flock, must be willing to actually risk his life to bring the last sacraments to a soul entrusted to his personal care.

"Similarly, a confessor must inform his penitent of his serious duty to fulfill even if the penitent will not accept the correction or the information. For example, if a penitent is using contraceptives in his marriage, the confessor must tell him he must stop. Because the Common Good of the Church is involved, a confessor of any soul has to answer to God for each soul whose confession he hears. He cannot leave a penitent in ignorance of his duty or leave the penitent in omission of his duty when the confessor knows the penitent is offending justice toward third parties.

"According to St. Alphonsus, the confessor would go to hell unless he repented, for not telling the penitent his duty. The confessor cannot leave the penitent in ignorance of his grave duty to third parties.

"The Pope's confessor is also held to this law of God. Not even the Pope can dispense the confessor from this obligation of telling the hard truth to his penitent, even if the penitent is the Pope himself. Just as the pastor of souls noted in the above example would commit a mortal sin for not trying (even at risk to his own life) to save that soul of his congregation, so too, the confessor would commit a mortal sin for not telling his penitent his grave obligation, even if the penitent does not want to hear it.

"So it would be at the risk of my own soul, as the Pope's confessor, if I did not insist with the Pope that he do the consecration or at least do all he could do (and there is much the Pope could do to bring it about) to eventually have the consecration done.

"So to repeat my answer, yes, I must insist and any confessor of the Pope who knows what I know is also bound to insist."

What if the Pope refused to make such a solemn undertaking after you insisted?

"Well, unless there was a significant new factor (and I cannot foresee there being one; I have so far answered every objection that any Cardinal, bishop, priest or layperson ever raised. After 15 years, there are not many reasons or factors I have not heard about) then I would have to tell him he would be bound before God to make such an undertaking and tell him that he was in danger of losing his soul in Hell if he didn't make such an undertaking."

And if the Pope still persisted, while offering no weighty, significant reason for his refusal. What then?

"I am afraid that my moral training would force me to tell the Pope that I could not help him in his refusal, for to do so would make me guilty of mortal sin. So, unless some more learned student of St. Alphonsus's Moral Theology could show me otherwise, I am afraid I would have to refuse the Pope absolution!"

Refuse the Pope absolution, did you say?

"Yes. It seems astounding but it is nevertheless true. The Pope is most seriously bound to obey Our Lady of Fatima even under pain of mortal sin. And his confessor if he knows Fatima like I do is bound to come to that conclusion and to refuse absolution as I would be as I explained above. I can see no other conclusion for his confessor or for that matter the confessor of each and every bishop, but the onus is on the Pope as the highest authority of the Church on earth, to set the date, to command the bishops. After the Pope gives the command and sets the date, then the onus would be on each bishop to obey, under pain of mortal sin. And each bishop's confessor would have to tell his penitent to obey or risk the loss of his soul in Hell for all eternity."

Then Father Gruner, this obligation of the Pope to consecrate Russia in the manner requested by Our Lady of Fatima is indeed most grave, is it not?

"Yes. Most certainly. Obedience to this request is necessary for world peace, the very existence of various (entire) nations and the salvation of millions of souls. To not bring peace to the world when we can do it, is a grave sin of omission. To not stop the annihilation of nations when I can, is indeed a grave sin against God and to use the phrase of a Catholic bishop regarding the annihilation of nations, 'a crime against humanity'. To not lift our hands in this necessary effort to save millions of souls would make me (and others who can) guilty of grave crime against God and man."

Your enemies suggest you insist on this consecration out of some sort of animosity to the Holy Father and the bishops. But Father Gruner, it seems, from what you have just said, that you are insisting in public on this out of a sense of obligation to the Church and the Holy Father.

"Yes, that is true. It is because 'the Charity of Christ presses us' that we cry out. Believe me, I would love to be able to retire in peace, to say my prayers, to read my library of books and have a very quiet life far away from all the battles that the enemies of Our Lady of Fatima insist on imposing on me in their profound ignorance of this full Fatima message.

"I estimate that many of us will be slaughtered in the certain and soon to be enslavement of the world if this request of Our Lady is not heard and obeyed in time. Besides, the moral law commits me to protect and support the Common Good of the whole Church by proclaiming Our Lady's full Fatima Message. Even against incomprehension, misunderstanding or outright malice of some powerful people.

"Despite my poor health, my distaste for much of this work, which pays me less than most priests in North America get, I continue, not because I am some sort of heroic person but only because I realize that the Church and more particularly the Pope and the bishops have no other real viable alternative.

"I hope it is plain to see in all this that I am certainly not against the Pope. I am perhaps one of his most loyal supporters. I am trying to save his neck in this life certainly and quite possibly in the next too.

"You see, it is Jesus Himself Who tells us to make these truths known to His ministers. That is, it is especially to those ministers, to the Pope and the bishops; those who are directly charged with this personal obligation to consecrate Russia, that Jesus directs us to inform when He says, 'Make it known to My ministers, given they follow the example of the King of France, in delaying the execution of My command, like him they will follow him into misfortune.'

"I, too, as His minister, would have this warning addressed to me personally if I refused to point out the truth of the serious moral obligation the Pope and the bishops have in the objective moral order. I, at least can say on this point, I have not hidden this fact from the Pope and the bishops out of false loyalty or party politics. On judgment day, they all will agree I told them plainly what their duty was.

"Not only are the Pope and the bishops likely to undergo some sort of persecution and even violent death because they delay the consecration but even more serious is the danger of hellfire they face for all eternity if they knowingly, deliberately, with full knowledge and consent do not do their duty to bring about the consecration of Russia.

"For bringing this possibility to their attention, I am indeed their best friend and loyal supporter. I am not looking for acknowledgment or thanks, but I must insist I am their best friend in order to counteract all my (and their) enemies who chant day in and day out in the corridors of power, in the Vatican and chancery offices in various parts of the world, that I am against the Pope.

"As Hitler said, 'Tell a lie often enough and it will stick.' No doubt, the powerful bureaucrats who either are unthinking, or power hungry or working explicitly for the devil, and who pass on this lie, not only hurt the Pope and the bishops but also seriously hurt themselves. To these ministers of Jesus, the warning also applies. They too, may see the same fate that befell the King of France fall on their own personal neck."

But Father, why do you say this so publicly? Why not just say it privately?

Father Nicholas Gruner looked at the picture of the Immaculate Heart of Mary, paused for a moment, and then said, "I am glad you asked that question. Apart from the fact that I do not have access to the Pope, there are other good reasons for saying this in public.

"I did have a personal appointment with the Pope. The time and date was set and I flew to Rome with Josyp Terelya. I paid his passage to Rome and obtained his travel documents for him, even paying for his English language interpreter to come too. But 24 hours or so before the appointment, it was cancelled. Subsequently I sought another appointment; I have gone to the Pope's personal friend from Poland, Cardinal Deskur but he couldn't or wouldn't help me see the Pope either.

"So, on July 12, 1995, we published an 'Open Letter to the Pope' which cost over $100,000. U.S. and asked the Pope to intervene against those who illegally and immorally tried to stop our bishops conferences. He read the letter but didn't do anything we can see or get in touch with us. I am certainly known to the Pope.

"There are many channels he could use to get in touch with me discreetly if he wants to; priest and bishop friends of mine see him but are loath to carry this message to him. It is obvious to me that I cannot get in to see him so I have no other means of reaching him except in the public forum. Although I cannot possibly anticipate here his every objection or question he has to what I perceive is his absolute, grave moral obligation to consecrate Russia, I, at least, can outline it in public sufficiently for him or his successor so that he will know his duty or at least be aware that he should look further into the crucial importance of the consecration before he rejects this one solution to all his problems.

"When the enslavement of Europe and the Americas and the rest of the world is in full swing, at least then maybe someone in authority, or in a position of influence will remember the one and only solution offered to this world.

"I may not survive all the attacks on me and on my reputation. I am growing weary of resisting all the lies, the incomprehensions, the outright malice by the very ones who should be helping not so much me but this cause of Heaven itself. But at least I should have a clear record for posterity, so that finally someone in the future will recognize the great gift of God that Our Lady is offering us in the full Fatima Message and the loving command that the Pope and the bishops together, on the same day, same hour, in a public, solemn way consecrate Russia to the Immaculate Heart of Mary.

"Besides not having access to the Pope and those in power, besides having almost all my efforts I make to have the bishops gather in meetings to hear the full Fatima Message being frustrated by a few loose cannon bureaucrats that up to now have not been reined in by the Pope, there are also other reasons for going public;

Not out of spite.

Not to prove I am superior in any way.

Not to embarrass the Vatican or the bishops.

Not to get even.

"These and similar motives would be wrong. But there are occasions when God Himself demands we go public, even to rebuke or to appear to rebuke our superiors. This is clearly taught by Sacred Scripture and also by the Doctors of the Church. There are examples in Church history which uphold this teaching in practice.

"To mention just a few examples, we have St. Paul rebuking St. Peter to his face in public when the faith was in danger because 'Peter was not standing in the truth'. (Gal.2:11) Did this mean St. Paul was against the first Pope, St. Peter? No. Was St. Paul within his right to correct a Pope? Yes. Was he wrong to do it publicly? No.

"We have Pope, Paschal II in the year 1111, being rebuked by bishops for his immoral and imprudent intention to appoint all bishops according to the will of the Emperor. Pope Pascal II, in 1116 agreed that his bishops were right and he was wrong.

"Theologians publicly rebuked Pope John XXII in 1333 A.D. for preaching heresy which was corrected with a solemn definition by the Pope in 1336. The Pope was wrong and the correction given in public by his inferiors was vindicated three years later by the Pope.

"St. Robert Bellarmine has written extensively on this point. St. Robert is a Doctor of the Church and a very staunch defender of the papacy, yet he clearly teaches there are times when even the Pope must be rebuked[1] in public by well informed inferiors.

"St. Thomas Aquinas, the greatest Doctor of the Church, also teaches the same thing. They both agree that if the common good of the Church is in danger, or if the Catholic Faith is in danger by a Pope's words or actions, then the Pope should be rebuked even in public by their subjects. Of course, if it applies to the Pope, the same holds true for rebuking bishops and in public as well.

"Today, the Church is in grave danger. The faith is in grave danger.

The Pope has spoken about this crisis and the battle between the Gospel and the anti-Gospel, between Christ and anti-Christ and that it is especially heightened in our time. Sister Lucy, in her last authentic public interview before she was silenced (See Appendix III) told Father Fuentes that we are presently in a decisive battle between the devil and the Blessed Virgin Mary. This is the time of a final battle when one side wins and one side loses definitively.

"As I said before, we are at the crossroads of history. The danger to the common good of the Church and the common good of all temporal society is indeed most grave, even if, as Pope John Paul II said in 1976, most of our contemporaries do not see it fully.

"The faith is in danger around the world, as Cardinal Ratzinger said in his book *The Ratzinger Report*. Since the definitive solution to these grave crises is in the hands of the Pope and the bishops, because only they directly can fulfill Our Lady of Fatima's command to consecrate Russia, then certainly the conditions laid down for speaking out publicly even if it appears to be a rebuke, is certainly present for me to rise up and insist publicly on the grave duty the Pope and the bishops have of obeying.

"The Pope himself said that 'the Message of Fatima imposes an obligation on the Church.' Indeed, it imposes a grave obligation, and there are grave consequences for ignoring such obligations."

Chapter 6

Do Not Extinguish The (Holy) Spirit Do Not Despise Prophecy

...(1 Thess.V:19-20)

Father Gruner, can you tell your reasons for insisting that the Pope and the bishops and in fact all of us have the grave duty to obey Our Lady of Fatima in all that She commands us?

"At the risk of repeating myself, I refer you to my speech on this subject that I gave to all the bishops, priests and lay delegates at our Fatima 2000 Congress held recently in Rome."

Opening Address at Fatima 2000 Congress, Rome 1996

It is very important to understand that there is a serious obligation to believe and to obey the full Fatima Message. This obligation is not only on each one of us, but on the Church. This is an obligation which is not, simply, because of pious devotion. Certainly our love for Our Lady should make us feel obliged and the fact that She is our Mother should make us feel obliged. But I would like to dwell not only upon devotional reasons but upon reasons which bind us strictly in justice and prudence. We find these reasons both in the natural law as well as in the light of Divine Revelation.

False Devotees' Objections

There are objections raised even by people who say that they promote the Message of Fatima. They say:

"You don't have to believe in Fatima; You don't have to obey Fatima; Of course, we devotees of Our Lady do that but we are not obliged to."

I would like that objection and that statement to be corrected. There is a strict obligation not only on those who believe Our Lady has a very special role, but everyone, especially the Church.

As I mentioned earlier, the Pope has said in his speech in Fatima in 1982, on May 13, that the Message of Fatima imposes an obligation on the Church. Although that should be good enough reason for us, it is not simply based on the statement of His Holiness.

Sacred Scripture Imposes an Obligation to Obey Fatima

The basis for saying that the Message of Fatima imposes an obligation is founded in Sacred Scripture itself. We find that in 1 Thess: 5:19-20, St. Paul says: "Do not extinguish the Spirit. Do not despise prophecy". In other words, to despise prophecy is the same as extinguishing the Spirit.

We cannot take the word of everyone, as well intentioned as they may be, every time they say "God has spoken to me". It may be true. But St. Paul goes on to say "test all things". So the onus is on us first of all to have an open mind that God could be speaking through the voice of prophecy.

But then we have the obligation, particularly the hierarchy has the obligation, to test whether that message indeed comes from God.

This is why I promote the Message of Fatima because the Church has tested Fatima and found it to be worthy of belief, unlike other apparitions that have come more recently. There are very few that I am aware of that are approved by the hierarchy of the Church since Fatima.

The Message of Fatima has been approved not only by the Church, which is certainly the pillar and ground of truth, but also by the great miracles, particularly the Miracle of the Sun, witnessed by 70,000 people.

St. Paul says "Hold fast to that which is good." And so we have an obligation to hold fast to Fatima. It has been found to be good. It is not only in Thessalonians that St. Paul speaks about this but you also find it when St. Paul talks about the Church.

Some people who ask if we have to believe and obey Our Lady of Fatima also ask: "Are you saying that Sister Lucy is more important than the Pope?" This is how some of our opponents would speak.

Father Joseph de Ste. Marie a professor of the Teresianum here in Rome gave a very interesting answer to that question. He points out that in Ephesians 2:20, the Church is established upon the foundation of the apostles and he points out that it is also founded on the prophets.

Listen, and Obey the Prophets

The prophets, Father Joseph points out, are the prophets of the New Testament. If you read the whole of the Acts of the Apostles, you find that together with the charism of the Apostles, is the charism of the prophets of the New Testament. The Church is founded upon not only the charism of the apostles, certainly, it is also of Divine origin; that is the Apostles and their successors, the bishops, were established as essential to the Church by Jesus Christ Himself. This is especially true of the Papacy. We are not in this talk even addressing the question, we are talking about the obligation to listen and obey the authentic voice of prophecy.

Three Kinds of Revelation

It is the role of the hierarchy to test, to find out, to determine whether a message comes from God. In fact, the Fifth Lateran Council, which took place around 1515, defined a solemn definition of the Catholic Church which says that the final interpretation of prophecy is left to the Pope of Rome. There are three kinds of authentic revelation recognized by the Church. They are: the public deposit of Divine Revelation contained in Sacred Scripture and Holy Tradition; private revelations; and public prophetic revelations. To not believe in the public deposit of Divine Revelation is a sin against the theological virtue of Faith.

Then there is what we call private revelation. That is, if I were to have a vision of Our Lady, which I've never had, which certainly I am not worthy of, but if I were to have had one and She told me to pray 15 decades of the Rosary, for myself, that would be a private revelation to me.

Certainly, no one except myself, should be expected to believe this private revelation. But as Bishop Graber of Regensburg, Germany, has pointed out a number of years ago, there is a third kind of revelation and that is what he called "public prophetic revelation". And that is distinct from private revelation and distinct from the deposit of faith.

That is what St. Paul is talking about in Thessalonians and Ephesians. As St. Thomas Aquinas points out in the second of the second part of the *Summa Theologica,* question 174 Art. 6 (note especially ad3) "God sends prophets to every generation, not to give a new doctrine but to remind the faithful what they must do to save their souls."

Intellectual, Professional Fads

Certainly God has used, and continues to use, many ways to reach us. But sometimes He has to overcome some obstacles to reach us. One of the things that is not only in theology, or only in the Church, but is a common experience of human nature is fads, intellectual fads.

My grandfather was a doctor, a researcher in cancer, and it was his view that the medical profession would go in fads. I would say the same thing for lawyers, no doubt and the same things for accountants. But I am pointing out that there is something human about the fact that certain theories or certain remedies in human activity are sometimes considered to be the only true methods, but later on when our popular understanding deepens, then new remedies are applied.

Let us illustrate this by taking some examples from the practice of medicine.

For a while, surgery was the answer to every problem. "Cut it off, cut it out" was the common solution offered to many problems. And then after a while it was pills, take this pill or that pill.

All of these practices have an element of truth in them. Not to knock medicine but sometimes they overemphasized one truth at the expense of another truth. And this can happen also in law. Sometimes we talk about the rights of the criminals and after a while the criminals have more rights than the victims do. And we see, certainly in American society, there is a swing now to point out that the victims have rights also and they should be safeguarded.

But I bring these examples up, not to speak about these other professions, but to speak about the fact that in the Church some times there are certain things which are emphasized in pastoral practice that are true, but are over-emphasized to the point of leaving out some other truths.

Prophets Meet Opposition

That is why God sends prophets to every generation; to remind the faithful of those things which are, shall we say, not that popular at the moment. And that is why prophets, historically, run into opposition. Because they are saying things often that are going against the present-day trends. If they weren't, so to speak, against the current, God would not need to send the prophet in the first place.

That is why it is important for us to remember the admonition of St. Paul: "Do not despise prophecy. Do not extinguish the Spirit." Because, whether it is we here or any other group in the Church, we can be made to feel overconfident of our cause by looking around us and saying "10 million Frenchmen can't be wrong". Trendy people can be seduced into thinking they are right because everyone else is doing it, believing it too.

As Cardinal Ratzinger points out, the truth is not arrived at by subjecting a question to a democratic vote, rather, the truth is the truth and it is for the mind to come to acknowledge the truth. That is why God sends prophets.

In turn, if we could put the argument the other way around, if God could send a prophet and work a great miracle, and we could say to ourselves in all good conscience, "Well that's okay, but it's only a private revelation. We don't need to pay attention. We have the Gospel. We have the Scriptures and Tradition and that's all we need." We are saying, therefore, that God cannot send us a message. We are not bound to listen to anything He says to us other than what we all agree among ourselves to hear.

Obviously that would be extinguishing the Spirit and despising prophecy. And there is a very serious admonition against that.

Even the Good Ignore Our Lady

Sister Lucy, speaking on December 26, 1957, one of the last times she has been able to speak publicly, said "Our Lady is very sad. Our Lady is very sad because neither the good nor the bad pay any attention to Her message."

Now it is understandable what She says about the bad. They have not seen the punishments of God fall on them. They just go about their merry way because they don't see any urgency or importance in Our Lady's words and they, of course don't pay any attention. I say "of course" because if they were good, you would expect them to pay attention. But if they are bad, well, that's what they are and therefore it is somewhat logical from their chosen approach to life to ignore Our Lady.

But what I find surprising in Sister Lucy's statement explaining why Our Lady is sad, is that the good ignore Our Lady's message. Nevertheless, she says that the good are doing this.

It is precisely, I believe, because the good have been sold a bill of goods. They have been told a lie. They have been told that they don't have to pay attention. They have been told they need not listen, they need not believe, they need not obey. And that is a most serious mistake.

"Only She Can Help You"

It is a mistake that could cost us our salvation. It will certainly cost us our freedom and cost us many things that we all hold dear. Our Lady has given us an offer that we cannot refuse. That is, "either you do what I say or you will die".

Now Our Lady is not going to kill us, but She is saying, because of the sins of mankind, up to the present time we are in a crisis of unprecedented proportions and as a result "only She can help you" out of it. Only She, not someone else. In a way, to perhaps even be shocking about this, not even God, because God has reserved this grace to Our Lady's intercession.

As St. Augustine points out: because God loves us, so much, because He is so good, God wants to give us certain great favors, great graces.

But God knows we do not deserve these graces. Still He wants to give them to us. But He will not give them except through the merits and intercession of the saints. That is because He knows two things: one, He knows we do not deserve them; secondly, He also knows that we will become proud if He gave them directly to us. That we will somehow think that "well, I did that. I deserve that grace."

Why Peace, Prosperity Entrusted to Our Lady Only

These graces are so extraordinary and so marvelous that God doesn't want these graces to become an occasion of pride for us. He also wants us to acknowledge that it is through the merits and intercession of the saints. He wants us to, after all, be grateful to His friends who have been able, by their prayers and merits, to obtain these things for us.

That is why we are told at Fatima that the peace of the world has been entrusted to the Immaculate Heart of Mary. That is why Our Lady can say, in all literal truth, "Only I can help you."

That is because we do not deserve this grace that has been promised to us, the grace of world peace, the grace of the conversion of Russia, and through the conversion of Russia, the conversion of the whole world, to the Catholic faith. But God wants to give it to us and He wants to give it to us in our time. God also wants it to be understood and known that it is only through the merits and intercession of Our Lady we will have obtained these graces.

Almost Deceivingly Simple

So when we finally do get the Consecration of Russia and world peace we must remember that it did not come through me. It is not through any of you, or all of us together. It is not even through the merits of the Holy Father, but it is the merits of Our Lady.

At the same time God also wants the whole world to see the importance of the unique position of the Holy Father and of the Catholic Bishops and in fact of the Catholic Church. And that's why He has insisted that it not only be the Holy Father but the Catholic bishops together with the Holy Father, so that the world sees the direct relationship between Russia being converted and the Pope and the bishops having made this act of consecration to the Immaculate Heart of Mary.

The people will do several things. They will say thanks be to God and Our Lady that we have received this grace of world peace. Thanks be to God the Son for becoming man and founding and sustaining His one true Church, the Catholic Church.

They will also say, thanks be to God for clearly indicating the power, the prestige, the importance of the Catholic Hierarchy and especially the primacy that the Pope has over the bishops of the Church. Because this Consecration will take place by the direct order of the Pope who commands the bishops, the people will then see that the Pope is not an equal among the bishops but that he is their superior. This action of the Consecration will clearly, publicly and definitively manifest to the whole world in a most miraculous way the will of God that the Papacy is founded by God and the Pope not only has the primacy of honor but also primacy of jurisdiction over all other bishops.

In the last analysis, God has given to the Church and the world this unchangeable plan of His to obtain world peace only by means of the Pope and Catholic bishops, consecration of Russia to the Immaculate Heart of Mary. Almighty God has so decreed to demonstrate to the Church and the world not only the necessity and importance of devotion to Our Lady, but also to demonstrate through this consecration of Russia and the consequent world peace, that He has founded only one Church, the Catholic Church and that He has established therein the hierarchy of the Catholic Church, and He has given the primacy of authority in the Church to the Pope.

The request was so simple it was almost deceivingly simple. Unless you stop and think about it for a while, it can almost pass you by, so that you might be tempted to think: "what else is there? There must be something more important".

And that is why Our Lady of Fatima, when She came at Tuy and gave this most important command to consecrate Russia She came in the presence of the Most Holy Trinity. When She appeared to the children at Fatima, She spoke on Her own. But when She spoke in the presence of the Most Holy Trinity, She spoke in God's name. Everything Our Lady says is what God wants Her to say. But when She gave Her request for the consecration of Russia, She said: "The moment has come in which *God* asks the Holy Father to make, together with all the bishops of the world, the consecration of Russia to My Immaculate Heart, promising to save Russia by this means."

Homes, Freedoms, Lives at Stake

And so, you can see that we have everything to gain by fulfilling Our Lady's requests and everything to lose by not fulfilling Her requests. It would also be prudent to fulfill Her requests, whether it is just because you love your country, or you love your family, or you love your freedom, or you love just to be alive, for any one of these reasons, or all of them together, just on the natural level it is obvious that it is the smart thing to do.

Not even addressing for the moment the great good of saving millions of souls, which is certainly even much more important than all these goods that I've just mentioned, but even on the natural level, I would say even an atheist can see he would have something to gain by promoting the Consecration of Russia.

Even Atheists Understand

I remember explaining this to an atheist one time, in 1984. He didn't believe in God, but he could understand nevertheless the prudence of carrying out this act of consecration. He said it was the first time he had seen any hope for the world. Even atheists understand it is most prudent to have the Consecration of Russia properly done just to take care of their lives, their persons, their homes that they paid 20 years' mortgage on or to safeguard whatever it is that they hold dear; if nothing else just being alive, and enjoying their freedom. All these things are at risk without Our Lady of Fatima's Message being heard and obeyed.

And so, even from an atheist's point of view it is perfectly prudent to put forward this act of consecration. If nothing else, what is going to be lost by doing it? Absolutely nothing. The worst that would take place, it would take half an hour of prayer of the Pope and bishops together to do the act of consecration. And with a bit more ceremony it might take an hour and a half. And that's all. The actual prayer would take less than five minutes to pronounce. And so from a prudential point of view there is everything to gain by doing it and everything to lose by not doing it.

Sacred Scripture Teaches us About Miracles

But apart from this human prudence, I would like to dwell upon some other reasons that we find in Sacred Scripture. Our Lord was asked by the Pharisees to work a miracle. They said, "work for us a sign in the Heavens and we will believe You. We will follow You." Our Lord said: "I will not do that. The only sign you will have is the sign of Jonas. That is the Son of man, after being three days in the bowels of the earth, will be raised up to life again."

But these Pharisees said they would believe had He worked a sign in the Heavens. Now the very sign that was refused to the Pharisees was the sign that Our Lady obtained from Her Son to prove to the world that this message indeed comes from God.

"As Low as Hell"

There is an obligation when we have a sign from God. This obligation is also spoken about by Our Lord. He says, in Scripture, "and thou Capharnaum and thou Bethsaida, do you think that you'll be raised as high as Heaven?" Our Lord answers His own question of these two cities, Bethsaida and Capharnaum, "No, you'll be cast as low as Hell." Very strong words.

Here are two cities that He says will be cast as low as Hell. Why does He say that? He explains Himself. He says: "Because if the signs worked in you had been worked in Sodom and Gomorrah, those cities might have done penance and stood to this day."

Sodom and Gomorrah, as you know, had fire rained down on them from Heaven because of the sins of homosexuality. And yet Our Lord says those cities of Sodom and Gomorrah, that Abraham could not find five just men. Those cities might have done penance had they seen the miracles, had they seen the signs that Our Lord worked in Capharnaum and Bethsaida.

And so to refuse to acknowledge such signs as Our Lord worked in Capharnaum and Bethsaida by not listening and obeying, is grounds for being cast as low as Hell. These are Our Lord's own words.

What Will God Say to Us?

What will Our Lord say then about the 20th Century? God has worked a miracle greater than He worked in Capharnaum and Bethsaida He worked the miracle that the Pharisees asked for that would convert them. He worked that miracle at Fatima. It is the first time, in the history of mankind, that a miracle had been predicted three months ahead of time.

It was on July 13, 1917, that Lucy asked for a sign because the pilgrims had been asking her to ask for a sign. She predicted on that day that God would work a miracle on October 13th, to prove, to demonstrate, to show that this message indeed comes from God.

There is a price to pay for ignoring, for not listening to, for not obeying the message, once God has given such a sign.

And so it is, I would say "foolish", "dangerous", if I cannot use the word "heretical", to say that we do not have to believe in Our Lady of Fatima. Not because Fatima itself is part of the deposit of faith, but because the deposit of faith tells us we have strict obligations to believe and obey prophetic messages such as the Message of Fatima.

An Important Theological Digression

Now there is an argument, or a line of reasoning, I would like to give you. But I am not relying on this argument to establish the point of my speech. Our obligation to listen, to believe, to obey Our Lady of Fatima does not rest on this line of reasoning. I have demonstrated above, other proofs for claiming our obligation, the Church's obligation to obey the full Fatima Message.

But it is nevertheless useful for us to reflect on this following line of thought. Pope Paul VI, who blessed our Pilgrim Virgin statue (here present) at Fatima in 1967, wrote the day before he went to Fatima, a very short encyclical, entitled *Signum Magnum*, which means "The Great Sign". Pope Paul VI starts off this encyclical quoting chapter 12 of the Apocalypse which reads: "I saw a great sign appear in the Heavens, a Woman clothed with the sun."

Pope Paul VI, in the first paragraph of that encyclical does not claim, but he suggests very strongly that the Woman clothed with the sun is not only Our Lady which Scripture scholars can demonstrate to you time and again, but it is Our Lady of Fatima that is predicted in chapter 12 of the Apocalypse. The Woman clothed with the sun is none other than Our Lady of Fatima.

If that is the case, and Paul VI would certainly like us to believe it, then the Message of Fatima, would in fact, be a part of divine revelation.

Now the Pharisees of the Old Testament claimed that they had Abraham for their father, they had Moses for their teacher, and who was this young man from Nazareth? They knew the law and He was just an "ignorant person" who wasn't even learned. And yet, in their very claim to be upholding Divine Revelation, and to be for God, they denied God Himself, and they in effect denied all the prophecies about Christ in the Old Testament. Our Lord said to them if you truly had God for your Father, then you would recognize Me because I am the image of My Father.

In the same way, we have people in our time who have told us over the last 30 years "You don't need Fatima. You have the Bible." And in their very claim of saying they have the Bible, they are clearly implying Fatima is not important.

I even had a professor here in Rome, at the Marianum, who said: "You don't have to believe in Fatima."

I stopped him and I said : "How do you know? How can you affirm categorically that Our Lady of Fatima is not the Woman clothed with the sun who was prophesied in Sacred Scripture? He couldn't answer me. I said: "Well then, if She is, then She is in Sacred Scripture, She is part of Divine Revelation, in its prophecy, and you cannot say that we don't have to listen to Our Lady of Fatima". He had no answer.

There ultimately is no answer to that argument. Even though I cannot demonstrate, without an infallible pronouncement from the Magisterium, that Our Lady of Fatima is the Woman clothed with the sun. And Pope Paul VI did not go that far, but he did clearly suggest that She was.

On the other side, no one can tell you that She is not the Woman predicted in chapter 12 of the Apocalypse. And if Fatima is truly a fulfillment of Biblical prophecy then She is part of Revelation.

St. Thomas points out, what I have to believe is everything that God reveals. The act of faith extends to all that God has revealed in the deposit of Revelation. And so, St. Thomas uses this very example, if you know that Scripture tells you that David had 70 sons, not 69, not 71, but that David had 70 sons, then you must believe that with Divine Faith.

Now lay people are not expected to know theology and all the books of Revelation as well as the priests, or bishops, or theologians. But if you know these facts, then you must believe them. Your belief in this historical fact is not the same kind of belief you have in history books in general. You would believe this historical fact with an act of the theological virtue of faith. Not because the book is an historical book, but because it is God's word, because God Himself has revealed it. Certainly the books are historical. But we must believe it with certitude not just say maybe I believe it. Once we know that God has revealed this we must believe it on the authority of God.

If we must believe with theological faith the fact that King David had 70 sons because God has revealed it to us, then we must also believe all the other facts we know are contained in Sacred Scripture with the same kind of faith. The fact of David's 70 sons is not ontologically as important as many other facts in Sacred Scripture yet we must believe it with theological faith.

Thus, it is even more important we believe facts relayed in Sacred Scripture of much more importance to us. Therefore if we also know that God has revealed that in the future He would send His Mother clothed with the sun, and that the fulfillment of that prophecy is Our Lady of Fatima; then we must believe that it is part of the Divine Deposit of Faith, that it is in Divine Revelation.

Now I'm not hereby saying you have to believe it today, because we don't have a pronouncement of the Magisterium on that. But we can also say to our opponents that you cannot affirm the contrary. Thus that professor who wanted to put me down could not answer, because I know there is no answer to that. And I do know that Pope Paul VI has suggested very strongly that, in fact, Our Lady of Fatima is none other than the Woman clothed with the sun in chapter 12 of the Apocalypse.

To Sum Up

To come back to our main point, whether or not the Fatima revelations are contained in prophecies written in Sacred Scripture; the fact of the matter is we MUST believe and obey Our Lady of Fatima. Our obligation still exists because we are told in Thessalonians "do not despise prophecy, do not extinguish the Spirit".

We are told that the Church is built upon the foundation of the apostles and the prophets of the New Testament. Sister Lucy, in her humility, does not talk of herself as a prophet. But strictly speaking, by the definition of the term she is a prophet. She has received the message from God to communicate to the Church at large and God has attested to this with a public miracle; a public miracle of the magnitude the world and the Church has not seen since the Resurrection.

We have Our Lord's own words which tell us that the people of Capharnaum and Bethsaida would be cast as low as hell for refusing to believe and be obedient to His message once He demonstrated it with great public miracles. And we have the First Vatican Council definition which tells us that the Catholic Faith is a light to the nations which can be known by two things independent of all scholarship.

I'm not knocking scholarship and scholarship certainly helps us, but independent of scholarship, even the most uneducated person, as well as the most educated, can know that the Catholic Church is the true Church and the Catholic Faith is the true Faith by two things. This is defined by the First Vatican Council. We can know these truths by public miracles and by public prophecies that have been realized. You will find them both there in the Message of Fatima. Therefore, if true miracles and true prophecies impose an obligation to believe the Catholic Faith, they also impose an obligation to believe the prophets that God has sent.

Our Age is in Grave Danger

So the obligation is serious and very important, we must remember Sister Lucy in her talk on Dec. 26, 1957 with Father Fuentes pointed out, that to resist the known truth is a sin against the Holy Spirit.

She also said at the same time that, speaking in a human manner, Our Lord with a "certain trepidation," seeing He had exhausted all other means of obtaining the attention and obedience of the Church and mankind, uses this one final means, which is His Mother. He finally tries one more time to get our attention and to get our obedience. But he is "afraid" to ask His Mother to come because if we refuse to pay attention to Her, if we refuse to give Her the due respect and honor that She deserves, then He must punish us more severely than if He had never sent Her in the first place.

The fact is that He sent His Mother six times to Fatima, together with the requests at Tuy and Pontevedra, for the Five First Saturdays and for the consecration of Russia. And if we refused these interventions of Our Lady, God, being Our Lord, the second Person of the Blessed Trinity, God the Son, being the good Son that He is, of His Mother, will vindicate the honor of His Mother. That our refusal of His words and His miracles, along with refusing to give the due honor to Our Lady, will make us more culpable than if we had never received the Message of Fatima.

It is meant to be a grace. It is meant to be a means of mercy for us. But if we refuse and if we believe those who say we have no obligation to believe and obey, then we turn the very means of grace for us, the very means of mercy for us, into a greater reason for our punishment.

Self-Evident Reasons Showing We Must Obey Fatima

Apart from the above reasons taken from Sacred Scripture, which demonstrates the Church's obligation to obey Our Lady of Fatima I want now to draw upon reasons which should be self-evident, based on the light of natural reason.

It would be very imprudent, if your next door neighbor came to you and said your house is on fire, call the fire department and rescue your children and you said, "well I don't have a pronouncement, a definition from the Pope that my house is on fire. Someone told me that you are not to be trusted. I am not going to listen to you. I am not going to go outside and look and see if maybe this person is right. I am not going to look. After all, I've had it said to me in a newspaper somewhere that you can't be trusted."

I think that anyone here who has a child, a house, or anything they consider valuable, if you were told there was a thief, or a fire, or something putting them in danger; you would at least take the precaution of verifying what was being said. At least that much. We are all children of Adam and Eve and we have an obligation to at least believe our fellow man, unless there are valid grounds for believing that he is not telling the truth.

Why We Must Believe 70,000 Witnesses

There are people who tell lies. But God has put in our heart, into human nature that even when people lie they betray somehow that they are not telling the truth. They change their voice, get nervous, they do all sorts of things. People cannot lie, except very practiced liars, without betraying the fact that they are lying in some way. Even when people are liars, the urge to tell the truth is such that even these people cannot lie all the time. It is impossible, morally impossible.

That is why out of the voice of many witnesses, you come to the knowledge of the truth. That is why, when we have 70,000 witnesses telling us that a miracle took place, when an atheist who is ridiculing the children and ridiculing all of the pilgrims who went to Fatima, was obliged to print on the front page of his paper, the next day, that he saw this miracle, we would be, to say the least, foolish to ignore what he says.

It would be a sin against prudence to say that all of these people, 70,000 of them, lied to us. There were people who were very simple and there were people who were very learned. There were people who were very Catholic and there were people who were very anti-Catholic. They all testified to the same thing. Even those who would be publicly embarrassed by having to reverse themselves, nevertheless testified to the truth, that this miracle took place. That is why the people of Capharnaum and Bethsaida, were guilty for not believing even though all of them didn't see the signs that Our Lord worked. But there were enough witnesses that the whole city knew that it took place.

We know if we go to a doctor or someone else, you believe this person when he tells you something if you have no reason to contradict or to question his testimony. And even though Fatima's and Our Lord's sign is contradicted, we have enough evidence to know that this is the truth. To resist the known truth is a sin against the Holy Spirit. If we continue and persist in this resistance to the knowledge of the truth then there is no forgiveness of that sin. And the final persistence, of course, is the persistence to our death.

A Serious Obligation

It is a very serious obligation. It does bind in conscience and the Pope was not making the statement lightly when he said the Message of Fatima imposes an obligation on the Church. It is founded in Scripture, it is founded in reason, it is founded in the miracles and the prophecies that we know have taken place and we know have been verified as having come from God.

If we can just ignore God when He sends us such a message, then we are despising prophecy, we are extinguishing the Holy Spirit, we are resisting the Holy Spirit. We are sinning against Him. And if we continue with this, (and when I say we, I presume that none of us here would have that attitude, but it is important to set it down in the record) that there is a price to pay, and that is hellfire.

Sinning against the Holy Spirit ends up by sending the person who commits it to Hell. It is a very serious obligation. It is not a light obligation. It is not just on me. It is not just on you. This obligation is imposed on the whole Church. The obligation to obey Fatima is fulfilled differently, depending on our position in the Church. But all of us must obey Our Lady of Fatima as Her message applies to our concrete circumstances.

The Position Outlined In This Talk Is Unchallenged For 8 Years

I have written about this obligation to believe and obey in my book which is translated into Spanish, Portuguese, French and English. I have spent about 75 pages of my book on it. I have sent that book to every bishop in the world and to every priest in Brazil. I am willing to send it to any theologian who promises to read it. Let any of them try to find a substantial error in it. It has been published now for over 8 years and there has not been one significant argument against what I have said about our obligation to believe and obey Our Lady of Fatima.

The only argument I have ever heard is that you don't have to believe private revelations. But Bishop Graber has pointed out that Fatima is not a private revelation. It is a public prophetic revelation. And all the arguments you hear about not having to believe Fatima are based on the false claim that Fatima is simply a private revelation.

Fatima is not a private revelation. 70,000 people do not constitute something that is private. 70,000 witnesses to a miracle announced three months ahead of time is a public miracle for the Church. It is a public prophetic message and it imposes an obligation on the Church and all of us are bound to do what we can to advance Our Lady's cause and to obey Her, first of all ourselves, and then to do what we can to get others to know, appreciate, love and obey Our Lady of Fatima and Her Message.

Our Lord says to "Make it known to My ministers". It is not Our Lady speaking now, it is Our Lord Himself saying "Make it known". That also is an obligation we have coming through the Message of Fatima.

BOOK III

TESTIMONIES

Appendix I

From the Fatima Network Website http://www.fatima.org
Reprinted with permission.

The Story of Fatima

The Blessed Virgin Mary, the Mother of God, appeared six times to three shepherd children ("the Three Seers")[1] near the town of Fatima, Portugal between May 13th and October 13th 1917. Appearing to the children, the Blessed Virgin told them that She had been sent by God with a message for every man, woman and child living in our century. Coming at a time when civilization was torn assunder by war and bloody violence, She promised that Heaven would grant peace to all the world if Her requests for prayer, reparation and consecration were heard and obeyed. **"If My requests are granted ... there will be peace"**

Our Lady of Fatima explained to the children that war is a punishment for sin and warned that God would further castigate the world for its disobedience to His Will by means of war, hunger and the persecution of the Church, the Holy Father and the Catholic Faithful. God's Mother prophesied that Russia would be God's chosen "instrument of chastisement," spreading the "errors" of atheism and materialism across the earth, fomenting wars, annihilating nations and persecuting the Faithful everywhere. **"If My requests are not granted, Russia will spread its errors throughout the world, raising up wars and persecutions against the Church. The good will be martyred, the Holy Father will suffer much and various nations will be annihilated."**

In all Her appearances at Fatima, the Blessed Mother repeatedly emphasized the necessity of praying the Rosary daily, of wearing the Brown Scapular of Mount Carmel and of performing acts of reparation and sacrifice. To prevent the terrible chastisement at the hands of Russia and to convert "that poor nation"... **Our Lady requested the solemn public Consecration of Russia to Her Immaculate Heart by the Pope and all the Catholic bishops of the world.**

She also asked that the Faithful practice a new devotion of reparation on the first Saturday of five consecutive months ("the Five First Saturdays").

The heart of Our Lady's Message to the world is contained in what has come to be called the "Secret" which She confided to the three child seers in July 1917. The Secret actually consists of three parts, the first two of which have been publicly revealed. The first part of the Secret was a horrifying vision of hell[2] "where the souls of poor sinners go" and contained an urgent plea from Our Lady for acts of prayer and sacrifice to save souls. The second part of the Secret specifically prophesied the outbreak of World War II and contained the Mother of God's solemn request for the Consecration of Russia[3] as a condition of world peace. It also predicted the inevitable triumph of Her Immaculate

Heart following Russia's consecration and the conversion "of that poor nation" to the Catholic Faith.

The last part of the Secret (often called the "Third Secret") has not yet been made public, but was written down by Lucy dos Santos, the last living Fatima seer, in 1944 and has been in the possession of the Holy See since 1957. Most informed sources speculate that this portion of the Secret concerns chaos in the Catholic Church, predicting widespread apostasy and a loss of faith beginning in the sixth decade of the 20th Century. **"You saw hell where the souls of poor sinners go. In order to save them, God wishes to establish devotion to my Immaculate Heart in the world ... If people do what I ask, many souls will be saved and there will be peace."**

At the time that She confided the Fatima Secret to the three seers, the Blessed Virgin also promised that God would work a great miracle the following October "so that all may believe." On October 13th 1917, in the presence of 70,000 eyewitnesses, a miracle was worked in the sky above Fatima at the exact moment and in the precise spot that the children had announced earlier. Witnesses recounted that the sun appeared to actually "dance" in the sky and seemed to fall to the ground before resuming its normal place in the heavens. **"On the last month, I will perform a miracle so that all may believe."**

This event has now become known as "the Miracle of the Sun"[4] and has been justly characterized as the greatest supernatural occurrence of the 20th Century. As one leading Fatima authority has noted, this great miracle "does not belong (only) to the domain of faith, or even that of science. Before all else it is an historical event."

The Catholic Church has officially endorsed the Fatima Message "as worthy of belief" since 1930. Five successive popes have publicly indicated their approval and belief in the validity and critical importance of the Fatima apparitions. Several popes have visited Fatima on solemn pilgrimage and Pope John Paul II has gone at least once in every decade of his pontificate. His Holiness has publicly credited Our Lady of Fatima for saving his life during an assassination attempt in 1981 (which, parenthetically, took place on the 64th anniversary of the first Fatima apparition). The following year, while in Fatima to give thanks for Her intervention, the Pope stated that "the message of Fatima is more relevant and more urgent" today than even when Our Lady first appeared. **"In the end, My Immaculate Heart will triumph. The Holy Father will consecrate Russia to me and she will be converted and a period of peace will be granted to the world."**

Belief in the Fatima apparitions and Our Lady's full Message are now widely synonymous with an orthodox adherence to the doctrines, rites and traditional practices and teachings of the Roman Catholic Church.

Many theologians believe that Our Lady's Message is uniquely designed for the difficult and trying times in which we live today and suggest that it is Heaven's intervention to save the world from war, hunger and need, the Catholic Church from apostasy and chaos and the souls of countless millions from eternal damnation. While stern in its warning of the terrible punishments for sin and disobedience, Fatima remains fundamentally a life-affirming and faith-building message of hope and peace for all Catholics and others of good will everywhere. **"Only I can help you ... My Immaculate Heart will be your refuge and the way that will lead you to God."**

Appendix II

The Message

by Oscar Gruner
January 28, 1926

The picture began by the appearance of a small glow of light, rounded in form, but indistinct at the edges. It gradually enlarged and brightened, and after attaining a size such as would be if one saw through an aperture a long way off, and yet quite clearly and sharply, shadows and shapes appeared from it until there was a definite picture; and the picture was of the altar-rail and the altar of the Oratory here at Hartley.

Very rapidly it became evident that there was a solitary young figure kneeling in the middle of the rail. It was Douglas. His head was bowed low over the rail.

The tabernacle suddenly became bright; It took the form of the first patch of light and very rapidly became intensely bright, so as to form the Light of the picture. It expanded also, and brightening every moment, became finally intensely bright. As it did so, the form of Our Lord became evident; robed in brilliant golden light; the raiment and He were one.

It was not like our robes which are separate from us. He came forward as He became distinct, and stepped down to the rail, down to the kneeling figure, and then seemed to stop right over him, and as it were envelope him, the upper part of our boy's body being quite lost to view in the blinding light of Our Lord's presence.

Then I perceived His Face, sharply visible in semi-profile, among the brightness which extended beyond and all round, almost like thick rays; and as He stooped over the boy, and seemed to embrace him, his shoulders, He seemed to be soothing him and comforting him, and embracing him, as a father might.

Throughout the time during which He lingered over the bowed form, there was a most wonderful fragrance, and yet more than a fragrance. It was like the most exquisite perfume ever to be conceived, combined with not a sense of smell, but a sense of touch; it was something to be felt; and at the same time it was not a touch but a sense of perfect peace and the most absolute security; like an absolute security which no storms without can touch, nor even the most riotous multitudes of man could touch; even were that around one, or the tempest of the ocean and one were within even sight of that Presence, one felt absolutely secure; it was not an atmosphere; it was peace itself; it was living peace.

It was even beyond peacefulness which a person might have in the midst of the most arduous human endeavor which one knew no man could shake. It was beautiful. One can only say it was beautiful. That odor of Peace was all between the place I saw, and right across the gulf down to me, and I was filled with it during the whole time His Form was visible.

After a while the Form changed; and it was no more His Form, but the form of the Host, still whiter, still brighter, and this seemed to move up and down once over the bending form, and blend with his head and shoulders; and then there was another pause in the picture.

After a further while, the light changed in form, and I became aware that our boy was now the center of a multiple form, which encircled him closely and on a level with him; they were angels' heads with little wings, like cherubs' wings; they were bending round our child - our child - and there seemed a movement among them with their heads - not exactly kissing, but bowing close and as it were breathing very gently upon him. And after this had proceeded a while they moved slightly apart from one another, and it was now clear that they formed a ring round the upper part of his body, and that a space formed, and that his head was in the center of the space.

Suddenly, at his (Douglas') left side, appeared the form of a most beautiful Lady; Her face was in semi-profile; there was a wonderful expression on it; infinite motherhood; the face was not young; the light She gave round Her was extremely intense, much more than that of the angels; and yet it was less intense than that of Our Lord, different really, it was not that peculiar sense of Almighty-security.

She stooped down to our boy and seemed gently to lift him up, his head lying in Her left elbow; I could not see his features; he was like a babe; and yet I was sure it was still he - still Douglas; he seemed to be sleeping, and yet aware of being in Her arms. His form was indistinct. As She held him thus, the circle of angelic forms rose a little with Her, and there seemed a movement of them all - away from the rail, and towards the Gospel side of the altar, and it was as when a person is carried from among a crowd and the crowd slowly makes as if to follow. At the same time She stood erect, nearly; and was in full profile; and for a moment I saw that Her profile was now exactly the profile of Our Lady of Hartley; but it was not a fancy; She was living; one could tell it was not a statue. The light of the whole scene centered in Her as She moved from the altar rail.

The details became indistinct for a short time now; but when it was all clear again, I saw that Our Lady had handed the soul of our boy into the care of a great multitude - a very great multitude of bright forms, forms like the angelic ones at the altar, but paler; where their features were visible, one could see they seemed sad - but a happy sadness.

They seemed to move greatly as She came; they moved eagerly forward to their new companion; it was a very active movement; and yet they did not seem to move away from their place. It was the movement of a sudden intense interest and eagerness to minister to the newcomer. But when the newcomer was among them he became like unto them; not like a baby-form; and he was quite lost to view to me; so dense was the crowd of beings who came round him.

Meanwhile, the picture had now quite changed again. Our Lady was not visible. There was a band of light across the whole picture which had become suddenly vast. Far away up on the right of me was the Glory, as if from the Tabernacle. And I perceived that this Glory was the Light of Our Lord, and it seemed to come, as it were, out of an ante-chamber. And without seeing beyond it I knew that, if one could enter that Glory, one would find oneself completely bathed in God, Who is beyond it.

The whole landscape, so to say, was formed of living beings. A vast canopy, the canopy of Heaven was between the picture and me; the distance between the bright Light far away above the Epistle side of the altar and the rail was now nothing but a vast concourse of people emitting a pale yellowish-white light, and all looking chiefly toward the Glory in the distance, the light of which was reflected in their faces - the faces were the faces of persons whose thoughts are intent on God. The forms which were nearest the Glory were very much brighter and I thought this was not because of a stronger reflection, but because they actually gave and had, and were, a stronger light.

After all this, the picture came to rest. The peculiar active movement, showing it was all alive, ceased and the whole faded from view and it remains clear, absolutely in every detail, to my mind as I write. And it seemed as though the soul had journeyed and found its position of equipoise, and was absolutely safe, feeling content.

There were other forms behind the paler ones, and these seemed to be those suffering much in Purgatory. The paler forms were those which were only yearning to be released, not suffering. The brighter and brightest forms were those of the saints.

So this was the "day of judgment"; when the Judge was Love, and the remedy imparted was the gift of Love, and the care and motherly nursing were each taking their part in the life of the soul now transferred into another sphere."

. . . (About 11:00 p.m. on the night of Jan. 28th; written down Feb. 4, 1926)

Attached to this document was a note -

"I read this: 'The Message of January 28, 1926 a few moments ago. It was written by my beloved Father-in-law, Dr. Oscar Cameron Gruner, concerning his beloved second son, Douglas. Doug had been killed accidently near Kerang, Australia just a short while before. He would have been 19 years old in February, 1926. My beloved husand, Malcolm, the elder of Baba's and Yellie's two sons, loved his brother dearly. They had a truly beautiful friendship."

. . . Jessie Gruner 9:30 a.m., Tuesday, November 5, 1985.

Appendix III

Reprinted with permission from *The Fatima Crusader* Issue 19.

A Prophetic Interview with Sister Lucy of Fatima

Introduction: This interview given by Sister Lucy to the Mexican priest, Father Fuentes on December 26, 1957 is extremely important especially today. We see with the benefit of looking back over 40 years to the time of this interview just how accurate Sister Lucy was regarding the defections and betrayals of so many priests and nuns. This plea of Sister Lucy is today for us all even more timely than when she gave it in 1957. Until the Pope allows Sister Lucy to again speak to the world we should treasure and ponder this important message.

When it was first published by Father Fuentes it drew widespread interest from many of the faithful around the world. However, as a result of the courageous publication of this serious message, Father Fuentes received a totally unmerited and unprecedented persecution from some anonymous officials in the Diocese of Coimbra, where Sister Lucy lives.

In light of various similar events in the more recent past, in other Curias, we should not be too surprised to learn that a nameless official of the Curia in Coimbra on July 2, 1959 released a statement to the world press saying that the report of Father Fuentes was not true. Common sense, as well as the principles of law, inform us that a statement made by an anonymous official has no real authoritative value.

Father Fuentes Defended: In Mexico, the Archbishop of Vera Cruz, His Grace Manuel Pio Lopez came to the defense of Father Fuentes. Cardinal Jose Garibi y Rivera, the Archbishop of Guadalajara also publicly defended Father Fuentes against the unjustified attack of unnamed diocesan officials. Whoever these persons were who did this, we know that it could not be a Cardinal or Archbishop because there was no Cardinal or Archbishop in that Portuguese Curia. Neither did the authors of this grossly misleading statement of the Curia of Coimbra ever have the courage to identify themselves.

First Father Alonso, the official archivist for the Bishop of Fatima in 1971, adopted the "official" position of the Curia of Coimbra. However, he too, after studying the matter in depth came to the defense of Father Fuentes by 1976. He then said, "The authentic text, which in justice is the only one attributable to Father Fuentes, in my opinion contains nothing which gave rise to the condemnatory note of Coimbra. Much to the contrary, it reinforces a doctrine which is very apt to piously edify the Christian people."

Father Alonso had ample opportunity to speak to Sister Lucy from 1971 to 1976 so as to come to a more accurate understanding of this affair. He, by 1976, knew that neither Father Fuentes nor Sister Lucy has misled the world by this statement of 1957 which we have published below.

Sources: This matter has been documented at length by Frere Michel de la Sainte Trinite in his recently published Volume III of his series '*The Whole Truth About Fatima*'. The text published here is *The Fatima Crusader's* translation of the Spanish and English texts published in Frère Michel's book 'The Third Secret' (Vol. III, pages 336-338).

The Report By Father Fuentes

"I wish only to tell you about the last conversation which I had with Sister Lucy on the 26th of December (last year). I met her in her convent. She was very sad, very pale and emaciated. She said to me,"

"No One Has Paid Any Attention"

"Father, the Most Holy Virgin is very sad because no one has paid any attention to Her message, neither the good nor the bad. The good continue on their way but without giving any importance to Her Message. The bad, not seeing the punishment of God actually falling upon them, continue their life of sin without even caring about the message. But believe me, Father, God will chastise the world and this will be in a terrible manner. The punishment from Heaven is imminent."

The Secret Not Revealed

"Father, how much time is there before 1960 arrives? It will be very sad for everyone, not one person will rejoice at all if beforehand the world does not pray and do penance. I am not able to give any other details because it is still a secret. According to the will of the Most Holy Virgin, only the Holy Father and the Bishop of Fatima are permitted to know the secret, but they have chosen to not know it so that they would not be influenced.

This is the Third part of the Message of Our Lady which will remain secret until 1960."

Russia, The Scourge Of God

"Tell them Father, that many times, the Most Holy Virgin told my cousins Francisco and Jacinta, as well as myself, that many nations will disappear from the face of the earth. She said that Russia will be the instrument of chastisement chosen by Heaven to punish the whole world if we do not beforehand obtain the conversion of that poor nation."

"The Decisive Battle" Between Mary and Satan: The Falling Away of Consecrated Souls and Priests

Sister Lucy also told me: "Father, the devil is in the mood for engaging in a decisive battle against the Blessed Virgin. And the devil knows what it is that most offends God and which in a short space of time will gain for him, the greatest number of souls. Thus the devil does everything to overcome souls consecrated to God because in this way, the devil will succeed in leaving the souls of the faithful abandoned by their leaders, thereby the more easily will he seize them."

"That which afflicts the Immaculate Heart of Mary and the Heart of Jesus is the fall of religious and priestly souls. The devil knows that religious and priests who fall away from their beautiful vocation drag numerous souls to hell... The devil wishes to take possession of consecrated souls. He tries to corrupt them in order to lull to sleep the souls of laypeople and thereby lead them to final impenitence. He employs all tricks, even going so far as to suggest the delay of entrance into religious life. Resulting from this is the sterility of the interior life, and among the laypeople, coldness (lack of enthusiasm) regarding the subject of renouncing pleasures and the total dedication of themselves to God."

That Which Sanctified Jacinta and Francisco

"Tell them also Father, that my cousins Francisco and Jacinta sacrificed themselves because in all the apparitions of the Most Holy Virgin, they always saw Her very sad. She never smiled at us. This sadness, this anguish which we noted in Her penetrated our souls. This sadness is caused by the offenses against God and the punishments which menace sinners. And so, we children did not know what to think except to invent various means of praying and making sacrifices."

"The other thing which sanctified these children was to see the vision of Hell."

The Mission of Sister Lucy

"Father, that is why my mission is not to indicate to the world the material punishments which are certain to come if the world does not pray and do penance beforehand. No! My mission is to indicate to everyone the imminent danger we are in of losing our souls for all eternity if we remain obstinate in sin."

The Urgency of Conversion

Sister Lucy also said to me: "Father, we should not wait for an appeal to the world to come from Rome on the part of the Holy Father, to do penance. Nor should we wait for the call to penance to come from our bishops in our diocese, nor from the religious congregations. No! Our Lord has already very often used these means and the world has not paid attention. That is why now, it is necessary for each one of us to begin to reform himself spiritually. Each person must not only save his own soul but also all the souls that God has placed on our path."

"The devil does all in his power to distract us and to take away from us the love for prayer; we shall be saved together or we shall be damned together."

Last Times

"Father, the Most Holy Virgin did not tell me that we are in the last times of the world but She made me understand this for three reasons."

The Final Battle:

"The first reason is because She told me that the devil is in the mood for engaging in a decisive battle against the Virgin. And a decisive battle is the final battle where one side will be victorious and the other side will suffer defeat. Also from now on we must choose sides. Either we are for God or we are for the devil. There is no other possibility."

The Last Remedies:

"The second reason is because She said to my cousins as well as to myself that God is giving two last remedies to the world. These are the Holy Rosary and Devotion to the Immaculate Heart of Mary. These are the last two remedies which signify that there will be no others."

The Sin Against the Holy Spirit:

"The third reason is because in the plans of Divine Providence, God always before He is about to chastise the world, exhausts all other remedies. Now, when He sees that the world pays no attention whatsoever then, as we say in our imperfect manner of speaking, He offers us with 'certain fear' the last means of salvation, His Most Holy Mother. It is with 'certain fear' because if you despise and repulse this ultimate means we will not have any more forgiveness from Heaven because we will have committed a sin which the Gospel calls the sin against the Holy Spirit. This sin consists of openly rejecting with full knowledge and consent, the salvation which he offers. Let us remember that Jesus Christ is a very good Son and that He does not permit that we offend and despise His Most Holy Mother. We have recorded through many centuries of Church history the obvious testimony which demonstrates by the terrible chastisements which have befallen those who have attacked the honor of His Most Holy Mother how Our Lord Jesus Christ has always defended the Honor of His Mother."

Prayer And Sacrifice and the Holy Rosary

Sister Lucy told me: "the two means to save the world are prayer and sacrifice."

Regarding the Holy Rosary, Sister Lucy said: "Look, Father, the Most Holy Virgin in these last times in which we live has given a new efficacy to the recitation of the Holy Rosary. She has given this efficacy to such an extent that there is no problem, no matter how difficult it is, whether temporal or above all, spiritual, in the personal life of each one of us, of our families, of the families of the world, or of the religious communities, or even of the life of peoples and nations that cannot be solved by the Rosary. There is no problem I tell you, no matter how difficult it is, that we cannot resolve by the prayer of the Holy Rosary. With the Holy Rosary, we will save ourselves. We will sanctify ourselves. We will console Our Lord and obtain the salvation of many souls."

Devotion to the Immaculate Heart Of Mary

"Finally, devotion to the Immaculate Heart of Mary, Our Most Holy Mother, consists in considering Her as the seat of mercy, of goodness and of pardon and as the certain door by which we are to enter Heaven."

Appendix IV

Reprinted with permission from *The Fatima Crusader* Issue 48.

Archbishop Milingo's Dramatic Speech

The following is an edited transcript of the talk Archbishop Emmanuel Milingo gave to the Second Bishops' Conference on World Peace in Mexico City, on Sunday, November 13, 1994.
Archbishop Milingo, former Ordinary of Lusaka, Zambia, now holds a high position in the Vatican itself. He has been living and working in Rome for over 10 years. He is not only one of the youngest men ever to be appointed Archbishop (at the age of 39) he has had vast experience in many different aspects of Catholic Church life.
Over 1,000,000 people have been personally inspired or touched by one or another of the Archbishop's apostolic works. Widely travelled, he came to the Bishops' Conference from the Vatican after a stopover of several days in Japan.

High Level Intervention

In one of the most electrifying presentations by the bishops present at the Conference, Archbishop Milingo gives us a living example of a true shepherd willing to fearlessly defend Our Lady of Fatima's message, the Catholic Bishops and our Fatima Apostolate's rights to meet and freely discuss Her message.

by Archbishop Emmanuel Milingo

Let us be very honest. The Fatima responsibility of the consecration is not in the hands of the bishops. It would happen instantly if the order to do it came from the Pope. The bishops would be there. If some objected, I'm quite sure it would not be many because the Marian Movement on the whole is suddenly having a lot of impact in the Church. I myself have witnessed twenty thousand people gathering in traditional processions. Thousands of people come.

Thousands Write The Pope

I also have received thousands of letters that were addressed to the Pope for the consecration of Russia to the Immaculate Heart of Mary. I myself have brought from my office directly to the Secretariat of State many, many, many of these letters since 1991.

Letters still come from all over the world asking for this consecration. I send them myself to the Secretariat of State. I am quite certain that is where they are stopped.

Abuse of "Obedience"

I really do not blame the bishops. If some resist, they are just a few. And letters like this (holding up a letter against the Fatima Peace Conference signed by a Secretary of State official) will make some of the bishops have no courage. They are unable to participate at a conference like this one.

But on the other hand, this letter from the Nuncio telling us not to come to this Conference shows, as a matter of fact, how one can misunderstand obedience. This says to those who came here, you were disobedient because an official letter told you not to come.

Then people tremble in their trousers. What a pity! It is a humiliation to a human being who is an apostle, a humiliation - intended to prevent him from fulfilling his duties according to his own personality and character. Because of a letter like this such a one will not come to this Conference.

It is sad. It is humiliating. It lowers the dignity of a human being to have a letter like this going around that actually prevents someone from coming to a conference for Our Lady. Meanwhile you have been chosen to be bishops to bear the responsibilities in your own dioceses. There you have got someone suspending your authority in carrying out all your duties and fulfilling your responsibilities.

Suspension of Authority

It is clear that they are living under suspended authority. No letter such as this should be able to affect how we govern in our own dioceses. Coming here to the Conference does not at all affect my policy in my diocese and does not at all touch my relation with the Church as a whole. I am going to a meeting. I go to other meetings, not only meetings about Fatima.

I go to different meetings, so why should I be controlled when I actually come to a meeting like this one. This is a great humiliation, as far as I am concerned, to circulate a letter like this to the bishops and actually pressure the bishops into not coming.

I came here purposely. Yes, purposely. I wrote back to the Secretary of State to say please will you send me a letter and let me have the permission that is needed. They wrote again. One letter had three signatures. I told my secretary, let them know I am going to the Fatima Peace Conference!

I Am An Apostle

Evidently, I'll be able myself to answer them very, very clearly because I am responsible for what I'm doing. I am not one whose authority is suspended. Not at all. I am an apostle. That means I accept full responsibility for what I'm doing.

If this letter represents their way to control us, it means that they don't trust the people to whom they have given authority.

And that doesn't do at all! That is not at all correct.

I Will Tell the Holy Father Myself

Therefore I am very happy to take this letter signed by the Papal Nuncio to the Holy Father. I'll be very open to him about it, because I have already gone this route.

I'll tell the Holy Father in writing. I will find channels through which to reach him and send this. I will explain about this, that I have been there, but I take full responsibility for coming here and I accept the consequences.

And I can assure you there will be no consequences. I will say if you have bishops who cannot carry out the message of Fatima, let we who are in the field, who do not have dioceses but have the people, have a chance. We may not be able to have a great influence on having the Consecration done tomorrow but we will be able to tell the people the demands of the Blessed Virgin Mary.

We are able to do that, to the last degree. We know how to present it and we continue to present it. Ours is not just a diocese, it's the world, and we do have thousands and thousands of people that we deal with.Therefore, with regards to the message of the Blessed Virgin Mary, we have occasions, we have opportunity, we are able to give that.

Catholics Being Swept Away

Basically I'd like to insist on this: that each and every one of us in this world must become evangelizers. The Kingdom of God demands violence, Pope Paul VI said already everyone must become an evangelizer. We are unable to make this happen.

That is why thousands of people, like in Zimbabwe, who have just come into the Church, now are going to evangelical groups. We have got in Italy a second religion, the Jehovah's Witnesses. Imagine that! And in France, Moslems, and so on. Why?

Because our own people are fixed in certain stages such as baptism, marriage, first communion and so on. But in between there is nothing to fill in. Therefore, they are swept away by so many other doctrines that come in. Consequently we find that they become victims.

Why? Because we are never able to make them disciples. Nevertheless, Jesus came to make disciples.

Standing on Your Own Feet

Not one of us will go to Heaven without holding a brother, a sister. Each and every one of us must step out of the crowd and stand on one's own feet strong enough to be a Christian, able to give testimony for that Christianity.

I know a man who was praying one day and the priest was confessing him - the power of the presence of God was shaking the priest even in the confessional. Imagine how powerfully God manifested Himself on that particular occasion!

We are acting as if this Catholic Faith were a private affair. This is not true at all. There is a lot still to be done even if the opening for the Consecration to be done is not yet there. Nevertheless, I think we can still go very, very far if we make each and every one of our Catholics concerned with the whole welfare of the world.

The world must be saved and it must be saved through each one of us.

To reach Archbishop Emmanuel Milingo, write him at his office:
The Pontifical Council for the Pastoral Care of Migrants and Itinerants, Piazza S. Calisto No. 16, 00153 Rome, Italy.

Appendix V

Reprinted with permission from *The Fatima Crusader.*

Regarding Communion In The Hand

It is noted that Father Gruner and other priests do not give Communion in the Hand. Further background to understand why is presented in this appendix.

Section 1: Why Communion in the Hand is Forbidden

Commentary by Father Nicholas Gruner, S.T.L., S.T.D. (Cand.)

The following is a commentary on the Regulations (See Section 3 of this appendix) allowing Communion in the hand under very restricted circumstances.

It must be remembered that Communion on the tongue is the law of the Church. Communion in the hand is an exception to the law (it is an "indult") which is not commanded but only allowed if all the conditions outlined by the Vatican are present. If the conditions are not present then the permission is not granted and Communion on the tongue only is permitted.

The seven conditions are based on two principles as the official document points out. These two principles are not something that the Pope could change even if he wanted to because they are based on Divine Revelation itself.

Every Occasion of Scandal Must Be Avoided

The first condition is that every occasion of scandal is avoided. Obviously if this practice causes some of the Faithful to lose faith in "the Real Presence" then this practice is not good for the salvation of souls because faith in the "Real Presence" in the Eucharist is necessary for salvation.

If the luxury of being able to receive Communion in the hand is going to cause the loss of faith and thereby the loss of souls for all eternity, can anyone fail to see that Sacred Scripture (which tells us to avoid scandal) and charity for souls would demand that this practice be forbidden. And so the Vatican document also makes this lack of scandal an explicit condition for allowing Communion in the hand.

In other words, in places, parishes or communities where the Faithful, even only one of the Faithful, would lose his faith in the Real Presence then in that place, even if the Bishop and the Vatican have given their permission, then by the very law and terms of the permission as well as by Divine Revelation itself, Communion in the hand in that place would be forbidden under grave obligation upon the minister of the Sacrament, the priest, the deacon and the extraordinary minister if there be one. It would bind the bishop, even the Pope himself in that place.

If some ministers do not follow this rule, their bad example does not change the rule, not even if the Pope were to give such example, this rule binds all, even the Pope.

The second principle which the Vatican document gives us is also based on Divine Revelation and cannot be changed by anyone not even the Pope himself because it is part of the unchanging Law of God.

All Danger of Irreverence Must Be Avoided

The second principle is that **"All danger of irreverence towards the Eucharist is avoided."** Since the Eucharist is the Body of Jesus Christ Himself Who is true God and true Man we are bound by the First Commandment to reverence and adore Him. To do the opposite would be the sin of sacrilege. Thus if one prudently fears that by giving Communion in the hand that sins of sacrilege will be committed then one must not give Communion in the hand.

Now as St. Paul explains it is the minister of the Sacraments who is personally responsible for their administration. He is responsible first of all not to the Pope, not to the bishop, not to the recipient of the Sacrament, but to God Himself Whose minister he is.

And it is for the minister to be found trustworthy as God's minister first.

Now it is precisely the minister, the priest who gives out Communion who is personally responsible to assess the situation. It is not the Pope or bishop, who are not present, but the minister who administers.

This is the principle of subsidiarity and is acknowledged explicitly enough when we read Norm No. 3, for who is to judge the attitude of the recipient in Norm No. 3 except the priest who, on the spot, administers the Sacrament. By the very nature of this norm it is not up to the bishop or Pope or Chancery official or other priest nearby but only the priest who actually administers the sacrament to the Faithful at that place and time who is personally responsible to judge the external attitude of the recipient.

Now you might ask what are some of the dangers whereby Communion in the hand might cause irreverence to the Holy Eucharist.

There are several very common ones. Especially and namely this: When a person receives Communion in the hand there is a very high probability that some Fragment of the Host will break off or come loose and remain in the hand after the communicant has put the Host in his mouth. Whereas there is little or no danger of Fragments breaking off and falling to the ground if he receives on his tongue. Now after some time the Fragment will fall off his hand and onto the ground where It can be trampled underfoot.

We know from the defined Dogma of the Catholic Faith that each and every Fragment which breaks off from the Host is "The Body of Jesus Christ - really present." So to drop a Consecrated Fragment on the ground is the same as dropping the Consecrated Host on the ground. Even if only done through negligence it is still a sin of sacrilege.

This danger of irreverence then is to be avoided by Divine Law. Not even the Pope can change this law. The Vatican document by including here the necessity of avoiding danger of irreverence is only reminding us of this Divine Law.

It is again the personal responsibility of the minister of the Sacrament be he the Pope, a bishop, a cardinal or a priest or deacon to see to it that all danger of irreverence towards the Holy Eucharist be avoided.

He cannot say the bishop commanded me or everyone else is doing it ... Before God he must answer for each and every act of administering the Holy Eucharist.

If he knows that the people receiving the Holy Eucharist in the hand do not look in their hands to see if there are any Fragments left after they consume the Host then he can be certain that some of the people will most likely have Fragments on their hands which will sooner or later be dropped. In which case for them their responsibility is clear. They cannot give Communion in the hand even if the bishop or Pope should order them to do so.

This is not to imply that Pope John Paul II has ever done such a thing. On the contrary, we are very grateful to His Holiness, Pope John Paul II, for resisting Communion in the hand in Italy. As one Italian major religious Superior pointed out, if it were not for Pope John Paul II, Communion in the hand would have been fully introduced in Italy by now.

Eucharistic Minister is Bound to Avoid Sacrilege

In fact in North America and most likely anywhere else in the world where Communion in the hand is given, not 100% of the people look into their hands to see if there are any Fragments for them to consume and therefore the minister of the Holy Eucharist is bound in public churches to avoid the danger of sacrilege and irreverence by not giving anyone Communion in the hand because he can be morally certain that some; likely most (but even some is sufficient reason) will not look in their hands after Communion. Consequently there will be at least a few, if not many, who will drop Fragments on the ground, thereby committing sacrilege and irreverence, even though it is only through negligence as Pope Paul VI taught in his Encyclical (Mysterium Fidei 1965, Sept. 3).

Since the minister knows this will happen he is not allowed by the very terms of this official document granting "the indult" of giving Communion in the hand. He is also bound by Divine Law in these circumstances to not give Communion in the hand even if his religious superior should command him.

With these two principles explained, the average reader should realize why Communion in the hand in practice is still forbidden by the current law of the Church even where the indult has "technically" been allowed. In other words the terms of the permission, both in Divine Law and in Church Law are so strict that almost never is it allowed in practice.

Before we finish we must recall that the person receiving Communion is also responsible to see that no irreverence is committed, but his responsibility does not excuse the minister from taking all the precautions necessary.

Section 2: Appeal To The Holy Father

The following correspondence further illustrates and illuminates the Church's teaching and law forbidding Communion in the hand and the persecution priests endure, who for reasons of conscience do not follow this practice.

J.M.J.

Dear Most Holy Father John Paul II, January, 1980

INTRODUCTION

A number of Catholic priests are suffering due to certain conditions prevailing in the Church at the present time. Because their conscience will not allow them to give Holy Communion in the hand, priests have been removed from their parishes, and priests are hampered in their work. Everyone is the loser, especially at this time when there is a great shortage of priests and the Faithful are as a result still further left with even less priests to actively care for them. We hope and pray that you will relieve this situation - so that priests will not be pressured to act against their consciences. We pray and hope that we will be able to continue, unhindered, our apostolic works for the Glory of God and Our Lady, and for the salvation of souls.

We pray and hope that you, Most Holy Father, will help us.

Some Reflections on Certain Theological Points

Is it not true that the ordinary minister of Holy Communion is the priest? (C.J.C. 845, 1; Council of Trent 13 c.8, 22 c.1) St. Thomas tells us:

"Accordingly as the consecration of Christ's Body belongs to the priests, so likewise does the dispensing belong to him." S.T. III, q. 82 a. 3

And is it not true that the minister is responsible to God for the proper administration of the Sacraments that he personally administers? But some priests ask themselves, "How can a priest be held responsible by God, if God (and the Church) does not also give to us priests the authority to dispense this Most Holy Sacrament according to God's law and the universal law of the Church?"

And is not the universal law of the Latin Rite still that the Consecrated Host be placed on the tongue of the communicant as the document *Memoriale Domini* (1969) says:

"... the Holy Father has decided not to change the existing way of administering Holy Communion to the Faithful.

"The Apostolic See therefore emphatically urges bishops, priests, and laity to obey carefully the law which is still valid and which has again been confirmed."

The Rights and Obligations of the Priest as Minister of Holy Communion

It seems then to a number of Roman Catholic priests that a priest is not ever obligated by Divine or Ecclesiastical law to give Holy Communion in the hand, even in those dioceses where the bishop has licitly given permission for the priests to give Holy Communion in the hand. As the indult given by the Holy See only dispenses a minister from the law of Holy Communion on the tongue, it does not command a minister to give Holy Communion in the hand.

Further, it seems that the indult to give Holy Communion in the hand allows this practice only under certain conditions, one of which is:

"Si deve fare attenzione a non lasciare cadere ne disperdere frammenti de Pane Eucharistico. Come pure si deve curare la conveniente mondezza delle mani ..." (A.A.S. 1969, p.547. Notiziae 1973, circa p. 295.) (One must pay attention to not let fall or disperse fragments of the Eucharistic Bread. As also care must be taken of the proper cleanness of hands ...")

Therefore it would seem that the priest giving out Holy Communion must judge if in fact the conditions set down by the Holy See for this indult are in fact present at the time he is distributing Holy Communion.

And it would further seem that if the priest is to obey the law of the Catholic Church for the Latin Rite he must not give Holy Communion in the hand, if in fact the necessary conditions for using the indult are not present.

Further, it seems that when the priest finds that to give Holy Communion in the hand would be against the law of God and his conscience, he would be obligated to not give Holy Communion in the hand. (As for example would happen when he is *morally* certain that the Faithful through ignorance or negligence will cause Consecrated Fragments to drop on the ground after they consume the Host.)

It further seems then that if a priest chooses to *not* give Holy Communion in the hand on some or on all occasions, he should not, on this account, be punished or hindered in his apostolic works by anyone, even by one or more Roman Catholic bishops.

Therefore I respectfully appeal to you, Most Holy Father. A number of Roman Catholic priests chose not to give Holy Communion in the hand for serious personal and pastoral reasons. As a result of this they in fact suffer serious losses. In the name of these who suffer, I appeal to you, Most Holy Father.

If it is possible, could you, Most Holy Father, give us priests *a public, authoritative declaration, which would be easily accessible to all priests and bishops,* declaring that no priest is to be molested, punished, or hindered because he declines to give Holy Communion in the hand.

Yours in Jesus, Mary and Joseph
Father Nicholas Gruner

His Holiness, Pope John Paul II, Vatican City, Rome, Italy.

Your Holiness: January 2nd, 1985

In January, of 1980, I wrote you a three page letter, copy of which is herewith enclosed, regarding Communion in the Hand and persecution that priests endure, who, for reasons of conscience, do not follow this practice. At that time, I asked for a public statement from Your Holiness, to allow priests to continue their Sacred Ministry and not be subjected to persecution by their superiors (Parish priests and bishops) for following their conscience regarding this matter.

In 1982, application was made to serve the Diocese of . . ., by Father Gruner. The bishop, Bishop . . ., would have welcomed my services but he imposed as a condition of my coming, that I give Communion in the Hand. I explained to him in person as well as by letter, that this was against the Law of God and of the Catholic Church, and, therefore, against my conscience. I also indicated that, although an Indult had been given by the Vatican to go against the Letter of the Canon Law when certain conditions were met (which the Divine Law itself demand be fulfilled), these conditions, in fact, are not being met and both the Divine Law and Canon Law do not permit me to give Communion in the hand without committing a sin. Enclosed is a copy of my letter to the bishop in question. As a result, the bishop did not accept my services, even though he had a shortage of priests. He did acknowledge by telephone that I truly had a problem of conscience.

A few years ago, the Archbishop of Kingston confided to me that Sacred Consecrated Hosts were found in his Cathedral after the Sunday Masses, because of the practice of Communion in the hand. I believe he reported this to the Canadian Conference of Catholic Bishops, but he wondered if his report about this matter ever reached the Vatican. **According to a report given to me, a priest who attended your Mass at Downsview, (Toronto, Ontario, September 1984) Father . . ., reported to a cloistered Redemptoristine Nun, Sister Emmanuel, that several people were engaged with the task of collecting the numerous Hosts left on the ground after the Papal Mass was over. As I understand it, the Hosts were gathered into garbage bags, and subsequently burned.** These are but a few of the many sacrilegious incidents that are occurring as a result of the practice of Communion in the hand. This shows, as well as by my own observation, that adequate Catechesis have not been given regarding Communion in the hand. Giving Communion in the hand without this adequate Catechesis is contrary to the Indult. A copy of our translation of this Indult is also enclosed. (See Section 3 of this Appendix.) Furthermore, the adequate care to see that the Host is not dropped on the ground as is commanded by Divine Law, as well as by Rule No. 5 of the Indult, has not been followed, as seen by the report of the Archbishop of Kingston, Archbishop Wilhelm, now retired.

It is not my place to judge what other priests or bishops do, however, I am responsible to God first of all in my administration of the Most Holy Sacrament, and, therefore, I cannot, in conscience give Communion in the Hand. Nevertheless, there is still widespread ignorance on the part of bishops and other religious superiors that somehow or other, I am 'not Catholic' or 'not obedient', because I follow the Law of God and of the Catholic Church in this matter.

Now, in 1985, a few years later, since the confusion regarding what a simple priest's obligations and rights are concerning this matter, I appeal to you once more. This time, I would ask for a simple letter signed by Your Holiness, expressing that Father Gruner and any Catholic priest living and working in a country in which the Vatican has permitted the practice of Communion in the hand, may, and indeed, must, if the terms of the Indult are not met, refuse to give Communion in the hand, and that no religious superior may penalize Father Gruner or any other priest for following the dictates of his conscience and the Rule of the Church in this matter.

Thank you Holy Father, for giving this matter your kind consideration. I pray to Mary, Our Mother, that your reply will better enable me to fulfill Her requests at Fatima.

Yours sincerely in Jesus, Mary and Joseph
Father Nicholas Gruner, S.T.L.

The above blanked out names and places were, however, made explicit to the Pope.

At first the Following Acknowledgment of Father Gruner's Letter Was Sent

Secretariat of State, Vatican City

Dear Father Gruner,

February 4, 1985

I am directed to acknowledge the letter of January 2, 1985 which you addressed to the Holy Father, and would inform you that it has been duly transmitted to the Congregation for the Clergy which is the competent office for attending to such matters.

Assuring you of my prayerful good wishes, I remain
Sincerely yours in Christ, Monsignor G.B. Re Assessor

Note: No other action has been taken other than calling a special Synod in 1985 which promised to correct the abuses following Vatican II but instead, in practice confirmed them and the persecution continues.

Section 3: The Official Post Vatican II Regulations Concerning Communion in the Hand

The following are the official rules that must be followed if Communion in the hand is to be given. If these 7 conditions are not present in a location, then it is always forbidden for a priest to give Communion in the hand.

This is a translation of the letter which the Sacred Congregation for Divine Worship[1] sends to those Conferences of Catholic bishops which have petitioned the Pope and which have received permission from His Holiness to allow the practice of giving Holy Communion in the hand. It is then the responsibility of each Ordinary, that is the Bishop or Archbishop in charge of a diocese to allow or not allow this practice within the confines of his territory. For those places where this practice is legitimately allowed, the Bishop Ordinary is advised that this practice be allowed only under the following conditions as set out by this letter of permission.

Unofficial Translation[2]

The instruction (in the preceding, "Memoriale Domini")[3] is completed in pastoral matters by this letter which concedes to Episcopal Conferences the indult[4] of distributing Holy Communion in the hand of the Faithful. This letter has all the conditions necessary for allowing the use of this indult.

Your Excellency,

In reply to the request presented by Your Episcopal Conference asking for permission to distribute Holy Communion by giving the Host into the hand of the Faithful, I hereby transmit the following communication:

While recalling the subject of the enclosed instruction of May 29, 1969, by which the traditional practice is maintained, the Holy Father has taken into consideration the reasons in support of your request and the results of the vote taken in this matter. He grants that, in the territory of Your Episcopal Conference, each Bishop, according to his prudence and his conscience, may authorize in his own diocese the introduction of the new rite for the distribution of Holy Communion. This is granted on condition that every occasion of scandal on the part of the Faithful and all danger of irreverence towards the Eucharist is avoided.

In this matter, the following norms are to be followed:

1. The new manner of giving Communion must not be imposed in such a way that the traditional practice is excluded. It is especially important that each one of the Faithful has the possibility to receive Holy Communion on the tongue, wherever the new practice is legitimately allowed, and at the same time as other persons who receive the Host in the hand. In effect, the two ways of receiving Communion may co-exist without difficulty in the same liturgical action. The purpose of the foregoing is so that no one will find in the new rite a cause to have his own spiritual sensibilities towards the Eucharist disturbed and so that this Sacrament, which is of its nature a source and cause of unity, does not become an occasion of discord among the Faithful.

2. The rite of giving Holy Communion in the hand must not be used without discretion. In effect, since we are dealing with a human attitude, it is linked with the sensibilities and the preparation of the one who assumes it. It is convenient therefore to introduce this practice gradually, beginning with groups and social environments (milieu) which are more suited and more prepared. It is above all necessary that the introduction of this rite be preceded by adequate catechesis, in order that the Faithful

understand exactly the meaning of the gesture and may perform it with the respect due to this most august Sacrament. The result of this catechesis must be such as to exclude any appearance that the Church is weakening in any way Her faith in the Eucharistic presence, and such that there is no danger of profanation or even the appearance of danger of profanation.

3. The possibility offered to the Faithful to receive in his hand and to put in his mouth the Eucharistic Bread must not offer to him an occasion of considering It to be like ordinary bread or something merely blessed; on the contrary, this possibility of receiving in the hand must[5] augment in the Faithful the sense of his dignity as a member of the Mystical Body of Christ, into Which he is incorporated by Baptism, and by the grace of the Eucharist, and this possibility also must[5] increase his faith in the great reality of the Body and Blood of the Lord Which he touches with his hands. His attitude of respect will be proportioned to how he carries out this sacred gesture.

4. Regarding the manner of doing this, the guidelines of the old tradition should be followed which make evident the ministerial function of the priest or the deacon so that he is the one who places the Host in the hand of the communicant ...[6] the Faithful receiving Communion must consume the Host before returning to his place. The part of the minister will be underlined by the customary formula: "The Body of Christ", to which the communicant will reply, "Amen."

5. Whatever manner is adopted, one must take care to not drop or lose any particles of the Eucharistic Bread, one must also take care to see that the hands are suitably clean, and that there be observed the proper composure of gestures according to the customs of the various peoples.

6. In the case of Communion under both species distributed by intinction, it is never permitted to place in the hand of the Faithful the Host which has been dipped in the Blood of the Lord.

7. Bishops who permit the introduction of the new manner of giving Holy Communion are requested to send after six months a report to this Sacred Congregation concerning the results of this concession.

I take this occasion to express to Your Excellency, my sentiments of profound esteem.
Signed by the Cardinal Prefect and the Archbishop Secretary

Footnotes To This Section Of The Appendix.

1. The Sacred Congregation for Divine Worship is now known as The Sacred Congregation for the Sacraments and Divine Worship. This Sacred Congregation has general competence over the ritual and pastoral aspects of divine worship in the Roman and other Latin rites. This Sacred Congregation supervises the discipline of the Sacraments without prejudice to the competencies of the Sacred Congregation for the Doctrine of the Faith and other curial departments.
2. Taken from the *Acta Apostolicae Sedis* 1969, pages 546-547.
3. In the volume for 1969 of the *Acta Apostolicae Sedis* the Instruction *Memoriale Domini* immediately precedes this letter. This Instruction confirms that the law of the Church for the Latin Rites is that Holy Communion is to be received on the tongue. In 1980, the Instruction *Inaestimabile Donum* issued by the Sacred Congregation for the Sacraments and Divine Worship, dated April 3, 1980, confirmed that the Instruction *Memoriale Domini* is still in effect.
4. An indult is a permission granted by a legitimate authority.
5. In order to permit the use of this indult, two "musts" are required in this paragraph, namely: the sense of dignity of the Faithful thus receiving must be increased, and the communicant's faith in the great reality of the Eucharist must be increased.
6. In the original norms laid down, the option of the Faithful himself picking up the Consecrated Host was mentioned but shortly thereafter this option was no longer allowed. It was definitely forbidden by authority of Pope John Paul II as can be seen in the Instruction *Inaestimabile Donum*, published in English in the June 1980 *L'Osservatore Romano*. This document was approved by Pope John Paul II in April 1980.

In This Appendix:

Section 1 First published in *The Fatima Crusader*, June-July 1989, Issue No. 28, pg. 34.
Section 2 Letter dated January 1980 to Pope John Paul II, first published in *The Fatima Crusader*, June-July 1989, Issue No. 28, pg. 36. Letter to Pope John Paul II, dated January 2, 1985, first published in *The Fatima Crusader*, Sept.-Nov. 1989, Issue No. 29, pg. 16
Section 3 First published in *The Fatima Crusader*, Issue No. 7, pg. 11, and republished June-July 1989, Issue No. 28, pg. 33.

Appendix VI

The ongoing, high level maneuvers of some Vatican bureaucrats engaged in keeping the full Fatima message from the Catholic Bishops of the world is shown forth by this recent letter.

February 26, 1997

His Eminence Bernadin Cardinal Gantin, Prefect
Congregation For Bishops,
Palazzo delle Congregazione
Piazza Pio XII 10
Roma 00193
ITALY
Re: Prot. 349/93, dated 26 October 1996
Your Eminence:

According to the attached letter from the Apostolic Nuncio of Australia, this Congregation recently circulated to the world's bishops a notice under Prot. No. 349/93, stating that they should not attend a conference sponsored by this organization in Rome Nov. 18-23, 1996, entitled "World Peace and the Immaculate Heart of Mary". The only reason you gave for this advice is that our conference was "absolutely without approval of ecclesiastical authority."

It seems reasonable to presume that this Sacred Congregation is familiar with the 1983 Code of Canon Law promulgated by the Holy Father. Thus, we presume that when you sent your notice about our Rome conference to the world's bishops, you knew that under Church law private associations of the faithful like ours *do not require* "approval of ecclesiastical authority" to hold conferences to which bishops are invited.

On the contrary, as you know, Church law guarantees the positive natural right of all Christ's faithful to hold meetings on Church affairs, and to form and conduct private associations for various apostolic works on their own initiative *without any ecclesiastical "approval" whatsoever.* Obviously, these rights apply to bishops, who are perfectly free to attend private congresses on Church matters. And we, as members of the laity, are free under Church law to communicate our concerns to the sacred pastors and to invite them to our conferences. [1983 Code of Canon Law, cann. 212, 215, 216, 278, 299 and, generally, 208-223]

Indeed, precisely because our apostolate is perfectly within the law of the Church, it has received expressions of support from over 1,500 bishops and more than 60 cardinals and patriarchs. A number of these prelates attended our Rome conference despite your *de facto* interdiction of our apostolate without due process of canon law.

- ***As a matter of justice, therefore, we must respectfully address to you the following questions:***

Why did you tell the world's bishops not to attend our conference because it is "absolutely without approval of ecclesiastical authority", when no such approval is required by the law of the Church?

- ***Why did you tell the world's bishops a half-truth—that our conference did not have "approval of ecclesiastical authority"—without telling them the whole truth: that no approval was necessary?***
- ***Why did you tell the world's bishops that "Father Gruner has convened" our conference, when in truth it was organized, paid for and conducted entirely by this organization of many members, of which Father Gruner is only one?***
- ***By what right did this Congregation advise every bishop in the world not to attend a perfectly permissible conference devoted to world peace and the Immaculate Heart of Mary?***
- ***By what right did this Congregation pass judgment upon a private association of lay faithful whose lawful activities are not even within your competence or jurisdiction?***
- ***By what right did this Congregation inflict severe damage upon the legitimate apostolic work of over 100 faithful lay Catholics, who labored for months to organize our conference in Rome and to secure the attendance of many benevolent bishops who support our work?***
- ***Can you point to any activity or publication of this organization, or Father Nicholas Gruner, which in any way offends faith or morals, so as to justify the extraordinary measure of a notice from this Congregation to all the worlds' bishops?***
- ***And most important:***
- ***Why does this Congregation busy itself with sending every bishop in the world misleading announcements about a modest Fatima apostolate and a morally upright priest like Father Gruner, while heretical organizations and unspeakable scandals multiply in the Church without any condemnation by this Congregation?***

We eagerly await your answers to these pressing questions. Meanwhile, we are directing a copy of this letter to the world's bishops to rectify the false impression this Congregation has created regarding our legitimate activities in the Church.

We hope to receive your reply soon. If none is forthcoming, we hope the world's bishops will draw the proper conclusions from your silence.

Respectfully yours in Christ,

National Committee for the National Pilgrim
Virgin of Canada

By: Coralie Graham, Executive Director

Note: This letter was sent to Cardinal Gantin by registered mail over three months ago. As of June 3, 1997, he had not replied to the above respectful questions.

Appendix VII

Reprinted with permission of the petitioners.

A Canonical Petition to His Holiness John Paul II

Feast of St. Michael, September 29, 1996

His Holiness Pope John Paul II,
Vatican City,

Your Holiness:

Pursuant to Can. 1501 et seq., we, Coralie Graham, Mairead Clarke and Mary Sedore, do hereby petition Your Holiness for redress of grievances against Respondents Jose Cardinal Sanchez and Archbishop Crescenzio Sepe, and their collaborators in the wrongful acts complained of in the accompanying formal Petition.

As explained more fully in the Petition, under Can. 1405 (1) 2, 3, Your Holiness is the only judge who is lawfully competent to hear this case, since Cardinals and, in penal cases, bishops, can be judged only by the Pope himself.

We lodge this Petition with Your Holiness as individual members of the faithful and as directors, members employees or supporters of the National Committee for the National Pilgrim Virgin of Canada and the Servants of Jesus and Mary, Inc., lay apostolates for the promotion of devotion to the Blessed Virgin Mary and Her message at Fatima. We proceed under an official interpretation of the 1983 Code of Canon Law, approved by Your Holiness, which states that members of a lay apostolate which does not have a juridical personality or even formal recognition in the Church may nevertheless pursue hierarchical recourses either singly or as a group. [AAS 80 (1988) 1818]

The Petition details Respondents' systematic abuse of ecclesiastical power and authority over a period of years. Acting totally outside the proper channels of canonical procedure, they have wrongfully interdicted our apostolate and calumniated its members before the entire Church. In the process, our apostolate has never been charged by Respondents with any canonical offense whatsoever, and we have therefore been deprived of any recourse against their actions except to present this Petition to your Holiness.

The wrongs detailed in the Petition are grave not merely because they injured us, but because they harm the Church as a whole by attempting to suppress an important apostolic work of the faithful (proclamation of the message of Fatima, which Your Holiness himself has proclaimed), and because Respondents have diminished the dignity and credibility of their respective offices by abusing them in the manner described.

We humbly request that Your Holiness admit this case, compel the respondents to join issue and then grant the relief we have requested against them.

Respectfully yours in Jesus, Mary and Joseph,

Mrs. Coralie Graham | Mrs. Mary Sedore | Mrs. Mairead Clarke

Respondents addresses are as follows:

Jose Cardinal Sanchez,
[Residence]
Via Rusticucci 13, 00193
Rome, Italy

Archbishop Crescenzio Sepe,
[Residence]
00120 Citta del Vaticano
[Office]
Congregazione Per il Clero,
Palazzo delle Congregazioni,
PiazzaPio XII, 3; 00193 Roma

A Canonical Petition (Libellus) to His Holiness John Paul II

-by-

Coralie Graham, Mairead Clarke and **Mary Sedore,** *et al,*
in their individual capacities as members of the faithful, and as directors, members, employees or supporters of the National Committee for the National Pilgrim Virgin of Canada and the Servants of Jesus and Mary, Inc.,
lay apostolates for the promotion of devotion to the Blessed Virgin Mary and her message at Fatima

Petitioners,

-against-

José Cardinal Sanchez
Mons. Crescenzio Sepe, and their collaborators in the wrongful acts complained of

Respondents.

Pursuant to Cann.
208-223
212
215
221
278
299
1326
1329, §1
1375
1389
1S70 § 2,
1334 § 2
1405 § 1, 2
1449 § 3
1501
1624

For Redress of Abuse of Ecclesiastical Authority and Calumny

Q. Whether a group of faithful, lacking juridical personality and even recognition envisaged in c. 299, §3, can legitimately make hierarchical recourse . . .

R. . . . *affirmative* as to individual members of the faithful acting either singly or together, provided they really have a grievance . . .

Decision of the Pontifical Commission
For Interpretation of Legislative Texts
—AAS 80 (1988) 1818

§

"Christ's faithful may lawfully vindicate and defend the rights they enjoy in the Church, before the competent ecclesiastical forum in accordance with law."

—Can. 221

§

"[T]he Roman Pontiff alone has the right to judge . . . [2°] Cardinals . . . [3°] and, in penal cases, Bishops."

—Can. 1405(1) 2° and 3°

Table Of Contents Of This Canonical Petition

Most Holy Father:

We humbly submit to Your Holiness this written Petition against His Eminence **José Cardinal Sanchez**, former Prefect of the Congregation for the Clergy, and **Mons. Crescenzio Sepe**, the Secretary of said Congregation ("respondents"). Under the law of the Church, you alone, Holiness, can judge grievances against cardinals and, in penal cases, bishops. [Can. 1405]

This Petition is made by us as individual members of the faithful, who have the right to seek hierarchical recourse as individuals for harm done by the respondents to the apostolate in which we are engaged. [Cfr. decision of Pontifical Commission for the Interpretation of Legislative Texts, AAS 80 (1988) 1818, construing Can. 299 §3]

We also make this Petition in accordance with our God-given right to appeal to the Supreme Pontiff—a right dogmatically defined by the Second Council of Lyons in 1274 and the First Vatican Council in 1870, and further codified in Can. 221 of the 1983 Code of Canon Law promulgated by Your Holiness.

I.
Brief Summary of this Petition

This Petition arises from respondents' unjust statements and actions against the apostolate in which we have been engaged for many years as active members of the Christian faithful: namely, the National Committee for the National Pilgrim Virgin of Canada, a Canadian organization, and its United States affiliate, Servants of Jesus and Mary, Inc., popularly known collectively as the International Fatima Rosary Crusade ("the apostolate").

The statements and actions of the respondents, including canonically groundless public "declarations" issued in the name of the Congregation for the Clergy, were designed to create the false impression in the minds of our ecclesiastical superiors, the world episcopate and the faithful at large, that our apostolate is illicit because it lacks "permission of ecclesiastical authority" to conduct its activities. Respondents are well aware that no such permission is required under the law of the Church. On the contrary, the law of the Church guarantees our right to engage in the apostolate as a private association of the faithful incorporated under civil law. [Cann. 212, 215, 216, 299 and, generally, Cann. 208-223]

Respondents' words and actions were further designed to induce our ecclesiastical superiors, the world episcopate, and indeed the entire Church, to shun our apostolate without just cause and without the canonical due process to which we are entitled as members in good standing of Christ's faithful.

II.
The Hardship Caused by Respondents' Acts

The apostolate is our life's work and a means of support for many of its employees, who number in excess of one hundred.

We, the petitioners, have labored for years in the apostolate, earning wages far less than we might receive in secular employment, working 12 to 16 hours a day, and often around-the-clock. Like Father Gruner himself, we have committed our lives to this work out of devotion to Our Lady, believing firmly that her message at Fatima is of crucial importance for the welfare of souls in this time of unprecedented crisis in the Church.

Respondents have abused the power and prestige of their offices in an effort to destroy everything we have built up over the years. We are concerned, of course, about the temporal hardship to ourselves and our fellow workers in the apostolate. But much more than this, we are concerned about the spiritual loss which could result to countless souls who stand to benefit from the deeper understanding of Our Lady's message at Fatima we have labored so hard to promote. Then, too, there are the many supporters of the apostolate who have donated their time and money, who have prayed and fasted, for the success of our work. We cannot allow their contributions to be rendered vain.

None of us has the power of a Cardinal or an Archbishop. We cannot issue a prestigious "declaration" or "announcement" from the Vatican to correct what has been said in the declarations and announcements of respondents against us, issued in the name of the Congregation for the Clergy. We can only ask Your Holiness to help us remedy respondents' abuse of their ecclesiastical authority before it causes even graver harm to our apostolate and those who benefit from it.

Thus, we respectfully implore Your Holiness to compel the respondents to make appropriate amends for their calumniation of our apostolate [Canon 1390 §3], and for their abuse of ecclesiastical authority [Can. 1389].

We further respectfully request that respondents and their collaborators be subject to the strict penalties envisoned by canon law for those who abuse their offices in the Church—not for the sake of vengeance, but to deter such abuse of authority in the future, so that other members of the faithful will not have to endure what we have endured at respondents' hands.

III.
Facts of this Petition

(A) History of the Apostolate

Our apostolate was founded as a civil corporation in Ottawa, Canada in 1974, under the auspices of His Excellency, The Most Reverend Michael Rusnak, then auxiliary bishop of the Eparchy of Toronto in the Byzantine Rite. (He is now Ordinary of the Byzantine Rite for Slovaks in Canada.) The Board of Directors of the apostolate was comprised entirely of laity until 1978, when Father Nicholas Gruner became a member of the Board of the apostolate after having served since 1977 as its Executive Director. Father Gruner was asked to serve by the Board after Bishop Rusnak insisted that a worthy priest be placed on the Board. The current Board of the apostolate consists of three priests, including Father Gruner, and two lay women—petitioners Coralie Graham and Mary Sedore. Petitioner Mairead Clarke is a member of the administrative staff of the apostolate. Since 1981 the apostolate has included Servants of Jesus and Mary, Inc., a lay apostolic group formed under the laws of the United States.

Father Gruner was ordained in Frigento, Italy in the Diocese of Avellino in 1976. In 1978 Father was given written permission by the Bishop of Avellino to reside in Canada, his home country. Since then Father Gruner has been engaged in the work of our apostolate with the full knowledge of three successive bishops of Avellino, none of whom has ever prohibited his work as a member of our Board.

Our apostolate is dedicated to the worldwide promotion of devotion to the Blessed Virgin Mary, and in particular Her message at Fatima. Our activities include exposition around the world of one of the Pilgrim Virgin statues personally blessed by your predecessor, His Holiness Paul VI, publication of *Fatima Crusader* magazine, various congresses and gatherings of the faithful regarding the Fatima message and its import for our time, and radio and television broadcasts concerning the Fatima message throughout North America. Many of these activities are conducted under the title of the International Fatima Rosary Crusade.

Under Father Gruner's stewardship, our apostolate has grown to the point where it now employs over 100 people, both Catholic and Protestant, has 100,000 active supporters around the world, publishes a magazine (*Fatima Crusader*) with a circulation of 500,000, and reaches a potential audience of many millions through Sunday television broadcasts throughout North America and daily radio broadcasts throughout the world.

Our apostolate also funds an orphanage in the Archdiocese of Hyderabad, India, having the care of fifty children; feeds a number of other children in Brazil; and distributes millions of scapulars and rosaries throughout the world.

Father Gruner and the apostolate have received blessings and good wishes from Your Holiness himself on several occasions, including your formal Apostolic Blessings in 1990 and 1993. Your 1990 Apostolic Blessing was extended personally to petitioners Coralie Graham and Mary Sedore.

Your Holiness, the apostolate is not merely Father Gruner's "personal initiative", as the respondents have said in one of their many improper and irregular public "declarations" in the name of the Congregation for the Clergy. Rather, the apostolate is the undertaking of many members of Christ's faithful, who believe it to be their proper apostolic work in the Body of Christ. We are confident that our apostolate is fully in keeping with the freedom of Christ's faithful to establish and direct associations on their own initiative for charitable or pious purposes under the law of the Church, and especially the Code of Canon Law promulgated by Your Holiness in view of the teaching of *Lumen Gentium* on the role of the laity in the Church. [Cann. 208-223; 299] Further, the same Code of Canon Law specifically recognizes the right of diocesan priests like Father Gruner to direct, and even establish on his own, apostolates such as ours. [Can. 278]

It is no secret, of course, that our apostolate expresses the concern of many of the faithful that Our Lady's request at Fatima for the specific consecration of Russia to Her Immaculate Heart has yet to be done by all of the world's bishops in union with the Pope, and that failing this consecration Russia will not convert but will continue to spread her errors throughout the world.

It is also true that our apostolate has implored the Holy See to disclose the Third Secret of Fatima to the world. We believe that the Third Secret is clearly an urgent warning for our time —a warning the entire Church was expecting to hear in 1960, only to receive the news that the Secret would not be disclosed. In the 36 years which have followed, it becomes ever more apparent that the Secret contains a warning and instructions of utmost importance to the Church in this time of unprecedented crisis.

The Consecration of Russia and the Third Secret are certainly matters of high controversy in the Church. Yet we know Your Holiness will understand that we cannot ignore our conscientious conviction that the good of the Church requires us to communicate to the sacred pastors and others of Christ's faithful our legitimate concerns about these matters. In so doing, we are only exercising that legitimate freedom of the laity enunciated *Lumen Gentium* (par. 37) and the current Code of Canon Law (Can. 212, etc.).

(B) The Present Controversy

In 1992, the respondents and others began a systematic effort to discredit and ruin the Apostolate, evidently because its activities are disfavored by respondents and other elements of the Vatican apparatus.

It is most significant that respondents have never attempted to interdict our apostolate in a manner consistent with canonical due process; for indeed there is nothing about our apostolate which could properly be interdicted under the law of the Church. Rather, the respondents, acting in their capacity as Prefect and Secretary of the Congregation for the Clergy, have used the Apostolic Nuncios, the pages of *L' Osservatore Romano* and *Avvenire*, and Vatican Radio to make "declarations" which effectively interdict us without due process by dishonestly implying that we are acting illicitly because our activities "do not enjoy the approval of competent Ecclesiastical Authority."

As the respondents must be presumed to know, the faithful do not need "approval of competent ecclesiastical authority" to conduct a private apostolate or hold a conference on Fatima. The Code of Canon law promulgated by Your Holiness recognizes the natural right of the faithful to meet and discuss their concerns about Church affairs without any prior ecclesiastical approval whatsoever. [Canons 212, 215 and 299] Thus, the respondents' "declarations" that the Apostolate's Fatima conferences are "without approval of ecclesiastical authority" are quite obviously designed to deceive the world's bishops and the faithful at large into believing that they would be guilty of serious disobedience to the law of the Church if they supported our work or attended one of our conferences.

Respondents can be expected to protest that nothing in their "declarations" is overtly false, and that they never meant to suggest there is anything illicit about the apostolate or our activities in futherance of it. Then let them explain, for example, why some 25 bishops urgently interrogated us about the canonical propriety of our Fatima Conference in Portugal 'discussed below' after respondents' "declarations" were issued, or why so many bishops have cancelled their trips to our conferences or rejected invitations following these "declarations".

It is clear, Your Holiness, that this campaign of deceptively ominous statements about "approval of competent ecclesiastical authority"—which approval respondents know full well is not required—amounts to a grave deprivation of our canonical rights without due process or just cause, and a gross abuse of respondents' ecclesiastical authority.

In combination with this tactic against our apostolate, respondents have further abused their ecclesiastical authority by blocking every offer of incardination Father Gruner has obtained from benevolent bishops around the world. At the same time, respondents directed the Bishop of Avellino not to excardinate Father in favor of a benevolent bishop. Then respondents directed the Bishop of Avellino to order Father Gruner to return to Avellino, after an approved absence of nearly 20 years, on grounds that he had "failed" to be incardinated elsewhere! *Your Holiness, the respondents have deliberately prevented Father Gruner from carrying out the very order they have instigated.* This abuse of their authority has harmed not only Father Gruner but ourselves.

In Father Gruner's own Petition to Your Holiness, which is intended to be presented simultaneously with ours, he sets forth the details of respondents' many illicit, extra-canonical interventions in his good faith efforts to be incardinated outside the Diocese of Avellino. We will point out here only the most recent case, involving the Archbishop of Hyderabad, in whose archdiocese our apostolate supports the orphanage already mentioned:

Your Holiness, on or about March 18, 1996 the Archbishop of Hyderabad, who is the *third* bishop to offer Father Gruner incardination since 1992, received a letter from the Respondent Sanchez, acting in the name of Congregation of the Clergy, pressuring him *to withdraw his formal decree of November 4, 1995 incardinating Father Gruner in the Archdiocese of Hyderabad.* This letter was summarized for us over the telephone by a functionary of the Archdiocese of Hyderabad. This functionary also disclosed that the Archbishop fears providing us with a copy of this secret letter without protocol number because "he would be putting the whole diocese in trouble". *In other words, the Archbishop fears an even greater abuse of ecclesiastical authority by respondents, this time directed against his entire archdiocese.*

How is it, Your Holiness, that the respondents can exceed the authority of the Congregation by dictating to an Archbishop whom he may incardinate in his own Archdiocese—especially when the priest in question has no canonical or moral impediments to the exercise of his priesthood. It should be noted, Your Holiness, that the Archbishop has tried to support the apostolate in its difficulties with certain elements of the Vatican apparatus. In his decree of incardination, dated November 4, 1995, the Archbishop declared that:

> "I hereby grant you all the faculties you need for continuing your God-given mission on earth . . God will give you great comfort and consolation through innumerable friends and well-wishers.
>
> Bureaucratic forces cannot stifle God's work."

Now, Your Holiness, the current Bishop of Avellino, acting under pressure from the respondents, has decreed (on May 16, 1996) that since Father Gruner "failed" to be incardinated in another diocese, he will be suspended from the sacred priesthood effective June 15, 1996 unless he returns to Avellino to live there in exile until his death—with no ministry, no salary and no provision for his old age. Father Gruner has appealed to the Congregation for the Clergy from that unjust decree, and has thereby avoided the proposed penalty for now. But his appeal will be considered by none other than respondent Mons. Sepe himself, who, together with respondent Cardinal Sanchez, the former Prefect of the Congregation, is the very person who has arranged for Father Gruner's exile to Avellino by improperly interfering with his incardination by the Archbishop of Hyderabad. This is truly a mockery of justice and due process.

Meanwhile, Father continues to function as the head of our apostolate. We who depend upon him for spiritual and temporal guidance in our work beseech Your Holiness to end this campaign to destroy our apostolate by illicit means which are designed to evade the just requirements of canon law.

(C) Our Open Letter to Your Holiness

Your Holiness will recall that one year ago on July 12, 1995, we published in *Il Messaggero* an Open Letter to Your Holiness from over 9,000 members of the faithful, regarding the injustices committed against our apostolate by those who would destroy it, and the efforts of those who surround Your Holiness to prevent you from responding to our earnest petitions. In the hope of avoiding scandal, we did not name the Vatican bureaucrats who were responsible. Indeed, we would not have published the Open Letter at all if the attacks against our work had not reached critical proportions.

Publication of the Open Letter was our last resort before having canonical recourse to Your Holiness. But the Open Letter has not deterred those who oppose communication to the faithful of the full Fatima Message, and who try to crush any organized effort by the faithful to petition for the Consecration of Russia and disclosure of the Third Secret. The attacks against our apostolate have only intensified, leading to the current injustices against us.

It is not personal pride in the Apostolate which has led us to this Petition, Your Holiness, but our deep and abiding conviction that the good of the Church requires that we continue this work.

Therefore, having no other canonical alternative but this Petition, we now present it to Your Holiness with the fervent prayer that you will intervene to remedy the wrongs done to our apostolate, so that we may continue our work without the stigma imposed upon us by respondents in a gross abuse of their authority and prestige in the Church.

IV.

Specification of Charges

(1) According to a purported decree of the Apostolic Signatura, dated May 15, 1995, (discussed below), on or about January 12, 1992 respondent Cardinal Sanchez issued a "declaration" in the name of the Congregation for the Clergy, stating that our apostolate had "not received any canonical recognition and consequently ought to be considered a personal and private initiative of [Father Gruner]". (Appendix 1) This statement is misleading, and therefore a calumny against us, because:

—No canonical recognition, permission or erection is required for the Apostolate [Cann. 212, 215, 216, 278, 299 and, generally, 208-223].

—The apostolate has never been Father's "personal and private initiative". It existed before he became a member of our Board, and over a hundred people are involved in its work. Our honorary chairman at the inception of the apostolate was the aforesaid Bishop Rusnak, on whose advice Father Gruner was asked to serve as a Board member. Your Holiness, the apostolate was the initiative of lay people, with Father Gruner contributing his efforts to an apostolate that was already underway.

(2) On October 8, 1992, respondents published another statement which appeared in *L'Osservatore Romano* and *Avvenire*, and was also broadcast on Vatican Radio, in which they again falsely "declared" that our Fatima conference in Fatima, Portugal "has not been approved by competent ecclesiastical authorities" and that "Father Nicholas Gruner does not have faculties from the Diocese of Leira, Fatima to perform ministerial acts." (Appendix 7) These calumnies were republished in the English edition of *L'Osservatore Romano* on October 14, 1992. (Appendix 8) They are calumnies against us because:

—The Bishop of Fatima actually did give permission for our conference on October 7, 1992. This permission was witnessed by three Archbishops: Toppo, Cardoso-Sobrinho, and Limon (now deceased). Archbishop Sobrinho can be seen on video tape referring to this permission on October 8, 1992 at the opening session of our Fatima Conference. Archbishops Cardoso-Sobrinho and Toppo are still acting as the ordinaries of their Archdioceses.

—Even without such permission, our conference was perfectly licit since, under the canons already cited, absolutely no permission is required for a private gathering of the faithful and bishops to discuss matters which concern the good of the Church.

—Father Gruner had no need of faculties to perform "ministerial acts" in the Diocese of Leira-Fatima in order to help organize a private conference of the faithful to discuss the Fatima message.

Thus, the October 8, 1992 "declaration" by the Respondents was a deliberate attempt to mislead the world's bishops and the faithful by creating the false impression that the Fatima conference in Fatima, Portugal was being conducted in violation of Church law, and without required "faculties", and that anyone who attended the conference would be violating a canonically valid *monitum* of a Curial office, when in truth the "declaration" by respondents lacked any canonical foundation whatsoever and was merely a gratuitous abuse of their authority and prestige in the Church. Respondents' 1992 "declaration" was issued without any canonical process to determine the liceity of our apostolate, or any opportunity for its members, including ourselves, to be heard in defense of our work.

(3) According to a letter from Apostolic Nunciature of the Phillippines (Appendix 9), on July 9, 1994 respondent Cardinal Sanchez issued a communiqué repeating and republishing the calumnies contained in respondents' October 1992 "Declaration" in *L'Osservatore Romano* and directed the Papal Nuncios to tell the bishops of the world "not to accept the invitations of [Father Gruner]" to attend the apostolate's Fatima conference in Mexico City in November 1994. The July 9, 1994 communiqué adds a new calumny: That the hierarchy of Portugal was "embarrassed" by our 1992 Fatima conference when it learned of Father Gruner's "irregular situation" in the Church. This, of course, is a blatant lie: There was nothing "irregular" about Father Gruner's situation; he had *express written permission* from his bishop to reside outside the Diocese of Avellino and his bishop had *never once prohibited h*is activities in our apostolate.

We have letters from India, Portugal, Mexico, the United States, Kenya and elsewhere (Appendix 11-20) reflecting this further illicit use of the nunicatures to "interdict" Father Gruner and our apostolate's Fatima conferences without any canonical due process or even notice to us. The repetition of these calumnies was all the more egregious because the respondents certainly knew by that date that the Bishop of Fatima had given permission for the 1992 Fatima Conference and that canon law authorized every one of our planned activities, none of which required Father Gruner to have any special "faculties to perform ministerial acts".

In connection with this deceptive propaganda, respondents used the Nuncio to Mexico to pressure Bishop Flores, Secretary General of the Mexican Episcopal Conference (CEM), to break a contract with us to use the meeting facilities of the CEM for our conference—after we had paid a deposit of $5,000 in good faith and spent many thousands more in reliance on the agreement for publicizing the event worldwide (including over 100,000 posters), delivering invitations to the worlds' bishops, travel arrangements for bishops and speakers at the conference and innumerable other expenses. We were forced to relocate the conference to a first-class hotel in Mexico City at an additional cost to the apostolate of approximately USA $20,000, plus approximately USA $10,000 for translation services at the hotel which were far more expensive than those of CEM.

Even those bishops who were not swayed by the misleading "announcements" and pressure tactics of respondents and their agents were still prevented from attending the conference when Bishop Flores, apparently acting at the behest of the respondents, instructed the Mexican Secretary of State to deny entry visas to bishops seeking to attend. Only a few bishops who had Vatican passports, or who requested visitor's visas without mentioning the Conference, were able to travel to Mexico City for the event.

The end result of this gross abuse of ecclesiastical authority was that the number of bishops who had attended our conference dropped from the 120 who had agreed to attend to less than ten bishops, who were able to overcome all the obstacles placed in their paths by respondents. Although the Conference went ahead as scheduled, our efforts were very substantially damaged. We were distressed and disheartened at this trampling of our rights by the members of your Curia, who clearly felt they could act with impunity and without regard to the effect their actions would have on many others besides their intended "targets", Father Gruner and our apostolate.

Even worse, there is the indignity of bishops being browbeaten and treated like children by respondents, who have completely disregarded the rights and prerogatives of the episcopate, and the duty of bishops to tend to the spiritual needs and listen to the spiritual concerns of the members of their flocks. Where is respondents' respect for the college of bishops? Do they believe that the entire world episcopate is subject to their personal authority and oversight? The authority of a bishop in his diocese is part of the divine constitution of the Church. With all due respect to the Congregation for the Clergy, Our Lord did not provide for the governance of the world's bishops by Respondents, reducing the bishops to the mere functionaries of the Curia.

(4) According to a letter from the Nuncio of India (Appendix 10), on or about January 3, 1996, respondents *again* repeated and amplified their calumnies in yet another communiqué issued to the world's bishops through the nuncios (and republished by the United States Catholic Conference) in response to our plans to hold a third Fatima conference in Rome later this year. (See, *e.g.*, Appendix 21-22) The January 1996 communiqué, quoted *verbatim* at Appendix 21, contains the following calumnies signed by respondent Mons. Sepe:

—That no bishop should attend the Fatima Conference in Rome because the Congregation for the Clergy has "volumes of dossiers in the archives" regarding Father Gruner.

The contents of the "volumes of dossiers in the archives" are not specified, but the false implication is that they contain evidence of canonical crimes or moral impediments on Father's part, when in fact Father has an unblemished 20-year record as a priest whose faithfulness to the Magisterium and moral probity are beyond question. His only "offense" was to "fail" to be incardinated outside the Diocese of Avellino, *after respondents themselves prevented him from being incardinated.*

—That the conference in Rome "includes activities which the Reverend Gruner has developed without ecclesiastical permission, and which are not sparing of any criticisms of Church authorities."

As high functionaries of the Church charged with the duty to know and follow canon law, respondents knew, or certainly should have known, that absolutely ***no*** "permission of ecclesiastical authority" is needed for us or Father Gruner to "develop activities" for a private conference of the faithful. On the contrary, the law of the Church (Cann. 212, 215, 216, 299 and many others) *positively encourage* such private initiatives by the faithful. Moreover, it was utterly false for respondents to state that the "activities" being planned for the conference in Rome are "not sparing of any criticisms of Church authorities."

The activities at our Fatima conferences have *never* been characterized by unsparing criticism of Church authorities. Rather, we have presented respectful resolutions and petitions regarding the Consecration of Russia and the Third Secret, which petitions we are entitled to present in accordance with our freedom of ecclesiastical discourse under Cann. 212, 215, 216 and 299, and the others cited. For example, we have included with this petition the Fourteen Resolutions adopted at our Mexico city Fatima Conference in 1994— *resolutions drafted with the assistance of seven bishops.* (Appendix 26-27)

The phrase "not sparing of any criticisms of Church authorities" is, therefore, a gratuitous calumny, designed to instill fear in the world's bishops that mere attendance at our conference would mark them as disobedient to "Church authorities"—that is, the respondents, who seek to interdict our activities without due process of canon law, or even an opportunity for us to be heard in our own defense.

—That the Bishop of Avellino has ordered Father Gruner to return to Avellino "so that this priest might not continue his harmful activities."

In truth, the order to return to Avellino makes no reference any "harmful activities" by Father, but is based solely on his alleged "failure" to be incardinated in another diocese, which incardination the respondents themselves have tried to prevent at every turn by illicit coercion outside the proper channels of canon law. The phrase "harmful activities" is another gratuitous calumny against our work. No "harm" to the Church from our activities has even been specified, much less proven canonically. Our activities involve nothing more than the sincere apostolic work of many faithful Catholics employed by the apostolate, only one of whom is Father Gruner.

(6) The "announcements", "declarations" and illicit private interventions and "arm-twisting" by respondents have inflicted grave harm on our apostolate. Unless respondents' abuse of ecclesiastical authority is repaired by corrective actions, which only Your Holiness can require of

them, the damage we have suffered will never be remedied. We believe we are entitled to have the good name of our apostolate restored by those who have unjustly damaged it in their zeal to convict and silence one priest, Father Nicholas Gruner, who himself has committed no offense whatsoever.

V.

Canonical grounds for Petition.

A. Only the Roman Pontiff himself alone can judge this Petition.

Can. 1405, §1 provides that:

"It is the right of the Roman Pontiff himself alone to judge . . .

2°cardinals;

3°legates of the Apostolic See and, in penal cases, bishops . . ."

Furthermore, "the incompetence of other judges *is absolute* in the cases mentioned in can. 1405." Can. 1406, §2.

Since Respondent Sanchez is a cardinal, whereas Respondent Sepe is a bishop in a penal case, Your Holiness has sole and exclusive jurisdiction over this Petition.

We are constrained by the law of the Church to seek relief from Your Holiness, and him alone, in accordance with the right of all Christ's faithful to "vindicate and defend the rights which they enjoy before a *competent* ecclesiastical court in accord with the norm of law." Can. 221, §1 We must, with all humility, turn to you.

1. This case having been lawfully introduced, a judgment must be issued after an investigation conducted by the judge *ex officio.*

Moreover, since judgment in this case is reserved by the law of the Church to Your Holiness alone, it is Your Holiness who, by his own decree in promulgating the Code of Canon law, is subject to the obligation to proceed with the case now that it has been legitimately introduced by this Petition. Can. 1452 §1.

The obligation imposed on the judge to proceed includes, even in matters judged by Your Holiness, the obligation to investigate the matter *ex officio*, and the judge can even supply for the negligence of the parties in furnishing proofs. Can. 1452 §2. Thus, Your Holiness ought to investigate on his own initiative the conduct of the respondents so as to uncover that evidence which has undoubtedly been concealed from us due to the extra-canonical and *ultra vires* manner in which respondents have acted.

With all due respect, therefore, we must insist upon our right to have this matter investigated and then judged by Your Holiness, under the law of the Church you have promulgated for the benefit of the faithful, including priests.

B. Respondents should be punished strictly for abuse of their ecclesiastical authority.

Can. 1389 provides that "one who abuses ecclesiastical power or function is to be punished in accord with the seriousness of the act or omission, not excluding deprivation of office. . ."

Respondents, acting as Prefect and Secretary of the Congregation for the Clergy, have clearly abused their authority by issuing public "declarations" to the faithful and the world episcopate falsely implying that we are functioning in violation of the law of the Church, when they know very well that our activities are perfectly licit and require no permission of ecclesiastical authority, given the rights of free association and expression on the part of laity and diocesan priests envisioned in Cann. 208-223, 278, 299, and others.

Respondents have used their power and influence in the Church to intimidate bishops and the faithful into shunning our apostolate, even though there is nothing illicit about its activities. Unable to find any basis in the law of the Church for interdicting our work per se, respondents have resorted to extra-canonical calumny and coercion in their effort to destroy our apostolate. What is more, even if there were some basis for interdicting our work—and clearly there is not—such interdiction would be within the competency of the Congregation for the Doctrine of the Faith. Respondents, as members of the Congregation for the Clergy, had no jurisdiction whatsoever to issue "declarations" effectively interdicting, and thus severely damaging, a private association of the faithful founded under the civil laws of Canada and the United States pursuant to Cann. 212, 215, 216 and 299. Our organization is in no way subject to respondents' gratuitous decrees and bulletins, issued from their office in Rome without canonical process or even prior notice to us.

In sum, respondents' actions were a patent abuse of their ecclesiastical authority in violation of Canon 1389. In justice, respondents should be strictly punished for abuse of their authority. Their actions have harmed not just Father Gruner, but all of us whose lives are devoted to the apostolate whose destruction respondents have plotted—there is no other word for it, Your Holiness. Under the law of the Church, only Your Holiness can impose upon respondents an appropriate punishment and due restitutionary measures.

C. Respondents should be strictly punished, and ordered to make reparation for, their false and malicious denunciations of our apostolate to ecclesiastical superiors and the faithful.

Can. 1390, §2 provides that "one who furnishes an ecclesiastical superior with [a] calumnious denunciation of an offense or who otherwise injures the good reputation of another person can be punished with an appropriate penalty"; and Can. 1390, §3 provides that "a calumniator can be coerced also to make a suitable reparation."

Respondents have calumniated us by falsely suggesting in "declarations" issued to the world episcopate and the faithful at large that our work is illicit for the lack of some required "permission of ecclesiastical authority", and that the head of our apostolate is functioning without required "faculties". Moreover, respondents falsely stated in the abovementioned "declarations" regarding the 1992 Fatima Conference in Portugal that our Conference had no ecclesiastical permission, when in fact permission had been given by the Bishop of Fatima, even though it was not required under Church law.

Respondents have labored to create, and have indeed created in the minds of many bishops and faithful, the false impression that our chosen apostolic work violates the law of the Church because we have not received *totally unnecessary* "permission of ecclesiastical authority", or because Father Gruner did not receive mythical "faculties to perform ministerial acts" in the dioceses where our private conferences have been held.

This is calumny, Your Holiness, because it uses "half-truths that convey the impression of what is untrue." [McHugh and Callan, *Moral Theology*, §2030 (c)]. Moreover, respondents calumniated us in our work by implying that the President of our apostolate, Father Gruner, is guilty of canonical crimes or moral impediments documented in "volumes of dossiers in the archives" of the Congregation for the Clergy, when in fact Father has never been charged with any canonical offense whatsoever, other than the "offense" of "failing" to be incardinated outside the Diocese of Avellino, which "failure" is the work of respondents themselves.

Your Holiness, justice requires that respondents be punished, and ordered to make reparation for, their systematic attempt to interdict our work without canonical due process, thereby violating our basic rights as members of Christ's faithful.

Here again, only Your Holiness can impose the penalty and order reparation to be made. At the very least, respondents should be compelled to undo the damage caused by their misleading "declarations" and "announcements" to the faithful and the world episcopate.

D. The penalties imposed on respondents should reflect the increased imputability resulting from the abuse of their offices.

Can. 1326, §1, 2° provides that

"A judge can punish *more severely than a law or precept has stated*: . . . 2° a person who has been given some dignified office or who has abused authority or office in order to commit the offense."

This canon contemplates an enhanced punishment based upon the increase of imputability which should result from the deliberate abuse of a high office in the Church. Because respondents have abused the authority of their respective offices to circulate calumnies against our apostolate and to browbeat bishops, priests and members of the faithful into shunning it without canonical due process, justice requires that they be punished all the more severely.

Certainly the abuse of a high ecclesiastical office entrusted to the holder by the authority of Christ's Church is among the gravest of offenses against God. That is why the cited canon calls for enhanced punishment in this case, not excluding removal from office.

E. The penalties imposed on respondents, as the principal authors of the offenses committed, should also embrace those who collaborated with them in committing the offenses, even if the collaborators cannot now be identified.

Can. 1329, §1 provides that:

"If the penalties established against the principal author are inflicted ones (*ferendae sententiae*), then those who collaborate to commit an offense through a common conspiracy but who are not expressly named in a law or precept are subject to the same or lesser severity."

Justice requires that those who assisted the authors of an offense in committing the offense, and without whom the offense could not have been committed, should share in the punishments inflicted. This canon envisions equal punishment for a violation of law committed by "several people working together, *e.g.*, conspiracy *to restrict legitimate church* freedom or the use of church goods, *or to intimidate various church personnel*." (Commentary, *The Code of Canon Law*, American Canon Law Society.)

This case involves precisely a conspiracy to "restrict legitimate church freedom" and "to intimidate church personnel" through the abuse of ecclesiastical office. The conspiracy has involved not only the acts of respondents, but many of the Papal Nuncios who have cooperated in bearing their messages and conducting their illicit private interventions against our work, as well as other members of the Curia and the various national hierarchies whom we are unable to identify because their activities have occurred outside the proper channels of canon law.

Accordingly, the penalties imposed on respondents *ferendae sententiae* should apply with equal force to all those who have collaborated with them in committing the offenses complained of.

VI.
Conclusion

It was Your Holiness himself who told the world during his May 13, 1982 pilgrimage to Fatima that "The message of Fatima is more relevant and more urgent today . . ."; that the message is "addressed to every human being"; that the message "*imposes an obligation on the Church.*"

No competent authority in the Church has ever stated that our apostolic work in promoting this very message is in any way contrary to faith or morals; nor could such a sentence ever be pronounced against us, for we are doing nothing more than what the law of the Church permits regarding the apostolate of the laity.

Your Holiness, we come before you as faithful Catholics engaged in a licit apostolate which is inspired in no small measure by your own respect for, and public statements about, the message of Fatima, however much we believe in conscience that the message has yet to be fulfilled by certain actions of the Holy See.

What we ask of Your Holiness in this Petition is that we be accorded the same rights accorded every other member of the Church under the Code of Canon Law Your Holiness promulgated: the right to be heard in the expression of our concerns about the state of the Church, and the right to be free from the abuse of ecclesiastical authority.

VII.
Prayer for Relief

WHEREFORE, we, the petitioners, request of Your Holiness the following relief:

(A) That respondents be subjected to a just penalty, including censure or removal from office, for abuse of their ecclesiastical authority in violation of Can. 1389;

(B) That respondents be subjected to a just penalty, including censure or removal from office, for their calumniation of our apostolate in violation of Can. 1390;

(C) That respondents be ordered by Your Holiness to make reparation for their offenses in the following manner:

(1) By publishing in *L'Osservatore Romano*, *Avvenire* and Vatican Radio, with the same frequency and in the same languages as prior statements by respondents in those fora, declarations advising, on the authority of Your Holiness, as follows:

(i) that we do not require permission of ecclesiastical authority to engage in the apostolate known as International Fatima Rosary Crusade, including conferences on Fatima to which bishops, priests, religious and the faithful are invited, nor is Father Gruner, our President, required to obtain such permission to function as head of the apostolate or to help organize its conferences;

(ii) that the conference to be held by the apostolate in Rome later this year likewise does not require such permissions, and that any bishop, priest, religious or member of the faithful is free to attend;

(iii) that all prior "declarations" or "announcements" purportedly issued by the Congregation for the Clergy suggesting that our apostolate lacked necessary ecclesiastical permission for its activities, including past and future Fatima conferences, are retracted;

(2) By issuing to every bishop and papal nuncio a statement, by authority of Your Holiness, containing the same information as set forth in paragraphs 1 (i)-(iii);

(3) By directing that all of the prayed for corrective statements and declarations be made unambiguously, unequivocally and with dispatch, so that any member of the faithful and any bishop who might wish to attend our Fatima conference in Rome can be apprized of the truth about the apostolate in time to make an informed decision about whether to attend.

(D) That respondents be ordered to provide us with copies of the prayed for corrective declarations and statements immediately, with express permission to publish them in any forum we deem appropriate for the remedy of their falsehoods against us and the apostolate;

(E) That respondents be ordered to refrain from any further public or private "announcements", "declarations" or other statements stating or implying in that there is anything illicit about the apostolate, our activities in furtherance of the apostolate, or the activities of Father Gruner as the apostolate's head, or that we, Father Gruner, or the apostolate lack "permission of ecclesiastical authority" for our activities;

(F) Such other relief as Your Holiness deems just and proper.

Respectfully submitted this 29th day of September, 1996.

Mrs. Coralie Graham　　　Mrs. Mary Sedore　　　Mrs. Mairead Clarke
et al.

Appendix VIII

Because the Apostolic Signature allowed its preliminary decision to be broadcast widely, it is necessary to publish here two documents that were instrumental in reopening that decision. These documents help set the record straight at this time of the ever coming closer final showdown between certain Vatican bureaucrats who apparently answer to no one and the full Fatima message as given by Our Lady.

SUPREME TRIBUNAL OF THE APOSTOLIC SIGNATURA

An Appeal from a Decree of the Congresso, dated May 15, 1995,
Refusing to Admit this Cause for Discussion by the Judges of the Plenaria
Protocol No. 25250/94 C.A.
-by-

[SUBMITTED ALSO UNDER Protocol No. 96002069]

Father Nicholas Gruner, S.T.L.; S.T.L. [Cand.]
Recurrent.

I. INTRODUCTION

Recurrent hereby appeals from a decree of the Congresso, dated May 15, 1995, and received by recurrent on October 28, 1996, refusing to admit this recourse for discussion to the judges of the Plenaria.

Recurrent hereby affirms that he has made this recourse within 90 days of his reception of the decree from his former advocate, Carlo Tricerri, who did not advise recurrent of the existence of the decree or provide him with a copy of it until October 28, 1996. On November 15, 1996 recurrent advised this Tribunal that he would file this recourse within 90 days of October 28, to which advice he received no objection from the Tribunal.

Recurrent affirms he was ignorant of how to appeal to the Plenaria, but has relied entirely upon his advocate, who never advised recurrent of the applicable time limits and procedures, and never took an appeal from the decree. [After he received the decree, recurrent was advised by a canonist that 90 days is the time limit for this appeal.] Based on advice from another advocate of this Tribunal, recurrent believes advocate Tricerri was unable to render effective legal assistance in this matter because of debilitating illness. Accordingly, recurrent hereby discharges advocate Tricerri from the cause and reserves the right to find a new advocate.

The decree *sub judice* leaves intact an order issued on January 31, 1994 by the Bishop of Avellino, His Excellency Antonio Forte. Said order directs recurrent to return from Canada to the Diocese of Avellino after an approved absence of over 16 years, without just cause, and canonically admonishes recurrent for completely unspecified "outrages" and "scandals".

Reliance Upon Related Recourse

For purposes of this appeal, recurrent hereby incorporates by reference, as if completely restated here, the facts and legal arguments contained in the related recourse already pending before this Tribunal under Protocol No. 96002069. A copy of the related recourse is affixed hereto.

II. GROUNDS FOR APPEAL

Recurrent appeals said decree on the following grounds:

A. In general, as to the decree itself:

(1) The decree served as the procedural predicate for a subsequent order by the Bishop of Avellino, issued May 16, 1996, which relies upon the decree and orders recurrent to return to Avellino in 29 days under penalty of suspension. Accordingly, the related recourse should be stayed until this recourse is decided.

(2) The decree is the obvious product of blatant bias and marked hostility on the part of the Prefect of this Tribunal, who has been working behind the scenes since at least 1989 to arrange the exile of recurrent to Avellino, even though three successive bishops of Avellino had no grievance against recurrent and no reason of their own to recall him.

Civil litigation in Canada has uncovered a letter from the Prefect to the Bishop of Avellino, dated October 27, 1989, in which the Prefect privately advises the Bishop to revoke recurrent's permission to reside outside the Diocese of Avellino and to threaten him with suspension and ultimately reduction to the lay state. Said letter instructs the Bishop to pretend that the idea of recalling and canonically punishing recurrent was the Bishop's own, and not the Prefect's. (Despite this letter, recurrent's permission to reside outside the Diocese of Avellino was not revoked until the above-noted order of Bishop Forte, dated January 31, 1994.)

(3) The decree contains no fewer than 12 manifest errors of fact and law. The decree uses these errors to support its false conclusions (both express and implicit) that recurrent's permission to live outside the Diocese of Avellino was revoked in 1989, that he was disobedient to legitimate precepts of his superiors, that he was deprived of "faculties", that he waived his right to be incardinated in an Indian diocese, that he has been living in Canada and conducting his apostolate in violation of the law of the Church.

(4) The decree, with all of its errors, was evidently released by this Tribunal for publication and distribution throughout North America, despite the supposed confidentiality of proceedings in the Signatura. The decree must be amended to reflect the true facts and law so as to restore recurrent's good name and priestly reputation.

B. In particular, as to the decree itself:

(1) The decree falsely accuses recurrent of "de facto independence" from ecclesiastical authority, when there is no factual dispute [see related recourse] that recurrent had both express and tacit permission from three successive Bishops of Avellino and various local ordinaries in Canada to reside in Canada and conduct his work there for over sixteen years. Furthermore, there is no such offense as being "de facto independent" from a bishop. It is perfectly legitimate to maintain incardination strictly as a *conditio iuris* while residing permanently outside the diocese of ordination with the bishop's permission, as the Congregation for the Clergy implicitly conceded in the related recourse. [It must be noted that the identical phrase "de facto independence" appears in the aforementioned 1989 letter of the Prefect, directing the Bishop of Avellino to revoke recurrent's longstanding permission to reside in Canada while pretending that this action was taken on the Bishop's own initiative.]

(2) The decree falsely implies that recurrent's apostolate has been conducted without some necessary "canonical recognition" and is an unlawful "private initiative". Absolutely no canonical recognition is required for recurrent's apostolate, and there is nothing unlawful about a "private initiative" by a priest in the field of apostolic work. [Can. 278] What is more, recurrent's apostolate was conducted with the express and tacit permission referred to above.

(3) The decree falsely accuses recurrent of disobeying a "precept" of the Papal nuncio, when no such precept was ever given, as the nuncio admitted in a letter and in a tape-recorded conversation.

(4) The decree falsely accuses recurrent of disobeying a "command" of the Congregation for the Clergy to be incardinated elsewhere or return to Avellino, and of ignoring a canonical admonition by the Congregation in that regard. In fact, the "command" and "admonition" were issued by the Prefect of the Congregation at the time (Cardinal Innocenti) in an *ultra vires* manner, usurping the authority of the local ordinary, who had issued no command or admonition himself. [See Can. 1339 §1] Accordingly, the "command" and "admonition" were dropped by Innocenti after recurrent objected in writing and appealed to the Pope. None of these facts is mentioned in the decree.

(5) The decree falsely states that plaintiff's permission to live outside of Canada was revoked by the Bishop of Avellino on November 15, 1989, when in fact it was not revoked until January 31, 1994 by the aforesaid order of Bishop Forte. The letter of November 15, 1989 makes no demand that recurrent return to Canada, and subsequent letters from successive Bishops of Avellino clearly presume the continuation of recurrent's 1978 permission to live outside the Diocese of Avellino. This false finding of "fact" is used by the decree to give the impression that recurrent was a "vagus" priest from 1989 to 1994, and that he was contumaciously refusing during that time a lawful order to return. There simply was no order to return, nor any revocation of the permission to remain outside the diocese, until January 31, 1994.

(6) The decree falsely states that by letter of July 18, 1989, the Bishop of Avellino at the time, His Excellency Gerardo Pierro, revoked "all faculties" he had given to recurrent, but the decree fails to note the obvious point that recurrent had no faculties in the Diocese of Avellino in the first place, and that the letter was, therefore, quite meaningless. Yet, said letter does affirm recurrent's

continued permission to reside in Canada while seeking a benevolent bishop to incardinate him elsewhere.

(7) The decree falsely states that recurrent failed to "contest" the so-called "revocation of all faculties" referred to in the previous paragraph, when there were no faculties to revoke and nothing to contest—as confirmed by the advice of a professor of canon law consulted by recurrent at the time the July 18, 1989 letter was issued.

(8) The decree falsely states that recurrent failed to "contest" a so-called "refused incardination" by Bishop Rego of India, when in fact there is no provision in the Code of Canon law for contesting a Bishop's refusal to incardinate. Furthermore, Bishop Rego withdrew his offer of incardination only because of *ultra vires* interventions by the then Prefect and Secretary of the Congregation for the Clergy, who systematically blocked recurrent's incardination by a series of benevolent bishops, which this Tribunal knows but which the decree does not reveal.

(9) The decree falsely asserts that recurrent failed to make recourse against the canonical admonition and threat of penal process contained in Bishop Forte's January 31, 1994 order to return, when the brief submitted to this Tribunal by recurrent's advocate, Carlo Tricerri, clearly objects to the *miramur* and threat of penal process as being utterly without foundation under Cann. 1339 and 1341, there having been no episcopal investigation, let alone proof, of the required, "scandal", "proximate danger of scandal" or other grounds for issuing an admonition under said canons.

(10) The decree falsely states that recurrent's forced return to Avellino did not involve a canonical penalty from which a recourse would lie, when in fact loss of residence and exile to a foreign diocese (which had denied recurrent any canonical mission and allowed him to establish his roots in Canada) are clearly penalties under Cann. 1336, §1, 1 , for example.

(11) The decree falsely states that there was "just cause" for recalling recurrent to Avellino because he "after so many years has not yet been incardinated in another diocese". This Tribunal is well aware that the former Prefect and current Secretary of the Congregation for the Clergy—through illicit, extra-canonical private interventions kept hidden from the record of these proceedings—have systematically blocked recurrent's incardination by a series of benevolent bishops who wished to foster his apostolate. This fact was not disputed by said prelates in the related recourse when it came before them. This Tribunal is also aware that said prelates have even attempted to coerce the Archbishop of Hyderabad into withdrawing his formal decree incardinating recurrent in his Archdiocese, which decree explicitly refers to a conspiracy by said prelates to deny recurrent his rights with respect to incardination by a benevolent bishop.

(12) The decree falsely states that there was "just cause" for recalling recurrent to Avellino because he was conducting "his own private work" "de facto independently of the legitimate ecclesiastical authority". As already noted, three successive bishops of Avellino freely allowed recurrent to engage in the apostolate for over sixteen years without objection; the apostolate also received express and tacit permission from various local ordinaries in Canada; and the phrase "de facto independent" is, in any event, quite meaningless and of no import canonically. Moreover, Can. 278 envisions the establishment and conduct of private associations for pious works by secular priests, without need of formal canonical recognition or approval.

C. In particular, as to the underlying order of Bishop Forte:

While this Tribunal's competence in contentious-administrative recourses is limited to the question whether the law was violated by the administrative act of a bishop, the norms governing contentious-administrative recourses do permit recourse from the *substance* of a bishop's administrative decision, as a violation of the law *in decernendo*, if

> "[I]t *could* be proven that the reasons given by the bishop were *substantially unfounded* ... [or] if canon law requires specific reasons for a particular type of decision ... and it *could* be proven that such requirements were not observed." [Norm 1(c)]

This case involves palpable violation of the law both *in decernendo* and *in procedendo* by the Bishop of Avellino for the following reasons:

> (1) Successive Bishops of Avellino admitted to recurrent that they themselves had no grievances against him and no reason to recall him to Avellino, but were acting solely at the behest of the aforesaid prelates. [Cfr. undisputed statement of facts in related recourse.] Thus, the January 31, 1994 order to return was *admittedly* without foundation, and therefore a *per se* violation of the law *in decernendo*.

Recurrent and three successive bishops of Avellino had clearly established a *modus vivendi* of many years duration which is not uncommon for priests today: Recurrent's incardination in

Avellino was maintained strictly as a *conditio iuris* while he was permitted to pursue his legitimate apostolic work. Indeed, the Diocese of Avellino manifestly never had need of recurrent's physical presence since he had never been given any canonical mission in the diocese. What is more, as noted in the factual recitation of the related recourse, it was *impossible* for recurrent to have a canonical mission in Avellino since he could not speak the dialect, was not permitted to hear confessions, and could not even deliver a sermon unless it was first totally written out by recurrent in Italian (in which he has never been completely fluent, let alone able to write ecclesiastical prose).

The aforementioned letter sent by the Prefect of this Tribunal to the Bishop of Avellino in 1989 proves conclusively that there would never have been a revocation of recurrent's permission to live outside the diocese had it not been instigated and orchestrated by the Prefect as part of a preconceived plan to silence recurrent and abolish his apostolate because it promotes legitimate views concerning the Message of Fatima which certain members of the Vatican apparatus, including the Prefect, vehemently oppose. [Cfr. related recourse]

In short, there was, by the Bishop's own undisputed admission in the related recourse, no "just cause" for recalling recurrent to Avellino pursuant to Can. 271§3.

(2) Since recurrent's "failure" to be incardinated by another bishop was caused entirely by the *ultra vires* interventions and abuse of authority by the aforesaid members of the Congregation for the Clergy, with the evident collaboration of the Prefect of this Congregation, the "failure" to be incardinated was not "just cause" recalling recurrent to Avellino after an approved absence of over sixteen years.

It is of utmost important to note that *there is no dispute in the related recourse* that recurrent's incardination by a series of benevolent bishops was systematically obstructed by the aforesaid members of the Congregation for the Clergy through unprecedented extra-canonical, secretive means (and with the evident collaboration of the Prefect of this Tribunal, who himself initiated the process of unjustly recalling recurrent to Avellino with his letter to the Bishop of Avellino of October 27, 1989). Indeed, even when recurrent succeeded in obtaining a formal decree of incardination from the Archbishop of Hyderabad, said prelates refused to accept it, and privately intervened once again to block recurrent's incardination by yet another benevolent bishop.

It is manifest, therefore, that recurrent's so-called "failure" to be incardinated in another diocese was not just cause for recalling recurrent since recurrent was indisputably not at fault for "failing" to be incardinated.

(3) Recurrent was manifestly not a "vagus" priest as falsely stated in the January 31, 1994 order.

The January 31, 1994 order manifestly errs when it asserts that recurrent must return to Avellino because he was a "vagus" priest. It is undisputed that recurrent had written permission to live outside the diocese as of the date of the order, and this permission negates as a matter of law the claim that recurrent was a "vagus".

(4) There was manifestly no basis for the canonical admonition and threat of penal process contained in the January 31, 1994 order.

On its face, the January 31, 1994 order fails to meet even the minimum requirements for the issuance of a canonical admonition and threat of penal process under Cann. 1339 and 1341. These canons, read together, require the following elements to be established before the admonition can be issued:

—the existence of a "scandal" caused by the cleric, "serious disturbance of public order", some other offense, or proximate occasion of an offense, or serious suspicion of same after an investigation,

—prior efforts at fraternal correction or reproof

The order specifies no "scandal", "serious disturbance of public order", offense or proximate offense whatsoever. [The only effort to provide any evidence in support of the admonition was Bishop Forte's reference to a complaint in 1978(!) from an unnamed party concerning some unspecified dispute *within recurrent's own apostolate*—which letter had never before been mentioned.] Indeed, it was not disputed in the related recourse that some two weeks before the order was issued Bishop Forte admitted to recurrent that he had *no grievance against recurrent.* The admonition of January 31, 1994 appears suddenly, as if from nowhere.

Of course, the record in this cause and in the related recourse is devoid of any prior effort at fraternal correction or reproof, as required by cited canons, because the completely unspecified "scandals" and "outrages" mentioned in the January 31, 1994 order *had never been mentioned even once in the preceding sixteen years.* There were in fact no scandals or outrages to mention.

For these reasons there was also no basis for the threat of penal process. Can. 1318 precludes a threat of *latae sententiae* penalties (under Can. 1341), except for "outstanding and malicious offenses". No offenses, let alone malicious offenses, were specified in the January 31, 1994 order or any other pronouncement of the Bishop of Avellino. In fact, recurrent has never been charged with any canonical offense whatsoever in the entire 20 years of his priestly life.

Thus, it is beyond dispute that Bishop Forte had no basis for issuing a canonical admonition and threat of penal process.

D. Request for Recusal

For the reasons set forth above, and in the related recourse, recurrent respectfully demands that the Prefect of this Tribunal recuse himself from this matter both as a matter of natural equity and pursuant to Cann. 1447, 1448, or be removed from the case pursuant to recurrent's demand under Cann. 1449.

E. Request for Documents

Recurrent respectfully requests that this Tribunal make available for inspection and copying by recurrent's advocate all correspondence and other communications between the Prefect, the successive Bishops of Avellino and any of the bishops who have offered incardination to recurrent at any time, and all such correspondence by the former Prefect and current Secretary of the Congregation for the Clergy, as well as any "declarations" or other documents pertaining to recurrent issued by this Tribunal, the Congregation for the Clergy or the Bishop of Avellino.

II. PRAYER FOR RELIEF

WHEREFORE, recurrent respectfully requests the following relief:

(A) A stay of the related recourse until this recourse is decided;

(B) Recusal of the Prefect from any further involvement in this recourse;

(C) Admission of this recourse to the judges of the Plenaria;

(D) Revocation of the decree *sub judice* and the underlying order of Bishop Forte;

(E) An order of this Tribunal directing the Prefect of this Tribunal, the former Prefect of the Congregation for the Clergy and its current Secretary, and their various collaborators, whomever they may be, from any further interference in recurrent's incardination by any and all benevolent bishops who will accept him;

(F) An order of this Tribunal directing the Bishop of Avellino to grant excardination to recurrent in favor of the Archbishop of Hyderabad or any other benevolent bishop who offers incardination;

(G) An award of damages in favor of recurrent and against the Prefect of this Tribunal, His Eminence G. Agostini, the former Prefect of the Congregation for the Clergy, His Eminence Jose Sanchez, and its current Secretary, His Excellency C. Sepe, the current Bishop of Avellino, His Excellency Antonio Forte, and their collaborators, for abuse of ecclesiastical authority and violation of law, both *in procedendo* and *in decernendo*, and transferring this matter to the First See to the extent that the claim for damages involves Cardinals.

Respectfully submitted this 27th day of January, 1997.

Father Nicholas Gruner, S.T.L; S.T.D. [Cand], Recurrent

January 31, 1997
Feast of St. John Bosco

His Holiness Pope John Paul II
Vatican City 00120
Rome, Italy

Re: **Recourses to Apostolic Signatura**
Protocol No. 25250/94 C.A.
Protocol No. 96002069

Most Holy Father:

In the above-noted recourses now pending in the Supreme Apostolic Signatura, I have made a request that the Prefect of the Signatura, His Eminence Gilberto Cardinal Agustoni, be recused from judging either matter.

The reason I am constrained to write to Your Holiness regarding this request is that under the authentic interpretation of Canon 1449, which governs recusal of who judges are Cardinals in the Signatura, including the Prefect, the request for recusal *must* be addressed to the Supreme Pontiff (*Response of the PCIV*/67-84, 01-07-1976, *AAS* 68 (1976) 635, *CLD* 8 [1973-1977] 1091-1902) I make this request under Cann. 1447 § 1 and 1449 on grounds of bias and marked hostility on the part of the Cardinal Prefect, and also on grounds of his disqualification under Cann. 1447, in that he has already rendered one adverse decision against me in this matter and therefore cannot continue to judge the case now that it has come before him again.

Your Holiness has been made aware of the facts of my case in the recourse I lodged personally with Your Holiness through the intercession of two benevolent bishops on November 20, 1996, at the end of the General Audience that day. There is no need to rehearse those facts here.

Suffice it to say that I am compelled to seek recusal of the Cardinal-Prefect from judging my recourses, because the facts establish that since at least 1989 he has been working behind the scenes, outside the proper channels of Canon law, to silence me and abolish the perfectly legitimate apostolate in which I have been engaged since 1978.

I am attaching to this letter as prime evidence of my contention a private letter form the Cardinal-Prefect (then Secretary for the Congregation of the Clergy) to then Bishop of Avellino, His Excellency Gerardo Pierro, dated October 27, 1989. I was obviously never supposed to see this letter, but by Providence it was discovered in the course of civil litigation in Canada. In this letter then Archbishop Agustoni, who is supposed to be the impartial judge in my case, carefully outlines the "stages" (as he himself put it) by which I was to be recalled to Avellino without just cause, under threat of "reduction to the laystate" if necessary, after an approved absence of over 16 years - during which time I had based my whole priestly life on an apostolate which no Bishop of Avellino had ever forbade me to conduct.

The Cardinal's letter concludes with the admonition that the Bishop of Avellino should pretend that the "stages" and decisions involved he presented as having originated in the mind of the Bishop, rather than being the plan of archbishop Agustoni. In this way, it was evidently hoped that Archbishop Agustoni could then judge any recourse I might make against what are really his own actions, while maintaining a false appearance of objectivity and fairness in his "deliberations".

Your Holiness will note that the letter is couched in terms of apparent solicitude for my priestly welfare and the good of the Church, combined with the accusation that I have failed to find a benevolent bishop to incardinate me, so that all my problems are my own fault. But facts which have arisen since the Cardinal's letter will, I am afraid, expose the insincerity of these expressed motives:

On November 4, 1995, Your Holiness, I was given a formal decree of incardination by Archbishop Saminini Arulappa of the Archdiocese of Hyderabad [second attachment], where my apostolate maintains an orphanage and where my priestly services and apostolic work are welcome by a very benevolent and holy prelate. The Archbishop has, in turn, been given a decree of excardination from the Diocese of Avellino, issued by Bishop Pierro a few months before Cardinal Agustoni began to interfere in my case with his 1989 letter.

This completed incardination into a "Third World" diocese in need of priests and financial support is *precisely* what *Pastor Bonus** directs the Congregation for the Clergy to encourage. Yet the former Prefect of the Congregation, Cardinal Sanchez, and its current Secretary, Abp. Sepe, have simply declared that this incardination by a benevolent bishop is *"tanquam non existens"*. So, Your Holiness, even when I finally succeed in doing what they have consistently blocked me from doing for years - becoming incardinated by a benevolent bishop - they declare the incardination non-existent! It is this decision of the Congregation which now comes before Cardinal Agustoni as Prefect of the Signatura.

If Cardinal Agustoni were truly concerned with my priestly welfare and the good of the Church, one would expect him to overrule the Congregation, declare my incardination in Hyderabad valid, and thereby fulfill the mandate of *Pastor Bonus* to assign priests to where they are needed and can have a canonical mission best suited to their particular gifts. Obviously, this will not happen: In 1995 Cardinal Agustoni sat in judgment on my first recourse against the order to return to Avellino *even though it was he himself who had instigated the order.* He then proceeded to issue an error-filled decree upholding the order to return as a valid exercise of the "bishop's" discretion, *when it was he himself who had told the bishop in a secret letter to order my return and to pretend that it was the bishop's idea*!

* Pastor Bonus is a legal document published by Pope John Paul II outlining the various duties of the Vatican Congregations and courts.

Your Holiness, how can I possibly expect justice now, from such a judge? Is it not completely clear that the Cardinal will simply confirm his own secret designs as expressed in 1989 and order me back to a diocese where it was impossible for me to have a canonical mission in the first place, and where the Bishop has never needed my services or given me any support in the past 20 years?

Permit me, Your Holiness, to quote from the decree of incardination issued by the most benevolent Archbishop of Hyderabad:

> **"Evil forces have conspired to put and end to your work of love.** But you go ahead trusting in the Lord. His love is steadfast and He will never fail, though you may be subject to many a trial and even ***persecution***. God will also give you great comfort and consolation through innumerable friends and well-wishers. ***Bureaucratic forces cannot stifle God's work.*** It is my prayer that you continue in your God-given mission in spite of great opposition."

You can see, Your Holiness, that there is an objective reality to the concerted illicit actions against me which have brought about my recourses, and also this request for recusal of the Cardinal Prefect from judging my case. The reality that I am being persecuted is readily seen by this distinguished prelate, who has been a bishop for 25 years, and he justly and fearlessly condemns it.

I will conclude, Your Holiness, by noting that in his secret 1989 letter outlining the plan for my "demise", the Cardinal patronizingly refers to me as "a difficult subject". No, Your Holiness, I am not a "difficult subject". I am only a loyal priest who knows his God-given rights and is not afraid to exercise them - because he believes in conscience that the good of the Church, the salvation of souls and peace in the world are aided by the work of all the faithful, including myself, in promoting fearlessly and publicly the whole Message of Fatima. As Your Holiness himself said at Fulda, knowledge of the Fatima message brings with it a responsibility. Given what I know by God's grace and His Providence, it is my duty to promote against all illicit opposition the Message of Fatima, despite my personal inclination to retreat and find some quiet haven away from the struggles my adversaries constantly impose upon me.

Your Holiness, the evidence speaks for itself. For Cardinal Agustoni to judge my recourses, even while he acts against me as an adverse party, would be a mockery of justice which would diminish substantially the credibility of the Signatura as a tribunal where priests can receive a fair hearing of their legitimate grievances against the abuse of power by prelates. Under Cann. 1447-48 the Cardinal should have recused himself in 1995, he did not. The case has come before him again, again he should recuse himself. He does not. Therefore, I must make this request.

Your Holiness, as my Father in the Faith, I am asking you for bread. I am begging you for the bread of a just hearing before an impartial judge. Please do not let them give me a scorpion instead.

In conclusion, I pray that Your Holiness will order the recusal of Cardinal Agustoni from my case - as only you are able to do under the law of the Church.

Humbly submitted,

Father Nicholas Gruner

P.S. I enclose as the third attachment my recourse to the Plenaria of the Signatura from Cardinal Agustoni's decree of May 15, 1995 (received by me only on October 28, 1996), which decree is a monument to the hostility and bias of the Cardinal in my case. I pray you will read this recourse in full since it summarizes in detail how truth itself is perverted in the effort to silence me without canonical due process.

P.P.S. This letter includes three attachments:

1. Letter of Cardinal Agustoni to Bishop Pierro, dated October 27, 1989 (2 pp).
2. Decree of Incardination issued to me by Abp. Arulappa, dated November 4, 1995. (1 p.)
3. My most recent recourse to the Signatura, dated January 27, 1997 (9 pp) and attached prior recourse tO the Signatura (39 pp.) and 23 attachments in two binders.

I will of course supply, any additional documentation or explanations Your Holiness might require.

Notes

BOOK I

Chapter 1: The Stars at Noon

1. Father Gruner, *Memories of My Mother*, The Fatima Crusader, Issue 47, Summer 1994, pg. 11.
2. Father Nicholas Gruner, *A Personal Thank You From Father Gruner*, The Fatima Crusader, Issue 30, Winter 1989, pg. 1.
3. William Thomas Walsh, *Our Lady of Fatima*, New York, The Macmillian Company, pg. 52.
4. *Fatima in Lucia's Own Words*, Sister Lucy's Third Memoir, pg. 104.
5. Ibid, pg. 102.
6. Ibid, pg. 104.
7. Ibid.
8. Frère Michel de la Sainte Trinite, *The Secret of Fatima Revealed*, pg. 7
9. Frère Michel de la Sainte Trinite, The Whole Truth About Fatima, Volume III, *The Third Secret*, Buffalo, NY., Immaculate Heart Publications, pgs. 479-481.
10. William Thomas Walsh, *Our Lady of Fatima*, pg. 80.
11. Ibid, pg. 145.
12. Ibid, pg. 148-149.
13. Ibid, pg. 149.
14. *Fatima in Lucia's Own Words*, Sr. Lucy's Third Memoir, pg. 102.
15. Ibid, pgs. 104-105, 107-108.
16. Frère Michel de la Sainte Trinite, Volume III, *The Third Secret*, Buffalo, NY., Immaculate Heart Publications, pg. 38.
17. Ibid pg. 42.
18. Ibid pg. 44.
19. Ibid pg. 45.
20. Ibid pgs. 47, 48.
21. Ibid pg. 47.

Chapter 2: The Beauty of Thy House

1. Pope Pius XII, From the Apostolic Constitution, *Munificentissimus Deus*, promulgated Nov. 1, 1950; Denzinger - The Sources of Catholic Dogma 2331-2333.

Chapter 3: Wound in the City

1. *The Life of Saint Margaret Mary Alacoque*, Bishop Emile Bougaud, pgs. 263-273, Tan Books and Publishers,Rockford,Il.
2. Frère Michel de la Sainte Trinite, Vol. III, *The Third Secret,* Buffalo, NY., Immaculate Heart Publications, pgs. 578-579.

Chapter 4: Gethsemane

1. This shrine is unique among all Our Lady's shrines. The Carmelites prayed to Our Lady, their perfect example, for guidance, and She led them to Aylesford, England, in 1241, with the help of Saint Simon Stock. One day, July 16, 1251, Simon Stock went to his cell there in Aylesford and prayed with all his heart for Our Dear Mother's intercession.
   Saint Simon Stock's cell was flooded with light when Our Lady appeared to him. She held the Scapular in Her hand, even as She wore it full size on Herself, and She made this, the Scapular, a sign of Her special love and protection for them.
   She said to Saint Simon, "This shall be to thee and to all Carmelites a privilege that whosoever dies clothed in this (Scapular) shall not suffer eternal fire. It shall be a sign of salvation, a protection in danger and a pledge of peace."
2. Frère François de Marie des Anges, Book One, *Fatima: The Astonishing Truth*, Immaculate Heart Publications, Buffalo, NY, pg 104; also, *Fatima in Lucia's Own Words*, Sister Lucy's Fourth Memoir, pg. 162.
3. Copy of document maintained in diocese of Avellino.
4. *Congratulations Father Nicholas Gruner,* The Fatima Crusader, Issue 53, Summer 1996, pgs. 1, 2; also, Picture of Father Gruner's Ordination, The Fatima Crusader, Issue 18, Oct-Dec 1985, pg. 13.
5. Father Nicholas Gruner, *A Canonical Recourse to the Sacred Congregation for the Clergy,* The Fatima Crusader, Issue 53, Summer 1996, pgs. 19-20;

also Father Nicholas Gruner, *Father Gruner's Letter to Cardinal Innocenti*, The Fatima Crusader, Issue 29, Sept-Nov. 1989, pg. 34.

Chapter 5: Whose Hands are Full of Bribes

1. *Introducing the new Executive Director,* The Fatima Crusader, Issue 1, Summer 1978, pg. 1.
2. *Recent Events,* The Fatima Crusader, Issue 3, Summer 1979, pg. 3.
3. *News Of The Apostolate*, The Fatima Crusader, Issue 5, Spring & Summer 1980, pg. 3.
4. *Recent Events*, The Fatima Crusader, Issue 3, Summer 1979, pg. 3.
5. *Recent Events,* The Fatima Crusader, Issue 2, Spring 1979, pg. 4
6. Ibid.
7. Ibid, pg. 5.
8. *The Fatima Crusader*, Issue 6, Christmas 1980, pg. 15; reprinted from *The Catholic Register*, an article written by Stan Koma.
9. *Recent Events,* The Fatima Crusader, Issue 2, Spring 1979, pg. 4.

Chapter 6: Power Play of a Locket Cult

1. Correspondence between Father Gruner and Archbishop Palmas.
2. Hamish Fraser, *Fatal Star*, Long Prairie, Neuman Press, 1986, pg. 159
3. *New Hope For the Fatima Apostolate in Canada*, The Fatima Crusader, Issue 6, Christmas 1980, pgs. 13-15.
4. Letter of invitation to delegates with original signature offically signed by Albert Setz-Degen, International Secretary of the Blue Army, dated Jan. 31, 1981, sent from Basel, Switzerland.
5. Frère François de Marie des Anges, *Fatima: Tragedy and Triumph*, first edition, pg. 153.
6. Ibid.
7. Frère François de Marie des Anges, *Fatima: The Only Way To World Peace,* pg. 91.
8. Letter of Father Gruner to Pope John Paul II, June, 1981, on file with Father Gruner's personal records.
9. Father Nicholas Gruner, *Father Gruner's Letter to Cardinal Innocenti*, The Fatima Crusader, Issue 29, Sept-Nov. 1989, pg. 35.
10. Father Nicholas Gruner, *Cononical Recourse to The Sacred Congregation for the Clergy*, The Fatima Crusader, Issue 53, Summer 1996, pg. 23.
11. *Fr. Gruner's Letter to Cardinal Innocenti*, The Fatima Crusader, Issue 29, Sept-Nov. 1989, pg. 35.
12. Ibid.
13. Written faculties from Archdiocese of Ottawa; of St. Catharines, and others for various times in the 1970's and 1980's are still on file with Father Gruner's personal records. Also present on file are faculties given in the 1990's.

Chapter 7: Before Communism Changed Its Name

1. Jean Madiran, The *Vatican-Moscow Agreement*, The Fatima Crusader, Issue 16, Sept-Oct 1984, pg. 5; originally published in *Itineraires*, Feb 1984, Paris, France.
2. Frère François de Marie des Anges, *Fatima: Tragedy and Triumph*, pg. 183.
3. Abbé Pierre Caillon, *Regarding the Consecration of Russia, Sister Lucy's Recent Authorized Statements*, The Fatima Crusader, Issue 13-14, Oct-Dec 1983, pg. 3; also, Abbé Pierre Caillon, *Fatima May 13, 1982 What Actually Happened? Was Russia Consecrated to the Immaculate Heart of Mary?* The Fatima Crusader, Issue 16 Sept-Oct 1984, pg. 22; also, published in Fidelite Catholique, April 1983, BP 217 - 56402 Auray Cedex, France; also, Stella Maris, No. 170, June 1983; also, "Ephemerides Mariologicae", 1983, pgs. 461-462.
4. Ibid.
5. Ibid.
6. Ibid.
7. Ibid; also, see the important footnote on this matter, Frère François de Marie des Anges, *Tragedy and Triumph*, chapter 4, footnote 125, pg. 226.
8. Abbé Pierre Caillon, op. cit.; also see the Papal Bull announcing the Holy Year, promulgated January 6, 1983.
9. John Haffert, *A Reported Interview with Sister Lucy*; also Hamish Fraser, *Last Minute News Flash,* The Fatima

Crusader, Issue 9-10, Oct-Dec 1982, pgs. 4, 5, 31.
10. Father Joseph de Sainte-Marie's January 16, 1983 *Letter to Hamish Fraser*; published in The Fatima Crusader, Issue 13-14, Oct-Dec 1983, pgs. 10-13.
11. Father Pierre Caillon, *Sister Lucy's Recent Authorized Statements*, The Fatima Crusader, Issue 13-14, Oct-Dec 1983, pg. 3.
12. Father Joaquin Maria Alonso S.T.D., Ph. D., Official Archivist of Fatima, *Meaning of the Consecration of Russia*, The Fatima Crusader, Issue 50, Autumn 1995, pg. 13. Previously published in Madrid, Spain in 1979.
13. Frère François de Marie des Anges, *Fatima: The Only Way to World Peace*, pg. 78.
14. Ezekiel: 33: 1-7.
15. St. Luke 10:16.
16. Pope Pius XI, Encyclical Letter, *Divini Redemptoris*, paragraph 58.
17. Ibid, paragraph 5.
18. Ralph M. Wiltgen S.V.D., *The Rhine Flows Into The Tiber*, pg. 274.
19. Ibid, pgs. 274, 275.
20. Malachi Martin *The Jesuits,* pg. 85-88.

Chapter 8: The Scaffold Rises

1. Father Pierre Caillon, op. cit., pgs. 22-23.
2. Father Paul Leonard, *The Plot To Silence Our Lady,* The Fatima Crusader, Issue 20, June-July 1986, pgs. 9-13; also Father Paul Leonard, *The Vatican Moscow Agreement Has Silenced Our Lady,* The Fatima Crusader, Issue 22, April-May 1987, pgs. 12-15; also Father Paul Leonard, *The Blue Army Leadership Has Followed a Deliberate Policy of Falsifying the Fatima Message,* The Fatima Crusader, Issue 22, April-May 1987, pgs. 26-28.
3. Father Joseph de Sainte-Marie's January 16, 1983 *Letter to Hamish Fraser*; published in The Fatima Crusader, Issue 13-14, Oct-Dec 1983, pgs. 10-13.
4. Hamish Fraser, *Address to International Fatima Rosary Crusade Symposium*, Vatican City, Nov. 24, 1985, published in The Fatima Crusader, Issue 19, Feb-April 1986, pg. 7.
5. Ibid, pg. 13.
6. Ibid, pg. 13.
7. Ibid, pgs. 13-14.
8. Father Paul Leonard, *The Vatican-Moscow Agreement Has Silenced Our Lady*, The Fatima Crusader, Issue 22, April-May 1987, pg. 12.
9. *Soul Magazine,* March-April 1986, pg. 9, cited in *The Fatima Crusader,* Issue 22, April-May 1987, pg. 12.
10. Father Paul Leonard, *The Vatican Moscow Agreement Has Silenced Our Lady*, The Fatima Crusader, Issue 22, April-May 1987, pg. 13.
11. Ibid pgs. 12-15; also, Father Paul Leonard, *The Blue Army Leadership has Followed a Deliberate Policy of Falsifying the Fatima Message,* The Fatima Crusader, Issue 22, April-May 1987, pgs. 12-15, 26-28.
12. Père Joseph de Sainte-Marie, *Letter to Hamish Fraser,* The Fatima Crusader, Issue 13-14, Oct-Dec 1983, pg. 10.
13. Father Paul Leonard, *The Vatican Moscow Agreement Has Silenced Our Lady,* The Fatima Crusader, Issue 22, April-May 1987, pg. 12.
14. Father Nicholas Gruner, *World Enslavement or Peace It's Up To the Pope*, Fort Erie, Canada, Fatima Crusader Publications, 1988. This book is a well-documented source of information to gain an indepth understanding of this vital point.
15. *The Catholic Church Betrayed,* The Fatima Crusader, Issue 17, Feb-April 1985, pg. 7.
16. Ibid, pg. 9.
17. Ibid, pg. 10.
18. Father Paul Leonard, *The Blue Army Leadership has Followed a Deliberate Policy of Falsifying the Fatima Message*, The Fatima Crusader, Issue 22, April-May 1987, pg. 27.
19. Mikhail Gorbachev, *Speech in Tashkent*, Richard N. Ostling, Time Magazine, Jan. 12, 1987; also published in the Uzbek daily Pravada Vostoka, and the report was cited in the Keston College News Service of December 11, 1986.

Chapter 9: The Network

1. See Appendix III for text of this interview of Sister Lucy with Father

Fuentes; also, Frère Michel de la Sainte Trinite, Vol. III, *The Third Secret*, pgs. 503-509; also Frère François de Marie des Anges, *Fatima: Tragedy and Triumph*, pgs. 26-32.

2. Frère François de Marie des Anges, *Fatima: Tragedy and Triumph*, pg. 31.
3. Frère Michel de la Sainte Trinite, Vol. III, *The Third Secret*, pg. 551.
4. Frère François de Marie des Anges, *Fatima: Tragedy and Triumph*, pg. 31; Frère Michel de la Sainte Trinite, Vol. III, *The Third Secret*, pg. 551.
5. *The Catholic Counter-Reformation, in The XX Century*, Issue 251, Oct 1992, pg. 4; Frère François de Marie des Anges, *Fatima: Tragedy and Triumph*, pg. 30; Frère Michel de la Sainte Trinite, Vol. III, *The Third Secret*, pg. 551.
6. See Book II, Chapter 1 of this work "Schism And The Common Good".
7. Cardinal Mindzenty, *Memoirs*, pgs. 412-13.
8. Ibid.
9. Acts 20:28-31.
10. Frère Michel de la Sainte Trinite, Vol III, *The Third Secret*, pgs. 701-702.
11. Dr. David Allen White, *The Mouth Of The Lion*, pg. 79.
12. Bishop Fulton, *letter to Father Gruner*, dated August 9, 1989, published in The Fatima Crusader, Issue 29, Sept.-Nov.1989, pg. 40.
13. *L'Osservatore Romano*, May 17, 1982, English Edition; also published in *The Fatima Crusader*, Issue 9-10, Oct-Dec 1982, pgs. 5-8.
14. Father Paul Leonard, *Incardination Offered on Condition of Silence,* The Fatima Crusader, Issue 29, Sept.-Nov. 1989, pg. 39.
15. Father Paul Leonard, *Some Vatican Officials Attempt to Silence and Suppress Our Lady of Fatima and Father Gruner,* The Fatima Crusader Issue 29, Sept.-Nov. 1989, pg. 4.
16. Father Nicholas Gruner, *Letter To Cardinal Innocenti*, The Fatima Crusader Issue 29, Sept.-Nov. 1989, pgs. 37-38.
17. See Appendix III of this book.
18. *Father Gruner in India*, The Fatima Crusader, Issue 18, Oct-Dec 1985, pg. 13, caption.
19. *The Fatima Crusader*, Issue 39, Winter 1992, pg. 20, caption.
20. *Father Gruner Speaks World- Wide On the Only Daily Radio Program Dedicated To Our Lady's Fatima Message*, The Fatima Crusader, Issue 30, Winter 1989, pg. 34.
21. *Soul Magazine,* Jan-Feb 1990, pg. 29.
22. Father Paul Leonard, *The Plot To Silence Our Lady Thickens*, The Fatima Crusader, Issue 31-32, March-May 1990, Pg. 5.
23. Ibid, pg. 5-6.
24. Ibid, pg. 6.
25. *The Fatima Crusader,* Issue 39, Winter 1992, pg. 13, caption.
26. Ibid, pg. 28, caption
27. Ibid, pg. 10, caption.

Chapter 10: To Make the Guitars Laugh

1. J. Kaess, *Strange Goings On In Fatima,* The Fatima Crusader, Issue 44, Spring 1993, pg. 35.
2. *The Catholic Counter-Reformation in the XXth Century,* Aug-Sept 1992, pg. 4.
3. Ibid.
4. Doctor Lacerda, Letter to Father Gruner, dated Dec. 20, 1991, published in *The Catholic Counter-Reformation in the XXth Century,* Aug-Sept 1992 Issue, pg. 5.
5. *The Catholic Counter-Reformation in the XXth Century*, Aug-Sept 1992, pg. 4.
6. Ibid.
7. Ibid.
8. Ibid, pg. 5.
9. Ibid.
10. Ibid, pg. 5.
11. Ibid, pg. 5, footnote 2.
12. Ibid, pg. 4.
13. Ibid.

Chapter 11: Ambush in Fatima October 1992

1. *Invitation to International Peace Conference*, reproduced in The Fatima Crusader, Issue 43, Winter 1993, pg. 16.
2. *L'Osservatore Romano*, Oct 7, 1992 - Italian Edition; also *L'Osservatore Romano*, Oct. 14, 1992, last page - English Edition.

3. *The Fatima Crusader,* Issue 43, Winter 1994, pg. 13, caption.
4. Ibid.
5. St. John 2:5.
6. *Police Report,* The Fatima Crusader, Issue 43, Winter 1993, pg. 9.
7. Ibid, pg. 9.
8. Ibid, pg. 9.
9. Ibid, pgs. 9, 28; also J. Kaess, *Strange Goings On In Fatima,* Issue 44, Spring 1993, pg. 34.
10. *The Fatima Crusader,* Issue 46, Winter, 1994, pg. 15.
11. Ibid.
12. *The Catholic Counter-Reformation in the XXth Century,* Oct 1992, pg. 1
13. Ibid, pg. 2.
14. Ibid, pg. 2; also, *The Fatima Crusader,* Issue 44, Spring 1993, pg. 36.
15. *The Catholic Counter-Reformation in the XXth Century,* Oct 1992, pg. 2.
16. Ibid, pg. 5.
17. *The Catholic Counter Reformation in the XXth Century,* Aug-Sept 1992, pg. 3, footnote 4.
18. *The Catholic Counter-Reformation in the XXth Century,* Nov. 1992, pg. 9.
19. *The Catholic Counter-Reformation in the XXth Century,* Oct. 1992, pg. 4.
20. Pope Pius XI, Encyclical Letter, *Divini Redemptoris,* Par. 58.

Chapter 12: The Incardination Game

1. Pope John XXIII, *opening speech* to the Second Vatican Council; also, Ralph M. Wiltgen S.V.D., *The Rhine Flows Into the Tiber,* pg. 15.
2. Pope Pius X, Encyclical Letter, *Pascendi Dominici Gregis,* paragraph 3, promulgated July 3, 1907.
3. Josef Cardinal Ratzinger, the autobiography, *La Mia Vita,* April 1997; also, *The Wanderer,* May 8, 1997, pg. 7.
4. *1983 Code of Canon Law,* Cans, 212, 215, 216, 299.
5. Can 290 of the 1983 Code of Canon Law states "After it has been validly received, sacred ordination never becomes invalid." A cleric can, however, lose the clerical state. This is not to say that the character of the priesthood is removed. *The Council of Trent,* Chap 3, Can 4, clearly teaches "... If anyone says that no character is imprinted by ordination: or that he who was once a priest can become a layman again: let him be anathema."
6. *A Canonical Recourse To The Sacred Congregation For The Clergy,* The Fatima Crusader, Issue 53, Summer 1996, pg. 21.
7. Ibid.
8. Ibid.
9. Ibid, pg. 22.
10. Ibid, pg. 23-24.
11. Ibid, pg. 24.
12. Can 384 of the 1983 Code of Canon Law states that the bishop "is to have a special concern for the priests to whom he is to listen as his helpers and counselors. He is to defend their rights..."
13. *A Canonical Recourse To The Sacred Congregation For The Clergy,* The Fatima Crusader, Issue 53, Summer 1996, pg. 24.
14. Ibid.
15. Ibid, pg 24-25.
16. Cann 270-271 of the 1983 Code of Canon Law detail Church law regarding incardination and excardination.

Chapter 13: The Balamand Connection

1. Iain Colquhoun, *What Happened in 1929,* The Fatima Crusader, Issue 47, Summer 1994, pg. 29.
2. Ibid.
3. *Eastern Churches Journal,* Vol. 1, pg. 18-25.
4. The second section of the Secretariat of State has the particular job of forming and maintaining relations with civil governments. *The 1997 Annuario Pontifico,* pg. 1814 describes the functions of the second section more in depth.
5. *Eastern Churches Journal,* Op. Cit., pg. 34.
6. *The Fatima Crusader,* Issue 33, Summer 1990, pg. 11.
7. Solange Hertz, *Beyond Politics,* Santa Monica, CA, 1995, pg. 170.
8. Ibid.
9. *Catholic Family News,* August 1995, pg. 13.

Chapter 14: Terrible Words

1. Father Alonso, *"Fatima Ante la Esfinge",* Madrid, Spain; 1979, pg. 97; also, Frère Francois de Marie des

Anges, *Fatima: the Only Way to World Peace*, pg. 78.
2. *Father Nicholas Gruner, Special Report - Second International Bishops Peace Conference*, The Fatima Crusader, Issue 48, Winter 1995, pg. 20.
3. Ibid.
4. Ibid, pg. 20-21.
4B. *Catholic Family News*, November 1996, pg. 4
5. Bishop Francis Clement Kelly, *Blood Drenched Altars*, pg. 102.
6. After Abbot Schullenberg, rector of the Guadalupe Shrine, on a radio broadcast in Mexico, expressed his unbelief in the reality of our Lady's appearance at Guadalupe, a storm of protest broke out causing him to resign his post.
7. Archbishop Emmanuel Milingo, *Archbishop Milingo's Dramatic Speech*, The Fatima Crusader, Issue 48, Winter 1995, pg. 20.
8. Ibid.
9. See Appendix IV of this book.
10. *Catholic Family News*, January 1995, pg. 7.
11. Bishop Francis Clement Kelly, *Blood Drenched Altars*, pg. 103.

Chapter 16: Window On The Arena

1. Msgr. Roche, *Pie XII devant l'histoire*, pgs. 52-53; also, *Inside the Vatican*, Jan 1997, pgs. 6-7.
2. St. Matthew 16:19.
3. The Second Council of Lyons (1274 A.D.) teaches, "Anyone who is aggrieved may appeal to it (the Holy Roman Church) in matters pertaining to the ecclesiastical court; and in all cases that require ecclesiastical investigation, one may have recourse to its judgement", Denzinger, thirtieth edition, paragraph 466; also, Vatican Council I (1870 A.D.) says "And because, by the Divine right of Apostolic primacy the Roman Pontiff is at the head of the whole Church, we also teach and declare that he is the supreme judge of the Faithful and that one can have recourse to his judgement in all cases pertaining to ecclesiastical jurisdiction", Denzinger, thirtieth edition, paragraphs 1830-1831; also, see 1983 Code of Canon Law, Cann 221; 1405 No. 1.

Chapter 17: The Letter

1. Father Laurentin made this statement on the Italian television talk show FORMAT-MISTERI, after Paolo Apolito challenged him on the topic; Giovanni Minoli, director; Lorenza Roschini, interviewer; Autumn 1995.

Chapter 18: End Game

1. Christopher A. Ferrara, Esq, Archbishop Shows: *"There is a Conspiracy Against This Priest"*, the Fatima Crusader, Issue 54, Winter 1997, pgs. 73-74.
2. Ibid, pgs. 74-75.
3. January 10, 1996 letter from Archbishop Arulappa is filed with Father Gruner's personal records.
4. Quoted from the letter of Archbishop Carlos Curtis, Apostolic Pro-Nuncio of Canada, Protocol No. 8007/95, taken from original letter from Archbishop Sepe.
5. The January 26, 1996 statement from the Bishop of Avellino to Father Gruner is filed with Father Gruner's personal records.
6. *Soul Magazine*, Vol 47, No 1.
7. Father Zweber of the local chapter of St. Paul, Minneapolis, Blue Army Newsletter.
8. Christopher A. Ferrara, Esq, op. cit., pg. 75.
9. The letter of Archbishop Arulappa to Father Gruner is filed with Father Gruner's personal records.
10. Christopher A. Ferrara, Esq, op. cit., pg. 76.
11. Ibid.
12 The Sept 20, 1996 decree of the Congregation for the Clergy, signed by Archbishop Sepe and Cardinal Sanchez, Protocol No. 96002499, pg. 11.
13. Archbishop Benedict To Varpin, *Welcome to Fatima 2000*, the Fatima Crusader, Issue 54, Winter 1997, pg. 32.
14. Pope Paul VI, discourse of June 29, 1972; also Frère François de Marie des Anges, *Fatima: Tragedy and Triumph*, pg. 273.
15. Amerio, *Iota Unam*, Sarto House, Kansas City, MO (1996), pg. 6. First published in Italy, 1985.

16. Msgr. Roche, *Pie XII devant l'histoire*, pgs. 52-52: also, Inside the Vatican, January 1997, pg. 7.
17. Thy Kingdom come, Thy Will be done on earth, as It is in Heaven.
18. The recusal request for a Cardinal must be referred to the Pope himself under Can 1449 according to the authentic interpretation of that Canon. (CF. Response of the PCIV/67-84, 01-07-1976, AAS 68 (1976) 635; CLD8 [1973-1977] 1091-1092).

Chapter 19: The Epilogue

1. *Fatima In Lucia's Own Words*, Sister Lucy's Third Memoir, pgs. 104-105.
2. Ibid.
3. Frère Michel de la Saint Trinité, Vol III, *The Third Secret*, pg. 505, See also Appendix III.
4. *The Fatima Crusader*, Issue 24, pgs. 2-3. *World Enslavement or Peace ...It's Up To The Pope* pgs. 23-31.
5. Sister Lucy op. cit. pg. 105.
6. See footnote 11, Chapter 4, Book II of this work. See also Appendix III of this book.
7. *L'Osservatore Romano* March 26, 1984, Italian edition. See this article photographically reproduced in the photo section of this book.
8. Pope Pius XII, *Evangelii Praecones*, 2 June 1951.
9. Jeremiah Chapter 6, V10; V14.
10. Ibid ch.6 v. 16.
11. Josef Cardinal Ratzinger, his autobiography, *La Mia Vita*, also *The Wanderer*, May 8, 1997 pg. 1.
12. Ibid, pg. 1.
13. Ibid, pg. 7.
14. See Appendix VII.
15. Because Jerusalem failed to heed the warning of the Prophet Jeremiah, in 580 B.C. it was defeated in battle and its leading citizen carried off into captivity for 40 years. In 70 A.D. Jerusalem was totally destroyed and there was not left "a stone upon a stone" (Matthew 24:2) because it did not recognize its Messiah and Savior, Who prophesied the fate of Jerusalem for its sin of unbelief.

BOOK II

Chapter 1: Schism And The Common Good

1. St. John 10:1-3.
2. Isaias 45:19.
3. St. Thomas Aquinas, Treatise on Law, *Summa Theologica*, I-II Q 90, Art. 4.
4. Galatians 2:11-14.
5. Galatians 6:10.
6. Apoc. 19:16: 1Tim. 6; 14-15.
7. St. Thomas Aquinas, *Summa Theologica*, I-II, Q 90, also, John A McHugh, OP and Charles J Callan, OP, *Moral Theology*, John F. Wagner Inc., New York City 1929, Vol. 1, pgs. 90-91.
8. John A McHugh, OP and Charles J Callan, OP, *Moral Theology*, Vol. 1, pgs. 467-470.
9. Galatians 2:14.
10. St. Thomas Aquinas, *Summa Theologica*, II-II, Q 33, Art. 4.
11. St. Robert Bellarmine, Tom IV, Proposition XVI.
12. Osea 4:6, Confraternity Edition
13. Pope Paul VI, Encyclical Letter, *Signum Magnum*, May 12, 1967.
14. Frère François de Marie des Anges, *Fatima: Tragedy and Triumph*, pg. 279.
15. The *"Jesus"* magazine published in Rome, Italy, in its Nov 11, 1984 issue quoted at length Cardinal Ratzinger on the Third Secret of Fatima and these remarks by Cardinal Ratzinger are analyzed and commented on by Father Joseph de Ste. Marie in *The Fatima Crusader*, Issue 18, Oct-Dec 1985, pg. S-4.
16. Frère François de Marie des Anges, *Fatima: The Only Way To World Peace*, pg. 91.
17. Frère François de Marie des Anges, *Fatima: Tragedy and Triumph*, pg. 28
18. Frère François de Marie des Anges, *The Only Way To World Peace*, pgs. 90-91.
19. Michael Davies, *Religious Liberty and the Secular State*, Catholic Family News, Aug. 1996.
20. St. Matthew 12:31-32.
21. *Fatima In Lucia's Own Words*, Sister Lucy's Third Memoir, pg. 105.
22. *Raccolta*, page 247, No. 339.

Chapter 2: Why The Open Letter

1. Exodus, Chapter 14.

2. Deirdre Manifold, *Fatima and The Great Conspiracy*, 7th Edition., pgs. 112, 137.
3. Exodus, Chapter14.

Chapter 3: The Truth Will Make You Free

1. *Fatima in Lucia's Own Words*, Sister Lucy's Third Memoir, Pg. 105; Fourth Memoir, Pg. 162.
2. John A McHugh, OP and Charles J Callan, OP, *Moral Theology*, Vol. II, pgs. 571-572, 580-581.
3. 1 Corinthians, Chapter 8.

Chapter 4: Historic Crossroads

1. Quoted by *The Wall Street Journal*, November 9, 1978.
2. Saint Augustine, *The City of God.*
3. St. John 12:31, 14:30, 16:11.
4. Genesis 3:15.
5. St. Matthew 12:30.
6. St. Mark 9:39.
7. An in-depth explanation of the perestroika hoax can be found in: Anatoliy Golitsyn, *The Perestroika Deception*, published by Edward Harle Limited, London, UK, 1995.
8. Floridi, S.J., *Moscow and the Vatican*, published by Ardis, Ann Arbor, 1986.
9. Frère Michel de la Sainte Trinite, Vol. I, *Fatima: Science and the Facts*, pg. 180. Note: Speaking of Herself in the third person before Our Lady of Fatima identified Herself on Oct. 13, 1917 as the Lady of the Rosary, She on July 13th said of Our Lady of the Rosary, "Only She can help you."
10. Father Fuentes interview with Sister Lucy Dec. 26, 1957. See Appendix III.
11. The exact words of Sister Lucy as quoted in the three paragraphs immediately preceeding the footnote number in the text is certified as accurate by two independent witnesses — Father Rocha and William Thomas Walsh as is further explained below. In his work, *Our Lady of Fatima*, pg. 226 published by The Macmillan Company 1948, as well as pg. 221 in the 1954 Image Books - Doubleday edition, Professor William T. Walsh quotes Sister Lucy as clearly specifying *Russia*, and not the *world* which must be the object of the consecration made by the Pope and the bishops. Also, both Father Rocha in 1986 and Professor Walsh in 1948, and in 1954, testify that the answer to the question asked of Sister Lucy by Professor Walsh, that if the consecration of Russia was not done, would that mean "every country without exception will be overcome by communism?", to which question Sister Lucy replied briefly, "yes". It is Father Rocha who goes on to specify that to the question, "Does that include the United States of America?", Sister Lucy answered in one word, "yes". Father Rocha was interviewed by Louis Kaczmarek, the guardian of the Blue Army Pilgrim Virgin Statue, in 1986, he published what he himself heard from Father Rocha's lips when he was pastor of Our Lady of Fatima Church in Ludlow, Massachusetts. The statements of Father Rocha are contained in the book, *The Wonders She Performs*, by Louis Kaczmarek, pg. 159, published in 1986. The statement of Sister Lucy's own words, as noted on the page, regarding the statements Our Lord made in Rianjo, was documented in Frère Michel de la Sainte Trinite's work, *The Secret and the Church*, pg. 464.
12. Frère François de Marie des Anges, *Fatima: The Only Way To World Peace*, pg. 91.
13. *Fatima in Lucia's Own Words*, Sister Lucy's Third Memoir, pg 105.
14. Frère François de Marie des Anges, *Fatima: The Only Way To World Peace*, pg. 91.
15. Ibid.
16. Ibid. pg. 78.
17. *L'Osservatore Romano*, May, 17, 1982, English Edition.
18. Frère Michel de la Sainte Trinite, Vol. III, *The Third Secret*, pg. 279.

Chapter 5: The Most Grave Obligation

1. St. Robert Bellarmine, Tom IV, Proposition XVI, pg. 470, Tom II, *de Romano Pontifice,* Chapter 29, pg. 417 ff.; also, St. Thomas Aquinas, *Summa Theologia*, I-II, Q 33, Art. 4.

Index By Person

Index By Subject

Select Bibliography

BOOKS

Floridi, Alexis Ulysses S.J. *Moscow and the Vatican*, Ardis Publishers, 1986

Francois de Marie des Anges; Frere. *Fatima: Intimate Joy World Event*, Immaculate Heart Publications, Buffalo, NY,

Book 1, *Fatima: The Astonishing Truth*, 1993

Book 2, *Fatima: Mary's Immaculate Heart and Your Salvation*, 1993

Book 3, *Fatima: The Only Way To World Peace*, 1993

Book 4, *Fatima: Tragedy and Triumph*, 1994

Golitsyn, Anatoliy. *New Lies For Old*, Dodd, Mead and Company, New York, NY 1984

Golitsyn, Anatoliy. *The Perestroika Deception* - The Worlds Slide Towards The 'Second October Revolution' (Weltoktober'), Edward Harle Limited, London, England 1995

Gruner, Nicholas; Father. *World Enslavement Or Peace ... It's Up To The Pope*, Fatima Crusader Publication, Fort Erie, Ontario, Canada, 1988

Johnson, Francis. *Fatima The Great Sign*, Tan Books and Publishers, Rockford, Illinois, 1980

Kelly, Francis Clement; Bishop. *Blood Drenched Altars*, Tan Books And Publishers, Inc., Rockford, Illinois, 1987

Lucia, (Lucy) dos Santos; Sister. *Fatima in Lucia's Own Words*, edited by Father Louis Kondor, SVD, Postulation Centre, Fatima, Portugal, 1976

Manifold, Dierdre. *Fatima And The Great Conspiracy*, seventh edition, Firinne Publications, Galway, Ireland, 1993

Michel de la Sainte Trinite; Frere. *The Whole Truth About Fatima*, Immaculate Heart Publications, Buffalo, NY

Vol. I, *Science and The Facts*, 1989,

Vol. II, *The Secret and The Church*, 1989,

Vol. III, *The Third Secret*, 1990

Trinchard, Paul; Father. *The Awesome Fatima Consecrations*, Metairie, Louisiana, 1992

Walsh, William Thomas. *Our Lady of Fatima*, The Macmillan Company, New York, NY 1948

MAGAZINES AND NEWSPAPERS

The Fatima Crusader Magazine, Issues 1-54, 452 Kraft Road, Fort Erie, ON, Canada, L2A 4M7

The Catholic Counter Reformation in the XXth Century, Maison Sainte Therese, 255, Chemin de la Resereve, Shawingan RR2, P. Que - G9N 6T6, Canada

Catholic Family News, MPO Box 743, Niagara Falls, NY 14302, USA